INTO THE CTHULHU-UNIVERSE

Lovecraftian Horrors in Other Literary Realities

Edited by

Steven Paulsen
and
Christopher Sequeira

This is a work of fiction. The events and characters portrayed herein are imaginary and are not intended to refer to specific places, events or living persons. The opinions expressed in this manuscript are solely the opinions of the author and do not necessarily represent the opinions of the publisher.

Into the Cthulhu-Universe: Lovecraftian
Horrors in Other Literary Realities

All Rights Reserved

ISBN-13: 978-1-923382-00-8

V1.0

All stories in this anthology are original and copyright ©2025, by the authors of each story, with the exception of the following reprints: 'Simbiyu and the Nameless' by Eugen Bacon in *Danged Black Thing* (Transit Lounge, November 2021). 'Dread Island' copyright © 2010 by Joe R. Lansdale, in *Classics Mutilated*, edited by Jeff Conner (San Diego: IDW Publishing). 'A Perfect Summer for Baseball, Tentacles, Mutants, and Love' by Barry N. Malzberg and Jack Dann in *Islands of Time* (Cemetery Dance Publications, March 2024).

Cover art by Dillon Naylor. Cover design by Greg Chapman.

This book may not be reproduced, transmitted, or stored in whole or in part by any means, including graphic, electronic, or mechanical without the express written consent of the publisher except in the case of brief quotations embodied in critical articles and reviews.

IFWG Publishing International
Gold Coast, Australia

www.ifwgpublishing.com

To my awesome son, Edward. Cthulhu fhtagn! Love you, mate. (SP)

To my pal and literary scholar, Les Klinger. Thank you for your friendship and support over the years, sir. A lot of what I have done owes success in part to your contributions, insight, and sheer enthusiasm. (CS)

Acknowledgements

Into the Cthulhu-Universe: Lovecraftian Horrors in Other Literary Realities is the brainchild of Christopher Sequeira. When he had the concept bouncing around in his head he mentioned it to a few writers and they were so inspired by the idea they began to submit stories before the project had even kicked off. That was when Chris asked me to co-edit the book. His enthusiasm was so infectious and the idea so cool I didn't take any real convincing to jump on board.

The concept we pitched to writers, from up-and-comers to grand-masters, was that we wanted a collection of literary mash-ups (but not in the true sense of a mash-up). Essentially, we asked them to pick any genre or even a particular literary work or character and introduce Lovecraftian tropes or Cthulhu Mythos elements to the story. They had free rein and the resulting tales, as you will find, are fabulous.

Chris and I are very proud of this book and grateful to all the wonderful creatives who have contributed to the project. We would like to thank Gerry Huntman (IFWG Publishing), who was quick to support the book; all the writers who have contributed stories; Jan Scherpenhuizen for his superb comic work; Dillon Naylor for his amazing cover art; and Greg Chapman for his talented book design. Last but not least, we want to thank everyone who reads this anthology and hope you enjoy the stories as much as we enjoyed curating and editing them. Unfortunately, due to ill health, Chris missed the final stage of the book's production, but this buffet of modern horror and fantasy would not exist without his creativity and passion.

Steven Paulsen
December 2024

Table of Contents

The Chaos Lords of Mars (Jonathan Maberry)..................1

Twas Brillig (Cat Rambo).......................................17

Sweet Music (Jason Nahrung)..................................25

Simbiyu and the Nameless (Eugen Bacon)......................35

The Meatamorphosis (Aaron Sterns)...........................49

Innsmouth Park (Jane Routley)................................75

The Queen's Solution (Peter Rawlik & Sal Ciano)...........89

Dread Island (Joe R. Lansdale)...............................107

Fhtagntastic Four (Christopher Sequeira &
   Jan Scherpenhuizen)......................................147

The Sleepwalker's Manifesto (Kat Clay)......................157

Creatures of the Night Train (Del Howison)..................171

A Perfect Summer For Baseball, Tentacles, Mutants,
   and Love (Barry N. Malzberg & Jack Dann)..............189

Three Bad Actors In A Silvery Room
   (Steve Proposch)..209

Fame Bites (Anna Tambour)...................................221

Leftovers (Jim Krueger)......................................231

The Power of F'thagn (Scott Driscoll).........................245

Hill-Runner and the Enemy From Behind
   the Curtain Of Stars (Gerry Huntman)....................255

The Colour Out of Hautdesert (JM Merryt)...................271

The Sign of Daoloth (Ramsey Campbell).....................287

Contributors..301

The Chaos Lords of Mars

An Adventure of John Carter of Mars

Jonathan Maberry

-1-

We rode our thoats nearly to death.

The eight-legged beasts were loyal, strong, and had great endurance, but it was clear to both Tars Tarkas and me that they were at the very end of their strength.

The chase through the desert had been a grueling and desperate one, and both of us felt that each passing moment was carved off our very flesh. And we each felt that it was our fault that this was happening. The memory of it all burned in my mind.

It started peacefully enough.

Sola, daughter of Tars Tarkas had set out on a journey to meet with representatives of a Thark tribe that had been living deep in the mountains far from most of their kin. Sola was acting as envoy for her father, hoping to negotiate a peace and to extend an invitation for them to join the unified Thark peoples. She brought a dozen soldiers and a handful of assorted aides, and set up a camp near the foothills of a small chain of stunted mountains.

Tars and I were hunting a small group of raiders in the same area, which was resolved quickly. The six raiders were no match for the Jeddek of the Thark people and me. They did not know who or what I was, having not seen a pale-skinned man on Barsoom rather than the red-skinned men of Helium. They did not know that the lesser gravity of this world gave my Earth-born muscles the effect of being a kind of Hercules, amplifying my strength and reflexes in every way. They brandished their weapons at our approach, and I plucked up a boulder and threw it over their heads, smashing it into a thousand shards behind them. When they turned back from gaping, they saw Tars Tarkas and I standing there with naked blades.

Perhaps they were brave enough in their way, but they were not bold enough for that kind of brawl. They threw down their weapons and fled, leaving us with a bloodless and certain victory.

"Well," said Tars Tarkas with a laugh, "that was easy. Perhaps all we'll ever need in battle will be you throwing stones."

"There's a good chance you scared them every bit as much as me," I replied. "You look fierce enough to bite the head off an *ulsio* and spit out its teeth."

"I'll try that next time. Come, John Carter. My daughter awaits."

By the time we found the camp, we realized with growing horror that something dreadful had occurred and that we were too late.

Far too late.

What we beheld was truly a scene out of a nightmare.

Bodies lay everywhere. None of them were whole. Every Thark had been butchered. Their thoats lay in pools of their own blood. A mated pair of *calots*—those fierce and loyal doglike creatures—were likewise sprawled and broken, their bodies torn open. Anyone familiar with scenes of battle could tell that each Thark and animal had fought to the very last.

Yet there were no traces of the fiends who had ambushed the caravan.

We searched among the dead; our minds blasted to horror by the devastation. Even a warrior as seasoned as Tars Tarkas was badly shaken, and all the more so as it became clear that his daughter, Sola, was missing.

We searched and searched, ranging far out from the camp but always returning with hearts that became heavier with fear and grief.

"Sola is not here."

A voice spoke behind us, and we whirled to see a soldier sitting with his back to a rock. When we'd arrived he had been slumped over, looking as dead as the rest. Like many of the dead Tharks, he was completely naked—his harness and weapons entirely missing. His body was rent by terrible wounds, and yet he raised his head and looked at his lord with desperation and pleading in his eyes.

"My Jeddek," he wheezed.

"Nils Nafron," said Tars Tarkas as we knelt on either side of the wounded Thark. "Who did this?"

Nils began to speak, but blood in his throat choked him and he lapsed into a wracking series of wet coughs that left him gasping. "My Jeddek," he said in a voice notably fainter than only a moment before, "we thought it was the group of the unaffiliated Tharks. That's what they looked like from a distance...but when they drew close they threw off their disguises and set upon us. They... they took...Sola..."

"*Who* took her? Who did this?" roared Tars Tarkas. "Was it the desert raiders? Was it the pirates of..." But his words trailed off as the soldier slowly shook his head. His eyes were clouded with pain and he had to fight for breath.

"They...they were demons...," he breathed.

Then he breathed no more.

Tars Tarkas placed his hand over the soldier's silent heart and we both bowed our heads for a moment. But a moment was all we could spare.

As we stood, Tars Tarkas looked around at the devastation.

"They slaughtered everyone," he said grimly. "Some of those soldiers were among our very best."

"And no trace of who or what did this," I mused. "Calling them 'demons' could mean anything. Madmen or monsters."

"Whoever they are," said the towering green giant at my side, "they have my daughter. They have Sola."

Emotion was not common among the Tharks, and they've spent centuries repressing and suppressing what they feel. Tars Tarkas, though the great leader of his kind, was different. He had the courage to let his feelings show. With that, he was a father who was terrified for his child. He was more than twice my height, but I laid a hand on his arm and offered what little comfort I could. Cold comfort, for all that.

"Then we'll hunt them and get her back," I snarled. "When we catch them they will know the scope and depth of their folly."

He stared down at me, his eyes bleak. "You've seen what they have done. What chance is left that Sola still lives?"

"There is every chance," I snapped. "If they wanted her dead, then she would lay amidst her retinue."

"You can't know that."

"Listen to me, my brother," I said, shifting so that he had to look me in the eyes. "Maybe they took her for ransom, and if so—if we can't steal her back—then the entire treasury of Helium is yours to spend to buy her safe return. Or…if she has been taken for some other purpose—slavery, extortion, whatever—then we will drown them in their own blood and bring her home."

"Drown *who*?" he countered, waving his arms around. "We don't even know who did this. There is blood aplenty but no bodies. These *demons* may be indestructible."

I smiled. "I have never met anyone or anything that can't be killed. You know this to be true. It may be their custom to carry their dead away. There are many mysteries here. Is this the opening move of a war? Was it a random encounter? We need to learn the truth. What we don't know, we will discover."

He stood there, trembling with mingled fear and rage, his heart and mind at war within him. I walked away a few paces to give him a moment to collect himself.

I knelt in the dust and studied the prints, separating out those of the Tharks and the more indistinct marks left by the enemy. Tars Tarkas' shadow fell across the ground in front of me.

"What have you found?"

I tapped the prints, which were rough and shapeless, and lacked consistency. If smoke could leave a trail in the sand, it would be like what we saw.

"Whoever they are," I said, "they went this way." He followed the direction of my pointing finger.

The sun was already setting, and darkness would fall like a

curtain over the desert.

"The moons will be up soon," he said. Tars Tarkas still looked stricken, but his courage was recovering because for him that was a very deep well. His hands absently touched the weapons that hung from his harness—short-sword and longsword. His radium rifle and spear were in their scabbards on his thoat. It was clear he was ready to fight. Eager for it. Hungry. He gave the horizon a fierce glower. "We can track them as long as the light lasts."

I rose and drew my sword and pressed the fist holding it to my heart. "We will find her, my brother, even if we have to chase them to the gates of hell. This I swear."

He studied my eyes for a moment, then gave a fierce nod. Dreadful fires ignited in his eyes. There was no need for any further discussion. We pulled ourselves into the saddle. In the hour during which we had searched in and around the camp, the hardy animals had greatly revived. We mounted and rode off.

-2-

The trail we followed was lit by the passing moons—gray Phobos and its paler consort, Deimos—as we headed toward a range of small mountains. The tracks were easy to follow for hours, and then the moons set and left us in starlit darkness. That made the chase much slower, but yet did not stop us.

An hour before dawn we came to the foot of one mountain that looked like it had once been the cone of a great volcano. Tars Tarkas held a finger to his lipless mouth, cautioning to silence. We slid from our mounts and studied the ground.

"This looks fresh," he said, touching the crumbling edges of another of those strange prints. "We are close. See, they vanish around yonder rock."

We tied our beasts to a stunted tree and crept to the edge of a house-sized boulder. Then we flattened out and peered around. The trail led across a space of bare sand and vanished into the black mouth of a cave. Two figures stood on either side of the cave mouth. Both were Tharks, but their harnesses were oddly nicked and battered—perhaps from the battle at the camp—yet neither warrior had visible wounds, though.

The night sky was dark, but in the thin atmosphere of Barsoom all the stars were brighter, more fixed and less twinkling than they would be to someone on Earth. It painted the intervening stretch of sand between us and them.

"They will see us coming," murmured Tars Tarkas.

I merely grinned, stood, checked that my blades and radium pistol were secure. Then I crouched, took a breath, and with all of my Earth-born muscular strength I leapt into the air in a high, curving leap that covered that distance. As I alit, I ripped my long sword and dagger free and the blades bit deep, taking one Thark across the throat and the other through the chest. They gasped and staggered and fell with no warning cry.

Tars Tarkas ran to catch up, briefly falling forward to use his smaller intermediary set of limbs as extra feet. It was an undignified thing for the Jeddek of the Tharks to do, but in that moment he was more father than leader, and that maneuver allowed him to cross the ground in half the time.

We knelt over the corpses, studying them, and I heard my companion gasp.

"This…this makes no sense, John Carter," he gasped. "I *know* these Tharks. That is Kors Karras, lieutenant of Sola's guard."

"Aye," I said, "and look here…this one is Nils Nafron or I'm a calot."

It was true. The dead Thark at my feet was the same one who had lived long enough to warn us of the attack by demons.

"And I saw Kors Karras lying dead back there."

We stared at each other in confusion and fear.

"Demons, indeed," said Tars Tarkas.

"We are your death," said Kors Karras, his eyes springing open. Then both of the dead creatures reached for us with bloody hands.

-3-

We both cried out in fear, I'll not deny it.

Here were dead Tharks, or some hellish copies of them, who had been lifeless hulks a moment before, now springing to their feet, tearing their swords from their stolen harnesses.

One stabbed at Tars Tarkas, the attack coming with shocking speed and force. But my friend was trembling with nervous energy already and that made his reflexes react at top speed. He fell back a pace, parrying a series of murderous cuts and stabs.

The one nearest me, the false Nils Nafron, grabbed my throat with one hand, my shoulders with two others, and drew a dagger with the fourth. The suddenness of the attack and the force of his surge knocked the dagger from my hand. Had I been an ordinary Barsoomian then my life would have ended there. But I had the advantage of my home-world's gravity to give me speed and strength. I caught the stabbing wrist and with a savage sideways jerk snapped the bones of his wrist. He did not scream or even grunt, but tightened his grip on my throat.

I kicked out at him, catching him on the hip and half-turning him, then I leapt forward, driving him before me so that he smashed into the unyielding rock wall. Bone snapped audibly, yet still there was no sound of pain. Loose dirt and pebbles, disturbed by the force of our impact, rained down on us.

I stepped back and slashed the Thark across the throat and then the middle, and such was my anger that the blades cut him nearly into three pieces. He froze, staring at me with eyes that expressed shock and something more. Something far stranger. Those large eyes seemed to lose their normal color and in place of the whites and the pupils and irises, there were stars. It was like looking into the heart of infinity. I was immediately entranced, seeing stars and constellations, exploding suns and streaking comets. Nor were any of those stars familiar to me—they were nothing I had ever seen on Earth or Mars.

Its mouth turned in an evil grin.

"Ware, creature of stagnant skin," it said. "You cannot kill that which is unkillable. Look upon your doom."

Beside me, Tars Tarkas was backing away from his opponent. He had cut the false Thark's head and sent it cracking against the wall. It lay there, its eyes looking up at us and, like its companion, those eyes were filled with the infinity of space.

Tars Tarkas stood there, panting, his blade dripping with blood that turned to something like black oil as the droplets fell.

Those drops did not soak into the sand, but instead grew legs like spiders and scuttled back toward the headless body and were absorbed back into it.

Worse still—much worse—the severed head grew a score of many-jointed legs and crawled toward its body. It, too, was re-absorbed and a whole and undamaged Thark rose once more. The one I'd cut to pieces had reassembled equally as fast and the two monsters stood shoulder to shoulder, blocking the entrance.

"What m-madness is this?" stammered Tars Tarkas.

"You are overmatched," sneered the creatures, their voices speaking in a harmony so perfect it was as if one directing intelligence spoke through them at the same time. "Flee now and pray to whatever gods you, in your ignorance, worship. Pray for mercy, though there is no such thing in this universe. There is no hope in all of the infinite dimensions, nor any in the dreamlands."

"What *are* you?" I demanded, backing away a few steps.

"We are the many who are one," they said. "We are slaves to our makers. We are *shoggoth* and we are infinite."

"Why do you appear in the aspects of the dead?" demanded Tars Tarkas.

"What are the dead to us but vehicles? What are they but one among uncountable forms open to us? We are the formless. We are risen from our ancient tombs, called back to life by the Elder Things. We are the children of chaos, formless and immortal. We are the sword and fist of entropy. We are *shoggoth*."

The word *tombs* struck a chord within me, and instantly I jumped high above them. Not to get behind them and into the cavern, but higher still to the edge of the ragged cliff from which the dirt and pebbles had fallen. I landed on fingers and toes, whirled and saw cracks both old and new in the sandstone. I raised both fists and brought the sides of them down on the far side of the largest crack. Once, twice, again, and again.

And suddenly a huge grinding noise filled the air and the whole front of the rock wall leaned out and then plunged down. Thousands of tons of stone landed on the two beasts—the two self-proclaimed *shoggoth*. Tars Tarkas, who was very familiar with my skills, understood what I was about and leapt to safety, but the shapeshifting monsters were buried under half a mountain. Dust swirled and eddied, but finally settled. There was no trace of the shoggoth. One massive slab of rock leaned against the cavern mouth, nearly blocking it.

I leapt down and picked up my fallen sword.

"What now?" asked Tars Tarkas. He had run back to fetch his radium rifle. But he answered his own question as he leaned close to examine the narrow gap. "I think we can squeeze inside," he said as he slung the rifle.

And so we did. It was no problem for me, but my friend had to push while I pulled, and when he stumbled into the cave there were large raw patches on his skin. It was not as dark as we expected, for firelight glimmered on the walls fifty yards from where we stood.

He touched my shoulder and stood still, his head cocked to listen.

I nodded, for I heard it, too. Voices raised in a kind of chant, though in what language they spoke was unknown to either of us. There was a melodic note that was oddly sweet and strangely compelling, and we found ourselves swaying slightly with the rise and fall of tone and rhythm.

Moving as silent as ghosts, we crept forward. There were no other guards, and I can understand why. How many others on Barsoom could have bested the two outside? These shoggoths— whatever that really meant—were arrogant in their confidence.

Arrogance is never a good trait for a warrior.

The closer we got, the stranger it all became. In the space of two dozen paces the meaningless chant became understandable. First as complete words and phrases, then in terms of understanding. Tars Tarkas glanced me and mouthed that it was in the common tongue.

I shook my head, though. I was hearing it in *English*. Hearing it, in fact, in the English as spoken in my home back in Virginia. The same distinct accent. I told my friend as much and we frowned at one another, perplexed, and unnerved because we both know that the language they actually spoken was neither Barsoomian nor English from Earth. Yet we understood it with perfect clarity.

"…the Elder Things, that they may wake from their dreams and claim their rightful dominion over all the uncountable worlds."

That was the fragment we heard, and it chilled us.

We both knew about conquest. We were each conquerors in our own right, and heirs to legacies of warfare from our mother cultures. What we heard was akin to a declaration of war mixed with an argument of rightful ownership of all.

We moved forward more quickly until we reached the mouth of the cave, and there we crouched. Below us, down a steep slope, were hundreds of forms. There were Tharks and Heliumites, Rykors and Plant Men, white apes and banths, apts and malagors, thoats and calots, and many other beasts the likes of which neither of us had ever beheld. Yet these were far outnumbered by forms that were stranger still. Giants with thousands of arms, squat octopoidal creatures with writhing tentacles, goat-headed men with gray skin and claws for hands, shaggy beast-men with scores of horns upon their grotesque heads, centipedes as long as boxcars, lobsters with human faces, and even worse horrors. Here and there among them were masses so bizarre as to have no real shape, but were instead lumps of black jelly from which gaseous bubbles rose and popped, and hundreds of eyes formed like pustules that flared with luminous green light before vanishing to leave the things blind and yet seemingly aware. These monstrosities were so strange, so obscene in nature, that it was difficult to behold without falling into madness.

These forms were not permanent, but came and went with the rhythms of the chants. At times four or five of the monsters would collide together and become one mammoth thing; at others a single beast would disintegrate into countless scuttling monstrosities. The sight of all this was an assault on our minds and the world itself seemed to be crumbing around us.

"These are not any gods of Barsoom that I've ever heard of," whispered Tars Tarkas. "And yet…"

"I know," I said. "I feel as if I *know* them. Somehow. Impossibly, because there is no way I beheld such horrors in my waking life."

He gave me a sharp look. "What about when you left your body behind on your world and traveled to Barsoom…however you did that. Did you see them in the outer darkness between worlds?"

I almost said no, but paused because his words struck a faint note within me. I had not been conscious of that transition between my life on Earth and my new life here on Mars. On Barsoom. And yet, there was a memory of the kind that lingers from a dream from which all other specifics have faded. A fragment that was partly a hazy visual image of some dream construct, and partly a nonspecific memory that was closer to a thought than to anything actually witnessed. It was so bewildering. The more I tried to clutch the memory and draw it to the front of my mind, the less I could *see* it with my mind's eye, while at the same time there was a flood of emotions —none of them wholesome—that filled every part of me.

Then Tars Tarkas gripped my arm with crushing strength.

"*Sola!*" he cried in a strangled voice.

I saw her then. His daughter lay stretched upon a rough altar, her six limbs bound to tall metal stands upon which torches blazed. She writhed and struggled against her bonds, but her shackles held her fast.

Tars Tarkas gripped his weapons and was about to break cover and make a dash for Sola, but I stopped him. He struggled against me, but though he was bigger I was stronger. I pulled him back and down.

"*Listen to me,*" I hissed. "She is bound and that cavern is filled with monsters. Besides, our blades are useless against them. We saw it at the camp and firsthand outside. If we just charge them then we will be overwhelmed and Sola will be lost."

My words hit him like a series of punches, but he gave a reluctant nod. With despair in his eyes he begged, "What then? There is no time to go seeking reinforcements. Apart from you bringing down the whole ceiling and entombing us all, what can we do?"

I slid my blades into their sheaths. "Blades are not the only weapons we have," I said as I drew my radium pistol.

"How will that be any better against monsters who can reform their own tissue even when hacked apart?"

I held up the pistol. "Because this doesn't cut flesh," I said. "It *obliterates* it."

"It does that to mortal flesh," he countered. "How do we know it will work on creatures such as these…these…chaos lords?"

"We don't know, my friend, but it is what we have left. If nothing else the bullets will explode and splash their flesh to the winds. If it does not kill them then at least it might buy us time to free Sola and escape. Then we can ride hard for home and return with a fleet to see how *unkillable* they truly are."

I crab-walked to the edge and pointed down. "You have the rifle and you're as good a shot as there is on Barsoom. Fire at the biggest ones first but leave the altar alone." I gestured to the ceiling. "Your crack about bringing the ceiling down isn't a bad one, but we have to get the timing right." I quickly outlined a wild plan and he nodded.

"For Sola," I said.

"For Sola."

-4-

I turned from him, surveyed the ceiling, tensed and leapt upward with every ounce of strength I possessed, flying high into the air, arms outstretched to reach for a stalactite. As I caught it, I turned to see Tars Tarkas moved to the mouth of the tunnel, the rifle to his shoulder as he opened fire. I clung there, watching to see the effect.

The radium bullets are really glass shells in which particles of radium float in gas. The range of those weapons is half a mile, but his targets were less than fifty meters away. The shell struck one of the shapeless masses, vanishing into the ruptured skin. There was a moment when the creature merely stopped and looked around to see what struck it. Then it threw back its head and howled with the first real pain we'd heard them utter.

All around the puncture wound the flesh was taking on a sickly green luminescence, with jagged lines of it radiating outward like slow lightning. Its cry was enormous—louder than any sound I had ever heard—and it shook the entire cavern. I had to cling on with all my might as the stalactite shuddered. Cracks appeared in the ceiling, whipsawing in all directions.

The shoggoths ceased their chanting and stared, none of them understanding what had happened.

"I *burn*," bellowed the injured one. "By the Elder Things, I burn!"

And so it seemed. The glowing green wrapped itself around it as the thing shambled off balance, striking dozens of smaller creatures.

Tars Tarkas fired again, striking another of the brutes. It howled, too, and the same luminescence appeared. Our plan was working far better than we could have hoped. With each shot, the largest monsters threw their screams into the air, and the cavern could not bear that force.

I felt the stalactite begin to crack and, as it broke free of the ceiling, I shoved against it to change the angle of its fall, lest it crush Sola. I rode it down and sprang off a second before it struck and crushed a dozen monsters. I dove and rolled and came up to my feet even as I drew my pistol.

Three monsters, each in a different nightmare form, rushed at me, but I pivoted and shot them all. They howled and collapsed backward, and from their reaction I could tell that accuracy was needed only to hit their flesh. That made sense, because as shapeshifters they would have no central nervous systems, skeleton, or organs. The radium exploded through them, though, attacking the changeable tissue from which they were made.

It was a shambles. Some of the beasts tried to flee, but it was soon apparent that the tunnel through which we'd come was the only exit. Tars Tarkas dominated that path, firing round after round. The rifle's magazine held one hundred rounds and he had a spare on his harness. My pistol had fewer, but I had three spare magazines.

Fear gave us speed. Outrage stoked our courage. The need to save Sola fueled our purpose. We fired and fired, filling the cavern with death. In truth, any one of them, even the smallest, could have killed us if we had fought them with steel. But the radium was different and its destructive power burned them from within.

It was a slaughterhouse.

Other stalactites were dropping now as the combined ear-shattering howls of the shoggoths broke the ceiling apart. Thousands of tons of rock dropped down, smashing the creatures into jellied pools, and though they tried to recover, a radium bullet waited for each.

I swapped my magazine but holstered my pistol and I leapt to the altar. Sola strained against the chains, though they seemed oddly delicate and ceremonial, yet she seemed unable to free herself. I waved her back, gripped the metal and, with a scream of my own, burst the shackles. Then I drew the gun with my right hand and wrapped a supporting arm around Sola. She was able to walk, though, and with her father's steady fire above and my pistol in hand we won our way to the slope.

He reached down and pulled his daughter up, while I bounded high and landed beside them.

Then we ran.

The cave was collapsing in on itself, bringing down a million tons of shattered rock. Clouds of dust and gas chased us all the way to the narrow entrance. I went through first, braced my back against the stone, and with all of my power, pushed. The obstructing slab moved ten inches and that was all it would ever go. Yet it was enough for father and daughter to squeeze through. With a grunt I jumped free and let the slab drop back. It cracked under its own weight and sealed the mouth of the cavern completely.

Even then we did not pause but ran for the thoats and galloped at full speed into the dawn.

-5-

We rode through the morning, with Sola clinging to her father. We did not know if any of the shoggoths survived. Nor did we want to check without an army of riflemen at our backs.

We did not return to the massacre at the camp, but pressed on.

Neither Tars Tarkas nor I paused to look at Sola, beyond checking her for wounds. Luckily, she was unharmed.

I say luckily, but looking back on it now, I know that we were not lucky. No, not at all. Had we thought to look at Sola, to stare into her eyes, we would have known the horrors yet to come. For her eyes swirled with infinite stars. Nor did we see her small and secret smile of pure, unnatural, and ageless malice…

TWAS BRILLIG

CAT RAMBO

In Wonderland's batwing-turreted red castle, where the Red Queen lived and her inconsequential spouse dreamed, in the Fifth Drawing Room, a dissatisfied mirror over the fireplace never showed the actual room, but instead any other room in the palace. The whys and wherefores of this are unknown, but so many of Wonderland's objects are prone to becoming animated, and their ways are as petty and malign as any human's.

This mirror's dissatisfaction would prove Wonderland's undoing. Mirrors can be many things, but one of them is doors, and doors can let things in.

In this room there was a carpet, red on burgundy on scarlet on crimson, that covered the floor. If you looked at it long enough, it would begin to seem as though roses were blooming from it, crawling up out of the surface. It was an unsettling carpet, and so the Fifth Drawing Room was seldom used. In the morning, the housekeeper would glance in to satisfy herself that everything was in order, and then move onto other duties, such as tending the lawn flamingos or making sure the clocks stayed in the right places and did not wander off.

And so no one noticed when the mirror finally showed the room it should, but with one crucial difference: that carpet.

The roses on its woven surface turned black. Their leaves

narrowed into daggers, and their thorns became more prominent than the blossoms. The roses swelled as they bloomed, and there were maggots at their cores. The petals were coated with flaky black ash that lifted into the air at the breeze's touch, floating out and away on it. It fell on the garden of living flowers outside the window. Their faces grew imbecile and unthinking, and they wailed where once they had quarreled and quipped. The gardeners tried their best with remedies of lime and phosphenes, and sprays of every variety, to no avail, watching the flowers die, one by one.

Wonderland is a place of the imagination, and so its corruption went quickly. Where in a "realer" world, the invasion might have taken place over the course of years, a matter of invasive species and over-exploitation of resources, it took only a week for Wonderland to fall.

Day one: The maids of the castle had all dreamed the same dream that night, they discovered when comparing notes in the morning. A road, thorn-edged, a black and vermilion sky, and from somewhere, something howling. Not a dog or wolf's howl, but an eerie ululation that seemed to come from all around them. They had felt eyes upon them, hostile eyes, and had awakened in the morning unrefreshed, feeling as though they had been chased down that road all night.

The White Knight, seeking the Jabberwock through a tulgey wood, came across a great black hole in the ground. It seemed to have recently appeared — several trees were in the process of toppling into it, crying out to their fellows as they disappeared.

The White Knight dismounted from a saddle jingling with mousetraps, a bee hive, and other sundry ingenious contraptions of his own device, and approached the hole. He stared down into it and tried to make something, anything, out. The darkness crawled and writhed, and he thought he could see a suggestions of undulating tentacles, a glimpse of a great beak edged with knives, an immense eye filled with ebon stars — but perhaps that was only his imagination. He took a lantern down from his saddle and lit it, then held it above the darkness, searching. Finally, he released it. It fell a few feet into the darkness and vanished as though it had never existed.

He went to report on this to the White Queen and King in their own white castle, but there was a lobster quadrille being held that evening, and everyone was engaged in preparing for it, and paid him no mind. He was used to that, being a gentle and ineffectual man, given to murmurs rather than shouts, but he wished he had the words to convey to them the deep sense of unease that had sunk into his core at first sight of the hole, and which still clutched at him with unrelenting, bony fingers.

He made his way to the White King and spoke to him, but the King only made a memorandum "very large hole" in his enormous memorandum book and sliding it back in his royal pocket, smiled brightly at the Knight as though everything had been resolved.

Day two: Still uneasy, the White Knight went to the Red Castle, despite all his misgivings about the rightness of the action. There are two factions in Wonderland, the Red and the White, and they never mix if it can be avoided. He wished the other White Knight was with him.

As he rode up, the frog-faced footmen regarded him with calm, unblinking disdain, doing so silently as he went up the steps and into the castle, past the fish-faced butler.

The Red Queen was holding court, and trying a case involving a dozen stolen orange marmalade tarts. She glanced briefly at the White Knight as he entered, but then went back to screaming at all participants in the case. At last, she ordered all of them to have their heads struck off, and beckoned to the Knight.

He walked forward. Where the White Queen was pale, the Red Queen was ruddy, dressed in scarlet satin and lace, and her hair was like a dying fire.

"There is a hole," he said to her without preamble.

"Bigger than the one in your head?" she said rudely. "Open your mouth a little wider when you speak, and address me as 'Your Majesty.'" She was a crass woman, and prone to sarcasm and violence, which is why he would have preferred to deal with the White Queen, even though they were both erratic and whimsical to a perilous degree.

"Wonderland is in danger," he said.

"From a hole? Don't be silly! Holes are everywhere!! The world is made of holes."

They argued for hours like this, employing words of a thousand meanings, and then making the words take on additional meanings, until the words wept beneath the weight of it all. Eventually he persuaded her to let him take her to witness it. She insisted on being accompanied by a troop of guards, and they went slowly, because several of the guards were not very good at riding and kept falling off their horses. Finally, though, they arrived.

The hole was twice as large as it had been the day before, the knight thought. And the roiling in its depths was still only glimpses through darkness, but they were glimpses nonetheless, ones that turned his stomach queasy if he looked at them too long.

The Queen stood by the edge of the hole, looking in, for a long and silent period.

"There is nothing to be done with this," she said in a quieter tone than any of them had ever heard from her, a voice that did not seem as though it could come from her.

Day three: The castle maids did not sleep last night, and when their numbers were counted, there was one less than there should be, but no one could agree who was missing. The Duchess served peppery soup to them all and plaintively asked if anyone had seen her child, who had vanished the day before and would never be found again.

Running an errand and late as always, the White Rabbit suddenly found himself hoisted up into the air by grim, rubbery-winged nightgaunts who gobbled and meeped among themselves but did not speak to him despite his screaming and imprecations.

Where they took him, no one knows. Later that day, the Mad Hatter and Dormouse sat at their tea table, and for once both of them were silent. When the Dormouse raised his teacup to his lips, it was with a shaking paw. Behind them, the March Hare's house, the ear-shaped chimneys sagged and the furry roof began to bow inward, rot creeping up from the floorboards to claim the interiors.

The messengers Haigha and Hasta were dispatched by the White King to scout and discover what they could of the disturbances. They did not return.

The Lion and the Unicorn fought along the bounds, up and down, up and down, and did not notice their transformation, which happened so imperceptibly that all they noticed was themselves slowing. Then a blow cracked the shining spiraled horn away, and another clanked off the furry mane, and then there were simply two statues, limbs entangled. The putrid ooze crept in over the boundaries, inch by slithy inch, and enveloped the stony forms.

The White Knight, coming across them, drew his bony mount to a halt and paused to contemplate them. He lifted his gaze a little and saw the other White Knight, a leprous reflection in the distance watching him. The two of them stood looking at each other while the sun rolled out of the sky and stars came out in unfamiliar patterns, as though the skies themselves had shifted. Finally they inclined their heads to each other, without exchanging a word, and then each turned back to his horse and went on his way, never to see each other again.

The trains of Wonderland, never on time in the first place, grew later and later, and then corrosion claimed the rails, and the engines no longer came.

#

Day four: The Tulgey Wood resisted infiltration, but the corruption came from the roots of the tumtum trees and crawled upward, darkening the trunks from a pleasant brown to an ominous ebon. Squamous worms writhed through the dark earth, and oily, iridescent liquid dripped from the fungus that sprouted in odd ovals on the ground, white mushrooms surrounding a scarlet one in every case, so from above it looked like a great, scarlet eye, staring blindly up into the sky.

The toves scuttled away, their limbs drooping and distorted, and the ground was strewn with the twisted corpses of rocking-horse-flies . The mome raths outgrabe for one last time, and the wood echoed with that peculiar sound, half bellow, half whistle, with a sort of sneeze halfway through, and then went silent. The Bandersnatches were caught and hung like pheasants to age before they would be consumed by eldritch gourmands, and the Dodo's small form swung from a large hook beside them, denuded of feathers.

The Jabberwock also screamed, crying defiance in the wood's depths, but shadowy hunters surrounded it, and when it slashed at them, its claws went through nothingness. It screamed again and again and far away, people drew the covers over their heads to try to cut that noise of despair and rage out. A barbed spear went into its side, then another. It whirled and snarled, but it could not overcome them, and eventually, the screaming stopped, and it gave one last burble. Those in bed went back to their restless dreams of wandering a place they had never seen, moss-choked hallways where no light had ever come, stony labyrinths with ice upon their walls, and dark stairways spiraling down into more darkness.

Day five: The ocean that borders Wonderland is technically part of it, and it too, began to fall. The sand shivered and blushed silvery, a pale and leprous color, and the waves left scrawled writings in the sand, symbols and letters that refused to fade when other waves tried to scrub the sand clean. In the deep waters, strange purple and green anemones blossomed, and any fish investigating them were drawn into their hearts to burn and dissolve. Jet black eggs and leathery sacs with curled corners washed up on the littered sand, smelling of brine and rot.

Fishermen came out of the water, men with damp skin, and odd markings on their necks, carrying tridents. They did not speak, but the rolling of their bulbous, protruding eyes was unsettling. Those who did not flee them immediately were killed, and scarlet letters joined the silver ones on the sand.

A rustling in the underbrush betrayed where the Cheshire

Cat sought its grin, working back through its footsteps, trying to locate where it might have slid off its face, but try as it might, the grin had vanished. The Cat wailed and caterwauled, but the warning was already far too late.

Sitting cross-legged on its mushroom, the Caterpillar contemplated its options, smoking its hookah, breathing out clouds of scented smoke. Of all of Wonderland's creatures, it was the one that had the most sense of what was happening, and this is why, after a time, it took out a pouch of tobacco, its color blue and violet with a pearly sheen, smelling of cardamon and lilies. It filled the bowl of the hookah and sparked it alight to take a deep lungful.

Exhaling, it watched a doorway take shape in the glowing smoke. Wriggling forward, it went through, and thus was the only creature to escape Wonderland's demise.

Day six: The White Knight traveled southward, trying to figure out what was happening. There are no cemeteries in Wonderland, so he did not know what it was that had appeared in the southwest corner of the demesne. He saw rows of gravestones, and stroking his beard as though to reassure himself, he walked through the rows, trying to puzzle out the inscriptions until he realized the words kept rearranging themselves, kept spelling out words he could not pronounce. In the center of the graveyard, he found a gazebo that might once have been white marble, but which was now darkened with black encrustations and scatterings of pigeon shit. In the center a plaque read:

"That is not dead which can eternal lie, / And with strange aeons even death may die."

When he turned, he saw the ghouls that had been creeping up on him: their eyes glowing a luminous green, the claws as dark and slimy as the layers of rot around him. They meeped softly, menacingly, as they crept forward.

He drew his sword and braced himself against the wall. But he was old, and it took very little for him to be overwhelmed, and in the end, the ghouls crept away, and where the knight had stood were bits of sundered armor and a red stain.

There was a final feast in the Red Queen's castle, where her

White counterpart joined her. Neither knew where their spouses had gotten to; neither cared. They introduced themselves to the soup, and then the joint, and then sat waiting for a pudding that never would arrive.

Every creature that dwells in Wonderland has a song that they will sing, should they ever encounter an Alice, and now all those still remaining sang, imploring for an Alice to come. But far away, an Alice beat her fists against an obdurate mirror that would not let her through. She could feel that something was terribly wrong, but this time Wonderland was closed to her, perhaps its last act of love.

Day seven: Wonderland's corruption was complete. Black roses, their hearts containing pallid worms, grew everywhere that the white and red roses had once bloomed. The White Knights were only white bones. And in the depth of ancient woods, once cool and pleasant, full of shaded avenues now bare to the searing sun, the jabberwock burbled no more.

Sweet Music

Jason Nahrung

The castle is old but the rock on which it stands is much older. The cliffs fall away on three sides, and from here on the southern balcony, the rough, serpentine road to the Pass is hidden from sight, the nearest town of Bistritz and smaller villages obscured by the serrated lines of crags and dark masses of forest, the clustered beech and pine scarred by chasms where rivers wend to the Black Sea. One such roils at the base of this pinnacle, the midday sun but a teasing glimmer should one care to squint over the moss-stained balustrade in that moment when it emerges from the thick morning mist only to vanish once more into the long, deep shadows of afternoon. So far below is it that not even an eddy's gurgle will reach the casual listener's ears; even to mine it is but a distant wet mumble, a begrudging mutter that it has somewhere better to be.

It sings my song, but the tune is played by another. At times I feel my life has been a mad dance called by other voices, whether the petty boyars and princes grasping for power, my scheming younger brother, or yes, the master tunesmith, the 'Mad Poet' Alhazred. Every footfall choreographed, every stumble preordained.

These crumbling stones are a far cry from the village in which I and my brothers grew up, that brief bucolic childhood of nobility supplanted by the magnificence of the Sultan's palace in Constantinople. The food, the cloth, the architecture, the accursed heat, the calls of the muezzins. Such an exotic gilded cage, a constant reminder that my younger brother, Radu, and I were hostages there to guarantee our father's obedience as Voivoide of Wallachia. Radu, even then a manipulative ferret of fair looks and velvet tongue, used his body to find favour with the Sultan, while I, whipped and denigrated for my refusal to kneel, trained tirelessly with sword and lance to equip myself for the struggle ahead. It came soon enough: my father overthrown and he and my older brother, Mircea, first in line, slain by craven Saxon boyars (their time would come). We were sent home, Radu and I, he with the favour and banner of the Sultan, me with a sword and a stolen book to fuel my claim.

What, you may wonder, could a book achieve that a sword could not?

This was no hymnal to summon God's grace, no mere compendium of military strategy. This tome, bound in leather of unknown origin and reeking of wrongness, promising all, was one of few surviving copies of the mystic writings of Abdul Alhazred. The Sultan prized the *Necronomicon* highly for the windows it opened into the past and future, though he baulked at the incantations that promised to not only open doors to other worlds but invite the denizens of those strange locations to step through, bringing with them the most unholy of powers.

When our departure was nigh, I enlisted the aid of a whore in poisoning and overcoming the guards, and a master thief to extract the book from its vault, then slew them both to cast the blame from me, a mere lad whose loyalty may have been doubted but whose whip-forged obedience was not. An uneasy façade I was happy to shed when once more ensconced in the forested, clouded mountains of home, but it served me well. I wonder still if the book may have called to me, ensuring the whispers of its existence (always whispers, low and conniving, convincing in their allure) reached my ears and the plan for its liberation took root. Mayhaps it shrouded the senses of the janissaries who failed to guard it and those who sought thereafter to solve the mystery of its theft. I had only to lay low and sympathise about the outrage for a few days before our caravan departed, ferrying Radu and me to our destiny.

How the Sultan must have chafed when he finally divined that his treasure had been lifted by his would-be vassal! At first, he sent spies to reclaim it. When they failed, hats nailed to their heads for the insolence, he sent an army, but that too fell against the ferocity of my soldiers' brutal resistance, the Turks' last courage quashed in the shadows of a forest of corpses. But he had another weapon at his disposal; there is no enemy as cunning as family.

Radu, with all the morals of an eel, wooed man, woman and boyar to his cause, and set about my undoing. It is no easy thing to rule a borderland territory flanked by the competing desires of two great empires; rather, to keep the peace is to dance on marbles, choosing one's partner as needs must to maintain one's footing. Radu and I were both lithe on our feet. Hard did we contest our meagre throne, and throughout those turbulent years, the book consoled me—when sword and followers failed, it would be steadfast.

Ah, the book…my greatest boon, my greatest torment. Worse than a genie's lamp, its promise of salvation carrying a scorpion's sting. It is gone now, lost to some thief's hands during one of my desperate flights, my string of incarcerations, and who knows to where Abdul Alhazred's infamous tome has flown, what enticement it whispers to its current owner, what doors its mystical histories will open. Will any rise to such heights, or lows, as I?

I often wonder, had I known how such a simple act of spite would alter the course of my life, would I still have gone through with it? Remembering Radu's final hours, how I stared down at my diseased brother, barely able to raise a hand yet closer to death than he realised … of course I would have. The chance to save my country, to preserve my seat and my line, to exact my revenge on those who wronged me, Radu being the foremost. What is a soul compared to this?

Maybe it is the book telling me the scales balance. Hard at times, to know the difference, between what I want to hear and what the *Necronomicon* wants me to hear. Though it is lost to me, its script still whispers, a sibilant zephyr both intoxicating and putrid bidding me hither and yon with visions of conquest, dreams of blood.

So the *Necronomicon* sang to me, at my lowest ebb, besieged on all sides and abandoned by all but the most loyal. There in the lowermost chamber of my castle, the bodies of my ancestors mouldering in the crypts beside me. The candles barely lit the dank catacomb air; the wick on my silver lamp unfettered by chimney or globe made a low serpentine hiss as I placed it on the reading table to light the pages. With held breath and bold hand, I unclasped the heavy cover. No sooner were the bonds undone than the book crashed open as though to a place held by an invisible ribbon. The lamp shuddered, flickered, shadows dancing, then steadied, lighting the record of a ritual from mists older and thicker than those that cling to the deepest chasm of my beloved Wallachia. The strange script sang in my mind, a promise of the power to destroy my foes, to grow stronger on their blood, to be untouchable (almost). If there was a finer print containing this caveat inscribed in the margins, between the lines, I saw it not. I traced the squirming ink with a shaking finger and uttered the mystical words as though they poured like wine from a jug without knowing or sensing; I drank the incantation's darkest promise. Blood dripped from my eyes and splattered like sealing wax upon the page. The terrible vision, rich with the aroma of earth and blood, overwhelmed my senses. A great roar overtook me, reverberating with screams of agony and exultation; I fell to my knees like a penitent as the room shook so that dust fell like snow, and I feared in some small portion of my remaining consciousness that the castle would fall upon me. The lamp, the candles snuffed out, but the text glowed in fiery script before me and I … I inhaled it. I inhaled it, and it consumed me.

The deal done, the cover slammed shut of its own accord, the thud resounding as though the door to Heaven itself had been closed and bolted against me.

I cared not. I had seen the craven machinations of Christendom, the Church as base a battleground for the whims of the power hungry as any palace. I had lived among the heathen, knew their god to be but another face of our own (that which had been my own, no more). Trust in God, the priests said, but what god would allow Mircea to be blinded and buried alive? Would allow Turkish boots to despoil our hallowed streets and fields? Would allow a child to be taken into servitude, a blade at his throat to compel the obedience of the father?

If the love of God would not protect my home, what about the fear of the Devil?

Oh yes, I opened the book. I accepted its offer. There was no going back.

When I awoke in the chamber, the servant I had bade guard the door was dead at my feet, the body cold and pale, its throat opened as though savaged by a winter wolf. And though not a flame flickered in that stygian hole, I could see the whole of the room as though it were open to the gloaming's grey light. How I loped to the battlements, taking stairs many at a time, strength flowing through me, my senses preternaturally alive—owl, hawk, wolf were senseless as stones by comparison.

Ah, but then the rub: as I cowered in the shadows, the bright balcony ablaze with agonising sunlight, it was revealed to me that there still stood one barrier between me and ultimate victory—the sun.

What mockery was this? To give with one hand, to take with the other? No better than the Hungarians who have taunted with cruelty and kindness! What good to have the power to destroy one's foes at night if one cannot hold the conquest by day?

My first thought was to experiment—why not make the night my day? Who could withstand an army of my own kind? It was not to be. I should not have been surprised in this failure, for no amount of gold, titles or favour appears sufficient to buy loyalty, the greedy always looking for the hand to feed and then to bite. A mere handful have I shared my power with, uninspiring all. It is as though the step from day to night quashes any essence that made them desirable companions, leaving only craven desires and the familiar capriciousness of their flesh-and-blood counterparts that has forever undermined me. One, a fine lady, has but recently offended me, daring to interfere with my great plan; I interceded only just in time, saving my inbound guest from her designs. Another, long ago, I found banal; I put him to the stake and allowed the dawn to have its way with him, a suitable warning to the others. Not that I could repeat the same with my three remaining companions, too dear to me for all that the 'sisters', as they term themselves, delight in testing my patience. Regardless, for all their cruel whimsy, they remain cowed and ultimately grateful for my gifts; mere shades of their warm selves, I love them yet.

An empire of night was, then at least, out of my reach. How could I, with my hobbled power, seek to foil Radu's ambition and drive the Turks from my land?

In my moment of despair, again, the Mad Poet showed me the way on the wings of blood-soaked visions. Who could I trust between dawn and dusk to occupy my chair, to fly my banner, lead my army?

Who better than my bother, Mircea. That he had died years before was but a minor inconvenience.

My land is as draped in folk tale as it is in mountain mists, and one such tells of a door at the top of the Răchițaua mountains that can move one through not just space but also time—if one has the key. Guided by visions, our journey to reclaim my beloved brother passed as though a key had turned in just such a door, transported to the destination of my vision: Castle Ferenczy, a relatively short distance hence astride its remote Transylvanian peak. My loyal Szgany drove our crudely covered leiter-wagon, the box with my brother's corpse alongside mine, which bore a lining of earth from the crypt in the lowest level of my family's ancestral home, and next to us a third, bearing our price.

If the journey itself was as if suspended somewhere between sleeping and waking—the tousle and toss of the crates, the itch of sunlight through cracks in the timbers, the release of night and the satiation at the end of the hunt across nondescript farms and villages, screams and corpses left in our wake—the days with the fanatical Bela Ferenczy were a fever dream. For all my unearthly power, I was in his shadow; his tales of wars in which he'd fought spanned centuries and exotic lands, though we shared a delight in putting the Turks to the sword. He appeared to acknowledge my nature in knowing glance and smirk but remarked not on it, soon consumed by his formulae and paraphernalia as he wrought his fearsome necromancy. The price of his exertions was much gold and the bones of an exalted wise man, reputed to have had the demon-given gift of future sight. But the result! Mircea, alive, those beautiful eyes, seeing; that loyal heart, beating; that keen mind, thirsting for news of his sleeping years!

Has there been such reunion? Not even in the pages of the *Necronomicon*, I swear; Mircea, laughing, swearing, drinking, returned through death's door and as vital as if the air had never left his lungs.

And quickly furious but not surprised at Radu's treachery. My brother fully supported my brazen plan, prepared to adopt my guise—we bore sufficient similarity, and with he dead these years, who else could he be when so proclaimed? Any who questioned would be suitably dealt with.

Oh, Mircea, so desperate to take the field once more, all while saddened that his revenge on those who had slain him I had already claimed. He was nevertheless pleased at the toll: the boyars and their families put to sword and chains, manors razed, their lands forfeited.

Once it was clear Mircea was as his old self, we were well pleased to leave the noisome, uncanny keep of Bela Ferenczy, to embark on our grand adventure to reclaim our birthright, between us ruling day and night.

Alas, the ploy was short lived, either betrayal or mischance finding Mircea caught in daytime by the invaders. A few treasured weeks with my brother, then, it was conveyed, he was cut down, into pieces, and believing it to be mine, his head sent in a trophy box to Constantinople.

It was as though the Poet's visions were one side of a mirror, the darker side revealed only when one had committed; the sweet followed by the bitter. Tears of joy turned to tears of blood.

With Mircea died my reign as voivode, but one ambition yet remained within my reach: Mircea, twice born, twice slain, would rest knowing his youngest brother would never again hold the title.

The journey to Radu's fortress was interminable, yet another reminder of the double-edged sword I now wielded. I railed at the bite of the sun, reducing me to infantile weakness when under the moon's soft light I am unmatched by man or beast. What is this half gift? Some reckoning of the god that I despise? An Achilles heel contained within the incantation, an error of Alhazred's recording, or a purposeful sabotage by a master afraid of creating a servant mightier than himself?

So to the leiter-wagon, escorted by Szgany in an undignified passage as little more than cargo to the proximity of my brother's castle.

Ah, but once there... The chill night air was replete with the reek of his unsated ambition, barely disguised by the stench of decay he had brought upon himself by his licentious politicking and debauchery.

The castle's precipitous stone walls presented no barrier to me. After days in a box anticipating this moment, I felt as if borne on the air itself as I scaled the brickwork no more hindered than a lizard.

And there he lay, remarkably alone, no wife or lover in his chamber, poorly, it would seem, struck down by his own weakness of character.

Oh, Radu, the 'handsome' no more, stirring from his syphilitic stupor as my shadow fell upon him. Swollen, weak eyes peered out, filled with surprise, horror, fury.

Delightful, to see the awareness dawning, that it would his brother's hand that sent him to his death.

I leaned over, his perfume of stale sweat and bodily waste greeting me as my lips met his throat, Radu unable to make so much as a fist, or raise a curse, a shout, a scream. Thin skin tore like muslin.

For a heady moment, no blood had tasted so sweet, but then

the contamination struck as the sourest of milks. Repulsed, I spat out the blood, yet another taste of victory spoiled in the taking. Radu's last insult, another twist of the Poet's jest.

Die, brother, I told him as his essence drained into the bedclothes, *and know that I live still. I will see your line turn to dust and your name overshadowed, while the world will know and fear me still.* So I have seen. The Poet may misrepresent but he does not lie.

Now, centuries later, here I stand, the wolves of the forest the best company I can find, while far away the world is turning, a distant hum and chatter teasing through my waking dreams. There is a path here, laid out by the Mad Poet: stay and dissolve into the lonely abyss as the castle crumbles around me, or fulfil the book's dark visions, seek yet the ideal companion of the night, be a harbinger for the forces spoken of in the *Necronomicon*. The book may be long gone from me but the visions call with inexorable power: a world of gaslight and finery, a hubbub of voices, streets teeming with life, congested like never before. Such a remove from this isolation, this detestation, the lies and propaganda of my foes that cling like the stench of the dead.

This world draws me, new technologies and sciences rising above the base superstition that hold my people in thrall.

I can taste it, almost reach out and close my fist upon it and loose its essence with my nails, squeeze it till it is nothing more than a husk. To feast upon it, drain it, make it mine.

As though sensing the auspicious night, the wolves take up a chorus, howls carried on a chill breeze through the vacant windows, echoing in the empty halls.

The memory of the ritual in the lowermost chamber surges forth, like a wraith ascending the dusty stairwells, draped in the scent of earth and blood. I turn, half expecting to see the sisters, or perhaps the forms of long-dead family and brothers in arms, but the chambers remain empty of all but the tension of expectation, a storm about to break.

I make my way to the stables, pull cloak and hat from their pegs and assume the mien of a humble driver.

It is the eve of St George's Day, 1893, the moon is a glimmer behind ranks of cloud that rumble with portentous thunder, and it is time to horse the calèche and attend the Pass. My guest is nigh, and it will not do to be late. The papers he bears hold the key to my escape, and the eldritch song in my veins will not have my footsteps falter. The wolves sing their sweet music; the unholy dance resumes.

Simbiyu and the Nameless

Eugen Bacon

The colour is full of shade and smells like crusts of fruit. Crushed guavas, warm wet clay—that's the sweetness and mushiness about the forest. A tepidness too. And then there's a whiff of soured yam, unwashed body. Something old sniffling in the shadows.

Eyes pore over your hollow within, ticking, ticking with your heartbeat. But the hollow is dead cassava dry—all surface and dust. What sound will fall when you press your ear to its longing? Perhaps nuances of self-reflection beckoning the moon's return.

You are eighteen months old.

A crunch of tyres, then squeals of children tumbling out of a foreign car. Your mother owns sandals but likes to walk barefoot. This is how she greets Aunt Prim, who is layered in batiks and swirling in a smell of flowers. She's approaching the boma under the blaze of an orange sun. Your cousins, Tatu and Saba, are giggling, whispering, nudging each other.

"Abana banu! These children!" Aunt Prim is all sharpness. Sharp eyes, sharp nose, sharp ears. "I heard what you said!"

She grabs a stick from the ground, makes to chase your cousins, but platform shoes don't take her far. Her tongue clicks. Her stick waves from the distance. Aunt Prim is nothing like you know. Because your mother is pillow-soft, her voice tender like the feathers of a baby bird. She's hooked you on her arm, your fat legs astride her waist. Her sweet brown eyes, her dancing dimples. She smells of sugar bananas—small and thin skinned—on her chest where you rest your head.

"Sissy Prim. What do you bring us from the city?"

"Flour, sugar and these two urchins. Look at them."

"Doing what?"

"Mischief. Can't you see?"

"Don't run it up. They are young. See how you make them hush like spirits."

"Evil ones."

Silence, then a scatter of feet. Titters spilling everywhere, as your cousins stampede around the hut in a shroud of dust.

"I swear!" says Aunt Prim. "Weye! Useless as mud."

Your cousins still running.

"Tatu!" She's the older one. "Wait 'til I catch you!"

"And then what?" asks your mother.

"She'll see."

"Don't fall on the child with a hammer."

"Mphyo!"

Your world is small yet familiar, framed in textures and shapes. Sometimes you see darkness and lizards, cats nudging and gliding between grown-up legs. You touch what you know. Listen to what you don't, but still touch it. Trust or instinct are not your diplomacy. It's all about repetition, endurance. Curiosity and hunger etched in your living.

"Tatu!" Your mother locates the cousin behind the fat waist of a mango tree. "Take Simbiyu."

"I don't want to."

"Because why?"

"It's hours of boring."

"Rubbish. Come on then, quick. Your mother won't eat you."

"But she might!"

You whimper a little as your mother loosens you from her hold, as she presses you onto Tatu's back. "Saba, go inside. Fetch me a wrap."

He runs.

She rubs banana smash off your face with spit and a thumb. She takes the floral wrap from Saba, secures you on Tatu's small back. "Now off you go. Stay away from the river. Be children. Be alive."

"Like a drum?" quips Tatu, kicking off her shoes.

You gurgle your glee and bop on your cousin's back. Her naked feet race away from the homestead, past a few huts, some goats and grumbling chickens, and into the tree line.

"Wait for me!" cries Saba.

It's an uneasy sanctuary for play. But Tatu has chosen it. She zips into the forest full of spidered twines and shiny leaves—green and swollen like avocados, but they smell of the watching dead.

"I don't want to go there," says Saba, stalling his feet.

"Iwe! Don't be a coward. Just come!" Tatu loops through the trees. She doesn't care that Saba has chosen to run back home. She unknots you, plants you against a slanted candelabra tree and its bad milk. A perch of white-backed vultures with sharp beaks are on the tree overlooking the river with its white wash where you'll likely die—not from the water's malice that is of a different kind, but from a bask of crocodiles burrowed in its mud and blinking to darkness.

The river is changing. You know this without knowing how, or why. Tatu doesn't notice. She's poking in the mud, digging for crabs. A black octopus climbs from the water's surface. A mist that whispers a name. You understand it. You're one with it, bopping your anticipation.

They find Tatu's husk, and you—crawling and full of play around her shrivel, babbling a name.

You are four.

Tumbling down the village with your little friend Uhuru from the hut next door. He's your companion now. Your mother is distant, busy with farming: yams, sweet potatoes and tomatoes to sell at her stall in the market.

You feel the shift in the air before you see it, before Uhuru's squeal.

Silence is a dog rooted on the ground, no heart behind it. Smell is a non-event whose jaw is wide open, eyes glassed in shock. It's the maggots that carry an answer—slipping in and out of intestines torn from the dog's belly. Worms coiling, uncoiling, negotiating with the corpse, draping around each other in a sepia slime of focus.

Uhuru sees the dead dog and its maggots, but you see more. He's unaware of the fragment—something broken—and it has chosen you. That something is the shade of a tree, a lurching darkness assembling, disassembling. A menace approaching, human, nonhuman, waving tentacles.

It's the octopus from the river. A shadow jerking and crawling like the maggots but with a story, and there you are. Your mouth is moving in silence, unfolding words that are a breath in a messy language full of space. And you're ready and available, full of history and a future, just unwilling to once more hear the name.

"Run!"

As if Uhuru needs encouragement.

You are five.

You don't remember much of what happened—it was a blackout. They say you were sitting at the edge of the forest, all giddy and merry inside the circle of a serpent's coil in broad daylight, mumbling a name.

The creature was lethargic, a swell in its belly. Village men pulled you out of the circle—only then did you cry like someone was ripping off your limbs. But the rock python was too lazy to move. They sliced out broken bones and what was left of Uhuru.

It changed how people saw you. Now, they whispered.

At first, they poured holy water and crossed themselves when you passed. In time, they forgot what you didn't.

You are seven.

You know how to mingle, but it's not a school day. You like the sweet and mushy forest near the river. It's cooler on the skin here. Oranges and purples in the bright green foliage, flowers drooping, sky-craning, leaning into you as you walk by.

The rogue sisal belongs near the candelabra tree but today it is here. Chorused trilling, squeaking birds. You adore nature in its glory. Look, a shrub, weather-trimmed to resemble the bum of a gorilla facing away. The *chwee chweee* of a cousin bird hushes with the cough of a giant bird flapping its wings above the broad star-face of wild cassava leaves. The sound of water running. You can smell it: wet soil and reed.

No one is here, just the birds and you. You forget tussles with harmless children who sometimes tease, and you all but hold back from calling up a name. You're nothing like them, the village tots like Juzi or Vipi or Bongo—never curious about the skull of a dead zebra, the neck of a fallen giraffe. You discovered them at the edge of the forest. You once saw a leopard drag away a child. People are afraid of this wilderness, not you. You've told no one about the cave and its dripping of warmish water near the shores of the murky river hiding crocs and snakes.

Today you're here where it's dry but cooler on the skin, the name of an entity in your head. But it won't come.

You are nine.

You are more and more in your head, but perhaps it's your mother's guilt or penance that farms you out to Aunt Prim. Your mother walks you miles and miles from the village and your river, from dawn to noon, until you reach a market. There, she haggles about the price of a ticket, and puts you in a bus.

"Your aunt will be there when you reach."

"But I'm hungry."

"Eat the oranges and casava in the handkerchief I gave you."

The bus pulls into a town station at dusk.

Aunt Prim is there, all right, layered in batik, swirling in a scent of leopard orchids and kudu lilies.

Slap!

"But I didn't do anything." Your hand on your cheek.

"That will put it right out of your mind to do anything," she snaps, and hauls you to her car.

"Where's Saba?"

"Boarding school, like you should be."

You look at her. You don't have to say the name in your head because you feel it. The octopus mist is swirling, swirling inside. All this way ... how did it come?

That night Aunt Prim wakes up to lizards crawling in and out of her hair, up and down her body. She sees a yellow-eyed cat sitting on the sill of her bedroom window, in the blackness looking at her.

The incident creates the grim reality of your tacit agreement with your aunt to be civil to each other. You do your chores, do your school, where students and teachers give you no mind, and you prefer it that way: left alone, except on the football field. Aunt Prim lets you be, and you let her be. Sometimes she gives you Saba's comic books: *The Adventures of Tintin*.

In this world, you run up tides and variations by intuiting. Your entity is here, a spectre that enfolds you when you close your eyes until you reach the edge of reason. In life's lessons, will your sixth sense do you solid? Or will it dot your portrait of purpose, all obscure?

Right now, you don't know. Each day is a swaying floor that smells of city, sea and trap. You should be angry, fatigued from it: who's scripting your part?

A dream with a name is your handhold.

You are thirteen.

A scout spots you playing football in a stadium. You're clean with the ball, hitting the scoreboard. The other team is wide, nowhere near. Your own team is a shocker, but you're the most valuable player.

The scout is leaning against a post, scribbling notes on a sheet held in a clipboard.

A blackbird with an orange beak hops on your path, vanishes into air.

A name that is peril and chance slams like a door in your head.

You are fifteen when they clear you for travel. Your scholarship has come through. Aunt Prim is still wary but today all teeth, a wad of money tucked between her breasts.

"Get settled there and send for your cousin Saba. You'll make us proud."

Does 'us' include your mother? You haven't seen her in years. Sometimes, you wonder about her, then forget. You lost your mother the day Tatu died. She stopped breastfeeding you that same evening, and her touch hardened.

"Jump in my car. I'll drive you to the airport," says Aunt Prim.

"I'll take a taxi."

The road to the airport is full of potholes. The foreign contractor used cheap tarmac, and someone put a lot of money in their pocket. It's midnight when you pull along the kerb to the international swing doors. "Keep the change," you tell the driver. The scout and the people he represents are either very generous or keen to have you. You step out of the cab and further from all you know. It's a story for no tabloid, only you are listening to its tale. You understand all you've lost forever, yet it's the answer for right now.

You arrive at the checkpoint without phoning your shoeless mother who may be waiting for your midnight news. For the first time you understand both dying and torment, and the yawning schism of passing over.

You're sullen all the way to Melbourne Tullamarine Airport.

Six a.m. A queue of people at customs. A thumb sucker catches your eye, barks his cry into his blonde mother's shoulder. Perhaps she's an expat. She's wearing a t-shirt that says: *African drumming: be alive.* It reminds you of Tatu.

The uniform's face when you reach him is a stop sign. He demands papers, gives you a look that says you don't have them. But you have them. There's no ambiguity in your compliance. Still, he enters a dangerous discussion.

"Empty your pockets." It's full of notes—jottings that remind you where to draw the line. "Your phone," he says.

"Enough," you say.

He starts to bark orders, but the smell of dead bones has a point. It also has a name. Alarms are beeping like mad. The uniform's mouth is opening and closing, like that of a fish out of water. His skin is losing lustre, in fact greying. Restraint, for you, will come with age. Today is a life behind you, and a fuckwit between you and the life ahead.

Your ride is a big white van with a sign: A hive of bees? A sack of guavas? Goget.com. The man driving it is not the scout. He's a scruffy white man with ash on his head and a back-turned cap. You saw enough tatty whites in the planes and the airports, stopovers in Dubai and Sydney, but attributed it to a lack of flying etiquette. Now here's another one who held up a sign to retrieve you at Arrivals. A sign that said: *Simba Yo*.

You tap him on the shoulder. "That's not how you say my name."

He grunts.

He's not a man of many words. He drives along the labyrinth of the metropolis. You reach the college campus, and he throws your swollen suitcase off the van.

You're not sure whether to tip him. You pull a note, mindless of its value, and offer it.

"Nah. Keep your money, mate. We don't do that in Melbourne." He reverses the van, drives away.

You report at the main office arranged with phones and computers. It has pale walls and high ceilings. Glistened trophies and framed certificates stare at you. The girl behind the desk is a topaz-eyed nymph with burnt-orange hair.

"You're early. Semester starts in a week."

You sign forms. She gives you a student card, keys to your room, an entrance fob and a map. "Not many students around, but you might bump into the odd teacher."

You drag your suitcase into the grey monolith that's your dormitory.

Later, you'll take a walk to acquaint yourself with this new world full of cars and shops, and houses built like wedding cakes; you saw a tiered one when Aunt Prim's friend got married. You'll discover a restaurant that serves wok-fried prawns with lemongrass, curry leaf and shrimp. You'll wash the food down with water, not a glass of white.

On your way back, you'll go past a young woman with a face

swallowed in sunnies, dragging a leash and Tintin's dog. She'll take one look at you and remember to remotely lock her car.

You connect early, though you don't know how to read her, the new one. She comes at you on campus, peering through a camera. She lowers the lens. Big gold eyes shimmering on her face.

"Yer 'ave a look like a man on a mission ter forget a past."

"I'm not sure," you say.

"Then yor name's Tipsy."

"It's whatever you like."

"Just messin' wiv yer. They call me Mali." She extends a lingering hand that fits in your clasp. She's attractive: full lips on a triangle face. Hesitant smile. Hair so black it's blue, braided in rows and tails on her head.

"I wasn't expecting that accent from a black girl."

"I'm not sayin' anyfink about yor accent." You look at her, amused. "I'm bloody well British. Media and Studio Design. Are yer also on a scholarship then, guv?"

She's wearing a sunflower flow, bohemian in style. It waves with the wings of a butterfly. She's a twist in your story now — your gut tells you this girl is important.

"I'm a lesbian," she breaks your heart.

Mali shines. The longer you know her, the shinier she gets. It's not just the gold in her eyes — sometimes she's splashed in a beam of light from the sun.

She introduces you to grilled hunky dory and deep-fried chips. You miss chicken hearts and gizzards, slowly stewed in a pot on a three-hearth stone. Simmered with four sprigs of coriander and natural pink salt from the flamingo lake.

You take Economics. The lecturer is easy on your requirements for tasks and assignments. What matters is the field. The coach teaches you to play a different kind of football that uses hands and feet. They call it footy. The game has marks: players climbing others in leaps to catch the ball. It has boundary throws. The coach makes you a forward, not a ruckman — you're athletic but don't have the height, even though you can fly.

First match, first quarter, you're a showcase: three goals on the spot. The octopus is in you everywhere, your hands and legs fully tentacled. Bounce, bounce, kick. On the field, like this, you're one with the team. Inside kick, handball pass. Clean disposals, no waste to the dying seconds. Off field, you're solo. Not counting Mali.

You are seventeen.

But today is its own narrative. The octopus is asleep.

Before you fall, the ball has legs and accuracy—for the other team. The field is yellow with night lights. Shadows and smells: sweat and feet. The other team's players are everywhere. The match is a brawl, short shorts as you fight. Shoulders and chests bulldoze you to the ground. Knees and shins find tiny gaps to the post. The other team's star player has a left foot that's a mongrel. Nothing you do bangs the ball your end.

Your coach is filthy about this, his hands and mouth severe. But your body is wrong, your kick a real mess. Your skin is ill-fitting—that's why you fall.

What you want to remember is the name in your head that stands you up. The name that comes when your mind connects with a memory and latches on to it. It makes you right, just so. The name that's a voice and a ghost and a storm all at once. The name that makes you slippery through the forward half as the other team gains metres and besieges you. The name that fuses the ground and the sky like a clash of heavens and hells on your shoulders. It's a release that floats your ball long and deep and the match is changed.

What the devil? It's great. Now you understand that the entity is not always harming, it's gifting too.

You are eighteen.

You celebrate with a trip on a leased car. A three-hour drive via the CityLink to the Hume Highway that merges onto the Northern Highway. Two hundred and thirty kilometres to Echuca.

"Blimey, right, I forgot the camera."

Mali—the lesbian friend you can't read—is all eyes and dimples that remind of your mother, yet not. She's the one driving, she has a licence.

Two years now, she's been giving the right vibes that could be wrong. She has slowly hijacked your life in a romance that will never take.

From when you first saw her, even as the campus grounds spilled with students—red ones, pink ones, olive ones—Mali and her cloaking of light are spottable anywhere. You find it refreshing to be around black skin, though she speaks funny and insists on pointing her lens at moving targets: birds, cars, people, you, mostly you. Saying, wow, wow, as if she sees something you don't.

Her photos of you are up close. A soldier's crop. Big square face. Thick black brows that are better less. A wide nose. A gobbling mouth—she caught you in a yawn. You wonder what she sees in you. Still you can't read her. She holds away from more. Or is it you holding away, unsure if she just really likes you, or is bi?

"As I were sayin", Simbiyu, me pops. He'd been married, wot— thrice?"

You look at her and see sparkles. She's shimmering.

"I never knew my father," you say. "Spoils of war."

"Scars, right, yer mean, isit?"

"Too good at reading me." You're thinking: Shouldn't she be the one?

"Yer make it sound terrifyin'."

You're in trackies, but the rented four-sitter is all shiny inside, gears and buttons. She glides, purring all the way down a lone country road, the sun bearing down, a scorch in your throat.

You were once a child with a lacking story, and now worry about what's too far gone for sadness or anger. But you already determine that what *should be* is a slaughtered treat. Nothing will resurrect the impossible. Work is never cut out for you. All you can do *now* is comfort yourself under the looming moon's unreadable gaze.

Mali drives long and north towards a country town with paddle-steamers on the Murray River. The evening sun is a watercolour on the horizon. Clouds frown malcontent into meantime lands.

Echuca is a ghost town. You're too late for the paddle-steamer, and everywhere is closed. Look, what's this: a pub named Parfitt. It's yet unpatroned but spilling with brash country music.

Please, no dogs, says a sign on the wall behind the service counter. But all you see is a memory far too big, a walking contradiction to nowhere stories. The pub with its fading décor is not the kind you pictured. A float of feathers lavishes fusty walls, but there's a hook for a coat. The man at the bar is wearing a sweater. He has eyes that could be your lost father's, his arms folded, legs akimbo. Box face, swirly curls all grey, the nose of a prince—all haughty like. He's built like a fridge but there's heat in his dislike. His eyes come and go to the sign on the wall, then at you.

You look around. There are no dogs, just you.

Mali is sparkling. "That says a bit. Like a bit."

You don't need to summon the name. You and the river octopus are one. Your head falls back, your tentacles spreading within, without. Your eyes close, your feet off the ground. Your eyes open to blinding light. You blink. All is changed. Fat toads are hopping on the counter, sliming the floor. Hundreds of lizards knocking glasses in slow-motion hours going without protocol. The man at the bar is making a noise that's a groan inside a croak. A toad is lodged down his throat. His legs have the shakes. He's deflating inside his sweater, a man-sized doll losing air. The desiccation in his skin … The shrivel of hair on his scalp. Centuries consume him. You look at your hands—you're a shadow. Your mouth is moving in silence, your body lurching darkness.

A voice inside the bright light says, "Me word. I don't 'ave me fuckin' camera, init? I knew yer were special."

You step back into yourself on solid ground, but your head is swirling. Suddenly you feel alone, and alone is not so fun anymore.

"Simbiyu." Mali's luminescence is reaching, your name is a caress on her lips.

As you wonder when she met her Cthulhu, she offers her lingering hand. You hesitate, then take it. She snatches you out of the pub and drives across a railway, past its station to a place you'll lean into each other, chest to shin, heads touching. Waiting—for what?

You'll spend the night at a family motel with wi-fi and free parking.

You are twenty-three.

Your team has been in the 'top four' years in a row: twice grand finalist and two cups to show for it. You are the most medalled player, constantly making headlines. You wear twice-shined moccasins. You own three cars and a tiered wedding-cake house on Summer Street in a leafy suburb.

You pay for Saba's tuition—he's family. *Wema hauozi*, says the adage. True: generosity never rots. You send money home to Aunt Prim and have built a storeyed house for your mother—what's family? She still walks barefoot, they say. You put electricity and tap water in the village. They finally cordon it from the wilderness when two elephants go rogue.

There's a sweetness in your bedroom, a mushiness in the air. A tepidness too. It doesn't matter when crushed guavas and warm wet clay show up, or when a whiff carrying ghosts of soured yam dumps itself with a scratch on your chin.

A crack of lightning, and the devil himself plods from twilight. Then he's you, and you're offside in your leap from the bed. You land knees and knuckles on the ground. Your skin heals and takes you back to yourself and your bed. The devil smiles and wets his parched throat from a brook as you lie awake counting words and dreams sprouting from a future that insists it knows what's best before sunrise.

You look at Mali, blanketed in silver light. Glittering in deep sleep beside you.

You remember with longing your once pillow-soft mother. Her sweet brown eyes and dancing dimples. Her voice, tender as the feathers of a baby bird.

You finally understand the nameless. And the darkness that rose from the river those many years ago—how it chose you. Because it's also you.

The Meatamorphosis

Aaron Sterns

As Gordon Pym awoke one morning from uneasy dreams he found himself transformed in his bed into a monstrous… shoggoth. He didn't even know the inhuman, guttural word that came to him, but just knew it to be true, like it had always lain dormant inside him waiting for chance release. *Shoggoth*.

He was lying on his gelatinous, somehow-now amorphous back, and when he lifted his head a little he could see his distended black-slimed belly rippling beneath the constraint of the quilt like a barely-contained bag of insects. His numerous legs—arms, tendrils?—which were pitifully thin compared to the rest of his bulk, waved uselessly out the sides of his bed.

What has happened to me? he thought. It was no dream. His room, a regular human bedroom, only rather too small, lay quiet between the four familiar walls. His scuffed dresser, bought and carried home like treasure from the Greenway river market, squatted against one wall beside the hallway door. The leather armchair his grandfather had left him, seat worn smooth with generations of comfortable contemplation, took up too much of one corner beside the second door to the shared bathroom. Above the table by the opposite wall on which his work folders lay—he was a medical instruments salesman and prone to much travel—hung the advertisement he had recently cut from a magazine of an absorbed young family laughing as they rushed inside before rain. Their house so large and covetous, perfect children, the angled wife looking back at her husband with a gaze as if seeing him for the first time. The husband grinning back, one hand still claiming the hood of his new Packard Twin 6 Roadster. It was no doubt Gordon's room.

His eyes turned away to the window, and the overcast Providence skyline beyond which made him even more melancholy. Outside, the traffic on Barnes Street filtered through the glass in a stream of muted bustle: town cars and rumbling milk carts, laughing children early to the nearby school, strolling couples shouting hallo to neighbours. He should just sleep a little longer and forget all this nonsense, Gordon thought, but it could not be done for he was accustomed to sleeping on his right side and in his present condition he could not turn himself over from his back, no matter how much he flailed his stunted limbs. He wasn't sure he was lying on his back, to be truthful. Or that he even really *had* a back any longer.

Beside the crater in his head that was once an ear his alarm clock began blasting its incessant childlike shriek. He managed to knock it off the stand where it shattered its plastic front on the thinly carpeted floor. Silence descended once more, though now the pressing awareness of his morning deadline took its place. Ah hell, he thought, what an exhausting job I've picked! Travelling about day in, day out, living out of a suitcase. It's a damn sight harder than doing the actual stocktaking and purchase orders in the office like Smith and Crofts and the other lazy sods. The devil take it all! As if in response to his heightened stress he felt a slight itching beneath the slope of his belly, but when he pushed higher up the bed to identify the source of discomfort he found only a concentration of white markings near where his groin (oh, my little friend!) should be, the nature of which he could not understand—though there was something inherent in the pattern, a stirring of pre-conscious thought that drifted into coalescence then snatched itself away, continuing to gnaw at him afterwards like a worm struggling to metamorphosise inside his brain. He thought hard to control one of his errant legs to scratch

THE MEATAMORPHOSIS

the irritation, then shied away at the instant jolt of discomfort as if he'd stuck his glistening limb in an electric socket, and was careful not to scrape his underside again.

His underside. How quickly he was accepting the fevered hallucination. It was this relentless getting up early, he thought, which made anyone quite stupid. A man needed his sleep. The other sales agents never worked as hard. Bishop, Lethbridge, Templesmith. Whenever Gordon came back to the hotels in the morning to write up the acquisitions he'd already secured, the others were always only sitting down to breakfast. Let *him* try that on with his manager. He'd be sacked on the spot. If not for Gordon's parents and sister he'd have given notice long ago. He'd have surely walked into the officious little cramped office above the warehouse and stood over *his* manager's desk and yelled down at *him*. But the mere thought filled him with a cold dread, and slime-sweat dripped into the sunken portals of his eyes and clouded his already hazy vision. He could not afford such fantasies while he still had to pay back the debts of his family's business failures—it would take another three or four years of miserly saving to be free of the scary loansharks who bankrolled his father's overambitious clothing factory—but then, yes then he'd quit without fail. For the moment he'd better get up, since his train went at six.

Yet when Gordon looked at the cracked alarm clock on the floor, its numbers still inexorably ticking over, he discovered he'd somehow already missed the train. It was six-fifteen. Dammit! he thought. How long had he lain struggling to rise, thinking useless thoughts? Or… perhaps it was his grasp on time. Even as he watched through the dulled fog of his new brain, the ticking numbers accelerated until his hold on them became meaningless. What even is time, but one human-centric interpretation of reality, a linear perception other beings more attuned to the atomic minutiae of the universe would understand as a fluid and unimportant filter lesser minds allow to consume and restrain them?

Now, where did that come from? Such strange musings were not helpful in the slightest, and must be stamped down if he were

51

to survive this morning. What was he to do now? The next train went at six-thirty; to catch that he would need to hurry like mad and his folders weren't even packed up, his clothes still hung over the back of the leather armchair, his hair must be a sight. Wait, did he still have hair? Perhaps he didn't have to worry about his errant rarely-cut curly locks any longer at least, but that just raised once more the issue of his appearance no longer quite matching... himself. How would he explain the waving tentacles, for one thing? How would one shake hands with a new client? Then there was the thought that even if he did catch a later train his manager would be irate the day's loadout would have to be pushed back. He'd been late once early in his tenure at the company, and his supervisor had berated him so long and so violently Gordon had begun to leak silent tears like a truant schoolchild, and had walked back head down from the little office to hide his snuffling shame. The other salesman sometimes still called him Baby Gordie amongst themselves, he knew.

All this must take an eternity to remember, for when Gordon next glanced at the clock it had struck a quarter to seven. He could only blink stupidly as the numbers flipped hungrily, further eroding his tenuous hold on time, and then there came a cautious tap at the hallway door. *"Gordie,"* said a voice—it was his mother's—*"it's nearly seven. Haven't you a train to catch?"* That increasingly-insipid, strangely-elderly voice! Gordon had a shock as he heard his own voice answering hers with his usual patience, unmistakably his own voice, yet with a guttural wetness beneath it like an undertone that left the words in their clear shape only for the first moment and then rose up reverberating round them to destroy their sense, so that one could not be sure you'd heard them rightly. Gordon wanted to answer at length and explain everything, but in the circumstances he confined himself to saying: "Yes, yes, thank you, Ma, I'm getting up now." The wooden door between them must have kept the change in his voice from being noticeable outside, for his mother contented herself with this statement and shuffled away.

Yet this brief exchange had alerted the other members of his family that Gordon was still in the house, and his stooped

THE MEATAMORPHOSIS

father was soon knocking too, gently, at first. "*Son?*" he called. "*What's the matter with you?*" And after a while in a deeper voice: "*Gordon? Gordon!*" Behind the bathroom door on the other side of the room his sister appeared in a low, plaintive tone: "*Aren't you well, brother? Are you needing anything.*" Then lower, her voice acidic with disappointment: "*Oh, what is it this time Gordon? How you hurt them so.*" He answered both at once: "I'm almost ready," doing his best to make his treacly voice sound as normal as possible by enunciating the words very clearly and leaving long pauses between them. But his concept of time being as it were the words dragged too long and did not convince them, and his father snorted and left, while his sister's voice turned impatient. "*Gordo? Open the door.*" However, he had no intentions of opening the door—or capacity to—and felt thankful for the prudent habit he had acquired while travelling of locking his doors at night, even at home.

He remembered that often in bed he had felt small aches and pains, probably caused by awkward postures on unfamiliar mattresses, which proved purely imaginary once he got up, and he looked forward to seeing this morning's delusions also gradually fall away. The change in his voice must be the onset of flu, yes, of that he had no doubt. Once he was dressed and had quietly eaten breakfast alone without fussing relatives, sanity— and reality—would once again prevail.

To shuck the quilt was easy enough; he had only to inflate himself a little and it slipped off by itself. But the next move was more difficult, because he was so... well, unformed, quite frankly. He would have needed arms and hands to hoist himself up, yet instead only had these multiple thin tentacles that never stopped waving in all directions and which he could not control in the least. When he tried to focus on one to straighten and brace against the wall it buckled with a snap of pain and a viscous goo seeped green from a small tear. It stung like a dog bite. Instead he had to synchronise his limbs, and when enough hit against the wallpaper at once he *shoved* and rolled in counterpoint away and felt his weight slipping, slipping off the bed. His head teetered over the edge and the hard floor loomed below and he realised too late his error, his hubris, and he saw himself falling in a great shift of mass and splattering like a ripe watermelon on the threadbare carpet. His parents and sister would come running and find the green goop painting his walls and bed and small work table like an explosion had gone off inside the little room. Of their son there would be no trace.

All this he saw as he rocked out into space and then his limbs instinctively folded into his bulk and he rolled off the mattress in a giant ball and landed with a muffled squelch below that hurt less than he expected, and the room spun as he kept rolling and came to a stop against the chair across the room. One chair leg dented his side in a gradual metallic burn and he pulled back and lay gasping for breath staring up at the ceiling. Deep within the house his family once again came running at the sound of cushioned impact.

"Gordon, did you fall? Gordon, open the door now!" His mother again, panicked. Just then, the little table above rattled as his desk phone chirruped its mating call. The room pulsed an electrical scream as the phone skipped and bucked across the table, already knocked off-balance by his hit, and danced off the edge and onto his belly with a wet slap. He looked down to see the curved black handset remain behind as the heavy base of the phone began sinking into his flesh, the little holes on the circular earpiece tinnying at him with the harsh voice of his manager's secretary: *"Mister Pym? Is someone there? Why, this is most irregular. I think he is playing games Mister Armitage—"* Unnerved, Gordon tried to swipe the phone off himself with his errant tendrils, but they only whipped like snakes across his skin, futilely slashing air, and the viscous jelly covering his entire surface washed over the black base like a tide and then the square of metal sank from view and the cutting female voice gurgled as the handset was pulled down after it and disappeared too. A sharp fizzing sound filled the air and a smell of scorched Bakelite hit his smell sacs as the cord now feeding into his belly was suddenly cut as if by acid. The only memory of the phone was a distant metal burn that began to thrum somewhere deep within like heartburn. At least the incessant annoyance of the machine now made no sound,

even though the whole event rattled Gordon with a severe bout of anxiety that took minutes—or was it hours?—to overcome. It only passed when *he* passed the phone, a compressed block of black mass expelling from an orifice somewhere halfway down his body like a bullet. It dented the skirting board and rolled to a stop, a mucus-covered square dark ball he tried not to look at again.

Gordon soon wished he *had* answered the call, even considered crawling over to the melted loadstone of black metal and somehow reattach the severed cord. The disparaging, instantly dismissive tone of his manager's secretary unsettled him. Had he already been fired, for being an hour late? Were the firm that callous? Did the world hate him so much it would punish him the instant he stepped out of line?

A moment later the hall phone bleated—a separate line from the sales line his company subsidised in his room—and he heard his sister answer, murmuring a moment, before her shuffled footsteps came to the hall door. *"Gordon. It's your manager, Mister Armitage himself. You're late to your first call. He says you'll lose the Royal Alfred order if you're not there in fifteen minutes. He says... he says this is the last straw."* For a moment Gordon imagined these words arising from deep inside his belly like the phone was still inside him, his manager's little ferret-faced mouth filling with slime as he berated Gordon before choking on his words and drowning. "But sir," Gordon suddenly said as loudly as he could, forced to defend himself against outrageous slander, "I'm just getting ready, about to open the door and leave. A queasy stomach, a bit of a head spin, has kept me from getting up. I'm dressing right this minute, will make the next train. I'll be ten minutes late to the hospital at most. They were later than that for my last meeting with them. But... but as for claims I'm somehow lazy or deficient in my job, my God, I worked for months paving the way for this order. Excuse my language, sir, I apologise, but I really must protest this attack on my work ethic. My elderly parents—who I now care for, I must remind you—instilled in me a diligence to any job I do, and I have worked tirelessly at the company. In fact... once I have closed this deal we... we should discuss the hours I've been performing."

Silence on the other side of the door. Then the electric-filtered squeak of his manager—strange that Gordon could hear the handset even from here, his hearing must be elevated—*"Did you understand a word of that? Is he being ill?"* His sister's reply: *"I'm sorry, I don't know what he's saying anything either."* *"Oh dear,"* cried then his mother in tears, *"He's sick and we're tormenting him! Gordon, open up!"*

Gordon distantly heard his father command his sister to hang up the phone and call a doctor this minute—*"Did you hear how he was speaking? That was no human voice,"*—and then yell at his mother to help him find his years-obsolete contacts book to locate a locksmith. *"Blast that boy and his secrecy."* But Gordon barely registered any of this. He had dragged himself to the dresser and further scratched its surface clawing up its face until he was standing unsteadily on a half-dozen thin legs. Dizziness threatened to take him but he fought his vertigo and focused on the door still an eternity away. He could not get there alone and grabbed the nearby precious armchair and hauled it bodily out before him, then slowly pushed it across the splintering floorboards. It left great screeching gouges in the wood that silenced his family in the hall, but at least the chair took enough of his weight that he was able to cover the distance in hiccupping bunnyhops. His legs threatened at any moment to give way beneath him but thankfully did not snap with the strain of his bulk. He did leave an embarrassing trail of slime though. He would ask for towels and insist on cleaning that himself.

Finally at the hall door he faced the difficult prospect of unlocking it with no hands. Nor did he seem to have teeth when he bent his frons—his flattened face—to the key in the lock, but his jaws were certainly very strong and he managed to grip the stinging metal with his mouth and work the tumblers beyond. Though he must be damaging himself—a thin brown liquid spilling over his chin from his shredded lips and dripping to the floor below—the excited chatter of his family outside spurred him on. *"Just listen to that, he's turning the key!"* *"Go on, Gordon."* *"I won't need the locksmith after all."* He felt a small thrill of almost-forgotten pride.

Gordon clenched his jaws on the stubborn key and worked his body around with all his meagre strength until it finally clicked and released him from his bedroom prison. Since he had to pull the door towards him, he was still invisible when it opened wide. He had to edge around its jutting scythe with his unfamiliar and awkward bulk, and was still grasping the chair for support when the first gasp hit him like a gust of wind: "Oh!" His mother was staring at him with her hand clapped over her mouth, little wizened eyes above like pinpricks of surprise, her morning hair yet undone and sticking up in all directions. She looked to her husband beside, but the once-imposing shabbily bearded man stood frozen, fists knotted as if he wished to knock Gordon back in his room, yet mouth working in gaping Os like a fish gasping for air. Gordon's sister leapt to her mother's side when the older woman collapsed to the floor, shooting her brother the look of silent disdain he had weathered so often in their interminable years on earth together.

"Well," said Gordon, knowing perfectly that he was the only one who had retained any composure. "I'll put my clothes on at once, pack up my samples and start off. If you will be so kind as to call my manager and inform him of my intentions, please? And perhaps aid me to open my dresser, for I do not feel quite... myself this morning, and seem to be having some troubles moving. And standing."

His family stayed motionless in the darkened hall like a Caravaggio tableau, his mother elegantly splayed on the floorboards, sister cradling, father overshadowing them with dramatic fist on heart, but at the guttural croaks emanating from their only son's blackened mouth hole they blinked and recoiled as if at a sudden stench, and when he flopped a stumbling step into the hallway towards their comforting embrace his mother screamed and scrabbled back up the corridor, then turned and bolted for her bedroom. She fumbled at its handle with about as much dexterity as Gordon had just shown, then threw herself inside. He could hear her great weeping cries as she buried herself in her bed.

His sister rose, her eyes growing bright with a dawning awareness as she took in Gordon's new visage, but his father was spurred by the attack on his wife's delicate senses and for a moment reverted to a commanding physicality decades in the past and the great protector straightened his looming height and looked to either side in the hall for something to grab, settling on a walking stick in the umbrella stand, and gripped its end with one suddenly-steady hand and leapt at Gordon, rapping his mucus-covered carapace and forcing him back into the room despite his sister's pleas. Gordon heard something crunch along his side and his legs buckled and he rolled backwards and then the door slammed shut.

Gordon lay curled on the floor for many minutes, bleeding heavily, but it wasn't that last image of his father's furious face as the slice of hallway closed that imprinted on his memory, nor the heavy cane thrashing down through the air at him, not even the way his wizening father recoiled at the crawling black blood that overleaped up the stick towards warm flesh before solidifying on contact with the air and fossilising in a clump like dried dog feces on its end.

No, it was his sister returning to his door once silence had settled on the house, her voice quickened with unusual interest in him as she pressed hard against it for a moment and whispered words that should mean nothing, yet picked further at some pre-existent lock within him that struggled to retain the last of his humanity.

Words from a time before humanity, a time before time, before existence itself.

"*Cthulhu fhtagn*, brother."

CHAPTER II

Gordon woke from troubled visions of a roiling great mass of bodies, slickened and viscous and leviathan, agitating at the thin membrane suppressing their vast birth. The jarring unreality of the dream—yet slightly comforting sense of shared community and mind—soon fell away as his fragile corporeality sounded itself once more. His left side felt like one single, long, unpleasantly tense scar from where his father had staved in his back with the sharp push of the walking stick. Though the blood had solidified on his skin it still

THE MEATAMORPHOSIS

bubbled and boiled beneath as it tried to mend the damage. Two tentacles hung limp and useless, and though he had many more would have to be vigilant to compensate his weight. He felt their loss keenly, like children.

As he fought the pain Gordon let his gaze trail around the darkened room, and its sad, sparse, alien furniture only added to his dislocation. He began to feel that the cramped, depressing room was no longer just his prison, but that *matter itself* disappointed him. *Why* had atoms arranged themselves in such a way to form this chair? *Why* a dresser? Why not a, a mathematically-beautiful swirl of wood? Or, or an endless hole in the wall that could store infinite items? Why were all these human creations so unambitious. So... ugly?

Something drew his attention back to the disheartening rectangle of door (*and why a rectangle of wood? Why not a sheet of cool, clear water that invigorated you passing through?*), and Gordon recognised a sweet scent from the past drifting in and up his smell sacs. He shuffled back across the floor with effort, then stopped, intrigued and a little frightened. Though the door was still closed, a small basin filled with fresh milk in which floated little sops of white bread sat just inside his room. Gordon suddenly registered his aching hunger and could have laughed for joy at his usually weekend-only breakfast appearing right when he needed it to recover from his egregious injuries. He bent his face into the beckoning liquid, then as quickly reared back—for although milk had been his favourite drink, and that was certainly why his sister had set it there for him—the taste now filled him with repulsion. He pulled away into the centre of the room to retch and heave, then curled into his little ball of lonely solace once more, wounds still smarting terribly and now without fuel to repair.

Listening hard, he could not make out the familiar huffing sounds of his father reading his newspaper in the living room across the hall, or his mother darning while she softly nattered to her husband regarding the neighbours and their latest social indiscretions: Mrs Haggarty talking to the widower Johnson while her husband was overseeing the sewing factory that kept her in such lovely dresses; or Father O'Halloran imbibing too much communion wine last Friday and falling asleep nestled in the rectory's hedge. With effort, balancing on his good side, Gordon cracked open the door enough to see out a sliver, and saw that the gas indeed was not on in the adjoining room. Muffled voices were coming from the kitchen down the hall instead, and he imagined his family huddled around the small dining table, brows furrowed as they wondered what to do now with their disappointing son, particularly if he could no longer provide for them. How would they support the household without their bonded slave? How would his mother afford her sickly bonbons? His father his ridiculous cough-syrup cognac? Or his sister her violin lessons that might one day elevate her to world orchestra tours, but for now cost almost as much as their rent every week, week after week. No doubt they were all tucking into what would soon become a dwindling supply of their cold meats and cheeses as they spoke, and Gordon's mouth hole salivated at the thought, then his insides shuddered and he nearly vomited at the memory of such heady tastes. If milk proved too strong for his stomach what chance did he have with the punching hit of salami? Nevertheless, it was some comfort to lie in the dark doorway and listen to their murmurings. He could at least feel some connection to the world this way, even if only aurally. He didn't expect a cuddle.

Once during the long afternoon he heard footsteps in the hall that faltered then retreated again: someone had apparently wanted to approach then thought better of it. With reluctance Gordon pulled himself back inside the room, close enough that he could listen for movement, but not so that he would ambush anyone glancing in the doorway.

He dozed throughout the quiet of night, watching as lights flared in little glows in the gap as the inhabitants of the house shuffled to bed before dark descended and the rest of the city slept beyond his window. Part of him remained unsettled at the prospect of the dreams returning, but he was too restless and unsure of his position in the household to fall into a deep enough sleep to suffer them, and his thoughts kept relentlessly churning over themselves.

Very early in the morning, it was still almost night, Gordon woke from his shallow slumber to a hunched figure peering in the doorway. His mother, hair in rollers, frayed dressing gown clutched tightly at her chest with white knuckles. With a last impulse of concern for her son—or perhaps guilt for having forced him to support his ailing parents when he had expressed such desires to travel, to England, to Australia, somewhere exotic and unexplored, for so long now—she searched the gloom, not seeing him at first. Then when she caught sight of him under the chair—well, he had to be somewhere, he couldn't have flown away, could he? and it was so comforting being confined by the legs of the chair, like back in the womb—she was so startled she hiccupped and slammed the door shut again.

It was some hours later before soft footfalls came from the side door and it creaked open to assess the room then shut once more. His sister must have noted the full saucer of milk, because some minutes later, or maybe hours as he no longer really grasped the passage of time, she ducked in from the hallway and whisked away the bowl and placed instead a sheet of old newspaper on which she threw a number of items to test his delicate digestion. The girl paused in silhouette, her body long and agile, those violinist fingers splayed in the dawning light like claws, and as a square of light hit her face Gordon saw a calculated ambition there, but also a flare of narrow-eyed doubt and before he could engage her she dashed out again.

Cthulhu fhtagn.

Gordon shuffled from beneath his womb retreat and blinked his many eyes at the harsh morning sun arcing through the high window. Avoiding its burning reach as well as he could, he skirted along the shadowed floor and inspected the bounty. To find out what he liked, his sister had left a whole selection of food arrayed on the paper in neat clumps. There were a few fresh carrots and a larger stack of old, half-decayed vegetables; bones from last night's supper covered with a white sauce that had thickened; some raisins and almonds; a piece of cheese Gordon would have called uneatable only days ago; and a dry roll of bread. Beside, she had set down the saucer again, but with fresh water this time that smelled somehow off to him. He nibbled the rancid vegetables and cheese, but devoured the bones, crunching them with his hard mouth and slurping out the spongey marrow. The fresh offerings and water however assaulted him with their mere presence, and when he had his fill he scuffed the paper over them and retreated to the shadows beneath the chair to lazily digest what was his first sustenance since all this had begun.

The key rattled as a signal of incursion, and Gordon retracted the errant tentacles extending beyond the legs of the chair so as not to cause offense to her sensibilities while his sister retrieved the leftovers. Slight attacks of breathlessness afflicted him and his array of eyes bulged a little out of his head as he watched his sister pause to consider the food that had been eaten and that which had not, give a little cluck of the tongue as her suspicions were confirmed, and then she swept up the remains with a broom and glanced over at him watching. She gave a jolt, confronted each time she saw him no doubt, then let loose a small smile.

"Even monsters must eat their vegetables, right brother?"

Once, she had told their parents he had been spooning the cold vegetables he loathed so much out the side window and his mother had beaten his backside with a spoon. His sister always delighted in reminding him since, when she was in a nicer frame of mind. Gordon guffawed a laugh that sounded more sinister and echoey than he intended beneath his cramped hollow and his sister stumbled backwards and fumbled for the door.

"No, sister! The meal has bloated me so much I cannot even move. See, the chair floats above, resting on my stretched back. Its legs hang off the floor. Can you not see I would have to scrape a layer off my flesh were I to move too quickly against this comforting wood? How can you think I should prove a threat?"

His sister only tore harder at the lock at his guttural bellowing, and she ripped open the door and ran before he could propel out from his hiding place at her, not that he would. He lay listening to her fleeing footsteps disappear up the hall, the meal rather tainted and heavy in his stomach now, like he'd stolen it. Like he hadn't earned the money to buy it in the first place.

THE MEATAMORPHOSIS

Money consumed his family more than the plight of their only son. His sister continued to provide his morning selection of rotting and half-consumed vegetables, or occasionally the sinewy remains of some unfortunate animal plundered over the dinner table the night before. Sometimes she threw in off-cuts of meat snuck from neighbour's bins, averting her face from the stench. And increasingly she stayed to watch him slink out from his haven and shovel up the offerings, and he'd grown comforted by her presence in his doorway. But she didn't talk to him again, and would flee if he attempted to do so. He soon stopped trying. Gordon's parents, however, were more concerned with his drain on their finances. Even though Gordon required no more than left-over scraps, his very presence was apparently costing them the last of the household's money. Once, he listened hard at the door and heard his father talking at the dinner table in his low, scratchy voice. *"If we had a paying tenant, that's all I'm saying. That would tide us over."* *"And where would you put... him?"* his sister asked, surprisingly defending Gordon for once. *"It's not like he can share a room with one of us."* *"Of course not, dear. Well... No, no of course not,"* his mother now, further away, distracted at the stove perhaps. *"But this can't go on forever, surely."* *"Meaning what?"* his sister had asked, but she received no reply.

At first his parents seldom ventured past his room to the front door, and never looked in when they did. Gordon stayed hidden as his father clomped up the floorboards and jiggled the bedroom's handle to ensure it was locked, or quickly shut the door if it was ajar airing out the increasingly-fetid smell. Only then would his mother venture from the kitchen and pass on to the weekly market. Lately though Gordon had begun to hear visitors to the little house: servicemen or bachelors with darning requests, once a bride-to-be distraught at a tear along one seam of her grandmother's gown, struggling parents with children's knees to be patched. All odd jobs once beneath his mother's talents when they'd had the factory, but now a lifeline. Gordon listened as his parents deferentially bobbed and bowed and acceded to their customer's haggling and admonitions of care. He could imagine his father's face turning impotent beet-red from the disrespect, and Gordon would smile to himself as the door closed on the demands and his father fumed into his beard back up the hallway while his mother trailed arms full of defective clothes pleading with him to *quiet, they might be loitering on our step listening for our complaint you old fool*. Sometimes a neighbour would try to ingratiate themselves inside, curious at the state of their son or suggesting medical investigation, but his parents would shoo them away with short shrift. Gordon thought they'd once said the sight was *"not that interesting really"*, or words to that effect. He imagined they'd said the same thing when the nursing mother had cooed maternal sentiments at Gordon's birth.

He'd almost escaped them once, when he was younger. He'd been betrothed to Jillian Armstrong then, the daughter of his father's foreman. A slight, nervy girl, she had nevertheless been enamoured with Gordon for some reason he'd never quite understood, hanging on his every word with luminous eyes. She made him feel taller, more ambitious. He in turn watched her paint, and would sit beside wondrous at the economical sweep of her oil brush, amazed as she created entire worlds from nothing. She grew in confidence with his support and began displaying her work at the fair, and even sold a piece. When he secured an entry job at an international brokerage he promised in two years he'd move up the ranks and be required to travel, and he'd take her to Paris first and they'd be married there. And then his father's factory collapsed beneath a weight of debt, like so many other manufacturing plants in Providence as the industrial revolution finally ran out of steam, and his parents revealed they'd made Gordon guarantor of the business and he was now liable for the accounts. They'd had to sell their manor house, and Jillian's father had stormed up to the door of their rental tenement one night and demanded Gordon release his daughter from her obligations, and Gordon had tried to plead with her around the bigger man's shoulders, but she'd stood silent and bereft of agency behind her father and that had been the last he'd seen her. At the risk of all four of his family losing the meagre accommodation left to them, Gordon had taken on the burden of the good provider, but he'd

THE MEATAMORPHOSIS

always longed to revert back to that time before it had all gone wrong, to revert to a time before his dreams were stolen without ever a word of thanks or respect.

At least the piecemeal work his parents now managed to secure quelled talk of evicting their albatross son, though Gordon grew more paranoid and would creep out from beneath the chair in the evening to press against the thin door and listen to their voices. He was strangely disappointed to find they stopped talking of him altogether after a time. They would talk of 'the Room', as in, "*throw these bones out in the room, they're picked clean,*" or "*have you mopped the room this week? You can smell it from the front door.*" Admittedly, the whole bedroom had indeed become tracked with the slime he emitted. Without his sister slopping water over the floorboards and wallpaper and even ceiling while he deferentially hid his visage from her view it became crusty and smelled of mold.

Yes, wallpaper, and ceiling. It was funny how Gordon had discovered his new abilities. For a while he gained strength with his new diet, and delighted in pelting around the room like an unleashed puppy. After he'd gnawed off the two injured tentacles which dangled uselessly and tripped him whenever he walked, the limbs so withered and forgotten it didn't even hurt when he yanked them free, he found he could skitter across the mucus-slickened floor with his remaining legs quicker than ever. After each meal-hit of sustenance he would giddily tear around the room while the rest of the house fell silent and waited for him to exhaust himself. Once he'd run too fast and hit the wall and climbed halfway up before realising he could effortlessly hold his own weight, and he kept going up onto the ceiling, where he hung lazily from the minute clawed hairs on the ends of his tentacles and surveyed his little world below.

He grew complacent, sometimes falling asleep upside down, and he was still resting beside the softly-chewed light fitting one afternoon perhaps a week later when his sister returned to clean his meal, but it was too late to retreat to his haven and at the sudden sight of him looming above she gave her first real shriek of fear. He retreated to the far upper corner and then, seeing he was no threat, she gave a little laugh of embarrassment and came back in from the hall.

"You are full of tricks," she said, and at first he faltered at the unfamiliar tone in her voice. Was that…admiration? She stood eyes wide with wonder and watched him perform, slowly at first so as not to disturb her, then racing faster and faster across the ceiling and along the walls in a denial of physics, like a hamster in a dimension-free cage, a spirit free of form. For what was matter now to contain him? He who no longer really felt part of this world, but instead straddled it with some other plane of existence that crept more and more into his dreams.

When he had exhausted himself he crept down to his little hiding spot beneath the chair, happy and spent, and lay panting as his sister's lilting laugh filled the room like the most beautiful music to his starved ears.

She came towards him and he tensed as she drew close and bent, yet he saw now she was no longer repulsed or scared by him, no longer scornful of his existence and achievements as his family had been for so much of his life. Instead she reached down and cradled the arched crown of his head, the first contact by another living being since waking that initial morning. "You are the key," she whispered.

He nestled into the unfamiliar weight of her hand for as long as he could. Felt its warmth sink deep into him. But when she finally pulled away little strands of jelly stretched up with her fingers and she had to flick them free to release herself. It felt like fireant bites to Gordon's head, and after she had left he could still feel the imprint of her hand burning into him.

When he woke in the morning a nasty dry scab had formed where she had touched him just above his eyes, right over his third ocellus eye hidden beneath the membrane of his slime-slickened skull. He barely sensed his morning breakfast being laid out, or his sister's calls from the doorway, her disappointment at his lack of engagement. By the time the sun was at its peak at noon, reaching its burning touch into the majority of the room and licking at the legs of his chair, the scab had consumed the mucus lubricating most of his head. His breathing became slow and ragged and his tentacles fanned out listlessly from the chair like uncontained hair.

As he curled against the discomfort racking through him, Gordon's fevered mind wandered. He'd always had a sense he was destined for something he wasn't fulfilling, and this long-felt void of achievement now returned with a vengeance. He felt a last impulse of restlessness to venture beyond the confines of his room more than ever, to travel like he'd always wanted. Not between hotel foyers and cramped rooms like he'd had to in his sales job, but to those worlds beyond he'd never known, that he'd promised Jillian. Yet he also knew he was now too weak to ever fulfil such dreams. That and his inconvenient bedroom-ridden transformation into a shoggoth in the first place of course.

Shoggoth. Cthulhu fhtagn.

What did these words mean? Why did he have a sense he should know them, that he has *always* known them, that they should evoke some deep-seated collective-unconscious memory that suddenly shifted all this into understanding. He was missing something, he knew, but couldn't decipher what that was.

Then soon he became too weakened to think much at all. The slime covering the rest of his entire exterior had now lost its slick viscosity as his sister's touch spread. As his body dried, little chunks of him began breaking off and collecting beneath the chair like dust bunnies, small sloughs of meat that drew his failing scent thinking them breakfast offerings only to realize they were discards of himself. His rows of eyes began to occlude, destined never to see into the other worlds for which they'd been made. His bloated thorax shrivelled like a mouse in a trap, back and will broken, and he began to desiccate with each passing hour.

He was dying, he knew, slowly but inevitably, unable to accomplish whatever new purpose he'd been given, a failure like he'd been all his life. If he'd been chosen to receive this… whatever he'd become as a gift, then he'd been the wrong man to choose. And he would die never understanding what any of this had meant.

But then does any of it mean anything? Is not life a mysterious joke, the meaning of which eludes us until it is too late and we realise we should not have been bothering with meaning?

He slept and these thoughts came to him less and less. He dreamed of the rolling masses. And wished he could join them.

Somewhere near the end he was vaguely conscious of his sister's presence floating above, panicked and confused before she raced out the front door, abandoning him he guessed, having invested so much of her energy the last weeks to sustain his leeching monstrosity that she could no longer stand the sight. Some time after that, Gordon's father opened the door and looked in at him, the old man thinner with age than ever, face gaunt beneath the long wisps of beard, only his eyes showing that fierce red weight of intelligence Gordon had long known. He stared at his son for a lengthy moment, forcing himself to confront the reality of what Gordon had become perhaps, but there was no compassion or regret in his eyes as he shut the door one last time. And although his mother evidently could not bring herself to see him, her heart too broken, it didn't stop her calling her old supplier on the phone for a bolt of cloth to fashion new drapes for his room, happy to wait "for a week or so for the room to clear". Gordon felt no surprise at this. By then he felt nothing at all.

CHAPTER III

"Oh, alright then. But they're choosing the second chair at four."
"Just come with me," Gordon's sister said to her guest. "And quiet, or my parents will hear."

"I cannot be late to rehearsal, my dear. And I still need to warm my fingers."

"Then you should have come when I first asked. Weeks ago. How can you be the head of the Society and baulk when your expertise is tested?"

"The Society? Well, yes, they are pleasant gatherings. But Magick is a lifelong pursuit of knowledge, and not an instant gratification that can be forced."

"I'm well aware of your idea of instant gratification."

"My dear, I resent the implications of your accusation—"

THE MEATAMORPHOSIS

Howard Bickerstaffe Jr broke off as the door opened, wrinkling his nose at the damp stench of rotting meat. Whipping a handkerchief to his fastidiously trimmed pencil moustache, his eyes darted left and right as they took in the dried slime-passages crisscrossing the floor and ceiling, the shredded furniture shoved against the walls, and then, most disturbingly, the greying multi-limbed ball lodged beneath the chair. In the hallway the cello he'd carefully placed against the hat-stand dislodged as he jumped back, and the expensive instrument slid down the wall and almost knocked over Gordon's sister's violin before she could catch it. Howard didn't notice.

"He was running everywhere before," Gordon's sister said softly. "But now... Don't you think he looks like what you've been teaching though?"

"Hmm?" Howard murmured, barely noticing her either.

"The Old Ones. The ones you all talk about in the rituals."

"The... Oh, oh right. Of course. Well, I'm not sure. It's rather a leap to assume a connection to the old gods, simply because he looks... like this. Maybe it's a form of teratoma. Or degenerative disease. And besides he, uh, appears quite dead, does he not?"

"No, he isn't! He can't be. Not yet. Please, I know I'm right." Gordon's sister grasped Howard's calf-leather gloves and he was barely strong enough to pull free. In fact, this close, without his hat on inside, she was quite a deal taller than his thin frame. He moved into the room to be free of the comparison and instantly regretted it.

This close to the... thing under the chair he began to see more of the detail. He'd at first assumed it to be some hastily-compiled hoax of butcher cuts and severed octopus arms, yet now could ascertain the soft expansion of breath of the flaking torso, only a few exhalations a minute but still enough to be discernable.

"You see the tentacles?" Gordon's sister said. "And the sets of eyes? Isn't that what the High Priest talked of once, in the creation ritual? The creatures the Elder Things created and sent to earth to build the pathways for their return. The shoggoths."

At the word the thing under the chair stirred. Gordon opened a third of his eyes. The room swam into focus.

"Shoggoths?" Howard repeated absently as he crouched and unfurled one of Gordon's tentacles with the end of his silver-topped cane. He blanched as congealed jelly rubbed off onto the metal.

"Yes, come on Howard. They were created to perform any task, assume any form, reflect any thought. Sent to this earth to build the ancients' hidden cities using the non-Euclidean geometry necessary to transform them to gateways when the stars align. Remember? Life on our world arose from cellular material left over from the creation of the shoggoths, that's what the High Priest said at the ritual. So in fact they are our mellifluous true form, rather than the clay-footed disappointment humans became."

"Broderick said that? Oh, yes, yes. Many of the old texts mention them. *Shoggoths*. But, and I am truly sorry to distress you here my dear, I believe they were categorised in von Junzt's *Unaussprechlichen Kulten* as the size of a bus. Not an… an over-sized cockroach."

As he leant over the curious mound of ill-formed limbs, Howard's excessive cologne hit Gordon's smell sacs like smelling salts. His array of eyes blinked and synchronised and swiveled up to the man squatting above. Howard stumbled backwards.

"But… but it's something like that, isn't it? Can't you do anything for my brother?"

"*Mon chéri*, I am a metaphysician, not a physician. Or a veterin-arian in this case. I'm not sure what—"

"All those nights. All those long rituals you and the other priests subjected us to. The Society of the New Flesh indeed—"

"Now I must take offence. You gave yourselves freely. We did not force any Magicks you were not willing to explore."

"You drugged me once! Tied me down."

Howard glanced at the doorway, moustache twitching. "Please be more discreet, my dear," he whispered, bringing her deeper into the room. "And you had an epiphany, yes? You saw there were other realms beyond ours that we could unlock for you. You must have, to believe it has incarnation here even in such a mundane domestic existence. I mean, your brother transforming into a god—" he chuckled and swanned a glove at the sickly thing unable to extricate itself from the dark beneath the chair, like some ghastly dying cat on its deathbed.

Gordon's sister stood in shadow, quiet, shoulders hanging. "He's the key. I know it. Perhaps because of how we treated him. His need to be seen unearthing some memory of our earlier forms in our cells. Maybe."

"He's certainly something, my dear," Howard said, rising and advancing on her with an oily smile. "Just not as interesting as you believe him to be." He took her in his soft animal-skinned hands and steered her to the door with gentle forcefulness, controlling her every move now. "It is sweet that you care for him so. But I am certain whatever it is he has become, he will soon be relieved of his torment, and once we have secured our spots in the orchestra we can both be rid of the shackles of your family responsibilities—"

"H' tharanak… l' ya."

On the threshold of the door the couple stumbled and glanced back at the multi-octaved utterance from beneath the chair.

"Did it… did he just speak?" Howard asked, clutching his conquest's hand too tight.

"Are you saying you don't understand? Then… that language in the rituals? Is that made-up?" The girl pulled her hand free and drew back a step.

"Certainly not," Howard huffed, feeling the doubt in her gaze like an emasculating knife. "Let us see if he says it again."

Howard pulled her back into the room, even though he'd been so close—*so close*—to extricating them from this tedium and finally getting to that damn rehearsal. Nevertheless, to humour her sweet face and sweeter form he lingered long enough for the dried husk on the floor to rattle another inhalation of breath:

"H' tharanak l' ya."

Gordon's sister stared at her brother. Something dark sparked behind her eyes. "I think I under—"

"It's telling us to leave it be," Howard cut in, slowly at first, then speaking with more conviction. "To let it die in peace. Yes, I know that, because we use that phrase in the funereal rites."

"No. That isn't it at all. I understand him."

"Whassat?" Howard mumbled, not really hearing her as he searched the creature for the source of its voice. Maybe there under that row of eyes? Maybe higher up? Is there a hole there? Then he shuddered at the thought of an orifice appearing amongst the folds of skin. It was enough to put one off carnal relations for life. Well, an afternoon at least. Thankfully, he'd be free of the sight soon regardless. "Is that so, my little one. And pray tell, what is it that your suddenly-articulate brother is oh so suddenly articulating? Despite being no longer human."

"He said, Bring him to me."

Howard turned too late, his mouth a little O of slow wit, and the violin smashed into his mouth and sheared loose a flap of skin from his chin and broke the lower jut of his jaw. He careened forward face-first and hit with a wet thud. Blood sprayed either side of his well-coiffed hair like a halo.

The girl stood over her suitor, her broken instrument hanging in numbed hands, face slackened as she stared at the fluids leaking from him. He was always repulsively leaking something. At least this time it wasn't on her.

With the last of his strength, her brother unfurled from beneath the chair and rolled over to expose his soft underbelly. His sister didn't understand at first, then gripped beneath the sweat-dampened armpits of Howard's arms and dragged his deadweight over. Then hesitated once more.

"I don't know what to do now."

"*Yogfm'll.*"

It sounded like her brother was sneezing, but the word translated in her mind like a divine bolt. "The stars." She almost glanced upwards, out the window, but something drew her gaze down instead, to her brother's exposed stomach. She'd seen the strange constellation of white spots on his groin before. He always seemed unusually coy about them, and would hide them if she looked too closely. Now he thrust his undercarriage up towards her. The speckling of spots triggered some ancient memory within her, a configuration of stars her forebears long in the past had once seen align in the sky before cataclysms nearly destroyed the planet. And now... and now the spots began to *move* on his skin, slowly forming and reforming into a series of complicated patterns mimicking interstellar patterns never seen in our universe, until at last they swirled in a hungry vortex that eddied with darkness and began to mesmerise her the longer she looked into it.

"*Yogfm'll*," Gordon prompted her, and she blinked and grabbed Howard's ears and dragged his weasel face towards the hole. She felt the gravity lick at her and leapt back in time, but Howard's face sucked tight against her brother's groin as if against a vacuum cleaner. A strange low hum filled the room as the skin began to slough off his cheeks and before it was over the man woke and clamped his hands either side of his face and tried to pull away screaming, and she saw the great multi-coloured stretch of matter as muscle and bone and brain pulp liquefied in a voracious stream of elongated meat, and she felt a moment of jealousy as the impromptu first sacrifice peered into the gateway hidden within the vessel of her brother—not a city created by planted shoggoths, but the unlocked human body itself—and then he gave one last existential shriek as he glimpsed the malevolent and uncaring dimensions beyond our own and his mind unravelled in an eternal moment of madness and awareness, and then he became pure thought as his body disappeared into the void of Gordon's stomach and the foppish empty clothes fell in a heap as the only reminder of his wasteful time on this earth. Gordon burped and grew.

Their father didn't come at the sound of Howard's muffled screaming, perhaps assuming it was Gordon in his last throes. By the time he did investigate hours later to see if the family was rid of its torment, Gordon's sister had rung the other women from the society, the disgruntled true believers such as herself who had believed they must wait for Howard their president and founder to endorse Gordon as their god. For though the Society proved ultimately empty and exploitative, it had stumbled on some correct truths. They could be thankful of that much. The once-imposing head of the family had been easy to catch. The coven of insatiable harpies had chased him back up the hallway and slashed his stringy old-man hamstrings and dragged him back to be fed to the stars.

Surprisingly, their mother put up more of a fight, barricading herself in her room as she had done so many nights during all this and grabbing a hatpin. They wrapped the bedspread over her like a chicken and hauled her bumping and caterwauling across the floorboards to her ascension.

Then one by one the Society fed themselves to their chosen destiny. Gordon's sister waited until last. By then Gordon had split the confines of the room and spilled out into the hallway and oozed partly through the window into the oblivious and uncaring world of Providence beyond. He would soon make his mark on it. Once she fed herself to him, he would crack the very walls and escape the house altogether, and then he could satiate himself with the first of the looky-loo neighbours and self-important passers-by, the bumbling authorities and attending council men, the fodder of the unwashed clogging the suburbs, and when he was large enough—not the size of a bus, that was as ill-informed and ignorant as much of the early writings of the esoterics she knew now somehow, but the size of Providence itself perhaps, for the ancient ones exiled from our world were vast in size, and so the Shoggoth gateway would somehow have to be just as large—then, then the first of the gods could step back once more into their rightful domain through the portal of flesh.

She smiled and took one of Gordon's engorged tentacles in her hands, stroking it in acceptance. His sweep of eyes followed her, loving, content, no longer unsure of himself or his worth in this world, as she brought her face down to his groin and brother and sister became one.

Innsmouth Park

Jane Routley

I first met the Marshes, mother and son, at the Plymouth Museum. My friend, Miss Lindsey, fell into conversation with Mrs Marsh while admiring some uncanny Polynesian ornaments in the Treasure Room. My friend was delighted then to be able to introduce me to Mrs Marsh. Mrs Marsh in turn introduced me to her son.

"The natural history room is my favourite part of the museum," said Mr Rowah Marsh, which made me instantly warm to him for it was my favourite too. We had a delightful conversation while poring over the cabinets of dried sea creatures and he had much of interest to say about the habits of octopus. Natural history is my passion. I had no qualms about giving Mr Marsh permission to write to me.

Mr Marsh was a shy quiet man. Perhaps this was not to be wondered at for he was more than ordinarily plain with a long narrow face, a too big mouth and eyes set too widely apart.

"How did you find him?" asked Miss Lindsey.

"I thought him very gentlemanly. And so learned. He has had a paper on the life of barnacles read at the Royal Society!"

"Dear Eugenia, only you would be impressed by that," said Miss Lindsey affectionately. "I am impressed because they are very wealthy. They own Innsmouth Park down in Cornwall. I suspect Mrs Marsh had come to Plymouth to seek a wife for her son."

Only now did I realize my old governess' true intentions. Dear lady. Dear friend. She knew my situation at home.

"It would be very pleasant to have a life partner who shared one's interests," I said, considering the possibility for the first time.

"You do not think him too ugly. Also, Mrs Marsh says the family suffer from skin aliments that can only be alleviated by extensive sea bathing."

"They both seemed very kind," I said. Kindness had become a priority for me. "And I would like to try sea bathing."

So it was that cards and letters were exchanged between my half-brother's wife and Mrs Marsh. The Marshes called upon our household and continued to do so. Mr Marsh and I had many a pleasant conversation about marine natural history and Mrs Marsh was a warm motherly presence.

My half-brother was typically derisive of my new suitor.

"A Cornishman," said he. "They're barely human. He looks like his mother mated with a fish. Goddamn, a fish mounting Mrs Marsh. That'd be a sight. Don't look at me like that, Amelia or I'll give you what for. You know he does."

He glared malevolently at his wife. The poor woman kept her eyes down—for all the good it ever did her. It is hard to believe that one could have so many of the outward trappings of birth and breeding and have so little of a gentleman's tone of mind as my half-brother did.

My life had been very happy until three years before when my parents were killed in a carriage accident. On that dreadful day my pleasant bookish life of study and collecting ended. My father's estate was entailed away to his son by a previous marriage. My sister Druscilla and I found ourselves completely dependent on our half-brother. Oswald Woodley had been brought up by his mother's family and he was a very different man from my gentle scientific father.

The day Oswald arrived, he called us to my father's study and said peremptorily, "It is a truth universally acknowledged that a spinster sister with a small portion is nothing but a burden to her relatives. I want you silly women married and out of my household as soon as possible." Then he burned my father's extensive collection of coastal plants and butterflies and sold his library.

Within the year my sister, the beauty of the family, accepted a proposal from Colonel Jenkins, a kindly but, it transpired, intemperate nearby landowner. I, being less pretty and of a bookish turn of mind, had fewer prospects. My only suitor was a Reverend Sheldrake, who at first seemed very suitable. Then I discovered that he allowed no reading matter in his house aside from the bible, because "my dear Miss Woodley, reading novels, and especially scientific journals, takes blood away from the womb and weakens the fairer sex for their proper role in life". I did not think I could face life under another autocrat without the consolation and variety that came from reading of the wider world. From then on, I did my best to prevent Reverend Sheldrake from proposing for fear of what would happen at home if I refused.

I gave serious consideration to finding work as a teacher or governess and applied to my old governess Miss Lindsey. Now happily retired on a small annuity, she was horrified at the idea of my embarking on such a cruel and thankless life. "Marriage is the only honourable provision for a well-educated young woman of small fortune," she said. Hence my introduction to the Marshes.

After making inquiries into the Marshes' fortune, my half-brother's attitude improved considerably.

"Innsmouth Park is a goodly property even if it is in the abysmal county of Cornwall. They own a saltworks and a fish cannery as well. Fish Face Fred is a great improvement on a mere Reverend Sheldrake."

So everyone, even the ever cautious Miss Lindsey, was pleased when the Marshes invited me to visit them at Innsmouth Park.

The only person who objected to the plan was Reverend Sheldrake.

"Do not go, dear Miss Woodley," he cried. "They practice many strange heresies in Cornwall and indeed in that very region. They include the abominable St Dagon in their communion."

And before I could prevent him, he finally proposed.

I thanked him politely for the honour of his proposal and told him with shameless insincerity that I would consider it. For I had every intention of securing Mr Marsh if I could.

My first view of the town of Innsmouth was not propitious. To reach it we travelled for some miles through dreary salt marshes. Autumn seemed to have come early here and a chill wind howled through the sedge and stunted trees. At last, a vast panorama of grey sea opened up before us. The land was so flat here that I felt it would take only a single great wave to seize the whole and drag it all into the sea's gaping maw. An overpowering odour of fish hung over the town, but it was the air of desolation that troubled me most. The larger houses at the town's edge were mostly shuttered, their gardens dank and overgrown. As we clattered past them on a rough potholed road, I saw that many of the cottages were shuttered too, with flaking whitewash and holes in the roofs. Where were the people? The streets of a prosperous town should have been bustling in the middle of the day, but all I saw were a few solitary figures shambling along distant laneways. As we passed the village inn, the Gilman Arms, I saw two elderly men, hunched on the benches outside, thick scarves around their heads. They must have been suffering from some skin complaint for the hands that held their pints were grey and scaly. Wide staring eyes and narrow grey faces looked up at us as we passed.

"By God they're an ugly lot in this part of the world," muttered my half-brother. "Fish face is positively good looking compared to this lot. Don't look at me like that, Eugenia. Of course I will guard my tongue in front of your suitor. Anything to have to stop feeding your useless little mouth."

I had hoped that the ever-ladylike Miss Lindsey would chaperone me on this journey but Oswald insisted on coming. I hoped he would not alienate the Marshes by exposing the brutish side of his nature and endured in wise silence the constant lament about costs and spinster sisters being a burden. Indeed, I derived some mean-spirited consolation from considering how much he would miss me when he longer had me to act as nursery maid to his children and to patch up my long-suffering sister-in-law after one of their many altercations. Although that second thought led to regret at how much that same sister-in-law would miss me.

On the sea front a couple of small fishing boats bobbed beside a drunken looking pier. Here at least were signs of prosperity. Figures rolled barrels in and out of large grim looking sheds and a group of women with aprons covered in blood, no doubt from fish gutting, came clattering out in clogs.

A small cluster of neat, whitewashed cottages surrounded an ugly church that looked as if someone had simply put a steeple on a warehouse. St Dagon's. I knew nothing of him and wondered what quaint provenance he would have.

Then we were out of the town and out of the salt flats too. The road sloped gently upwards through coastal heathland (a wonderful place for bird watching as I well knew) and before us was a rocky headland. As we turned I caught my first glimpse of the house that might be my future home. Tall and grey, it was a forbidding prospect. The high stone wall that surrounded it seemed to shut out the land rather than the vast expanse of grey sea beyond.

The beautiful rose garden and shady trees inside the walls were a relief after the grim surrounds. A pleasant well-raked gravel drive led to the front of the house. This sign of civilization and prosperity relaxed me and as we alighted from our carriage I was relieved to note that we could not smell fish.

Mother, son and two servants were on the stairs of the house to greet us. Both servants had the greyish skin and long faces of the locals. The man servant, who sullenly shambled away with our bags, was particularly ugly with stringy orange hairs hanging from his balding scalp. But Mrs Marsh was all affability and after we changed out of our dusty travelling clothes, she served us the finest Darjeeling tea in the drawing room. Rowah Marsh quickly drew me into conversation about his latest acquisition, Louis Renard's book about fish, crayfish, and crabs.

We were not to see Mr Marsh Senior, who was an invalid and shuttered away upstairs. The excuse made my brother protest.

"You may apply to me on any matter of business, Mr Woodley, and I shall pass the message to my husband," said Mrs Marsh "He trusts me in all things."

"More fool him," muttered my brother, who had no great opinion of women's capacities. Mrs Marsh showed us around the house, which was a rambling place with many shut up rooms "for the family is not as large as it once was."

"But there is room for it to become larger again," she said, smiling so meaningfully at me, that I blushed. Rowah seemed unaware of the exchange. He was looking out of the window at the sea.

Those rooms that were open were tastefully decorated and comfortable. The Marshes had always been great seafarers and many nooks held fascinating and slightly sinister artifacts from the South Seas—skilfully carved statuettes with tentacles and human legs, cunningly wrought ceremonial daggers, a ship in a bottle being swallowed by a kraken. Despite such gruesome trophies, I liked the house and looked forward to learning more about its objects and the countryside and people around. I loved the sea and would be delighted to live close to it.

Later Rowah took me down the set of stairs that were carved into the cliff face to where a series of large rock pools were cut out of the flat damp rocks.

The mirror still pools were like little gardens, full of soft mermaid's hair seaweed and bright green sea lettuce. Tiny fish and crabs darted through long kelp strands like deer in a terrestrial park. I was filled with admiration.

"I would love to be able to swim though that garden," I cried.

"My dear Miss Woodley, I would be delighted to teach you," he said taking my hand. "Would you allow me to? Would you make a life here with me?"

There was a rare warmth in his eyes, though his hand was very cold.

A proposal already! I was full of delight at the idea of spending my life here, studying and collecting. I would regain the life I had lost.

"Oh yes. I will," I cried.

We returned to the house and the congratulations of our families.

Yet as I sat at dinner, I did wonder how I would go along being married to Rowah Marsh. I had become used to his plainness, but he was so reserved. The only time he became animated, and when I felt any true connection to him, was when we were speaking of the sea and sea creatures.

I cast a sideways glance at Oswald taking yet another glass of the Marshes' fine claret and reminded myself of what awaited me at home if I baulked. Better to be a scullery maid than face that. If Mr Marsh was deficient in feeling, I felt certain he would at least not beat me or prevent me from pursuing my interests. And I would have Mrs Marsh as a mother-in law. Her kindness soothed the heartache left by the death of my own mother.

Though my mind was unquiet, I was tired after our travel and the rhythmic pounding of the waves lulled me quickly to sleep.

I swum though a swaying forest of kelp, light and free in the water. Before me a great city of coral. "We are home," said my companion. He took my hand. A gold ring shone on his cold webbed fingers matching the one on my own. I looked up. Not at a person but at a sea creature.

I woke with a start. A reddish light was winking, winking, balefully on the horizon.

Rising to pull the curtain, I noticed shapes bobbing among the glassy waves below. Rounded shapes. I peered more closely and became certain that they were swimming figures coming from the direction of the village. An uneasy chill went through me. There were so many and what were they? Surely not the villagers swimming at this time of night.

I shook myself. The excitements of the day were prompting strange imaginings in one who prided herself on being very sensible. Wonder replaced unease as I realized that the swimmers were most likely seals, common on this coast, going out to sea for their night's fishing. I was witnessing a glory of nature and all from my own bedroom window.

A cloud went across the moon then. When it was gone the shapes had gone too. But the red light out in the sea kept on winking, winking, balefully.

Unable to truly sleep again, I was at the window once more in the very early morning trying to read in the pale light of dawn when I saw Rowah Marsh, pattering across the garden carrying a string of fish. He was soaking wet and his shirt clung immodestly to his body, revealing his physique I had never seen so much of a man before and the sight left me feeling almost as breathless as my vision of nature's wonder the night before.

"I must see Mr Marsh," hissed my Oswald in my ear.

"But you saw him at breakfast."

It had been a pleasant meal. Mr Marsh, full of freshness and vigour, had described the many fine fish he had seen feeding in the seaweed gardens beneath the headland. He had touched my hand and promised again teach me to swim so that I might see these fish as he did.

"Not him, you stupid woman," snapped Oswald. "Mr Marsh Senior. Men should deal with men. I do not like that Marsh virago. She keeps refusing to change the marriage contract. And I am entitled to some recompense for feeding and housing you."

"Are you wishful to borrow money?" I asked. Foolishly, I realized immediately afterwards.

But he was not as angry as he usually was.

"An infusion of cash would be helpful at this time," he said. "Has Fish Face set a date yet?"

"No."

"Well hurry up. Use some of the womanly wiles God gave you. The sooner I can leave this place the better."

"You don't like it here!"

"Of course not," he snapped. "The people are inhumanly ugly, the girls are unfriendly and the countryside ill-omened. If you insist on marrying into this family, I shall not be visiting you here."

It was not the discouraging prospect he seemed to think it was.

I found Mrs Marsh in her small sitting room overlooking the rose garden and told her apologetically that my brother was insistent upon seeing Mr Marsh Senior.

"I will see what I can do. My husband is very ill, but he will want to meet his son's fiancée."

"May I ask the nature of his illness?" I inquired anxiously. My one great fear on marrying was illness — to be exact the unspeakable, unnameable illness my poor sister Drusilla had contracted from her philandering husband, jovial Colonel Jenkins. An illness which had left her housebound — covered in the most dreadful sores the year before and sickened since with the mercury treatment.

"You may. In fact, it is probably time I told you of our family's condition. As my mother-in-law told me when I married Mr Marsh."

She put aside the strangely wrought surplice she was embroidering for the priest of St Dagon and rang for tea.

"This family has always been devoted to the sea. The tale goes that centuries ago in return for good fishing off this coast the people hereabouts formed an alliance — a marital alliance — with a clan of sea monsters who lived on reefs off the coast," she said.

"Regardless of whether you believe such fanciful tales — and you and I are too well-educated to subscribe to such superstition — the truth of the matter is that something in the blood line of the Marsh family causes the health of many of the Marshes to degenerate as they age.

"Their eyes can no longer bear sunlight, their skins become scaley and grey, deep creases appear in their necks, and they take on other abnormalities that make them hideous for ordinary people to look on. They tend to withdraw from society and lock themselves in their houses, coming out only at night to bath in the sea to relieve the skin condition. This hereditary illness is widespread in Innsmouth which is why the town seems so quiet during the day. After the sun goes down it is quite busy."

My feelings upon hearing this story were overwhelming. The room reeled around me. Mrs Marsh poured me some more tea and after looking at me, added a dash of something from the sideboard. The strong spirit made me splutter but bought me back to my old sensible self.

"Will Rowah undergo such a change?"

"Given his love of the sea, I fear so. But he has about twenty years to go before he is forced to retire to his room and forgo all human contact and in that time you could be very happy together. And the illness does not cause pain. Nor will it shorten his life.

"I feel it only fair to tell you this and yet I do hope this news will not make you turn your back on my poor Rowah. For he is most desirous to marry you, though he is of a shy disposition and would not show it. But we have met very few women he feels so comfortable with and who, indeed, share his interests so deeply. And the illness of the Marshes requires that they find serious and capable wives who can manage their estates. I feel certain you are such a one.

She squeezed my hand.

"I have been very happy with Mr Marsh and I believe, even considering a mother's partiality, that my dear Rowah will make you a kind husband. You will have all the advantages of your own establishment and all the money to buy any books you would like. And someone who will respect your intelligence and share in your interests in a way I suspect no one does at the moment."

She looked at me with such understanding in her eyes. I saw that without being told she knew everything about my wretched fearful life at home with Oswald and perhaps even about the Reverend Sheldrake. As she held my hand I found myself weeping.

At dinner that evening Mrs Marsh told us that Mr Marsh was well enough to receive us. So afterwards, we mounted the stairs to the distant closed room where the invalid lay.

I was struck instantly by the smell of the sea. The pungent scent of salt mixed with the iodine reek of seaweed was present throughout the house but in this room, it was almost overpowering.

Indeed, in the dim light of the single candle I thought at first the hunched figure on the bed was a pile of seaweed. Then, as my eyes grew used to the darkness, I saw that a person sat up against the pillows but was hunched so deeply into blankets, scarves and shawls that his face was hidden by hooded blackness.

Words bubbled clumsily forth from under those blankets as if the speaker was speaking underwater. But the meaning was clear.

Mr Marsh Senior insisted I sit by him, took my hand in his heavily gloved one and told me that he had heard many fine things about me and that he would be delighted to welcome me into his family.

I looked across the bed at Rowah and he smiled at me with his too big smile, and Mrs Marsh nodded encouragingly. The welcome in their expressions and Old Mr Marsh's kind words filled me with warmth, despite the fact that his hand felt so cold, so very, very cold even through his gloves.

"Come. Give me the pleasure of joining your two hands together for I doubt I will see it done any other time," said Old Mr Marsh. "I fear I am not long for this world."

I stretched out my hand and on the other side of the bed Rowah stretched out his.

It was at that moment that my Oswald struck.

"Ha! Enough of this charade! Who are you really, Sir?" he cried, as he leapt at the bed, seized the shawl and flung it away.

The figure on the bed reared up. I saw everything. I saw the grey scaly slimy skin, the slitted neck, the huge crest of scales. Hideous glassy eyes glared with terrifying cold anger at my brother.

Then blessed blackness claimed me. I fainted (the first time I had ever done such a thing).

When I awoke I was lying on the couch in Mrs Marsh's small cosy sitting room. A fire burned in the grate. Mrs Marsh was holding my hand.

Terror filled me. I struggled to sit up.

JANE ROUTLEY

"There, there, my dear. Do not move. You are safe. You have had a shock. It took me thus too when I met my own father-in-law."

There was something soothing in her voice and in the warm and pleasant surrounds. I drank the cordial she offered me and it brought warmth back into my veins. I suddenly felt much stronger.

"Now you have seen the worst of it," comforted Mrs Marsh.

"Yes," I said.

He had looked so inhuman.

"Is this to be the lot of Rowah?" I said, with trembling voice.

"I fear so," said Mrs Marsh. "For my poor son dreams often of the sea and of great forests of seaweed and cities of rock and coral. Poor Mr Marsh is so changed. He is almost another person. But he has not become cruel. He has never been cruel to his wife and I doubt my son would be either. And I think you know enough how important kindness is in a husband."

At length under her soothing and sensible tone I was able to reorder my feelings and calm my terror enough to remember Oswald and apologize for his behaviour.

"Where is my brother?"

"He has taken it very badly. I fear for his sanity. We have carried him to his room. Do you feel strong enough to sit with him, Miss Woodley? It may help to bring him out of his state."

I nodded dutifully. Oswald was after all family.

My half-brother lay on his bed staring into nothingness, eyes fixed, mouth slightly agape, a look of blank horror on his face. His body was slack and still as if all hope had left it. We decided that I should sit up alone with him and Mrs Marsh should withdraw to a nearby room. I was not sure how much I would comfort him, but I would at least be familiar.

The exertions of the day had left me exhausted. As I sat by the bed I could not help but doze.

Still I heard my brother muttering. I woke to see him out of bed.

"The blood taint! They shall not pollute our women!" he shrieked as he leapt at me.

Then his hands were around my neck and he was squeezing

my throat. His terrible, bulging, mad eyes filled my vision.

I managed to scream and saw the lighted open door over his shoulder. I am not quite sure what happened then.

Someone pulled him from me. There was a struggle between Rowah and Oswald. The window was open. I know Oswald screamed, "Lie in your own filth for all I care." I know he screamed again and that suddenly he was gone. I ran to the window. Rowah and Mrs Marsh tried to stop me, but not before I saw Oswald's crumpled body leaking blood onto the terrace two stories below. And that baleful red light winking, winking, out at sea.

Blackness came down for the second time that night.

The Marshes showed me every consideration in the following days as I lay in bed alternatively weeping and staring into space. Rowah came every day to my bedside and read to me from Gilbert White's *Selbourne*. When I was enough myself to ask him why he had chosen that particular book, he said, "Because it contains nothing of fish. My mother was afraid you might have become...averse to sea creatures."

I looked into my heart. "That has not happened," I said.

"Then you are still willing to become my wife? Despite... everything?"

I considered. He would never be an affectionate husband, but what sensible woman looks for that in marriage? Of all the gentlemen I had met since my parent's death, he still seemed the least likely to raise his hand to a woman. He did not seem to have the passion for such a thing. And Mrs Marsh had already promised me I would be able to send money to my sister and sister-in-law should they need it.

But could I live with the prospect of his change? I looked around at the comfortable room and the books of natural history on the table.

"Yes," I said and took his chilly hand.

Because, as a very wise woman once said, Mr Marsh "offered me as much chance of happiness as most people can hope for on entering the married state."

The Queen's Solution

Peter Rawlik and Sal Ciano

I suppose, Raymond, it's time that I told you about some rather curious business that occurred some years back. I don't mean to be coy my dear—I know that you've suspected something for quite some time—you've always been a clever man, all those books you've written attest to that. In contrast, I am, and always have been, a woman of Victorian sensibilities, even these days I still prefer my black brocade dresses with their Mechlin lace, and of course my black lace gloves and cap. It may not be fashionable, but it wears well and never fails to garner me the respect that I deserve—that I have earned.

Now, what was I saying? Ah yes, I was saying that it was not my intention to be coy but I must admit that I am rather pleased with how it has all ended up, spending my twilight years—watching people and understanding their human nature and developing my talents as an amateur detective of a kind. It has been most satisfying to solve all these problems— these mysteries—that perplexed the minds of men who were supposedly so much cleverer than I. That was what started the whole thing, a mystery—you should remember; you were there, but then again it was so long ago, and now that your memory isn't what it once was, I will recount the details for you.

My part in the tale I shall relate, is rather small, but the events of those bygone days had a profound impact on my life. They were—and I say this with no sense of exaggeration—the most pivotal of days and set me on the very path I still walk to this very day.

For me, the whole affair began in October of 1918. I was sitting in the corner of the drawing room at West Hall in Little Auburn, dressed much like I am now, knitting something out of yarn. We were there to celebrate your safe return from the Great War. Among those attending with us were your father George West, his friends Lord Roderick Beauclerk and his wife Lady Christabel, that girl you were seeing, Evelyn Summers—I always liked her—a sensible young lady, the adventuress Rowena Ventnor, and that man you had brought back with you from France, Doctor Herbert West—a distant American cousin you had suggested.

Also present were the Withers, the family that served as housekeepers in West Hall for years: the stout butler Arthur, his willowy wife Ruth the housekeeper, and their daughter the gangly Estelle, who worked as nursemaid to your father.

Anyway, I was sitting there knitting while Ruth served tea. And we were discussing the book you had written, *Letters From The Front Lines*, and the fact that it had been recently accepted for publication by Wetherton University Press—a great achievement, but as you were soon to find out such achievements come with the expectation of more.

"You should write a murder mystery!" exclaimed Rowena Ventnor as she sipped her martini, "From what I can tell they seem to be all the rage."

Evelyn Summers gulped her lemonade and waved her free hand awkwardly with a boneless flop. "She's right Raymond, everyone is reading them, they are all I see in the shops these days."

You shook your head, Raymond, and said, "It's not really what I want to do. I want to write about real people, doing real things, things that regular people can relate to."

"You mean romance novels," suggested Lady Beauclerk. "My husband calls them parlor pornography."

THE QUEEN'S SOLUTION

Lord Beauclerk was suddenly uncomfortable. "I just meant that the genre as a whole is meant to invoke a response from women, much the same way that the writings of de Sade and Wilde are meant to invoke a response from men."

You smiled. "Of course, Lord Beauclerk, and you are quite right, but I'll remind you that regardless of its artistic merits romance and erotica can be quite profitable."

"If making money is your end, then why not write mysteries?"

You thought about that for a moment, I watched you turn it over and over in your head, but then your eyes lit up and you had your answer. "Most of what you call mysteries are really what one might better term 'True Crime'. It's been a viable genre for decades, starting I suppose with Dupin and perfected I suppose by Watson's accounts of Holmes. Now of course we have that bloody Catholic priest and that funny little Belgian."

"Also a Catholic," noted your father derisively. "Two men with too much time on their hands."

"But isn't that the very thing that all detectives have in common?" suggested Rowena. "Isn't leisure time what they need? Doctor West, you're a scientist, you have a logical mind, what do you think?"

"He's a medical doctor Rowena, not a professor," you quickly rejoined.

"Actually Raymond," retorted your friend, "I am a researcher in the medical field. I am a practicing physician, true, but I have done extensive research in a variety of other areas of medicine."

You were taken aback. "I would have never guessed; in what field do you specialize?"

Doctor Herbert West took a long pause and then smiled wryly, "You might say that I'm interested primarily in human longevity."

"Interesting," said Rowena as she leaned forward. "So, answer the question Doctor West, these geniuses who research the most puzzling of problems, and solve the most baffling crimes, where does leisure fit into their lives?"

"Hmm," muttered the American, pushing his round spectacles up his nose and then running a hand through his prematurely white hair. "It is true that the logical mind needs time, but not, as you say, for leisure. Men of science like myself, and I suppose these detectives, must—by the natures of our twin professions—undertake a very particular and rigorous course of study: first through reading the published literature and then by observing the world in relation to these works, drawing logical conclusions. On occasion, making such observations, and drawing appropriate conclusions takes time. To the layman all of this may look to be leisurely, but I assure you that the mental processes that must be undertaken are quite laborious and require great clarity of mind." He reached down for his cup. "Which is why I drink only tea and coffee, and avoid alcohol."

"I've heard a rumor that Mister Holmes was fond of a solution of cocaine," interjected Evelyn. "That he was addicted to the rotting stuff, that it allowed him to think in a rather accelerated manner."

Doctor West shook his head. "I've actually met Mister Holmes, just a few weeks back, and I saw no evidence of addiction. I can assure you that his mental acuity is still very much intact and as functional as ever. But this is beside the point. Chemical stimulants and depressants may help or interfere, but ultimately it is cognition coupled with observation and experimentation that it is preeminent. For these processes time is essential, and thankfully Dupin, Holmes and all the others like them have been granted positions that remove from them the concerns of everyday life."

Rowena was clearly annoyed. "You say men, Doctor West. Is it your position that only men are capable of such introspection?"

West shrugged. "It is my experience that the female mind is often too occupied with the mundane drudgery of common life: cooking, cleaning and the like. When not engaged in such work, they fill their time with what is generally described as idle gossip."

"For a man who seems to have gotten so much right about one thing, Doctor West," I interjected but kept my eyes focused on my knitting, "you are surprisingly wrong about the other."

"What exactly do you mean, Aunt Jane?" you asked respectfully.

THE QUEEN'S SOLUTION

"Forgive me a moment I've just dropped a stitch. Doctor West is correct in saying that time is essential to the deductive mind, and he is also correct that being relieved from the drudgery of everyday life may also be essential. However, what he fails to acknowledge is that in almost every one of these cases, without women to tend to their needs most of these men wouldn't be able to carry out their studies." I took a breath. "As for idle gossip: what one might see as a rude habit, others might describe as immersive observations of village life, which might be considered its very own field of study."

The drawing room was suddenly quiet. I suppose no one expected the elderly spinster to speak her mind. I raised my eyes to take in their expressions, reveling a bit in the mild scandal my comment had wrought. "When I was a young girl, the women would gather together to hang the day's washing. Housekeepers and housewives together, and it was their way to talk about what they had seen and heard in the days and nights before. It was the publican's wife that knew what time James Barker had left The Ragged Mare, and Jenny Mead—always a bit of an insomniac— that saw him open his door two hours after that. This being a small village the walk should have only been a half an hour at most. So where was Mr. Barker all that time? Madeline Williams supplied the answer when she pulled a man's vest—Barker's vest—out of the Widow Singleton's basket and hung it up to dry." I looked back down at my knitting. "I suspect that in the villages of England, and probably throughout the world, women know more about what goes on in the lanes and behind closed doors than any constable or detective."

Rowena Ventnor let out a raucous guffaw. "Well said Jane, well said." She glanced about the room. "You've given them something to think about for the night."

The conversation went on, albeit in another direction. Your father described a visit from the local medium—a woman named Arcadi, if I recall correctly—and her attempt to establish contact with your dear departed mother. I had met the very same self-proclaimed medium years earlier, and frankly she was an insufferable woman, something of a clown, going on and on about the multitude of pale green ghosts she said haunted whatever crumbling pile she was standing in. Nonsense of course, but she wasn't the first spiritualist I had met, and she was far from the last. I never had much use for such people, but somehow, they have become a staple of British society, at all levels. Proof, I suppose, that fools abound, good breeding or not. Not long after that Estelle brought us all a nightcap, which I recall was a very fine sherry, and then all the guests scattered to their various rooms to retire for the evening.

The next morning, I rose early, as was my nature, and had a light repast in the kitchen. After two cups of strong tea, I went on a stroll about the grounds, an activity that had become my customary morning routine. The morning was rather glorious, the air was crisp, and a cool breeze blew over the lake. The sun shone through the grey clouds in great shafts of light that were warm and pleasant to pass through as I perused the manicured gardens. As is the way of most estates the tended portions of the grounds soon gave way to wilderness, or at least the illusion of wilderness. The path that I trod was well-kept, there was a curious lack of litter and deadfall, but I was surrounded by a multitude of great trees including oaks, elms and birches that played host to all manner of life, or so the birdsong suggested.

Not far into the wood I spied the edifice known as the Temple of Hypnos, a folly built by Lord Theodore West over two centuries earlier. Built as a circular colonnade without any walls, the family used it as a retreat to escape the summer days. But the cold marble, so welcome in the heat of July, was intolerable in October's icy grip. No one came to the place out of season, so I was as surprised as anyone to see a man sitting on the steps. I recognized him almost immediately. He was still wearing the same clothes that he had worn at dinner the night before. He was still, and did not respond to any of my calls nor move as I approached. As I mounted the stairs I saw the mist of my own breath, but noted that none rose from your father. I was careful, and put my years of training to good use, touching his wrist only once. He was cold, very cold, and I detected no pulse. There was no doubt your father was quite dead.

THE QUEEN'S SOLUTION

As quick as I could I made my way back to the house. Down the well-kept paths, past the manicured trees, and out of the dark forest, and into the open fields and the warm sun. My breathing was rapid, much faster than I felt it should have been as I was in top physical condition, but that is to be expected I suppose, as it is not every day that one finds a body in the woods. I had seen dead bodies before they were after all an occupational hazard, but it had been years since my last and I had quite forgotten the electric thrill that comes with being intimately close to death. So, I can, therefore, assure you that I was not panicking, and I certainly was not running. My pace could best be described as brisk, it is not wise for a woman of more than six decades to move too quickly. As I moved into the manicured gardens I turned east and had to raise my hand to block the glare of the light. There was a shadow, someone stood between the sun and myself, I couldn't tell whom.

"Mr. West," I blurted out, hazarding a guess as to who could be there in the blinding sun. The form felt cold and threatening but still I entreated the shadowy figure for help. "In the folly. He's dead."

Whoever it was said nothing, but simply moved to one side, stepping behind a hedgerow. I didn't see anything that could have identified the person. Despite feeling like the form was vaguely masculine, I honestly couldn't have told you whether it was a man or a woman. The figure was completely gone by the time I shook off the momentary sun blindness and so I continued on my way, moving as fast as my old legs could carry me. By the time I made it back to the house, my heart was pounding, my breathing was ragged and there seemed to be a tremendous weight on my chest. I burst into the kitchen and—in between gasping breaths—I explained the situation to Mrs. Withers and told her to call the local constabulary. While that was undertaken, Mister Withers escorted me to my room where I sat down in an overstuffed armchair to recover from my exertions. I looked at my pocket watch—it was just a few minutes after eight. It felt like there was something stabbing into my jaw. I closed my eyes and tried to breathe through the pain. After a few moments the agony subsided and the exertions of the past hour got the better of me, causing me to succumb to the whisperings of Hypnos and slip into a brief and welcome pain-free oblivion.

I was roused, moments later it felt like, by the sound of Estelle Wither's voice as she called to me through the door, informing me that the constables had arrived. They wanted to speak to me in the drawing room. I let her know that I would be down in a few moments. As I struggled to my feet I felt a pinch in the back of my neck. Just then the hall clock chimed ten, and I realized that I had been asleep for nearly two hours. Sleeping deep like that was a behavior that was definitely not in my nature. My exertions had taken quite a toll, I thought. I was stiff and sore and now had a pinched nerve in my neck as well. "No good deed goes unpunished," I muttered to myself as I readied myself to receive the constables.

Constables Gently and Foyle were very different men. Foyle was slight, and average with a Sussex accent and charm about him. He called me 'Ma'am' several times as we spoke. Gently was larger, with a rough Norfolk accent. His hands were large, like a boxer's, and his nose was definitely that of a boxer's, having clearly been broken several times by the flattened, bent look of it. Neither could have been more than thirty years old, and I suspected them both to be much younger than that.

"Madam," spoke Foyle politely now that the pleasantries of introduction had concluded. "The staff said you asked them to call us after finding a body in the folly?"

I nodded. "Yes, quite right, my brother-in-law, George West."

"The thing is, Madam," chimed in Gently gruffly, "we've been out to the folly. There was no body. There was nobody living or dead there at all. In fact, Miss Ventnor told us that she was in the turret this morning, not long after you returned, and saw George West running out of the woods and toward the brook."

"That notion is quite ridiculous," I said, trying my best to chastise them for even considering the notion. "My brother-in-law is well into his eighties, he doesn't run anymore, hasn't for years." The two constables looked at each as if they were deciding to acknowledge my point, but I wasn't done with them

THE QUEEN'S SOLUTION

yet. "May I suggest we undertake a search immediately?" There was some hesitation on their part so I expanded my position. "If I am wrong, and I imagined the whole thing—which is highly unlikely—you will have my sincerest apologies, but if I am right, and the body I saw in the folly was indeed his, then George West is dead, and whomever Miss Ventnor saw was likely involved in either his death or interfering with a corpse. Given those two scenarios might I suggest that humoring a little old lady for a few hours might be in your best interest?"

This was logic neither of them could dispute. You'll most likely recall that you, Doctor West and Mr. Beauclerk were all recruited to the cause and the search for George West was soon underway. It did not last long. The search party, minus both constables, returned just before midday with unsettling news.

George West, or at least his body, had been found—not in the folly as I had suggested, but on the banks of one of the many brooks that ran through the estate. He had, according to Beauclerk, drowned, but this was perplexing because that area of the brook was only a foot or so deep. There had been a witness, one of the local boys who had seen the man earlier. He related that George had been wading about in the water splashing about wildly, apparently chasing after a trout that had caught his eye. The constables surmised that George, in pursuit of the fish, had lost his footing, fallen into the brook, hit his head on a rock, and been knocked unconscious, with drowning being the inevitable result.

Rowena—who had been rather fond of George—and had been for many years since your mother's death—found this explanation rather unsatisfying as George had never been fond of fish in general, and was repulsed by trout in particular. Once again, I raised the notion that a man in his eighties would engage in such behavior was rather ridiculous. Rowena agreed, but then reiterated that she had seen a man running from the wood towards the brook. She was sure that it had been George. The man had worn George's jacket, but as to the question of how he could have moved that quickly, and in that peculiar lopping manner, this she could not explain. Frankly, neither could I.

It was about then that Lord Beauclerk suggested that regardless of the manner of his death, or the events that led up to it, George West was dead, and that made you Raymond—his only heir—likely master of the house. The solicitor would have to be called, papers filed, the estate duty paid. There was an ominous silence over this last point that was only interrupted when Rowena suggested that she needed to go see Mrs. Withers about organizing lunch.

You and Lord Beauclerk retired to the study, Evelyn Summers and Lady Beauclerk went out to sit in the garden, while Doctor West noted that he had some work to do in one of the workshops that you had set up for him as a laboratory. I wandered into the drawing room, sat down in the corner chair, and worked on my knitting. Knitting is, in its own way, rather important to my mental processes. I find the routine rather soothing, but at the same time it focuses my mind and allows me to draw connections between the various unconnected things that surround me. Both are acts of putting things in order, of making something out of nothing, and seeing if it will hold together. As the knitting patterns come together so too do my deductions, weaving themselves together as neatly my scarves or caps or a tea cozy. One cannot simply pull disparate facts together and draw whatever conclusion one so desires. All the various pieces—all the clues—must be properly put together and only then will the truth reveal itself, woven from threads of truths and secrets brought to light.

I had not always been a deep thinker, indeed in my youth I would say I was a frivolous girl, but as I grew older, I began to become more meditative about the time I had left and the times I'd already had, and with this came a sense of quietude, and contemplation. I tended only to speak when I had something to say and often would consider a question such as "How do you do today?" far longer than the average person before answering as truthfully as I could. Some might have considered my lack of speed an indicator of senility, a byproduct of my age, but this would have been an error. I was merely being introspective. As our earlier conversation had suggested, it was time to think that all great detectives needed, and as the proverbial little old lady I had time in abundance.

I found myself for the first time ever being put into the position of having to solve a mystery—I was hesitant to call it a crime—for had anything untoward really happened? George had been dead when I had found him—of this I had no doubts. How then had he been seen running from the woods toward the brook? How had he been seen at the brook? Why was it that the police thought that he had drowned? These were the primary things that went through my head as I sat there with my skein of yarn and my needles trying to make something complex out of the simplest of things. Of course there was one more thing that I had to consider, the individual who I had encountered on the way back from the woods. Who had that been? Obviously, it had to have been one of the houseguests, it could not have been one of the staff — after all I had encountered the entirety of the Withers family when I had returned to the kitchen. And it could not have been Rowena Ventnor as she had been in the turret. That left the Beauclerks, Miss Summers, you dear nephew, and your friend Doctor West.

One might have thought you, Raymond, had the most motive for killing your father. You were his heir and the will left the entire estate to you. However, what we did not realize then was just how insolvent your father had become. Your father had been what they called land-rich, but with his passing the exact state of his bank account was made clear. The windows of the drawing room were open, as were the windows of the study, and so as I knitted I listened to bird calls and—more importantly—I overheard the urgent whisperings of Lord Beauclerk to you about debt and surmised that this house was not going to be in the family much longer, a thought confirmed when I heard your rejoinder that you knew all this already and that you'd hoped to pay back the debt with the proceeds from the next book, that this would ruin you. Ultimately this prophecy proved true; you could not pay the estate duties, and the Crown seized the property. You were forced to make do with the income you garnered from writing your books. If you had killed your father then it was perhaps the least profitable death ever. This eliminated you as a suspect in his murder.

But I wasn't looking for a murder suspect, was I? What was it I was looking for? George was dead, I was sure of it. How then had he come back to life? When I worked as a nurse, I had observed doctors reviving the recently deceased, particularly those who had drowned, taken an excess of pills, or other such events. What I had not seen was a doctor revive a patient who had been dead for an extended period of time. And George had been so very cold; he must have been dead for hours. What doctor would have the skills necessary for such a feat? My mind wandered back to what Doctor West had said he was studying—human longevity—what exactly did that entail? I decided I would have to make discrete inquiries, perhaps after lunch.

The midday meal was cream of mushroom soup, followed by roast duck with a side of baby carrots, and potatoes au Gratin. It was a fine meal and we all complemented Mrs. Withers on the lengths she had gone to under a trying circumstance. She took the compliment with expected humility. Afterwards her husband served a warm Darjeeling tea. I made sure that everyone else was occupied while I quietly rose from the corner and slipped out the side door. I don't think anybody even noticed I was gone.

It did not take me long to make my way across the grounds to the workshop that you had designated for Doctor West's laboratory. As I had expected the door was locked, but it was my sister that had set about modernizing this estate and I knew quite well how she used whelks to hide spare keys in the gardens by the doors. It didn't surprise me in the least that George had done nothing to change that bit of my sister's legacy.

Inside, I was surprised at how tidy and organized the place was. Doctor West was apparently quite fastidious. The majority of the space was made up of shelf after shelf of specimen jars. I could see whole sections that were devoted to plants, others to fungi, and even more to animals both whole and in part. All of these were labeled in Latin, which made identifying them rather difficult, but I recognized samples of foxglove, jimsonweed, and destroying angel mushrooms. I assumed that the rest of the samples were equally as toxic. Doctor West was seemingly

THE QUEEN'S SOLUTION

obsessed with a variety of poisons. For a man who claimed to be interested in longevity, he certainly had managed to collect a wide variety of ways in which to kill people.

On a desk in the corner there was a small black valise and a journal. The valise was locked, but the journal was open and the last entry was just earlier that morning. I sat down and over the next half hour familiarized myself with the last few weeks of Doctor Herbert West's experiments. West it seemed was engaged in both the experimentation on and the vivisection of animals. As he was not a British citizen there was no possibility of him obtaining a state license as required by the Cruelty to Animals Act of 1876. His acts of experimentation were therefore a crime, although the details were vague. West spoke in detail about administering some sort of chemical—he referred to it as his reagent—to various subjects and then observing their reactions and occasionally examining their internal organs. Each experiment was preceded by a series of codes or abbreviations that I could not interpret. I assumed that these identified the animal species and its pre-existing conditions. Next to these were various dosages of his reagent, which were administered in various manners, often by injection directly into the brain. He had even carried out not one but two experiments that very morning. The first had been at quarter till eight, and the second around half past nine. There was however a minor difference. The first experiment had used West's standard reagent, and the subject's reaction had included a failure to respond to any verbal command followed by extreme violent thrashing before the subject escaped his sight. The second subject was dosed with something called the Queen's Solution, and West noted that the subject had responded favorably and was expected to make a full recovery.

I was rather perplexed, how had Doctor West found the time to carry out these experiments? One had run off, but where was the other, the one that had made a full recovery? There were no cages in this room, no pens outside either. Where was he keeping his test subjects? For that matter, what animals was he experimenting on in the first place?

101

I put the journal back where I found it and made my way back to the main house. I was thinking the whole time, pondering what I had seen in West's laboratory and what bearing it might have had on the issue at hand. It was a long walk back, plenty of time to think. To look at the pieces and see how they fit together. It wasn't until I was mounting the stairs back into the house that I saw something that might have explained everything. The Beauclerks were sitting on the patio overlooking the garden. Lord Beauclerk was so still, his head hanging down over the table, I thought for a moment he was dead. I thought to myself that two deaths in one weekend seemed excessive, but then his wife reached out and touched his arm. He pushed the chair back as he stood up and jumped about in fright from the sudden and rude arousal.

Lady Beauclerk looked over at me and waved. "Sorry," she called out, "sometimes he sleeps so soundly it's like waking the dead."

I'm sure my eyes grew a little wide as I let out a little gasp of surprise and decided that it was time to confront Doctor Herbert West.

I found him in the library sitting in a chair reading a mouldering copy of something called *A Restitution of Decayed Intelligence* by one Richard Verstegan. He didn't notice me at first but then looked up and smiled as I crossed the room and sat down in the wingback chair just across from him.

He returned his focus to the book. "I find it remarkable what one can find in the libraries of old European homes."

I smiled and looked about the room. "You're looking at generations of accumulation, sometimes with purpose, but mostly just the byproduct of indiscriminate buying. Basil West, who lived here back at the beginning of the nineteenth century, was rather fond of studies in British architecture, but his son Christopher, was more interested in penny dreadfuls. George collects—collected—Chinese manuscripts." I turned back and looked him in the eye. "You are right, it is amazing what you can find just by looking about." I pulled my knitting out and began to work on it, the needles clicking sharply. "I've been to your laboratory; I've read your journal."

He closed the book and set it down with some force. "I assumed I was renting a private room."

I forced a smile. "I doubt that the issue of violating your privacy will be a primary concern for the authorities."

He laced his fingers together and brought them to his thin lips. "Is there a need to involve them?"

I looked down at my needles making sure that I hadn't dropped a stitch. "Tell me about your reagent."

Doctor Herbert West leaned forward. "It's my life's work, a chemical formulation that works to reanimate the dead. My first qualified success was about twenty years ago. Since then, I've made a significant amount of progress under conditions that were less than ideal. You have no idea how difficult things have been, the stress and strain that I have had to endure to obtain test subjects and reagent components. It was difficult enough when I had the support of a university, in private practice it has been sufficiently more trying."

"Two decades. How many people have you successfully— what was that word you used—reanimated?"

"Over two decades, a handful, six at the most." He sighed despondently. "There are mitigating factors, variables that affect the process: Age, cause of death, freshness of the subject, even gender."

"It was you I passed in the garden?"

"Yes."

"And you used this reagent on George West this morning, after I found him in the folly?"

"Yes."

"But the reanimation was unsuccessful?"

West grimaced. "It was a qualified success. The body reanimated. Autonomic functions were restored, as was motor control, and motivation. However, there was no evidence of conscious thought. He didn't respond to any questions or directions. There was no evidence of language recognition." He took a deep breath. "It happens sometimes. If the brain suffers an extended period without oxygen, the higher functions essentially fail to recover. After reanimation George West was little more than an animal.

I'm surprised he lived long enough to make it to the brook. Drowning was probably the least painful way for him to die."

I nodded. He wasn't wrong. "What is the Queen's Solution?"

Doctor West pulled his chair forward. "The Queen's Solution is a rather special version of the reagent. A colleague of mine, Major Sir Eric Moreland Clapham-Lee, developed it shortly before he died. He called it the Queen's Solution for two reasons: the first being that it was extraordinarily expensive, the base being a rare Kor oil from Africa."

"And the second?"

"It was only effective on post-menopausal women, which frankly makes it rather limited in application and usefulness." He chuckled. "Clapham-Lee thought that only someone like Queen Victoria would be a proper recipient, let alone afford it."

I frowned. "You still have access to this version of the reagent?"

A wicked look came across Herbert West's face. "An interesting inquiry, what happens if I say yes?"

"I was thinking that perhaps an accommodation could be made."

"An accommodation?"

"An arrangement."

"What did you have in mind?"

I looked up from my knitting. "You supply me with a dose of the Queen's Solution, and I won't inform the authorities about your experiments."

"You want to use the Queen's Solution?"

I narrowed my eyes. "I'm considering it."

"For what purpose?"

"To prove you wrong Doctor West, to prove all of you arrogant men wrong. The other night you suggested that all the great detectives are men, comfortable men who have the luxury of time to develop methods that allow them to solve the most heinous of crimes. I want to join their ranks and prove that if given the same opportunities, women can be their equals, perhaps even their betters."

"You don't need the Queen's Solution to do that."

"I do. I'm into my sixth decade. I have no illusions that I have little time left here. If I am going to make a mark, a significant mark, I'm going to need more time. I need a way to extend my life." I put my knitting back into my bag. "I need you to inject me with the Queen's Solution."

It was then that Doctor Herbert West said to me the words that would forever change my life. It explains how I've outlived three of my nurses, including Estelle Withers. How over the course of fifty years I've solved dozens of crimes and made myself one of the preeminent detectives in the world. It also explains why I'm standing here, forty years your senior watching you struggle for breath on your deathbed. I wish there was something I could do for you, Raymond. You really are my favorite nephew, and you've always taken care of me, but all I can do is try and find a way to comfort you and explain what has happened.

You see West told me he had used the last of the Queen's Solution that very morning. After he had experimented on George, he had discovered an older woman who had suffered a massive coronary, not an ideal situation but one he was willing to take advantage of. This was the second test subject that he had documented in his journal that morning the one he wrote had recovered fully. He had used the last of the Queen's Solution to reanimate her.

I stood up to leave then and apprised Doctor West that I was going to inform the authorities. I didn't even reach the door before he began laughing. "Stop! Stop. There's more to tell," he laughed. It was a dark almost satirical laugh.

"Why should I stop? Stop laughing," I spoke in as controlled a manner as I could but I was seething.

"For a woman who wants to be a great detective, you are not off to a fantastic start," he said, tears of mirth gleaming in his eyes. "You cannot even solve the mystery of your own resurrection." His laughter filled the room as he howled at the look of shock and terror and horror that filled my eyes. I had died.

You see Raymond, it all became so clear then to me. That pain that I felt as I stumbled back to the house, the subsequent nap, the "pinched nerve" ... I was the last and latest recipient of the Queen's Solution.

West's laughter slowed and then stopped. He leaned forward.

"So, you see there is no need for you to involve the authorities madam: Your wish is granted," he said with a grin. "I look forward to seeing what you do with all the time in the world."

DREAD ISLAND

JOE R. LANSDALE

This here story is a good'n, and just about every word of it is true. It's tempting to just jump to the part about where we seen them horrible things, and heads was pulled off and we was in a flying machine and such. But I ain't gonna do it, 'cause Jim says that ain't the way to tell a proper yarn.

Anyhow, this here story is as true as that other story that was written down about me and Jim. But that fella wrote it down made all the money and didn't give me or Jim one plug nickel of it. So, I'm going to try and tell this one myself like it happened, and have someone other than that old fart write it down for me, take out most of the swear words and such, and give you a gussied-up version that I can sell and get some money.

Jim says when you do a thing like that, trying to make more of something than it is, it's like you're taking a drunk in rags and putting a hat on him and giving him new shoes with ties in them, and telling everybody he's from uptown and has solid habits. But anyone looks at him, they're still gonna see the rags he's wearing and know he's a drunk 'cause of the stagger and the smell. Still, lots of drunks are more interesting than bankers, and they got good stories, even if you got to stand downwind to hear them in comfort.

If I get somebody to write it down for me, or I take a crack at it, is yet to be seen. All I know right now is it's me talking and you listening, and you can believe me or not, because it's a free country. Well, almost a free country, unless your skin ain't white. I've said it before: I know it ain't right in the eyes of God to be friends with a slave, or in Jim's case, an ex-slave that's got his free papers. But even if it ain't right, I don't care. Jim may be colored, but he has sure-fire done more for me than God. I tried praying maybe a dozen times, and the only thing I ever got out of it was some sore knees. So, if I go to hell, I go to hell.

Truth is, I figure heaven is probably filled with dogs,'cause if you get right down to it, they're the only ones deserve to be there. I don't figure a cat or a lawyer has any chance at all.

Anyway, I got a story to tell, and keep in mind—and this part is important—I'm trying to tell mostly the truth.

Now, any old steamboater will tell you that come the full moon, there's an island out there in the wide part of the Mississippi. You're standing on shore, it's so far out it ain't easy to see. But if the weather's just right, and you got some kind of eye on you, you can see it. It don't last but a night—the first night of the full moon—and then it's gone until next time.

Steamboats try not to go by it, 'cause when it's there, it has a current that'll drag a boat in just like a fella with a good, stout line pulling in a fish. I got word about it from half a dozen fellas that knew a fella that knew a fella that had boated past it and been tugged by them currents. They said it was all they could do to get away. And there's plenty they say didn't get away, and ain't never been heard of again.

Another time, me and Tom Sawyer heard a story about how sometimes you could see fires on the island. Another fella, who might have been borrowing the story from someone else, said he was out fishing with a buddy and come close to the island, and seen a post go up near the shore, and a thing that wasn't no kind of man was fastened to it. He said it could scream real loud, and that it made the hairs on the back of his neck stand up. He said there was other things dancing all around the post, carrying torches and making a noise like yelling or some such.

Then the currents started pulling him in, and he had to not pay it any more mind, because he and his buddy had to row for all they was worth to keep from being sucked onto the island.

When we got through hearing the story, first thing Tom said was, "Someday, when the moon is right, and that island is there, I'm gonna take a gun and a big Bowie knife, and I'm going to go out there. I'll probably also have to pack a lunch."

That danged old island is called Dread Island, and it's always been called that. I don't know where it got that name, but it was a right good one. I found that out because of Tom and Joe.

Way this all come about, was me and Jim was down on the bank of the river, night-fishing for catfish. Jim said there was some folks fished them holes by sticking their arms down in them so a catfish would bite. It wasn't a big bite, he said, but they clamped on good and you could pull them out that way, with them hanging on your arm. Then you could bust them in the head, and you had you something good to eat. He also said he wouldn't do that for nothing. The idea of sticking his hand down in them holes bothered him to no end, and just me thinking on it didn't do me no good either. I figured a gator or a moccasin snake was just as likely to bite me, and a fishing line with a hook on it would do me just as good. Thinking back on that, considering I wouldn't put my hand in a hole for fear something might bite it, and then me going out to Dread Island, just goes to show you can talk common sense a lot more than you can act on it.

But anyway, that ain't how this story starts. It starts like this.

So, there we was, with stinky bait, trying to catch us a catfish, when I seen Becky Thatcher coming along the shoreline in the moonlight.

Now Becky is quite a nice looker, and not a bad sort for a girl, a breed I figure is just a step up from cats. Jim says my thinking that way is because I'm still young and don't understand women's ways. He also explained to me their ways ain't actually understandable, but they sure do get a whole lot more interesting as time goes on.

I will say this. As I seen her coming, her hair hanging, and her legs working under that dress, the moonlight on her face, I thought maybe if she wasn't Tom's girl, I could like her a lot. I'm a little ashamed to admit that, but there you have it.

Anyway, she come along, and when she saw us, she said, "Huck. Jim. Is that you?"

I said, "Well, if it ain't, someone looks a whole lot like us is talking to you."

She come over real swift like then. She said, "I been looking all over for you. I figured you'd be here."

"Well," I said, "we're pretty near always around somewhere or another on the river."

"I was afraid you'd be out on your raft," she said.

"We don't like to go out on the water the night Dread Island is out there," I said.

She looked out over the water, said, "I can't see a thing."

"It looks just like a brown line on top of the water, but it's sharp enough there in the moonlight," I said. "If you give a good look."

"Can you see it too, Jim?" she asked.

"No, Miss Becky, I ain't got the eyes Huck's got."

"The island is why I'm looking for you," she said. "Tom has gone out there with Joe. He's been building his courage for a long time, and tonight, he got worked up about it. I think maybe they had some liquid courage. I went to see Tom, and he and Joe were loading a pail full of dinner into the boat. Some cornbread and the like, and they were just about to push off. When I asked what they were doing, Tom told me they were finally going to see Dread Island and learn what was on it. I didn't know if he was serious. I'm not even sure there is an island, but you tell me you can see it, and, well … I'm scared he wasn't just talking, and really did go."

"Did Tom have a big knife with him?" I asked.

"He had a big one in a scabbard stuck in his belt," she said. "And a pistol."

"What do you think, Jim?" I asked.

"I think he's done gone out there, Huck," Jim said. "He said he was gonna, and now he's got that knife and gun and dinner. I think he's done it."

She reached out and touched my arm and a shock run through me like I'd been struck by lightning. It hurt and felt good at the same time, and for a moment there, I thought I'd go to my knees.

"Oh, my God," she said. "Will they be all right?"

"I reckon Tom and Joe will come back all right," I said, but I wasn't really that sure.

She shook her head. "I'm not so certain. Could you and Jim go take a look?"

"Go to Dread Island?" Jim said. "Now, Miss Becky, that ain't smart."

"Tom and Joe went," she said.

"Yes, ma'am," Jim said, like she was a grown woman, "and that proves what I'm saying. It ain't smart."

"When did they go?" I said.

"It was just at dark," she said. "I saw them then, and they were getting in the boat. I tried to talk Tom out of it, because I thought he was a little drunk and shouldn't be on the water, but they went out anyway and they haven't come back."

I figured a moment. Nightfall was about three or four hours ago.

I said, "Jim, how long you reckon it takes to reach that island?"

"Couple of hours," Jim said, "or something mighty close to that."

"And a couple back," I said. "So what say we walk over to where Tom launched his boat and take a look. See if they done come in. They ain't, me and Jim will go take a gander for him."

"We will?" Jim said.

I ignored him.

Me and Jim put our lines in the water before we left and figured on checking them later. We went with Becky to where Tom and Joe had pushed off in their boat. It was a pretty far piece. They hadn't come back, and when we looked out over the water, we didn't see them coming neither.

Becky said, "Huck, I think I see it. The island, I mean."

"Yeah," I said, "there's a better look from here."

"It's just that line almost even with the water, isn't it?" she said.

"Yep, that's it."

"I don't see nothing," Jim said. "And I don't want to."

"You will go look for him?" Becky said.

"We'll go," I said.

"We will?" Jim said again.

"Or I can go by myself," I said. "Either way."

"Huck," Jim said, "you ought not go out there. You ain't got no idea what's on that island. I do. I heard more stories than you have, and most of it's way worse than an entire afternoon in church and having to talk to the preacher personal like."

"Then it's bad," I said, and I think it was pretty obvious to Becky that I was reconsidering.

Becky took my arm. She pulled herself close. "Please, Huck. There's no one else to ask. He's your friend. And then there's Joe."

"Yeah, well, Joe, he's sort of got his own lookout far as I'm concerned," I said. I admit I said this 'cause I don't care for Joe Harvey much. I ain't got no closer friend than Jim, but me and Tom was friends, too, and I didn't like that he'd asked Joe to go with him out there to Dread Island and not me. I probably wouldn't have gone, but a fella likes to be asked.

"Please, Huck," she said, and now she was so close to me I could smell her, and it was a good smell. Not a stink, mind you, but sweet like strawberries. Even there in the moonlight, her plump, wet lips made me want to kiss them, and I had an urge to reach out and stroke her hair. That was something I wasn't altogether understanding, and it made me feel like I was coming down sick.

Jim looked at me, said, "Ah, hell."

Our raft was back where we had been fishing, so I told Becky to go on home and I'd go look for Tom and Joe, and if I found them, I'd come back and let her know or send Tom to tell her, if he hadn't been ate up by alligators or carried off by mermaids. Not that I believed in mermaids, but there was them said they was out there in the river. But you can't believe every tall tale you hear.

All the while we're walking back to the raft, Jim is trying to talk me out of it.

"Huck, that island is all covered in badness."

"How would you know? You ain't never been. I mean, I've heard stories, but far as I know, they're just stories."

I was talking like that to build up my courage; tell the truth, I wasn't so sure they was just tall tales.

Jim shook his head. "I ain't got to have been. I know someone that's been there for sure. I know more than one."

I stopped walking. It was like I had been stunned with an ox hammer. Sure, me and Tom had heard a fella say he had been there, but when something come from Jim, it wasn't usually a lie, which isn't something I can say for most folks.

"You ain't never said nothing before about that, so why now?" I said. "I ain't saying you're making it up 'cause you don't want to go. I ain't saying that. But I'm saying why tell me now? We could have conversated on it before, but now you tell me?"

Jim grabbed my elbow, shook me a little, said, "Listen here, Huck. I ain't never mentioned it before because if someone tells you that you ought not to do something, then you'll do it. It's a weakness, son. It is."

I was startled. Jim hadn't never called me son before, and he hadn't never mentioned my weakness. It was a weakness me and Tom shared, and it wasn't something I thought about, and most of the time I just figured I did stuff 'cause I wanted to. But with Jim saying that, and grabbing my arm, calling me son, it just come all over me of a sudden that he was right. Down deep, I knew I had been thinking about going to that island for a long time, and tonight just set me a purpose. It was what them preachers call a revelation.

"Ain't nobody goes over there in they right mind, Huck," Jim said. "That ole island is all full of haints, they say. And then there's the Br'er People."

"Br'er People," I says. "What in hell is that?"

"You ain't heard nothing about the Br'er People? Why, I know I ain't told you all I know, but it surprises me deep as the river that you ain't at least heard of the Br'er People. They done come on this land from time to time and do things, and then go back. Them fellas I know been over there and come back, both of them colored, they ain't been right in they heads since. One of them lost a whole arm, and the other one, he lost his mind, which I figure is some worse than an arm."

"You sure it's because they went out to Dread Island?"

"Well, they didn't go to Nantucket," Jim said, like he had some idea where that was, but I knew he didn't. It was just a name he heard and locked onto.

"I don't know neither them to be liars," Jim said, "and the one didn't lose his senses said the Br'er People was out there, and they was lucky to get away. Said the island was fading when they got back to their boat. When it went away, it darn near pulled them after it. Said it was like a big ole twister on the water, and then it went up in the sky and was gone."

"A twister?"

"What they said."

I considered a moment. "I guess Br'er People or not, I got to go."

"You worried about that Miss Becky," Jim said, "and what she thinks?"

"I don't want her upset."

"I believe that. But you thinking you and her might be together. I know that's what you thinking, 'cause that's what any young, red-blooded, white boy be thinking about Miss Becky. I hope you understand now, I ain't crossing no color lines in my talk here, I'm just talking to a friend."

"Hell, I know that," I said. "And I don't care about color lines. I done decided if I go to hell for not caring about that, at least you and me will be there to talk. I figure too that danged ole writer cheated us out of some money will be there too."

"Yeah, he done us bad, didn't he?"

"Yeah, but what are these Br'er People?"

We had started walking again, and as we did, Jim talked.

"Uncle Remus used to tell about them. He's gone now. Buried for some twenty years, I s'pect. He was a slave. A good man. He knew things ain't nobody had an inkling about. He come from Africa, Huck. He was a kind of preacher man, but the gods he knew, they wasn't no God of the Bible. It wasn't no Jesus he talked about, until later when he had to talk about Jesus, 'cause the massas would beat his ass if he didn't. But he knew about them hoodoo things. Them animals that walked like men. He told about them even to the whites, but he made like they was little stories. I heard them tales when I was a boy, and he told them to me and all the colored folks in a different way."

"You ain't makin' a damn bit of sense, Jim."

"There's places where they show up. Holes in the sky, Uncle Remus used to say. They come out of them, and they got them some places where they got to stay when they come out of them holes. They can wander some, but they got to get back to their spot a'fore their time runs out. They got 'strictions. That island, it's got the same 'strictions."

"What's 'strictions?"

"Ain't exactly sure, but I've heard it said. I think it means there's rules of a sort."

By this time we had come to the raft and our fishing lines, which we checked right away. Jim's had a big ole catfish on it.

Jim said, "Well, if we gonna go to that dadburn island, we might as well go with full bellies. Let's get out our gear and fry these fish up."

"You're going then?" I said.

Jim sighed. "I can't let you go out there by yourself. Not to Dread Island. I did something like that I couldn't sleep at night. Course, I didn't go, I would at least be around to be without some sleep."

"Go or don't go, Jim, but I got to. Tom is my friend, and Becky asked me. If it was you, I'd go."

"Now, Huck, don't be trying to make me feel bad. I done said I'd go."

"Good then."

Jim paused and looked out over the river.

"I still don't see it," Jim said, "and I'm hoping you just think you do."

We cooked up those catfish and ate them. When we was done eating, Jim got his magic hairball out of the ditty bag he carried on a rope around his waist. He took a gander at it, trying

JOE R. LANSDALE

to divine things. That hairball come from the inside of a cow's stomach, and Jim said it had more mystery in it than women, but was a lot less good to look at. He figured he could see the future in it, and held stock by it.

Jim stuck his big thumbs in it and moved the hair around and eyeballed it some, said, "It don't look good, Huck."

"What's that hairball telling you?" I was looking at it, but I didn't see nothing but a big ole wad of hair that the cow had licked off its self and left in its stomach before it got killed and eat up; it smelled like an armpit after a hard day of field work.

Jim pawed around some more, then I seen his face change.

He said, "We go out there, Huck, someone's gonna die."

"You ain't just saying that about dying 'cause you don't want to go, are you?" I said.

He shook his head. "I'm saying it, 'cause that's what the hairball says."

I thought on that a moment, then said, "But that don't mean it's me or you dying, does it?"

Jim shook his head again. "No. But there ain't no solid way of telling."

"It's a chance we have to take," I said.

Jim stood for a moment just looking at me, shoving that hairball back into his pants pocket.

"All right," he said. "If that's how it is, then put this in your left shoe."

He had whittled a little cross, and it was small enough I could slide it down the side of my shoe and let it press up against the edge of my foot. Jim put a cross in his shoe too. We didn't normally have no shoes, but some Good Samaritans gave them to us, and we had taken to wearing them now and again. Jim said it was a sure sign we was getting civilized, and the idea of it scared me to death. Civilizing someone meant they had to go to jobs, and there was a time to show up and a time to leave, and you had to do work in between the coming and leaving. It was a horrible thing to think about, yet there I was with shoes on. The first step toward civilization and not having no fun anymore.

I said, "Is that cross so Jesus will watch over us?"

116

"A cross has got them four ends to it that show the four things make up this world. Fire, wind, earth, and water. It don't do nothing against a regular man, but against raw evil, it's supposed to have a mighty big power."

"But you don't know for sure?" I said.

"No, Huck, I don't. There ain't much I know for sure. But I got these too."

Jim held up two strings, and each of them had a big nail tied to it.

"These supposed to be full of power against evil," he said.

"Ain't the nails on account of Jesus?" I said. "Them being stuck in his hands and feet and such. I think I was told that in Sunday school. It's something like a cymbal."

"A cymbal? Like you hit in a band?"

"You know, I ain't sure, but I think that's what I was told."

"I don't see it being about no cymbals," Jim said. "Iron's got magic in it, that's all I know. It had magic in it before anyone ever heard of any Jesus. It's just iron to us, but to them haints, well, it's a whole nuther matter. Here. Loop this here string over your neck and tie the other end back to the nail. Make you a necklace of it. That ought to give you some protection. And I got some salt here in little bags for us. You never know when you might have the devil on your left, which is where he likes to stay, and if you feel him there, you can toss salt over your left shoulder, right into his eye. And we can use some of it on something to eat, if we got it."

"Finally," I said, "something that sounds reasonable."

When I had the nail around my neck, the cross in my shoe, and the bag of salt in my pocket, and my pocketknife shoved down tight in my back pocket, we pushed off the raft. Moment later we was sailing out across the black night water toward Dread Island.

The water was smooth at first, and the long pushing poles helped us get out in the deep part. When we got out there, we switched to Jim using the tiller and me handling the sails, which is something we had added as of recent. They worked mighty good, if you didn't shift wrong; and, of course, there had to be wind.

It had been pretty still when we started out, and that had

worried me, but before long, a light wind come up. It was just right, filling that canvas and pushing us along.

It didn't seem long before that line of dark in the water was a rise of dark, and then it was sure enough an island. Long and low and covered in fog, thick as the wool on a sheep's ass.

The raft started moving swift on account of it was caught up in a current, and before we knowed it, we was going through the fog and slamming up on the bank of Dread Island. We got out and used the docking rope to drag the raft on shore. It was a heavy rascal out of the water, and I thought I was gonna bust a gut. But we finally got it pulled up on solid ground.

Right then, there wasn't much to see that was worth seeing. The fog was heavy, but it was mostly around the island. On the island itself it was thin. Off to my right, I could see briars rising up about ten feet high, with dark thorns on them bigger than that nail I had tied around my neck. The tips of them were shiny in the moonlight, and the bit of fog that was off the water twisted in between them like stripped wads of cotton. To the left, and in front of us, was some woods; it was as dark in there as the inside of a dog's gut.

"Well, here we is all ready for a rescue," Jim said. "And we don't even know they here anywhere. They may have done come and gone home. They could have come back while we was frying catfish and I was looking at my hairball."

I pointed to the mud gleaming in the moonlight, showed Jim there was a drag line in it.

"That looks like the bottom of a boat," I said.

Jim squatted down and touched the ground with his fingers. "It sure do, Huck."

We followed the drag line until we come to a patch of limbs. I moved them back, and seen they had been cut and was thrown over the boat to hide it.

"I figure this is their boat," I said. "They're exploring, Jim. They done hid the boat, and gone out there."

"Well, they didn't hide it so good," he said, "'cause it took us about the time it takes a duck to eat a June bug to find it."

We got a big cane knife off the raft, and Jim took that and cut down some limbs, and we covered the raft up with them. It wasn't a better hiding place than Tom and Joe's boat, but it made me feel better to do it.

With Jim carrying the cane knife, and me with a lit lantern, we looked for sign of Tom and Joe. Finally, we seen some footprints on the ground. One was barefoot, and the other had on shoes. I figured Tom, who had been getting civilized too, would be the shoe wearer, and Joe would be the bare-footer.

Their sign led off in the woods. We followed in there after them. There was hardly any moon now, and even with me holding the lantern close to the ground, it wasn't no time at all until we lost track of them.

We kept going, and after a while we seen a big old clock on the ground. I held the lantern closer, seen it was inside a skeleton. The skeleton looked like it belonged to an alligator. Inside them alligator bones was human bones, all broke up, along with what was left of a hat with a feather in it, a boot, and a hook of the sort fits on a fella with his hand chopped off.

It didn't make no sense, but I quit thinking about, because I seen something move up ahead of us.

I wasn't sure what I had seen, but I can tell you this, it didn't take but that little bit of a glance for me to know I didn't like the looks of it.

Jim said, "Holy dog turd, was that a man with a rabbit's head?"

I was glad he said that. I had seen the same darn shadowy thing, but was thinking my mind was making it up.

Then we saw movement again, and that thing poked its head out from behind a tree. You could see the ears standing up in the shadows. I could see some big white buckteeth too.

Jim called out, "You better come out from behind that tree, and show yourself good, or I'm gonna chop your big-eared head off with this cane knife."

That didn't bring the thing out, but it did make it run. It tore off through them woods and underbrush like its tail was on fire. And it actually had a tail. A big cotton puff that I got a good look at, sticking out of the back of a pair of pants.

I didn't figure we ought to go after it. Our reason for being here was to find Tom and Joe and get ourselves back before the light come up. Besides, even if that thing was running, that didn't give me an idea about chasing it down. I might not like it if I caught it.

So, we was standing there, trying to figure if we was gonna shit or go blind, and that's when we heard a whipping sound in the brush. Then we seen torches. It didn't take no Daniel Boone to figure that it was someone beating the bushes, driving game in front of it. I reckoned the game would be none other than that thing we saw, so I grabbed Jim's arm and tugged him back behind some trees, and I blowed out the light. We laid down on our bellies and watched as the torches got closer, and they was bright enough we could see what was carrying them.

Their shadows come first, flickering in the torchlight. They was shaped something odd, and the way they fell on the ground, and bent around trees, made my skin crawl. But the shadows wasn't nothing compared to what made them.

Up front, carrying a torch, was a short fella wearing blue pants with rivets up the side, and he didn't have on no shirt, His chest was covered in a red fur and he had some kind of pack strapped to his back. His head, well, it wasn't no human head at all. It was the head of a fox. He was wearing a little folded hat with a feather in it. Not that he really needed that feather to get our attention. The fact that he was walking on his hind paws, with shoes on his feet, was plenty enough.

With him was a huge bear, also on hind legs, and wearing red pants that come to the knees. He didn't have no shoes on, but like the fox, he wasn't without a hat. Had a big straw one like Tom Sawyer liked to wear. In his teeth was a long piece of some kind of weed or another. He was working it from one side of his mouth to the other. He was carrying a torch.

The other four was clearly weasels, only bigger than any weasels I had ever seen. They didn't have no pants on at all, nor shoes neither, but they was wearing some wool caps. Two of the weasels had torches, but the other two had long switch limbs they was using to beat the brush.

But the thing that made me want to jump up and grab Jim and run back toward the raft was this big nasty shape of a thing that was with them. It was black as sin. The torch it was carrying flickered over its body and made it shine like fresh licked licorice. It looked like a big baby, if a baby could be six-foot tall and four-foot wide. It was fat in the belly and legs. It waddled from side to side on flat, sticky feet that was picking up leaves and pine needles and dirt. It didn't have no real face or body; all of it was made out of that sticky black mess. After a while, it spit a stream that hit in the bushes heavy as a cow pissing on a flat rock. That stream of spit didn't miss me and Jim by more than ten feet. Worse, that thing turned its head in our direction to do the spitting, and when it did, I could see it had teeth that looked like sugar cubes. Its eyes was as blood-red as two bullet wounds.

I thought at first it saw us, but after it spit, it turned its head back the way it had been going, and just kept on keeping on; it and that fox and that bear and them weasels. The smell of its spit lingered behind, and it was like the stink of turpentine.

After they was passed, me and Jim got up and started going back through the woods the way we had come, toward the raft. Seeing what we seen had made up our minds for us, and discussion about it wasn't necessary, and I knowed better than to light the lantern again. We just went along and made the best of it in the darkness of the woods.

As we was about to come out of the trees onto the beach, we seen something that froze us in our tracks. Coming along the beach was more of them weasels. Some of them had torches, some of them had clubs, and they all had hats. I guess a weasel don't care for pants, but dearly loves a hat. One of them was carrying a big, wet-looking bag.

We slipped back behind some trees and watched them move along for a bit, but was disappointed to see them stop by the water. They was strung out in a long line, and the weasel with the bag moved in front of the line and the line sort of gathered around him in a horseshoe shape. The weasel put the bag on the ground, opened it, and took out something I couldn't recognize at first. I squatted down so I could see better between their legs, and when I did, I caught my breath. They was passing a man's battered head among them, and they was each sitting down and taking a bite of it, passing it to the next weasel, like they was sharing a big apple.

Jim, who had squatted down beside me, said, "Oh, Huck, chile, look what they doing."

Not knowing what to do, we just stayed there, and then we heard that beating sound we had heard before. Off to our left was a whole batch of torches moving in our direction.

"More of them," Jim said.

Silent, but as quick as we could, we started going away from them. They didn't even know we was there, but they was driving us along like we was wild game 'cause they was looking for that rabbit, I figured.

After a bit, we picked up our pace, because they was closing. As we went more quickly through the woods, two things happened. The woods got thicker and harder to move through, and whatever was behind us started coming faster. I reckoned that was because now they could hear us. It may not have been us they was looking for, but it was darn sure us they was chasing.

It turned into a full-blowed run. I tossed the lantern aside, and we tore through them woods and vines and undergrowth as hard as we could go. Since we wasn't trying to be sneaky about it, Jim was using that cane knife to cut through the hard parts; mostly we just pushed through it.

Then an odd thing happened. We broke out of the woods and was standing on a cliff. Below us, pretty far down, was a big pool of water that the moon's face seemed to be floating on. Across from the pool was more land, and way beyond that was some mountains that rose up so high the peaks looked close to the moon.

I know. It don't make no sense. That island ought not to have been that big. It didn't fit the facts. Course, I reckon in a place where weasels and foxes and bears wear hats, and there's a big ole thing made of a sticky, black mess that spits turpentine, you can expect the facts to have their problems.

Behind us, them weasels was closing, waving torches, and yipping and barking like dogs.

Jim looked at me, said, "We gonna have to jump, Huck. It's all there is for it."

It was a good drop and wasn't no way of knowing what was under that water, but I nodded, aimed for the floating moon and jumped.

It was a quick drop, as it usually is when you step off nothing and fall. Me and Jim hit the water side by side and went under. The water was as cold as a dead man's ass in winter. When we come up swimming and spitting, I lifted my head to look at where we had jumped from. At the edge of the cliff was now the pack of weasels, and they was pressed up together tighter than a cluster of chiggers, leaning over and looking down.

One of them was dedicated, 'cause he jumped with his torch in his hand. He come down right in front of us in the water, went under, and when he come up he still had the torch, but of course it wasn't lit. He swung it and hit Jim upside the head.

Jim had lost the cane knife in the jump, so he didn't have nothing to hit back with. He and the weasel just sort of floated there eyeing one another.

There was a chittering sound from above, as all them weasels rallied their man on. The weasel cocked back the torch again, and swung at me. I couldn't backpedal fast enough, and it caught me a glancing blow on the side of my head. It was a hard-enough lick that for a moment, I not only couldn't swim, I wouldn't have been able to tell you the difference between a cow and a horse and a goat and a cotton sack. Right then, everything seemed pretty much the same to me.

I slipped under, but the water, and me choking on it, brought me back. I clawed my way to the surface, and when I was sort of back to myself, I seen that Jim had the weasel by the neck with one hand, and had its torch arm in his other. The weasel was pretty good-sized, but he wasn't as big as Jim, and his neck wasn't on his shoulders as good neither. The weasel had reached its free hand and got Jim's throat and was trying to strangle him;

he might as well have been trying to squeeze a tree to death. Jim's fingers dug into the weasel's throat, and there was a sound like someone trying to spit a pea through a tight-rolled cigar, and then the next thing I knowed, the weasel was floating like a turd in a night jar.

Above, the pack was still there, and a couple of them threw torches at us, but missed; they hissed out in the water. We swam to the other side, and crawled out. There was thick brush and woods there, and we staggered into it, with me stopping at the edge of the trees just long enough to yell something nasty to them weasels.

The woods come up along a wall of dirt, and thinned, and there was a small cave in the dirt, and in the cave, sleeping on the floor, was that rabbit we had seen. I doubted it was really a rabbit back then, when we first seen it in the shadows, but after the fox and bear and weasels, and Mr. Sticky, it was hard to doubt anything.

The moonlight was strong enough where the trees had thinned, that we could see the rabbit had white fur and wore a red vest and blue pants and no shoes. He had a pink nose and pink in his big ears, and he was sleeping. He heard us, and in a move so quick it was hard to see, he come awake and sprang to his feet. But we was in front of the cave, blocking the way out.

"Oh, my," he said.

A rabbit speaking right good American was enough to startle both me and Jim. But as I said, this place was the sort of place where you come to expect anything other than a free boat ride home.

Jim said slowly, "Why, I think I know who you are. Uncle Remus talked about you and your red vest. You Br'er Rabbit."

The rabbit hung his head and sort of collapsed to the floor of the cave.

"Br'er Rabbit," the rabbit said, "that would be me. Well, Fred actually, but when Uncle Remus was here, he knowed me by that name. I had a family once, but they was all eat up. There was Floppsy and Mopsy and Fred, and Alice and Fred Two and Fred

DREAD ISLAND

Three, and then there was… Oh, I don't even remember now, it's been so long ago they was eaten up, or given to Cut Through You."

There was a roll of thunder, and rain started darting down on us. We went inside the cave with Br'er Rabbit and watched lightning cut across the sky and slam into what looked like a sycamore tree.

"Lightning," Jim said, to no one in particular. "It don't leave no shadow. You got a torch, it leaves a shadow. The sun makes a shadow on the ground of things it shines on. But lightning, it don't leave no shadow."

"No," Br'er Rabbit said, looking up and out of the cave. "It don't, and it never has. And here, on this island, when it starts to rain and the lightning flashes and hits the ground like that, it's a warning. It means time is closing out. But what makes it bad is there's something new now. Something really awful."

"The weasels, you mean," Jim said.

"No," Br'er Rabbit said. "Something much worse."

"Well," Jim said, "them weasels is bad enough. We seen them eating a man's head."

"Riverboat captain probably," Br'er Rabbit said. "Big ole steamboat got too close and got sucked in. And then there was the lady in the big, silver mosquito."

"Beg your pardon," I said.

"Well, it reminded me of a mosquito. I ain't got no other way to explain it, so I won't. But that head, it was probably all that remains of that captain. It could have been some of the others, but I reckon it was him. He had a fat head."

"How do you know all this?" I said.

Br'er Rabbit looked at me, pulled his paw from behind his back, where he had been keeping it, and we saw he didn't have a hand on the end of it. Course, he didn't have a hand on the one showing neither. He had a kind of paw with fingers, which is the best I can describe it, but that other arm ended in a nubbin.

The rabbit dropped his head then, let his arm fall to his side, like everything inside of him had turned to water and run out on the ground. "I know what happened 'cause I was there, and

JOE R. LANSDALE

was gonna be one of the sacrifices. Would have been part of the whole thing had I not gnawed my paw off. It was the only way out. While I was doing it, it hurt like hell, but I kept thinking, rabbit meat, it ain't so bad. Ain't that a thing to think? It still hurts. I been running all night. But it ain't no use. I am a shadow of my former self. Was a time when I was clever and smart, but these days I ain't neither one. They gonna catch up with me now. I been outsmarting them for years, but everything done got its time, and I reckon mine has finally come. Br'er Fox, he's working up to the Big One, and tonight could be the night it all comes down in a bad way. If ole Cut Through You gets enough souls."

"I'm so confused I feel turned around and pulled inside out," I said.

"I'm a might confused myself," Jim said.

The rain was really hammering now. The lightning was tearing at the sky and poking down hot yellow forks, hitting trees, catching them on fire. It got so there were so many burning, that the inside of our cave was lit up for a time like it was daylight.

"This here rain," Br'er Rabbit said. "They don't like it. Ain't nobody likes it, 'cause that lightning can come down on your ass sure as it can on a tree. The Warning Rain we call it. Means that there ain't much time before the next rain comes. The Soft Rain, and when it does, it's that time. Time to go."

"I just thought I was confused before," I said.

"All right," Br'er Rabbit said. "It ain't like we're going anywhere now, and it ain't like they'll be coming. They'll be sheltering up somewhere nearby to get out of the Warning Rain. So, I'll tell you what you want to know. Just ask."

"I'll make it easy," I said. "Tell us all of it."

And he did. Now, no disrespect to Br'er Rabbit, but once he got going, he was a dad-burned blabbermouth. He told us all we wanted to know, and all manner of business we didn't want to know. I think it's best I just summarize what he was saying, keeping in mind it's possible I've left out some of the important parts, but mostly, I can assure you, I've left out stuff you don't want to hear anyway. We even got a few pointers on how to decorate a burrow, which seemed to be a tip we didn't need.

126

The rain got so thick it put those burning trees out, and with the moon behind clouds, it was dark in that cave. We couldn't even see each other. All we could do was hear Br'er Rabbit's voice, which was a little squeaky.

What he was telling us was, there was gonna be some kind of ceremony. That whoever the weasels could catch was gonna be a part of it. It wasn't no ceremony where there was cake and prizes and games, least not any that was fun. It was gonna be a ceremony in honor of this fella he called Cut Through You.

According to Br'er Rabbit, the island wasn't always a bad place. He and his family had lived here, along with all the other brother and sister animals, or whatever the hell they were, until Br'er Fox found the stones and the book wrapped in skin. That's how Br'er Rabbit put it. The book wrapped in skin.

Br'er Fox, he wasn't never loveable, and Br'er Rabbit said right up front, he used to pull tricks on him and Br'er Bear all the time. They was harmless, he said, and they was mostly just to keep from getting eaten by them two. 'Cause as nice a place as it was then as measured up against now, it was still a place where meat eaters lived alongside them that wasn't meat eaters, which meant them that ate vegetables was the meat eater's lunch, if they got caught. Br'er Rabbit said he figured that was just fair play. That was how the world worked, even if their island wasn't exactly like the rest of the world.

It dropped out of the sky come the full moon and ended up in the big wide middle of the Mississippi. It stayed that way for a few hours, and then come the Warning Rain, as he called it, the one we was having now; the one full of lightning and thunder and hard falling water. It meant they was more than halfway through their time to be on the Mississippi, then there was gonna come the Soft Rain. It didn't have no lightning in it. It was pleasant. At least until the sky opened up and the wind came down and carried them away.

"Where does it take you?" I asked.

Br'er Rabbit shook his head. "I don't know I can say. We don't seem to know nothing till we come back. And when we do, well, we just pick up right where we was before. Doing whatever it was we was doing. So if Br'er Fox has me by the neck, and the time comes, and we all get sucked away, when it blows back, we gonna be right where we was; it's always night and always like things was when we left them."

He said when that funnel of wind dropped them back on the island, sometimes it brought things with it that wasn't there before. Like people from other places. Other worlds, he said. That didn't make no sense at all to me. But that's what he said. He said sometimes it brought live people, and sometimes it brought dead people, and sometimes it brought Br'er People with it, and sometimes what it brought wasn't people at all. He told us about some big old crawdads come through once, and how they chased everyone around, but ended up being boiled in water and eaten by Br'er Bear, Br'er Fox, and all the weasels, who was kind of butt kissers to Br'er Fox.

Anyway, not knowing what was gonna show up on the island, either by way of that Sticky Storm—as he named it 'cause everything clung to it—or by way of the Mississippi, made things interesting; right before it got too interesting. The part that was too interesting had to do with Br'er Fox and that Book of Skin.

Way Br'er Rabbit figured, it come through that hole in the sky like everything else. It was clutched in a man's hand, and the man was deader than a rock, and he had what Br'er Rabbit said was a towel or a rag or some such thing wrapped around his head.

Br'er Rabbit said he seen that dead man from a hiding place in the woods, and Uncle Remus was with him when he did. Uncle Remus had escaped slavery and come to the island. He fit in good. Stayed in the burrow with Br'er Rabbit and his family, and he listened to all their stories.

But when the change come, when that book showed up, and stuff started happening because of it, he decided he'd had enough and tried to swim back to shore. Things he saw made him think taking his chance on drowning, or getting caught and being a slave again, was worth it. I don't know how he felt later, but he sure got caught, since Jim knew him and had heard stories about Dread Island from him.

"He left before things really got bad," Br'er Rabbit said. "And did they get bad. He was lucky."

"That depends on how you look at it," Jim said. "I done been a slave, and I can't say it compares good to much of anything."

"Maybe," Br'er Rabbit said. "Maybe."

And then he went on with his story.

Seems that when the storm brought that dead man clutching that book, Br'er Fox pried it out of his hands and opened it up and found it was written in some foreign language, but he could read it. Br'er Rabbit said one of the peculiars about the island is that everyone—except the weasels, who pretty much got the short end of the stick when it come to smarts—could read or speak any language there was.

Now, wasn't just the book and the dead man come through, there was the stones. They had fallen out of the sky at the same time. There was also a mass of black goo with dying and dead fish in it that come through, and it splattered all over the ground. The stones was carved up. The main marking was a big eye, then there was all manner of other scratchings and drawings. And though the Br'er Folk could read or speak any language possible, even the language in that book, they couldn't speak or read what was on them stones. It had been put together by folk spoke a tongue none of their mouths would fit around. Least at first.

Br'er Fox went to holding that book dear. Everyone on the island knew about it, and he always carried it in a pack on his back. Br'er Bear, who was kind of a kiss-ass like the weasels, but smarter than they was—and, according to Br'er Rabbit, that was a sad thing to think about, since Br'er Bear didn't hardly have the sense to get in out of the Warning Rain—helped Br'er Fox set them stones up in that black muck. Every time the storm brought them back, that's what they did, and pretty soon they had the weasels helping them.

Fact was, Br'er Fox all but quit chasing Br'er Rabbit. He instead sat and read by firelight and moonlight, and started chanting, 'cause he was learning how to say that language that he couldn't read before, the language on the stones, and he was teaching Br'er Bear how to do the same. And one time, well, the island stayed overnight.

"It didn't happen but that once," Br'er Rabbit said. "But come daylight, here we still was. And it stayed that way until the next night come, and finally before next morning, things got back to the way they was supposed to be. Br'er Fox had some power from that book and those stones, and he liked it mighty good."

Now and again he'd chant something from the book, and the air would fill with an odor like rotting fish, and then that odor got heavy and went to whirling about them stones; it was an odor that made the stomach crawl and the head fill with all manner of sickness and worry and grief.

Once, while Br'er Rabbit was watching Br'er Fox chant, while he was smelling that rotten fish stink, he saw the sky crack open, right up close by the moon. Not the way it did when the Sticky Storm come, which was when everything turned gray and the sky opened up and a twister of sorts dropped down and sucked them all up. It was more like the night sky was just a big black sheet, and this thing with one, large, nasty, rolling eye and more legs than a spider—and ropey legs at that—poked through and pulled at the night.

For a moment, Br'er Rabbit thought that thing—which from Br'er Fox's chanting he learned was called Cut Through You—was gonna take hold of the moon and eat it like a flapjack. It had a odd mouth with a beak, and it was snapping all the while.

Then, sudden like, it was sucked back, like something got hold of one of its legs and yanked it plumb out of sight. The sky closed up and the air got clean for a moment, and it was over with.

After that, Br'er Fox and ole One Eye had them a connection. Every time the island was brought back, Br'er Fox would go out there and stand in that muck, or sit on a rock in the middle of them carved stones, and call out to Cut Through You. It was a noise, Br'er Rabbit said, sounded like something straining at toilet while trying to cough and yodel all at the same time.

Br'er Fox and Br'er Bear was catching folk and tying them to the stones. People from the Mississippi come along by accident; they got nabbed too, mostly by the weasels. It was all so Br'er Fox could have Cut Through You meetings.

Way it was described to me, it was kind of like church. Except when it come time to pass the offering, the sky would crack open,

DREAD ISLAND

and ole Cut Through You would lean out and reach down and pull folk tied to the stones up there with him.

Br'er Rabbit said he watched it eat a bunch a folk quicker than a mule skinner could pop goober peas; chawed them up and spat them out, splattered what was left in that black mud that was all around the stones.

That was what Br'er Fox and Br'er Bear, and all them weasels, took to eating. It changed them. They went from sneaky and hungry and animal-like, to being more like men. Meaning, said Br'er Rabbit, they come to enjoy cruelty. And then Br'er Fox built the Tar Baby, used that book to give it life. It could do more work than all of them put together, and it set up the final stones by itself. Something dirty needed to be done, it was Tar Baby done it. You couldn't stop the thing, Br'er Rabbit said. It just kept on a coming, and a coming.

But the final thing Br'er Rabbit said worried him, was that each time Cut Through You came back, there's more and more of him to be seen, and it turned out there's a lot more of Cut Through You than you'd think; and it was like he was hungrier each time he showed.

Bottom line, as figured by Br'er Rabbit, was this: if Br'er Fox and his bunch didn't supply the sacrifices, pretty soon they'd be sacrifices themselves.

Br'er Rabbit finished up his story, and it was about that time the rain quit. The clouds melted away and the moonlight was back. It was clear out, and you could see a right smart distance.

I said, "You ain't seen a couple of fellas named Tom and Joe, have you? One of them might be wearing a straw hat. They're about my age and size, but not quite as good-looking."

Br'er Rabbit shook his head. "I ain't," he said. "But they could be with all the others Br'er Fox has nabbed of late. Was they on the riverboat run aground?"

I shook my head.

Jim said, "Huck, you and me, we got to get back to the raft and get on out of this place, Tom and Joe or not."

"That's right," Br'er Rabbit said. "You got to. Oh, I wish I could go with you."

"You're invited," I said.

"Ah, but there is the thorn in the paw. I can't go, 'cause I do, come daylight, if I ain't on this island, I disappear, and I don't come back. Though to tell you true, that might be better than getting ate up by Cut Through You. I'll give it some considering."

"Consider quick," Jim said, "we got to start back to the raft."

"What we got to do," Br'er Rabbit said, "is we got to go that way."

He pointed.

"Then," he said, "we work down to the shore, and you can get your raft. And I'm thinking I might just go with you and turn to nothing. I ain't got no family now. I ain't got nothing but me, and part of me is missing, so the rest of me might as well go missing, too."

Jim said, "I got my medicine bag with me. I can't give you your paw back, but I can take some of the hurt away with a salve I got."

Jim dressed Br'er Rabbit's paw, and when that was done, he got some wool string out of that little bag he had on his belt and tied up his hair—which had grown long—in little sheaves, like dark wheat. He said it was a thing to do to keep back witches.

I pointed out witches seemed to me the least of our worries, but he done it anyway, with me taking my pocketknife out of my back pocket to cut the string for him.

When he had knotted his hair up in about twenty gatherings, we lit out for the raft without fear of witches.

Way we went made it so we had to swim across a creek that was deep in places. It was cold water, like that blue hole we had jumped in, and there was fish in it. They was curious and would bob to the top and look at us; their eyes was shiny as wet stones in the moonlight.

On the other side of the creek, we stumbled through a patch of woods, and down a hill, and then up one that led us level with where we had been before. In front of us was more dark woods. Br'er Rabbit said beyond the trees was the shoreline, and we might be able to get to our raft if the weasels hadn't found it. Me and Jim decided if they had, we'd try for Tom's and Joe's boat

DREAD ISLAND

and wish them our best. If their boat was gone, then, there was nothing left but to hit that Mississippi and swim for it. We had about as much chance of making that swim as passing through the eye of a needle, but it was a might more inviting than Cut Through You. Least, that way we had a chance. Me and Jim was both good swimmers, and maybe we could even find a log to push off into the water with us. As for Br'er Rabbit, well, he was thinking on going with us and just disappearing when daylight come; that was a thing made me really want to get off that island. If he was willing to go out that way, then that Cut Through You must be some nasty sort of fella. Worse yet, our salt had got all wet and wasn't worth nothing, and we had both lost the cross in our shoes. All we had was those rusty nails on strings, and I didn't have a whole lot of trust in that. I was more comfortable that I still had my little knife in my back pocket.

We was coming down through the woods, and it got so the trees were thinning, and we could see the bank down there, the river churning along furious like. My heart was starting to beat in an excited way, and about then, things turned to dog doo.

The weasels come down out of the trees on ropes, and a big net come down with them and landed over us. It was weighed down with rocks, and there wasn't no time to get out from under it before they was tugging it firm around us, and we was bagged up tighter than a strand of gut packed with sausage makings.

As we was laying there, out of the woods come Br'er Fox and Br'er Bear. They come right over to us. The fox bent down, and he looked Br'er Rabbit in the eye. He grinned and showed his teeth. His breath was so sour we could smell it from four feet away; it smelled like death warmed over and gone cold again.

Up close, I could see things I couldn't see before in the night. He had fish scales running along the side of his face, and when he breathed there were flaps that flared out on his cheeks; they was gills, like a fish.

I looked up at Br'er Bear. There were sores all over his body, and bits of fish heads and fish tails poking out of him like moles. He was breathing in and out, like bellows being worked to start up a fresh fire.

JOE R. LANSDALE

"You ain't looking so good," Br'er Rabbit said.

"Yeah," Br'er Fox said, "but looks ain't everything. I ain't looking so good, but you ain't doing so good."

Br'er Fox slung his pack off his back and opened it. I could see there was a book in there, the one bound up in human skin. You could see there was a face on the cover, eyes, nose, mouth, and some warts. But that wasn't what Br'er Fox was reaching for. What he was reaching for was Br'er Rabbit's paw, which was stuffed in there.

"Here's a little something you left back at the ceremony spot." He held up the paw and waved it around. "That wasn't nice. I had plans for you. But, you know what? I got a lucky rabbit's foot now. Though, to tell the truth, it ain't all that lucky for you, is it?"

He put the paw in his mouth and clamped down on it and bit right through it and chewed on it some. He gave what was left of it to Br'er Bear, who ate it up in one big bite.

"I figured you wouldn't be needing it," Br'er Fox said.

"Why, I'm quite happy with this nubbing," Br'er Rabbit said. "I don't spend so much time cleaning my nails now."

Br'er Fox's face turned sour, like he had bitten into an unripe persimmon. "There ain't gonna be nothing of you to clean after tonight. And in fact, we got to go quick like. I wouldn't want you to miss the meeting, Br'er Rabbit. You see, tonight, he comes all the way through, and then, me and my folk, we're gonna serve him. He's gonna go all over the Mississippi, and then all over the world. He's gonna rule, and I'm gonna rule beside him. He told me. He told me in my head."

With those last words, Br'er Fox tapped the side of his head with a finger.

"You gonna get ate up like everyone else," Br'er Rabbit said. "You just a big ole idiot."

Br'er Fox rose up, waved his hand over his head, yelled out, "Bring them. And don't be easy about it. Let's blood them."

What that meant was they dragged us in that net. We was pressed up tight together, and there was all manner of stuff on the ground to stick us, and we banged into trees and such, and it seemed like forever before we broke out of the woods and I got a glimpse at the place we was going.

Right then I knew why it was Br'er Rabbit would rather just disappear.

We was scratched and bumped up and full of ticks and chiggers and poison ivy by the time we got to where we was going, and where we was going didn't have no trees and there wasn't nothing pretty about it.

There was this big stretch of black mud. You could see dead fish in it, and some of them was mostly bones, but there were still some flopping about. They were fish I didn't recognize. Some had a lot of eyes and big teeth and were shaped funny.

Standing up in the mud were these big dark slabs of rock that wasn't quite black and wasn't quite brown, but was somewhere between any color you can mention. The moonlight laid on them like a slick of bacon grease, and you could see markings all over them. Each and every one of them had a big ole eye at the top of the slab, and below it were all manner of marks. Some of the marks looked like fish or things with lots of legs, and beaks, and then there was marks that didn't look like nothing but chicken scratch. But, I can tell you this, looking at those slabs and those marks made my stomach feel kind of funny, like I had swallowed a big chaw of tobacco right after eating too many hot peppers and boiled pigs' feet, something, by the way, that really happened to me once.

Standing out there in that black muck was the weasels. On posts all around the muck right where it was still solid ground, there was men and women with their hands tied behind their backs and then tied to rings on the posts. I reckoned a number of them was from the steamboat wreck. There was also a woman wearing a kind of leather cap, and she had on pants just like a man. She was kind of pretty, and where everyone else was hanging their heads, she looked mad as a hornet. As we was pulled up closer to the muck, I saw that Tom and Joe was there, tied to posts, drooping like flowers too long in the hot sun, missing Bowie knife, gun, and packed lunch.

When they seen me and Jim, they brightened for a second,

then realized wasn't nothing we could do, and that we was in the same situation as them. It hurt me to see Tom like that, all sagging. It was the first time I'd ever seen him about given up. Like us, they was all scratched up and even in the moonlight, you could see they was spotted like speckled pups from bruises.

Out behind them I could see parts of that big briar patch we had seen when we first sailed our raft onto the island. The briars twisted up high, and the way the moonlight fell into them, that whole section looked like a field of coiled ropes and nails. I hadn't never seen a briar patch like that before.

There were some other things out there in the muck that I can't explain, and there was stuff on the sides of where the muck ended. I figured, from what Br'er Rabbit had told us, they was stuff from them other worlds or places that sometimes come through on the Sticky Storm. One of them things was a long boat of sorts, but it had wings on it, and it was shiny silver and had a tail on it like a fish. There was some kind of big crosses on the wings, and it was just sitting on wheels over on some high grass, but the wheels wasn't like any I'd ever seen on a wagon or buggy.

There was also this big thing looked like a gourd, if a gourd could be about a thousand times bigger; it was stuck up in the mud with the fat part down, and the thinner part in the air, and it had little fins on it. Written on it in big writing was something that didn't make no sense to me. It said: HOWDY ALL YOU JAPS.

Wasn't a moment or two passed between me seeing all this, then we was being pulled out of the net and carried over to three empty posts. A moment later, they wasn't empty no more. We was tied to the wooden rings on them tight as a fishing knot.

I turned my head and looked at Jim.

He said, "You're right, they ain't no witch problems around here."

"Maybe," I said, "it's because of the string. Who knows how many witches would be around otherwise."

Jim grinned at me. "That's right. That's right, ain't it?"

I nodded and smiled at him. I figured if we was gonna be killed, and wasn't nothing we could do about it, we might as well try and be cheerful.

DREAD ISLAND

Right then, coming across that black mud, its feet splattering and sucking in the muck as it pulled them free for each step, was the Tar Baby.

Now that he was out under the moonlight, I could see he was stuck all over with what at first looked like long needles, but as he come closer, I saw was straw. He was shot through with it. I figured it was a thing Br'er Fox used to help put him together, mixing it with tar he got from somewhere, and turpentine, and maybe some things I didn't want to know about; you could smell that turpentine as he waddled closer, spitting all the while.

He sauntered around the circle of folks that was tied to the posts, and as he did, his plump belly would flare open, and you could see fire in there and bits of ash and bones being burned up along with fish heads and a human skull. Tar Baby went by each of them on the posts and pushed his face close to their faces so he could enjoy how they curled back from him. I knew a bully when I seen one, 'cause I had fought a few, and when I was younger, I was kind of a bully myself, till a girl named Hortense Miller beat the snot out of me, twisted my arm behind my back and made me say "cotton sack," and even then, after I said it, she made me eat a mouthful of dirt and tell her I liked it. She wasn't one to settle an argument easy like. It cured my bully days.

When the Tar Baby come to me and pushed his face close, I didn't flinch. I just looked him in his red eyes like they was nothing, even though it was all I could do to keep my knees from chattering together. He stayed looking at me for a long time, then grunted, left the air around me full of the fog and stink of turpentine. Jim was next, and Jim didn't flinch none either. That didn't set well with Tar Baby, two rascals in a row, so he reached out with a finger and poked Jim's chest. There was a hissing sound and smoke come off Jim. That made me figure he was being burned by the Tar Baby somehow, but when the Tar Baby pulled his chubby, tar finger back, it was him that was smoking.

I leaned out and took a good look and seen the cause of it—the nail on the string around Jim's neck. The Tar Baby had poked it and that iron nail had actually worked its magic on him. Course, problem was, he had to put his finger right on it, but in that moment, I gathered me up a more favorable view of the hoodoo methods.

Tar Baby looked at the end of his smoking finger, like he might find something special there, then he looked at Jim, and his mouth twisted. I think he was gonna do something nasty, but there come a rain all of a sudden. The Soft Rain Br'er Rabbit told us about. It come down sweet smelling and light and warm. No thunder. No lightning. And no clouds. Just water falling out of a clear sky stuffed with stars and a big fat moon; it was the rain that was supposed to let everyone know it wouldn't be long before daylight and the Sticky Storm.

The weasels and Br'er Fox and Br'er Bear, and that nasty Tar Baby, all made their way quick like to the tallest stone in the muck. They stood in front of it, and you could tell they was nervous, even the Tar Baby, and they went about chanting. The words were like someone spitting and sucking and coughing and clearing their throat all at once, if they was words at all. This went on for a while, and wasn't nothing happening but that rain, which was kind of pleasant.

"Huck," Jim said, "you done been as good a friend as man could have, and I ain't happy you gonna die, or me neither, but we got to, it makes me happy knowing you gonna go out with me."

"I'd feel better if you was by yourself," I said, and Jim let out a cackle when I said it.

There was a change in things, a feeling that the air had gone heavy. I looked up and the rain fell on my face and ran in my mouth and tasted good. The night sky was vibrating a little, like someone shaking weak pudding in a bowl. Then the sky cracked open like Br'er Rabbit had told us about, and I seen there was light up there in the crack. It was light like you'd see from a lantern behind a wax-paper curtain. After a moment, something moved behind the light, and then something moved in front of it. A dark shape about the size of the moon; the moon itself was starting to drift low and thin off to the right of the island.

Br'er Rabbit had tried to describe it to us, ole Cut Through You, but all I can say is there ain't no real way to tell you how it looked, 'cause there wasn't nothing to measure it against. It was big and it had one eye that was dark and unblinking, and it had a beak of sorts, and there were all these ropey arms; but the way it looked shifted and changed so much you couldn't get a real handle on it.

I won't lie to you. It wasn't like standing up to the Tar Baby. My knees started knocking together, and my heart was beating like a drum and my insides felt as if they were being worked about like they was in a milk churn. Them snaky arms on that thing was clawing at the sky, and I even seen the sky give on the sides, like it was about to rip all over and fall down.

I pressed my back against the post, and when I did, I felt that pocketknife in my back pocket. It come to me then that if I stuck out my butt a little and pulled the rope loose as possible on the ring I was tied to, I might be able to thumb that knife out of my pocket, so I give it a try.

It wasn't easy, but that thing up there gave me a lot of will power. I worked the knife with my thumb and long finger, and got it out, and flicked it open, and turned it in my hand, almost dropping it. When that happened, it felt like my heart had leaped down a long tunnel somewhere. But when I knew I still had it, I turned it and went to cutting. Way I was holding it, twisted so that it come back against the rope on the ring, I was doing a bit of work on my wrists as well as the tie. It was a worrying job, but I stayed at it, feeling blood running down my hands.

While I was at it, that chanting got louder and louder, and I seen off to the side of Cut Through You, another hole opening up in the sky; inside that hole it looked like a whirlpool, like you find in the river; it was bright as day in that hole, and the day was churning around and around and the sky was widening.

I figured then the ceremony was in a kind of hurry, 'cause Cut Through You was peeking through, and that whirling hole was in competition to him. He wouldn't have nothing to eat and no chanting to hear, if the Sticky Storm took everyone away first.

You see, it was the chanting that was helping Cut Through You get loose. It gave him strength, hearing that crazy language.

From where we was, I could see the pink of the morning

starting to lay across the far end of the river, pushing itself up like the bloom of a rose, and that ole moon dipping down low, like a wheel of rat cheese being slowly lowered into a sack.

So, there we were, Cut Through You thrashing around in the sky, the Sticky Storm whirling about, and the sun coming up. The only thing that would have made it worse was if I had had to pee.

Everything started to shake, and I guess that was because Cut Through You and that storm was banging together in some way behind night's curtain, and maybe the sun starting to rise had something to do with it. The Sticky Storm dipped out of that hole and it come down lower. I could see all manner of stuff up there in it, but I couldn't make out none of it. It looked like someone had taken some different mixes of paint and thrown them all together; a few light things on the ground started to float up toward the storm, and when they did, I really understood why Br'er Rabbit called it a Sticky Storm; it was like it was flypaper and all that was sucked up got stuck to it like flies.

About then, I cut that rope in two, and pulled my bleeding hands loose. I ran over to Jim and cut him loose.

Br'er Fox and the others didn't even notice. They was so busy looking up at Cut Through You. I didn't have the time, but I couldn't help but look up too. It had its head poking all the way through, and that head was so big you can't imagine, and it was lumpy and such, like a bunch of melons had been put in a tow sack and banged on with a boat paddle; it was leaking green goo that was falling down on the ground, and onto the worshipers, and they was grabbing it off the muck, or off themselves, and sticking their fingers in their mouths and licking them clean.

It didn't look like what the Widow Douglas would have called sanitary, and I could see that them that was eating it, was starting to change. Sores, big and bloody, was popping up on them like a rash.

I ran on around the circle to Tom and Joe and cut them loose, and then we all ran back the other way, 'cause as much as I'd like to have helped them on that farther part of the circle, it was too late. On that side the ground was starting to fold up, and their

DREAD ISLAND

posts was coming loose. It was like someone had taken a sheet of paper and curled one end of it. They was being sucked up in the sky toward that Sticky Storm, and even the black mud was coming loose and shooting up in the sky.

On the other end of the circle, things was still reasonably calm, so I rushed to Br'er Rabbit and cut him loose, then that lady with the pants on. Right about then, Cut Through You let out with a bellow so loud it made the freckles on my butt crawl up my back and hide in my hair, or so it felt. Wasn't no need to guess that Cut Through You was mad that he was running out of time, and he was ready to take it out on most anybody. He stuck long ropey legs out of the sky and went to thrashing at Br'er Fox and the others. I had the pleasure of seeing Br'er Fox getting his head snapped off, and then Br'er Bear was next.

The weasels, not being of strong stuff to begin with, started running like rats from a sinking ship. But it didn't do them no good. That Cut Through You's legs was all over them, grabbing their heads and jerking them off, and them that wasn't beheaded, was being pulled up in the sky by the Sticky Storm.

I was still on that side of the circle, cutting people loose, and soon as I did, a bunch of them just ran wildly, some right into the storm. They was yanked up, and went out of sight. All of the island seemed like it was wadding up.

Br'er Rabbit grabbed my shoulder, said, "It's every man for his self," and then he darted along the edge of the Sticky Storm, dashed between two whipping Cut Through You legs, and leaped right into that briar patch, which seemed crazy to me. All the while he's running and jumping in the briars, I'm yelling, "Br'er Rabbit, come back."

But he didn't. I heard him say, "Born and raised in the briar patch, born and raised," and then he was in the big middle of it, even as it was starting to fold up and get pulled toward the sky.

Now that we was free, I didn't know what to do. There didn't seem no place to go. Even the shoreline was starting to curl up.

Jim was standing by me. He said, "I reckon this is it, Huck. I say we let that storm take us, and not Cut Through You."

We was about to go right into the storm, 'cause the side of

it wasn't but a few steps away, when I got my elbow yanked. I turned and it was Tom Sawyer, and Joe with him.

"The lady," Tom said. "This way."

I turned and seen the short-haired lady was at that silver boat, and she was waving us to her. Any port in a storm, so to speak, so we run toward her with Tom and Joe. A big shadow fell over us as we run, and then a leg come popping out of the sky like a whip, and caught Joe around the neck, and yanked his head plumb off. His headless body must have run three or four steps before it went down.

I heard Tom yell out, and stop, as if to help the body up. "You got to run for it, Tom," I said. "Ain't no other way. Joe's deader than last Christmas."

So we come up on the silver boat with the wings, and there was an open door in the side of it, and we rushed in there and closed it. The lady was up front in a seat, behind this kind of partial wheel, looking out through a glass that run in front of her. The silver bug was humming, and those crosses on the wings was spinning. She touched something and let loose of something else, and we started to bounce, and then we was running along on the grass. I moved to the seat beside her, and she glanced over at me. She was white-faced, but determined-looking.

"That was Noonan's seat," she said.

I didn't know what to say to that. I didn't know if I should get out of it or not, but I'll tell you, I didn't. I couldn't move. And then we was bouncing harder, and the island was closing in on us, and Cut Through You's rope legs was waving around us. One of them got hit by the crosses, which was spinning so fast you could hardly make them out. They hit it, and the winged boat was knocked a bit. The leg come off in a spray of green that splattered on the glass, and then the boat started to lift up. I can't explain it, and I know it ain't believable, but we was flying.

The sun was really starting to brighten things now, and as we climbed up, I seen the woods was still in front of us. The lady was trying to make the boat go higher, but I figured we was gonna clip the top of them trees and end up punched to death by them, but then the boat rose up some, and I could feel and hear the trees brush against the bottom of it, like someone with a whisk broom snapping dust off a coat collar.

With the island curling up all around us and starting to come apart in a spray of color, being sucked up by the Sticky Storm, and that flying boat wobbling and a-rattling, I figured we had done all this for nothing.

The boat turned slightly, like the lady was tacking a sail. I could glance up and out of the glass and see Cut Through You. He was sticking his head out of a pink morning sky, and his legs was thrashing, but he didn't look so big now; it was like the light had shrunk him up. I seen Tar Baby, too, or what was left of him, and he was splattering against that big gourd thing with the writing on it, splattering like someone was flicking ink out of a writing pen. He and that big gourd was whipping around us like angry bugs.

Then there was a feeling like we was an arrow shot from a bow, and the boat jumped forward, and then it went up high, turned slightly, and below I seen the island was turning into a ball, and the ball was starting to look wet. Then it, the rain, every dang thing, including ole Cut Through You, who was sucked out of his hole, shot up into that Sticky Storm.

Way we was now, I could still see Tar Baby splashed on that gourd, and the gourd started to shake, then it twisted and went as flat as a tapeworm, and for some reason, it blowed; it was way worse than dynamite. When it blew up, it threw some Tar Baby on the flying boat's glass. The boat started to shake and the air inside and out had blue ripples in it.

And then—

—the island was gone and there was just the Mississippi below us. Things was looking good for a minute, and then the boat started coughing, and black smoke come up from that whirly thing that had cut off one of Cut Through You's legs.

The boat dropped, the lady pulling at that wheel, yanking at doo-dads and such, but having about as much luck taking us back up as I'd have had trying to lift a dead cow off the ground by the tail.

"We are going down," she said, as if this might not be something we hadn't noticed. "And there is nothing else to do but hope for the best."

Well, to make a long story short. She was right.

Course, hope only goes so far.

She fought that boat all the way down, and then it hit the water and skipped like it was a flat rock. We skipped and skipped, then the whirly gigs flew off, and one of them smashed the glass. I was thrown out of the seat, and around the inside of the boat like a ball.

Then everything knotted up, and there was a bang on my head, and the next thing I know there's water all over. The boat was about half full inside. I suppose that's what brought me around, that cold Mississippi water.

The glass up front was broke open, and water was squirting in around the edges, so I helped it by giving it a kick. It come loose at the edges, and I was able to push it out with my feet. Behind me was Tom Sawyer, and he come from the back like a farm mule in sight of the barn. Fact was, he damn near run over me going through the hole I'd made.

By the time he got through, there wasn't nothing but water, and I was holding my breath. Jim grabbed me from below, and pushed me by the seat of my pants through the hole. Then it was like the boat was towed out from under me. Next thing I knew I was on top of the water floating by Tom, spitting and coughing.

"Jim," I said, "where's Jim?"

"Didn't see him come up," Tom said.

"I guess not," I said. "You was too busy stepping on my head on your way out of that flying boat."

Tom started swimming toward shore, and I just stayed where I was, dog paddling, looking for Jim. I didn't see him, but on that sunlit water there come a big bubble and a burst of something black as the Tar Baby had been. It spread over the water. It was oil. I could smell it.

Next thing, I felt a tug at my leg. I thought it was one of them big catfish grabbing me, but it wasn't. It was Jim. He bobbed up beside me, and I grabbed him and hugged him and he hugged me back.

Dread Island

"I tried to save her, Huck. I did. But she was done dead. I could tell when I touched her, she was done dead."

"You done what you could."

"What about Tom?" Jim said.

I nodded in the direction Tom had gone swimming. We could see his arms going up and down in the water, swimming like he thought he could make the far shore in about two minutes.

Wasn't nothing to do but for us to start swimming after him. We done that for a long time, floating some, swimming some. And I'm ashamed to say Jim had to pull me along a few times, 'cause I got tuckered out.

When we was both about gone under, a big tree come floating by, and we climbed up on it. We seen Tom wasn't too far away, having gotten slower as he got tired. We yelled for him, and he come swimming back. The water flow was slow right then, and he caught up with us pretty quick, which is a good thing, 'cause if he hadn't, he'd have sure enough drowned. We clung and floated, and it was late that afternoon when we finally was seen by some fishermen and pulled off the log and into their boat.

There isn't much left to tell. All I can say is we was tired for three days, and when we tried to tell our story, folks just laughed at us. Didn't believe us at all. Course, can't blame them, as I'm prone toward being a liar.

It finally got so we had to tell a lie for it to be believed for the truth, and that included Tom who was in on it with us. We had to say Joe drowned, because they wouldn't believe Cut Through You jerked his head off. They didn't believe there was a Cut Through You. Even the folks believed there was a Dread Island didn't believe our story.

Tom and Becky got together, and they been together ever since. Five years have passed, and dang if Tom didn't become respectable and marry Becky. They got a kid now. But maybe they ain't all that respectable. I count eight months from the time they married until the time their bundle of joy come along.

Last thing I reckon I ought to say, is every year I go out to the edge of the Mississippi with Jim and toss some flowers on the water in memory of the lady who flew us off the island in that winged boat.

As for Dread Island. Well, here's something odd. I can't see it no more, not even when it's supposed to be there.

Jim says it might be my eyes, 'cause when you get older you lose sight of some things you used to could see.

I don't know. But I think it ain't out there no time anymore, and it might not be coming back. I figure it, Br'er Rabbit and Cut Through You is somewhere else that ain't like nothing else we know. If that's true, all I got to say, is I hope Br'er Rabbit is hid up good, far away from Cut Through You, out there in the thorns, out there where he was raised, in the deep parts of that big old briar patch.

Fhtagntastic Four

Story: Christopher Sequeira

Art and Captions: Jan Scherpenhuizen

Edits: Jason Franks

Fhtagntastic Four

Fhtagntastic Four

FHTAGNTASTIC FOUR

AS THE MAN KNOWN AS *MR PHTANGTASTIC* ATTEMPTS TO *IGNORE* THE QUESTIONS OF THE *THING-ON-THE-DOORSTEP* AND DECIFER HIS OCCULT TOME, WAVES OF *CORRUSCATING POWER* (OUR FAVOURITE KIND) RADIATE OUTWARD FROM THE *AWE-INSPIRING BEHEMOTH* WHO SEEMS TO HOLD THE VERY *FATE* OF THE *EARTH* IN HIS TENTACLED APPENDAGES.

A *STRANGE* AND *TERRIFYING* PROCESS OF *DEVOLUTION* TAKES PLACE...

SO CLEAR NOW, *ALEX JONES* MAKE *BEST* PRESIDENT...

JEWISH SPACE LASERS!

AND *EVERYWHERE* THESE *ARCANE OCCULT RAYS* REACH...

LOREM IPSUM DOLOR SIT AMET, CONSECTE-TUR ADIPISCING ELIT, SED DO EIUSMOD...

OH NO! HAS ROOD GONE TO THE *DARK* SIDE? THAT'S PLACE-HOLDER TEXT...

WHAT SHOULD WE DO? *DRINK BLEACH?*

ROOD! THE SPELL'S NOT PROTECTING US! THE THING-ON-THE-DOORSTEP IS *DEVOLVING*...

WADDAYA MEAN... I *ALWAYS* DRANK BLEACH, IT'S MY GUILTY *PLEASURE*...

OH...

153

FHTAGNTASTIC FOUR

155

THE SLEEPWALKER'S MANIFESTO

KAT CLAY

WE, THE KINETIC SOMNAMBULISTS, DECLARE:

1. OUR WORLD IS A DREAM DECLARED REALITY BY LANGUAGE.
2. DREAMS AND THEIR ARTS ARE PORTENTS OF THE FUTURE. THEREFORE, NO MAN HAS A PAST. NONE SHALL ASK ABOUT THE THINGS THAT HAPPENED YESTERDAY.
3. RIGID SYMBOLISM IS A CONSTRUCTION OF OLD ART. IN THE NEW ART, DREAM LOGIC APPLIES. OBJECTS AND PEOPLE ARE NEVER AS THEY SEEM.
4. ART IS A PROBLEM OF TRANSLATION. DREAMS DO NOT SPEAK THE LANGUAGES OF MEN. WE DEMAND A NEW LANGUAGE OF VISUALISATION, ONE FREE OF LINGUISTIC STRUCTURES.
5. LANGUAGE IS THE TYRANNY THAT GIRDS A FALSE EARTH.

I.

I re-read the manifesto on the *Fleche d'Or*, shooting across the landscape as fast as my mind could carry me, my heart already in the arrondissements of Paris. I had been invited by the author, Anton

Depoiteaux, to join his cadre of Kinetic Somnambulists, and I was determined to prove myself worthy of the invitation, memorising those rules and lines as if they were the oaths of an ancient order.

I was a painter of dreams, a sculptor of the things unseen. No one would dare use the word renaissance in our radicality—but I saw my work as that of Tiresias, eyes covered, yet communing with the dead. I saw beyond the veil and sought to distil the very essence of the subconscious into original visualisations. My Dream Facilitator had caught Depoiteaux's eye, and warranted the letter I clutched in my hand, inviting me to display the work at the *Galerie de Cauchemar* in Montparnasse.

I was the face of the New British Art, he wrote, and this was where I would make my name, because art was old in London and new in Rome and full of dreams in Paris. I was drunk on the vitriol of the age. I cursed my forebears. I hated upon that which was old; I despised myself for ageing. I was an imitation of my heroes: Apollinaire, Breton, Tzara.

Depoiteaux promised that unlike the Surrealists, we could reach the dreams so rigorously analysed by Freud, to make the subconscious visible, to define the indefinable. The ba-dum of the train wheels propelled me towards that promised future.

So, by the time I reached *Gare du Nord*, hopped up on leftover cocaine and a lack of sleep, my drowsy eyes lit with fire at the sight of the morning city. I declared myself the new king of the arts, born of ego and a borrowed suit.

"C'est ici, le royaume des rêves," I shouted, spooking the pigeons into flight. For art had an immediacy seen in these fragmentary moments: the bird caught in motion upon a grey sky, the ringing strike of a clock tower marking eleven-thirty, the crotchety man looking up with disdain from his café at this bright young thing. To the old, my vitality was a reminder of what had been lost in living.

I made my way to the apartment, suitcase in one hand, dragging the Dream Facilitator in the other. I had been promised accommodations as part of the commune of Kinetic Somnambulists. Yet no one greeted me; Depoiteaux left a note with the key. Disappointingly, he had been called away on urgent business and would catch up with me at the exhibition.

I slept all day, troubled by visions in that gloaming consciousness where fatigue meets insomnia. For Paris had brought with it its own oneiric mysteries; a violence in my dreams, of a city beyond this one, of a reversed Paris where even the stars could be seen under the electric skies. This world glimmered like the diamonds in a jewellery box, powered by the burning of creation itself.

Between the buildings that bloomed from the ruins of the old, I caught sight of an immutable structure. A ziggurat, a stark building made of intersecting lines, each layer defined by a singular obsidian slab. Within its rectangular entry, a void darker than the walls itself. How did I know it was a temple? For no-one worshipped there.

II.

By Sunday, the *Galerie de Cauchemar* was open for business. It was a darkly ordained place, neither heaven nor hell, but built from the limbo of the subconscious.

Fake roses bloomed from a stuffed mallard's beak. A *poubelle* spewed torn pages of the literature of the old guard. A dining table served barbed wire, the lines and trenches of the war marked out in its fine veneer. The arts were an esoteric confidence game; a world where a ceramic toilet could sell for a fortune, if only you said it was something else. Where, or from whom, these works had come, I knew not. I had seen not a soul in the commune of Kineticists, although I had heard movement in the building—the occasional shout, door slam, and the low grunt of perfunctory sex.

I set up the Dream Facilitator at the centre of the room; the machine built from dissonant parts mounted on a wooden tripod. At the apex sat a broken camera, its sagging accordion proboscis propped up with a tuning fork. A Brodie helmet crowned the box, giving the machine the impression of a one-eyed soldier forever observing at his post. An art born of war and false faith in the infallibility of modernity. It would never work, but it never needed to. For art was more about conviction than truth. It stood, imposing, illuminated by a spotlight at the head of a velvet chaise.

My art was as much performance as sculpture itself. When the hour turned midnight, I took to the stage. A hush descended, punctuated by the dim chime of crystal glasses.

"Freud was wrong. Dreams are not expressions of unacknowledged fears and desires. They are not a representation of the subconscious. Rather, we are the subconscious, the dreams of a world beyond this one."

I confess, I revelled in the eyes upon me, those black spheres lit with a tiny spark of white from the spotlight. They followed me everywhere, as if the crowd were not a group of individuals but a singular creature blinking in the dark.

My provocations were not the false statements of one who sought attention, although I drank from their gaze as one would a deep and heady wine. For I only declared that which was hinted at in sleep; who has not caught glimpses of a world beyond this one in the night's passing?

"But you do not believe me," I said, reading the mutters from the back row of surrealists. "Let me show you the real world."

The performance was not yet complete; I placed the helmet on my head as a priest anointing a king. I rolled my sleeve up and withdrew a large needle from a case; that heady flash as opioids ran thick through my veins, I lay down, hands crossed over my chest, and fell languorously into the gloaming world.

I cannot describe what the audience saw, only that which I dreamed.

In this world, I walked the streets of a Paris so familiar and yet unreal.

When we think of Paris, we recall its decadence; those magnificent edifices memorialising history — triumphal arches, columns, and architraves. Here, Paris had become the world promised by the modern architect. Razed and built new, parks and vistas surrounded by buildings that defied the laws of physics. Yet still it remained unmistakably Paris. Those remarkable, swirling signs of the Paris Métro, now read *Niatiloportèm Sirap,* stairs leading to a train which skirted the clouds and stars through pyramids to touch the ceiling of the world. *Sirap,* this city, unashamedly new, a rejection of all that had come before.

THE SLEEPWALKER'S MANIFESTO

My feet felt light upon the stairs, passing people who seemed more vibrant than the world from which I had just come. Women whose bodies had been replaced with clocks, their fingers ticking time on pianos that hung from swinging pendulums.

A man with a camel's face passed me an umbrella; when it opened, the underside showered me with fountain pens. One pierced my open palm. Blood came from my hand too easily. I sucked it and it tasted as marmalade, sweet and orange. All while I ascended those stairs to the whirling *Ortèm*.

From the train's high vantage, I spied the familiar streets, now reversed. *Ilovir ed Eur, Segsov sed Ecalp, Seèsylè-Spmahc*. And at its centre, that luminous temple which beckoned me to worship at its altar to a god yet unknown. There are no words to describe the pull which this shrine had on me. Led by an invisible hand, I needed to uncover what was worshipped in this edifice, for it contained a secret of the world that I might harness for my art, thus declaring my immortality among the greats. The world would know my name as a Picasso or Gauguin. A new Da Vinci born of dreams.

In pursuit of this destination, I tumbled from *Ortèm* station to *Ortèm* station, switching lines, trying to read the tangle of signs which pointed this way and that, always encircling the temple at the centre of *Sirap* but never arriving at its destination. Where the streets were populated with the whimsies of the world, the temple repulsed any approach. Whenever I came close, the architecture of the new would rise to meet me. A row of obelisks sprouted through a park of glass trees. I ran straight into this wall and woke, as one does with the slap of icy water, jerking suddenly from the lounge.

There was no applause; a fraught fear ran through the crowd. What had they seen when I had been in *Sirap*? The plan had been to perform, yet I had seen something beyond my comprehension.

The crowd dissipated into whispering groups, and it was not long before I found myself drinking at *Le Bœuf sur le toit*, lurking between mirrors, cigarette and pipe smoke, surveilled by a painting of a disembodied eye.

I watched the crowd from the bar, arm casually laid against

its wooden boards. A lone man's hand emerged from an evening cape, each swipe of the fingers parting the world, so that none touched him as he passed. Was he a man? For his long black hair fell straight as a curtain from a delicately featured face. He stopped beside me, turning to face that world which danced and drank as if it had not seen a portal opened to dreams.

The man sat beside me and lit a cigarette, puffing closely from nicotine-stained fingers.

"Your machine is a fraudulent dream factory. A performative statue at best, like the static idols carved by pagans, worshipped by fools." He spoke English in the same way I wished I spoke French: a soft lilt to his accent, his mouth pursed tight, the words passing through his thin lips as a cold draft in a warm room. An intimacy in the tightness around his mouth, the muscles pursed as if to kiss or to speak. It was the problem of language. What was said could be undermined by the symbolic desires of the body.

My eyes did not stray from the drunken patrons before me, swirling movements caught in the yellow glow of my drink, the crystal glass in my hands.

"Fancy yourself an art critic, do you?" I said.

He shook his head at the edge of my vision. "What if I told you that you could open a waking portal between here and the dream world? A métro station of the mind, if you will. But you need a psyche for it to work."

I could not tell if the man was a lunatic, a charlatan, or a true believer. For I had made this machine as a mockery; and here he believed it could be made to pass the veil of the subconscious.

"I suppose you are a purveyor of psyches? Tell me of your wares; do mental maladies and hysteric women come at a discount?"

At that, I dared to look at him. The man grinned wickedly, his smile reaching from each side of his deep cheeks. "Bombast is beautiful on the poor. It deflects from the frayed silks they wear."

He waited for my reaction; I gave him none. His grin settled as he bent close to my ear. The loudness of the party justified his proximity, nothing more.

The Sleepwalker's Manifesto

"I am sorry it has taken me so long to introduce myself in Paris. I wanted to see your Dream Facilitator for myself, before I decided whether to initiate you into the group. I am Anton Depoiteaux."

"And if I had not passed your test?"

"You would have been back on the train to London tomorrow morning."

"What convinced you to let me stay?"

He pulled out a fountain pen and scratched out a design on a napkin. Despite the bleeding ink, it was the strange temple from my dream. I snatched the drawing from under him, the pen squiggling away a line, his clammy hand lingering next to mine for too long.

"Will you call on me tonight?" I asked, part of me wanting to dissect that which lay underneath that cape of darkest night. He shook his head, although not displeased with my appraising look.

"Consider me a noctambule of the space between the two worlds, Paris as it exists between midnight and the first hour. Come find me at that intersection."

He turned away. I knew I should not follow. I knew that to find him invited a thrilling danger that I would not come back from. But I could not help but watch Depoiteaux disappear in the crowd, as the stars are hidden by the brilliant arrival of the sun.

III.

In the weeks following, insomnia kept me from those hours reserved for dreaming. I longed to go back to *Sirap*, yet my body would not allow it, trapped in restless sleep. I would wake, thinking that Depoiteaux was watching me from the shadows of the apartment, that sinister, inexplicable feeling that someone was there when they were not. I would check the corners and cupboards, looking for that pale hand, those delicate features to emerge from an interstitial place. All I found were empty walls and unfinished art, the Dream Facilitator hulking under a sheet to keep it from taunting me further.

Drawings of the temple's singular face proliferated through the apartment. At each angle, it showed a different side, but still retained that same, immutable rigidity.

KAT CLAY

Yet it seemed the more I longed to go back to *Sirap*, the less the door would open for me. Like the flâneur, I took to meandering the streets in a dim homage to Baudelaire, crossing cobblestoned alleys electricity failed to reach.

I searched for Depoiteaux in these places, for it seemed that he was a man that existed in the frisson of movement and chaos. I looked through dance clubs, music loud, waiting for that hand to emerge from the black cloak and reveal the secrets of the Dream Facilitator to me. I stood at intersections waiting for his appearance in those passing crowds. I searched through directories and address books. I asked at nearby cafés and the Hôtel de Ville for his address, even going so far to ask at the Salpêtrière, in the case he was truly a madman. None had heard of him.

In my fatigue I staggered along the dark banks of the Seine, lines of yellow lights disrupted by the passing of pleasure boats, under the storied sandstone buildings, shutters closed to the night. A profound sadness swept over me. I had so willingly declared Freud was wrong but could not deny dreams as places of immense pleasure—if I could not spend another hour in Depoiteaux's company, I could enact the lusts that consumed me in my dreams.

Sandstone walls fenced me on one side, and I thought of jumping into that water, if only to sleep forevermore. Standing at its edge, precariously balanced on the river walls, if you looked carefully, you could see a reflection of the street signs, a signal that *Sirap* was ever-present, if out of reach. Strangely, like *Sirap*, those historic monuments and buildings did not reflect in those shifting waters. Only the emanations of an all-consuming light, and the points of distant stars in the darkness.

Stumbling with this revelation, I tripped and fell backwards, grazing my wrist on the firmament. In *Sirap,* my blood had tasted like marmalade, here it scented of iron. I sat on the side of the street, caressing this wounded hand, as the world passed around me. In a mirror of my pale member, another hand emerged from the folds of the cape of night. And so, my lips found not my flesh but his. I milked the tips with my tongue, the cloying, addictive taste curdling in my mouth. With this hand came a body. I sat at his feet, curled around his legs, clutching his palm. Depoiteaux had found me.

IV.

Depoiteaux took centre stage in the apartment, the lines of the oriental rug drawing my eyes towards his sallow frame, his eyes focussed completely on me. "Art is a way to express that which cannot be spoken. In putting things into language, we declare what they are. If we do not declare them, they exist in a precarious state of pre-existence. This is the place where the door to *Sirap* opens."

"That's all very well and good, but how do we get there?" I said.

"Have you never heard of the phenomena of sleepwalking? Where one is caught between the state of waking and dreaming. It is innocent enough, under the right circumstances. Although the ego's desire for pleasure sometimes takes hold..." He said these words in a honeyed tone, and I did not notice as he pulled a fob from his pocket. My gaze fixed upon him as he swung that chain from side to side. "Hypnotism is the path which opens the gate to waking dreams. What time is it?"

"Eleven-thirty."

"What time is it?"

"Eleven-thirty."

"What time is it?"

My limbs became weary with the sensation of sleeplessness. I was in that half-state, where the mind is semi-aware of what is happening, but the body reacts as an automaton. Bleary-eyed, I did not know if I was dreaming or waking.

From this half state, my body awoke. The floor opened under us into a staircase made of feathers. Each step down was as walking on a cloud, my clothes transformed to the finery I deserved, but could never afford. Depoiteaux stood resplendent. It was as if he was a refraction of light in our world, yet dreams revealed his true self; warmth tinged his skin, his palm caressing my back when no one was watching. I thought of my behaviour at the Seine, and felt a terror, that my dreams betrayed my subservience to this man, the way I lapped at his fingers as if he were my lover. It was foolishness; for had that not been a dream?

As if reading my thoughts, "No, it was a desire. But *Sirap* is a land of impunity. What is shameful in the real world carries no burden in dreams. It is why so many people travel here, never to leave."

There was a vitality to our fervour in *Sirap*, that of the excitement of my first day in Paris, when everything was new, and the world was open and possibilities endless. We drank from martini glasses as big as fountains at the bar of feathers, where wine poured freely from toucan beaks. A pelican dripped caviar onto a plate, his gobbet warbling with unknown song.

Dancing girls made of mechanical parts kicked high along the bar, and our seats moved along a conveyor belt further underground, an open room where it rained upwards, sparks of lighting striking wherever we danced among the clouds. I realised I had not seen the temple since we arrived. Had Depoiteaux been guiding me away from its view? I asked as much, and he said, one eye cocked. "You wish to see the temple?"

Deep in my cups, I nodded; even in the dream world, alcohol gave me the discombobulating sensation of vertigo. Soon, wine turned to pleasure, and a red wooden door opened upon those dreams which linger at the dark edges of our subconscious. My guide stood at the lintel, a circus master, a tour guide, a seer.

Inside stood a gallery of sculptures of the human form, silhouetted by candlelight. Each stood on a dais in those poses of classical antiquity; a hand arched over the head, a body tucked into an athlete's actions. It was only as I got closer, my footfall echoing in the large room, that I noted the slight tremble to these poses. These were sculptures of the living.

On closer inspection, their bodies had been pulled apart and re-sculpted. A hand attached backwards, the thin seam of a scar marking the surgical incision. Legs: one forward, one backward. Eyes that twitched and revolved in on themselves, the white spheres chilling my soul. I cannot describe my horror at those strange, reversed men of *Sirap*, scars writ large on their bodies. No desire transfused my body for their nakedness, only repulsion.

From Depoiteaux's dark cloak glinted a ceremonial knife, its curved blade etched with words from a language I could not decipher. "To worship at the temple requires sacrifice. Are you willing to pay the price?"

I knew then that Depoiteaux's singular desire was to dissect me and rebuild my body in the manner of these men before me. Whether these were mere constructions of a broken psyche, or reflected real-world transformations, I did not wish to discover the answer. In my hubris, I had longed to use sculpture as a language of the unspeakable. To my terror, he succeeded where I had not.

I ran from this dream place, from that haunting darkness, from the pale hand that pursued me, Depoiteaux traversing through the shadows of this nightmare. The white hand emerged from doorframes and windowsills, his body threatening to follow as it grasped at my coattails. From these penumbral ways came Depoiteaux, ceremonial dagger slashing at my clothes.

Stumbling, I whirled down flights of stairs that led to a cloakroom where women had been turned inside out, their bodies made of mutated muscle, walking backwards without skin. Through a hall where abstract paintings threw sharp, painterly lines at me, until my clothes flowed behind me as ribbons on an ethereal wind.

A familiar sight at the end of that nightmare gallery. *Niatiloportèm Sirap*. A train could take me far from the reaches of Anton Depoiteaux.

The corridor opened on an underground station, white and green tiles circling in a rotunda of incomprehensible angles. Through this whirl of time and space, the *Ortèm* slowed to a halt, that breath of opening doors reminiscent of a high-hat played with soft sticks.

The train was empty, wooden seats beckoning me to rest, to sleep. I stood, clutching a handrail until my knuckles turned white, as if this were the only thing preventing me from falling into a great chasm to my death. The train picked up speed through hyperbolic geometries, stars falling past the windows in a multitude of colours. In a primordial act of *a priori* knowledge, the stars whispered their names to me as they passed: Aldebaran, Beta Persei, and the Hyades. In return, I promised I would

KAT CLAY

dedicate myself to the worship of the temple god, if only the train would deliver me from this nightmare.

If I had not clung to my handhold, my body would surely have collapsed upon that celestial conveyance, to perish amongst the stars. But it was not to be. For one glorious moment, as all have experienced when an underground train breaches the sunlit world, the great violet sky rendered me momentarily blind from its brightness.

As the train slowed, it pulled into a grand courtyard of ashen tiles, a remnant of the once great civilization that lived here, now filled with the depraved creations of its usurper. The doors opened in reverent silence. I stepped upon the expansive platform, gossamer tendrils of darkness snatching at my leather shoes, only to break away as I approached the great ziggurat of my vision. My dreams had heard my cry for sanctuary, for in the hum of an ancient language, the words warned that the unholy Depoiteaux could not step within this place.

The only entrance: a grand arch. Close up, it was etched with unknown letters from a language no man had seen. In my pursuit of the new, I found something older than man. A mode of communication beyond art and imagination.

I descended those stairs, down through an obsidian corridor, where no seam between the rocks could be found. As a sculptor, I knew what it was to carve from stone, but these constructs had been rent by a power unknown; no mark showed from mason's tools or an architect's plan. The bottom of this stair opened upon a room lit by iridescent stars, continuing into infinite galaxies reflected from ceiling to floor. I stood upon a path which charted through this cosmos and was overwhelmed by an awe-sundering feeling of loneliness. These stars were light and the absence of light, they were all things and nothing at once. They would consume me if I let them. Perhaps I already had become food for those devouring stars.

At the end of this path stood a marble dais, devoid of statuary. I ascended those brief stairs and stood at its apex.

Truly, this was a temple.

But no one worshipped here. It was consecrated to a peculiar form of god, one which desired worship by all but only ever received the worship of one.

This temple was dedicated to the self. I looked upon the great expanse of absent worshippers before me and felt the emptiness of my narcissism. Despite my desire for the world's adoration, I remained a performative statue atop a dais, only to be worshipped by fools.

The scales fell from my eyes; what hubris we artists have to think we can entrap the universe in a symbol? To declare, this is the thing, when all around us swirls a world which demands fealty and fear.

The dais I stood on was no place for a god. It was a plinth of submission to the building that enclosed me on every side and trapped me in its grand foundations. For what did the imposing, implacable nature of these edifices say, but I am here, I have been here, and here I will remain? No man could move these mountains, no builder could excavate their foundations. These had grown from the dreams of something greater than man.

Terrified, I ran from this place, but the floor on which I ran was no longer straight but constantly curving, my body walking forwards into the flat surface of the floor, into that galactic infinity.

The world fell dark, save for the brief spotlight upon my iron crown.

V.

Nervous laughter. Applause. I sat bolt upright, having passed through the veil of stars into the glimmering lights of my performance.

A white hand glinted in the blinking afterburn of my eyes. Before he could find me, I threw the helmet from my head and smashed the Dream Facilitator. The crowd's murmur halted, pierced with the screech of metal on metal, the tuning fork ringing a dissonant note. When it was done, springs and wire littered the floor, my cold and sweaty face contorted with rage.

I ran into the late streets, desperate for the cool air, the slap of jazz in a distant café, the petroleum scent of heavy traffic, the glow of the electric lights. Oh, this city and its hedonism. I longed to be nothing at all amongst the crowds. An anonymous man, moving between lives and languages of expression, never needing to be acknowledged. "*Il est fou,*" shouted a woman, as I broke into a delirious run, desperate for a vision of those grand monuments of the Paris I knew. Tumbling, my feet staggered in a broken run, hitting shoulders, shouts, furious café owners, bowling through the green and cream chairs, knocking over wooden tables and placards, until I was convinced that these objects were not declarations of a false world, but exactly what they were. And never would I declare them to be otherwise, for to play with the very definitions of language is to invite a state of non-existence in the mind, to unhinge the very subconscious from its being.

I laughed, frightened by this very realisation. Language was an anchor to protect us from the terror of an undefined world. The Dream Facilitator was never about the object itself, but the words used to convey us from one place to another.

I stumbled, drunk on life through those dark streets, until I found a train station to take me home. Not to the apartment, but back to London, back to the safety of the old. I would sculpt mythic heroes for royal families. I would paint Eurydice and Lot's wife, turning to look at the forbidden, forever changed. Even Tiresias, once a woman, once a man, blinded and blindfolded by dreams.

My pocket watch read eleven-thirty when I was woken by the conductor, my breath fogging the glass windows of the hastening train. Without thinking, I pressed my ticket into the official's white gloved hand. "*Est-ce que votre premiere fois à Sirap?*" he asked.

I paled, the ba-dum of electric wheels hurtling me towards a future I had only dreamed of.

CREATURES OF THE NIGHT TRAIN

DEL HOWISON

"So, like a forgotten fire, a childhood can always flare up again within us." —*Gaston Bachelard*

They were laughing and pillow fighting so rambunctiously that the children never realized there was somebody standing in the hall outside their room. That is until the door started to slowly creak open. Juliet screamed, and the two boys stopped in mid-swing, frozen like a tableau caught in a single spotlight, dead center on the stage. As the door slowly moved inward a set of fingers appeared, grabbing the edge of the wood, adding leverage to the arc of the creaky hinges. The children watched, unmoving, their eyes wide with fear and wonder. When a head popped around the side of the door, they all gasped and jerked backwards.

"Papa," the kids shouted in unison, the two boys rolling on the bed in laughter and the granddaughter running up to Grandpa for a big hug.

Papa laughed and hugged her, then playfully shook his finger at the boys.

"You are making such a racket that your parents cannot even hear the television. They sent me up here to punish you for your misbehavior." But he couldn't hold the fake expression of scorn any longer and broke into a big grin. "You are supposed to be getting ready for bed. Is there problem?"

Juliet looked up from where she had her arms wrapped tightly around his legs.

"We're not sleepy, Papa. Tell us a bedtime story."

"Yes, yes," the boys joined in. "Tell us a story and then we'll be tired and go to sleep."

Grandpa rubbed his chin, feeling the scruff from not having shaved that morning, or any morning earlier in the week. That is some of the lazy fun he treated himself to now that he was retired.

"Let me think," he said. "It is late. I don't know if I can make something up."

"Then don't make something up," Juliet said.

Papa crouched down to her level. "What do you mean?"

She put her hand next to his ear and whispered, "Tell us something scary that really, happened to you."

Papa scowled at her.

"No, I cannot tell you something frightening. Then you would have bad dreams that would wake you up and you would never get back to sleep."

"Tell us about the time you and your friends went deer hunting, and a bear chased you."

"No," Grandpa said. "I've already told you that story."

The two boys began cheering and yelling. "Something scary! Something scary!"

Grandpa stood up and waved his hands. "Shhh. Your father will come up if he hears you and then there will be no story. He will be mad at both you and me."

The children grew quiet.

"If I tell you a story," he said looking back and forth between them. "Do you promise you will go to your beds? Juliet, afterwards you'll go back to your room. There will be no more disruptions?"

Juliet glanced at her brothers and touched grandpa's leg. "Yes, we promise."

He clapped his hands. "Ok then. Everybody, change into your pajamas and climb into bed. Tyler and Toby, you share a bed and

CREATURES OF THE NIGHT TRAIN

Juliet you use the other one. I will tell you a tale of the Creatures of the Night Train. It is something that happened to me. Something so *scary*," he lowered his voice to a whisper, "that I have never told anybody because just thinking about it makes me frightened all over again."

"Ooh," the boys said. Their eyes grown large as black plums.

Papa clapped his hands again. "Now get ready!"

He looked at the three expectant faces in the beds before him. Blankets pulled up to their chins, the wall sconce fighting the darkness while the rain and wind slapped at the window. On the bedside table lay a copy of *Dagon* by H. P. Lovecraft. Grandpapa walked over and picked it up. He grinned at the garish cover.

"So, this is what you are reading these days?"

"Have you ever read it, Papa? There are monsters and all sorts of creepy things."

"Oh yes. I have met some of them with my own eyes!"

"You have? How old were you?" Toby asked.

"A long time ago when I was your age," he began.

"Grandpa, how did you get to be so old?"

"It was a miracle," he said.

"Why don't you tell us that story?" Tyler asked.

"About how I got to be so old? No. Because it's too long. But I am going to tell you the tale of when I was able to meet The Lovecraft monsters."

"Ooh," the boys said again and pulled the blankets even tighter about their chins and Grandpa began to tell his tale.

The darkness was so deep from the clouds covering the full moon that it seemed like I was trying to see inside a black cave. I only knew where I was outside by the occasional lantern light from a nearby barn or the golden warm light through a farmhouse window. I tried to stay on the dirt road, fearing that if I stepped off it, I would lose my way in the night and never find my way home. I knew I'd be doomed if I strayed. Maybe I'd be lost forever. Never wander from the path. I had no choice but to continue walking through the depths of night. I was hoping my friend Danny would be at Cowles Corner where we planned to meet up.

Two days earlier I had seen a paper flyer laying damp in the grass concerning a traveling sideshow coming to town. ONE NIGHT ONLY! it said. SEE HERETOFOR UNKNOWN SECRETS OF THE WORLD! it shouted at me. MONSTERS OF THE DEEP. At the bottom of the flyer was a drawing of some oddly shaped monstrosity. I picked the flyer up and showed it to Danny that day. We couldn't decide if it was a badly drawn animal or a real monster. But it sucked out the breath of our imaginations and it gave us a thrill in the pit of our stomachs.

Since they were going to set up in Nelson Green's empty pasture about a mile outside of town, they would have to pull in on Wednesday night. The pasture seemed like the most likely place to set up a circus tent. It hadn't been planted this year and sat fallow. What better place? How would they be coming? Down main street from the train stop in horse-drawn wagons? Would they have a calliope, and lions, beautiful circus performers in sparkly costumes and parade through town on their way to setting up a big tent? We had seen pictures of all the colors and glory in books. I didn't know the difference between a circus, under the big tent and a sideshow, which was designed for an entirely different purpose. But I soon found out and it changed my life. We had so many questions. We agreed to sneak out of the house at midnight of their arrival and meet at the crossroads. We would face the dangers together...as long as our parents didn't catch us.

I had heard the lonesome chugging of the train as I lay in bed on the night, window open. The sounds of a train could carry a long way at night. It came with the other nocturnal noises and grew in volume as it approached town. The train had to be them. I didn't know what time it was, but I knew it was the middle of the night. I slid out of bed fully clothed. I had climbed into bed that way to be ready in a hurry when the time came. Tying my shoes, I looked under my bedroom door to make sure there was no light. My parents must have been asleep. I went to the window. And stopped. Was I doing the right thing? From outside I could hear the chugging as the fantastic grew closer. It called me. It touched my very soul. So, I sat on the windowsill with my legs hanging down. My decision was made. I pushed myself off the ledge, dropped to the ground and into the great unknown.

About 15 minutes later, even with the darkness, I could tell I was almost at the crossroads. I stopped and did our secret bird-whistle. If Danny was there, he would whistle back. It was our covert signal. We were best friends. We would argue and fight, even bring a little blood. But we would do things together because there were only about seven kids within a square mile of that countryside. We didn't like each other, but we were best friends.

I put my hands on either side of my mouth and puckered up. The sound pierced the night, much louder than I'd hoped for. I hadn't wanted anybody else to realize we were there.

"Make the whistle for us, Papa," Juliet said.

Grandpa shook his head.

"It's too loud and will disturb your parents," he said. He leaned in conspiratorially. "But, maybe tomorrow when we're outside, away from the house I'll do it for you. Then you can use it as your secret signal too."

The children smiled, knowing they were going to have a hidden knowledge from their parents that they couldn't get in trouble for. They had no idea then that they would share that bond for the rest of their lives. Grandpa looked back at the bedroom door as if making sure their parents were still downstair watching TV. When he seemed satisfied, he turned back to the kids and continued his tale.

I could still hear the groaning of the train as it settled into the last curve before the station where it would stop to unload. We would need to hurry if we were to see anything tonight. A loud whistle pierced the night. Danny had answered the call. In a couple of minutes his footsteps scuffed along the dirt road, and he came up beside me panting.

"Sorry," he said. "I had a hard time getting away without my parents knowing. This had all better be real. I'm not gonna get my ass whipped for nothing."

"That's okay. You're here now."

"Man, it's dark. I can hardly see your silhouette in front of me."

I turned and faced the direction of the track. There was a distant screech of metal as the train seemed to come to a stop. Then a hiss of steam as if the locomotive was letting out a sigh. I turned back to Danny.

"I can smell it. Can you smell it?"

"Maybe that's me," Danny said wiping his forehead. "I got really hot trying to find my way here in the darkness. I'm all sweaty."

I shook my head. "Nope, you smell like a hot kid. I smell the train."

Danny turned his head in the direction of the tracks and breathed deeply. The smell was there. He just wasn't getting it. He couldn't smell adventure. Grease and oil, burnt fuel, a smell almost like burnt charcoal, and something else. Something organic. Something living like the smell of my aquarium when I open the top to feed my snake. The train made a metallic grunt in the distance and began moving again.

"The train is going away," I said.

"It sounds like it is going right out into Farmer Green's field," Danny shook his head. "But there's no track that way."

We looked at each other. Astounded. We headed off the road, jumping a wire fence and trudging through the pasture in the direction of Green's meadow. The morning would be appearing in just a few hours. The clouds shifted, uncovering the face of the moon, and the light turned the area from pitch black to a dark grey. At least we were able to navigate or we would have truly fallen in a hole or walked into a barbed wire fence crossing the pasture. As it was, travel was hard enough. Even though we sloughed through the weeds and bushes as fast as we could, it was slow going. We both were sweating profusely, and the plants and bugs seemed to be clinging to our skin and clothes. No matter how much we wiped our faces the sweat rolled down our faces and stung our eyes. Gnats and other flying bugs seemed to seek refuge in our nostrils and mouth, and we did our best not to breathe them in. Even the light breeze did nothing to keep the insects away.

"Eeww," Juliet said. "That's gross."

"Yes, it was. I think I spit out insects for days after that," Grandpa said.

Eventually, after hopping one more fence, we saw it. It was a wonder to our eyes. Beautiful and terrible at the same time, it slowly chugged into place, a living entity. As it did the track behind it disappeared, since there had never been rail passageway at that location in the first place. In front of the engine the rails would show up, like a mirage, and the train would slowly continue its roll to a final stop. A procession of about a dozen railroad cars, like the tail of the beast, strung out behind the engine. Each one was a large flatbed type car with what looked like a cage secured on top of it. They were huge enclosers almost the size of small houses and I couldn't imagine them slowly moving along the tracks cross country. But there they were. Danny punched me in the shoulder in case I wasn't looking.

"Look, look," he said.

"Ow," I rubbed my arm. "What did you think I was doing, you sloppy scum farmer."

I pushed him.

"Cut it out psycho pus clown."

He pushed me back and we were about to get into it when the iron monster let out another deep breath of steam and came to a complete stop. A tableau in mid-punch, we stared at the locomotive.

"What do you think is in those cages?"

"Monsters. I'm sure of it," I said. "I can smell them."

"Really?"

"Yes."

"How do you know what monsters smell like?"

"Like dirty socks or your farts."

Danny looked at me. "You're a worm whistle, you know that?"

"I'm gonna kick your butt."

"Just try it."

"I will," I said, and we stood there staring at each other. "But first we need to find out what is in those cages. Then you're a dead man."

"Ha," Danny said. "I'm shaking in my boots."

It was hard to tell what the iron cages contained as the sides were covered with canvas tied at the base with strong cables running through grommets and latched to eye bolts in the metal edge of the flatbed. Only a small portion of metal bars peeked out when the cracked tarpaulins moved with the vibration of the train or from a breath of air. Most of the canvas was old and rent and the torn pieces would move easier than the heavy grommeted pieces secured to the flatbeds.

Slowly, we walked through the field down towards the train. There was nobody in sight. A caboose stood at the backend of the string of cars and a light shone through the window of the cupola. Shadows moved back and forth inside but were never discernable as humans. Only something moving about that must be passing in front of the lamps. The gambrel roof of the lookout angled queerly and seem to be in desperate need of repair. The stygian appearance of the rest of the cars made the low-lit window stand out in defiance against the dark shadowy caravan. As we watched no face appeared in the window, so we continued our slow approach towards the string of cars.

The reptilian putridness that I had picked up on earlier, was more emphasized with our closer proximity and we could hear groaning and strange noises coming out from the other side of the coverings. Danny was pinching his nose shut trying to keep the foul odor out. But I'm sure it was to no avail. It was that odd combination of wet and dry smells together, sweet and sour, like a toad. We walked slowly, fearful yet inquisitive. Somewhere in the back of my mind a strong voice said: "Come closer, child. Don't be afraid. We have a new world to show you." It was a hypnotic pull, drawing us in. When I turned to look, I could tell it was calling Danny also. He walked as if in a trance, zombified and I called out to him to try and snap him out of it.

"Danny, what are you doing?"

He continued on as if he were deaf. I grabbed him by the arm and shook him. "Danny!"

He stopped and slowly looked at me.

"Did you hear that?" He spoke slowly as if English was his second language, and he was making sure to pronounce each word precisely.

I pulled up a handful of wet weeds and waved them in front of his face, sprinkling the water on him. It wasn't much but it was the only thing I had.

"I heard them. If you don't listen; they can't make you do things."

Everything was starting to feel like an old science fiction movie. Those were fun. But this was scaring the crap out of me. Yet, as a teenage boy I needed to know what was there. I was this close and hadn't come for nothing.

Grandpa looked at the three mesmerized children on the beds in front of him. They were totally immersed in his tale.

"You know what they say? Curiosity killed the cat."

Juliet waved a finger at him.

"But you're not a cat," she said.

Grandpa smiled. "I am not. Thank goodness."

We now stood about ten feet from the first flatbed behind the engine in the row. The bars and cage were much higher than the perception we had while looking at them from a distance. Even though the train sat still, there was a creaking, as of something large pacing accompanied by grunting and a rocking of the car from side to side. Something giant was moving about in a restless manner that suggested to us an unhappiness with being locked up. The voice, or should I say voices, that beckoned us were much louder now that we were next to the train. It seemed that Danny and I had figured out their beckoning calls. We were no longer captives to their vocal summons.

"Inquisitive, nosey, or downright meddlesome?"

The basso voice came from behind us, and we turned to see

a rather tall gaunt man standing there. He was wearing a long car coat and brown dress pants all topped by a grey fedora with a teardrop creased crown. He smiled, showing a silver metal tooth. In his left hand he held a silver-headed cane, the handle was carved into an obscure looking octopus creature. Its tentacles ran a short ways down the shaft past the band of the cane as if to secure the head onto the wood. He reached up and tucked the ascot he wore tighter into his shirt with his cadaverous fingers and pulled the coat closer about his upper body.

"Damn cold at the dew point, isn't it boys?"

"I'm sorry," I said. "We didn't hear you walk up."

"Obviously," he smiled, and his teeth seem a bit too long for his face. He looked up at the train and sighed with what sounded like satisfaction.

"Do you know what you are staring at?" He hissed his words as much as spoke them and curled his tongue upwards across the surface of his front teeth. It appeared like he was try to wipe the words off of his mouth in case they were as slimy as they sounded when he spoke.

Danny shook his head. "No, but I'd like to find out. Is this a sideshow?"

The man looked down and laughed. "It is more like a side door into your mind. Come, I will show you."

We walked closer to the railway.

"It is really the preposterous, inconceivable wanderings of a diseased writer's mind. As these insane creatures flowed from his consciousness, they arrived on the printed pages of a book. Others read these grotesques which he had transcribed, and they were given life by thousands of neophyte imaginations. This train belongs to the repugnant imagination of Lovecraft, and dare I say his followers, appreciatives."

"I've read some of his books," I said, feeling the rising excitement in my chest.

The man stooped down as to be eye level with me. He placed his long boney hands on my shoulders. I could feel the cold emanating from them, through my clothes, and chilling my skin.

"There is nothing so beautiful as a read book," he said. "But the consumption changes the reader."

He stared at me for what seemed an eternity and finally stood back up.

"Who are you?" Danny asked.

"For lack of a better moniker, I am the Ringmaster. However, we have no rings like a circus. Think of me as your guide. I am Dr. Alfred Clarendon. I wear several hats here." He laughed a husky, smokers laugh. "The Several Hats of Dr. Al. Let me take you on a little tour of these abominations. They are held tight in their cages by the bars of rationality." He pointed at me. "Having read some of his words you may recognize a few of the various creatures."

He stood alongside the first flatcar. We remained somewhat behind him, fearing a first attack but hoping that if there was one, he would block or slow down the assault. He stood still, revealing nothing until we felt certain he'd frozen into a statue. Then he shook his arms out, as if he was unwinding, while we stared at the tenting draped over the bars.

"I've got experience," he grimaced. "Look at me. Look at my face. Every line, every crease reveals mileage. You only learn from failing. That is why I have so many scars to match. I have failed." He smiled. "But I am fine now."

The battered canvas flapped and rippled at its base. Out from underneath edged a tentacle reflective with an oozing gelatinous substance. It flicked, raising the tip skyward as if trying to pick up a scent like an elephant's trunk. It was almost comical until the ghastly wail blurted from behind the material. The doctor reached out his hands, palms up and stretched his arms toward the beast. As he did so the canvas slowly vanished, and we were left staring at a writhing heap of tentacles with no other discernable feature. The thought that struck me was that something had eaten a dinner of tentacles and then heaved it up. The sound came from within and each time prior to its call the mass would swell up bladderlike, gathering air and then let loose with its mournful call.

"You are looking at Kassogtha. Cthulhu's mate and handily his sister. She calls to her children, fearing they've been devoured by their father. Do not get too close lest you become part of her digestive system."

As we watched it twisted and distorted, a giant pile of worms, and then let go with another bellow. I feared the entire countryside would be awakened by the sound. Yet when I turned around the entire landscape had been cloaked in a fog and completely disappeared from sight. I turned back and Dr. Alfred stood with palms reversed, facing the ground. The covering slowly reappeared to engulf the cage once more. When it was finished, we walked over to the next car. The doctor performed the same bit of hand magic, realizing the same results.

"Meet Ghast," he said. "Normally a pack creature, but I believe you only need a singular specimen to understand. They shun sunlight as it proves deadly to them."

The creature before us had long kangaroo shaped legs and feet. A faintly humanoid face lacked the features of ears and nose, so it breathed with its mouth open, showing repulsive teeth that had a slight backwards shark angle to them. Escaping the bite would be nearly impossible.

The doctor took in a large breath.

"Ghasts have an unnerving effect upon me. They need to be fed constantly and if I am tardy in those duties they fall into cannibalism. That's the reason we keep them as separate as possible."

The floor of the car was befouled and discolored, and I could only imagine what had created those begrimed markings. He again made his hand motion, covering the cage and we moved along to the next display. Upon revelation we were face-to-face, or should I say eye-to-eye with a blobish creature that continuously slammed itself against its prison confines. An extra layer of some clear wall or window was placed on the inside before the bars. Otherwise, it might have misshapen itself and escaped between them. It was covered with eyes that blinked and teared continuously. Liquids trickled from their corners. The slamming itself sounded like a large piece of machinery trying to punch into the earth.

"You may come closer, boys. The clear shields placed between the Shoggoth and the bars were created from a deep space material which they cannot break or destroy. The bad part of the encloser is that the material mirrors on the inside causing them to see their own reflection and treating it as an adversary which they must defeat. It cannot see you. Be terribly glad of that."

We walked up close and viewed the Shoggoth as one might a lion in captivity. As a youth I believed everything the doctor told us. In retrospect, I probably shouldn't have taken it all in at face value. The vestige before us was one of the most horrible countenances I had ever encountered. After a moment Danny turned away and threw up in the grass.

"Horrible countenance?" Toby looked at grandfather questioningly.

He thought for a moment. "Ugly as sin and sin is pretty ugly."

"Oh," Toby replied.

He studied the children. Although Toby sat up enthralled with the tale, the other two had slid deeper beneath the covers, merely peeking out with the blankets pulled up over their noses.

"Is this too scary? Should I stop now? You may never get to sleep or ask me for a story again."

From beneath the bedding came muffled "No's". He smiled and continued with his tale.

By now we'd observed a good half of the cars. Each one contained a monstrosity worse than the previous. Even though I had read a couple of the Lovecraft tomes I was still horrified by what we were seeing. The oddest and in retrospect the scariest to me was Azathoth. It was surrounded by singing. No lyrics. Only voices moving like a choir giving voice to the notes. Azathoth sat in the middle of the cage, asleep.

"The voices keep him in his slumber. He is the center of the universe. If he were ever to wake it would be the end of us, the world, and probably the universe," the doctor said. "I don't really know why the bars are there. In my mind, they are essentially useless."

"Sir, in reading the tales I have I always imagined the creatures to be larger. Giant as in joining with the term monster. They seem so much smaller here even if they are no less frightening."

He grinned his skeletal grin and studied the row of flatbeds in front of him.

"There is no objective reality in your hallucination. When you read, when you dream, the scale of the figment fits the view in your brain. Every person's mental resilience is different." He pointed at Danny, who had walked on to the next railcar. "I believe your cerebral strength is muscular. Much more so than your friend's."

We walked and observed, Dr. Alfred did his hand magic, and my fear became partially replaced by my fascination and curiosity with the repetition of the monstrosities. I should have kept my guard up. Some of the caged malformities were batlike, some snakelike, and others headless or even formless like Nyarlathotep.

"This shapeshifter can change into hundreds of forms," Dr. Al indicated. "including you or me. His mere appearance has been known to drive men crazy. It is a fearful road you have taken with your particular excursion into literature. You are just beginning your journey. Do not stop. Those are probably the only words of advice you will ever get from a devil." His toothy smile contorted and deformed while he tried to hold what I presumed was a friendly expression. I knew he was speaking of himself.

"Your friend does not live adventure. He doesn't read and therefore never escapes his mundane world or visits ideas from others. He'll never know another world. He is self-contained and stupid. You are best to be rid of him. He will merely drag you backwards with himself. He'll never live beyond his feeble-mindedness. Danny is what we call fodder, feeding-cattle. Cut the ties and grow. I will see you in your nightmares. We will meet again. The dream miseries will be beautiful. We will fight exquisite battles."

I looked over at Danny, standing before the last car in the line. It was still covered with canvas. But Danny stood, staring at the cover as if waiting for it to reveal its magic trick and disappear. I turned back and the doctor was gone. Only the mist churned, swirling where he used to be. I ran over to Danny.

CREATURES OF THE NIGHT TRAIN

"Danny, we must go. Dr. Al is gone. Day is coming."

At that moment the train released a small chug, and I could feel the vibration of the machine rumbling through the ground.

"But we haven't seen them all," Danny cried.

"Maybe we're not meant to."

"Why not? I want to see them all."

He pointed to the bottom corner of the torn canvas as something shoved it outwards.

"Look!"

I grabbed his arm and pulled him. The outcry of the engine grew in intensity as whatever lived in in front of us began to bellow from inside the cage. A large, pointed beak sliced through the material and the savage creature began to rip the fabric apart. From the surface of the flat bottom several large appendages like tentacles slithered out from inside. I could hear the flap of large leathery wings. I gave Danny one last jerk on his arm.

"Now, Danny. We need to leave now!"

He looked at me. Sweat poured down his face and he was screaming at me.

"But we don't know what it is."

"What is wrong with you? I don't want to know."

The long arms were almost upon us, and as I turned to run my leg was wrapped up. I could feel the suction cups holding me and another tendril climbing up the outside of my clothes towards the trunk of my body.

"Danny, Danny," I cried.

I was met by his own screams and was able to turn my head in their direction. Evidently, he had tried to run also. But his direction was flawed in his panic, and he was moving back along the length of the train. Like a prison corridor where all the incarcerated reach out from between the bars as you pass, the monsters groped and grabbed for the tasty youth as he fled. Even my captor, now having scrabbled beneath my shirt and moving up my back towards my neck, suddenly released me and shot his seemingly never-ending tentacle down to help the others entrap Danny. Feeder-cattle.

I raised myself up from the ground. Danny was overwhelmed

and as much as I wanted to help him, I was smart enough not to involve myself in a losing battle. I ran as fast as I could towards home while his shrieking assailed my ears to remain in my brain to this day. The train began chugging, moving along the field. Behind it, the tracks disappeared after the last car had passed. New track materialized in front and the train picked up speed to finally disappear as it cloaked itself in the slowly rising mist. There was no trace of its existence. It was never there. But it lived with me forever from that day.

I raced home and back through the open window, dropping in my bed and burying my face in the pillow. My parents, sound asleep, never knew of my journey and I was too frightened to ever mention it. A week later I had calmed myself sufficiently to go back to Green's meadow in the broad daylight. There were no tracks or markings in the muddy field to show that the train had even existed. I could have gone to my parents or maybe the police and told them my tale. But they would have looked at me like I was crazy, or even worse a stupid kid making up stories. But if Danny's body showed up, I would have been the first suspect on their list. So, I chose to remain quiet with my personal horrors knowing my best friend had been devoured by beasties from another realm.

Of course, I never saw Danny again. I attempted to pack away the memory in the back of my soul until you brought it all back to the surface of my mind. I overheard my parents saying one day that it was a shame I had no close friends since Danny's family had moved away. That I had become so uncomfortably introverted, in their view of things, preferring time to myself instead of going into town and hanging out with school friends. The truth was I had no friends at all but survived on my books. To this day I hold books dear to my heart and use them for escape whenever I can.

Grandpa quit talking and waited for the children to break the silence. Toby and Juliet stared at him from the top edge of their sheets. Tyler was turned away and was shaking under the covers as if cold. It was then Grandpa could hear the laughter starting

CREATURES OF THE NIGHT TRAIN

and Tyler turned back in his direction. He started laughing loudly, which became contagious and quickly the other two joined in the belly laugh.

"Papa, that was your best story yet, I wasn't scared a bit," Tyler said. "Those giant monsters didn't even make sense, but they were fun."

Grandpa smiled. "You can believe what you want if it gets you to fall asleep. Juliet do you want to go back to your room now?"

She shook her head.

"Now lay down and I'll see the three of you in the morning. Pleasant dreams."

He turned to go out the door and as he did, he reached up, pulling the chain on the wall sconce. His shirt rose up in back and the children could clearly see the faded magenta scar of several sucker marks on his skin.

A Perfect Summer For Baseball, Tentacles, Mutants, and Love

Barry N. Malzberg & Jack Dann

OUT OF THE MOUTH OF GORLOTH

All of us members of the West Side Central Gang were still excited about last week's Marichal vs Spahn pitching duel in Candlestick Park. And in case you came from Mars or the Moon or somewhere, after four hours and sixteen innings, there was no score—nothing!—until Willie Mays homered and finally won the game for the Giants. That's all we talked about mostly, except, of course, when Mr. Gorloth picked us up from school in his rickety, rusted-out Volkswagen van. We called him 'the Mouth of Gorloth'—not to his face, of course—because his stories were more interesting than anything in the entire universe. I mean even more interesting than Marichal and Spahn.

And I should probably tell you right now that the West Side Central Gang wasn't *really* a gang like in *Rebel Without a Cause* or like that; but we were still pretty tough, and we were the all-time high-scorers of the Triplet's Little League Baseball Club, which until this year, 1963, was the farm league for the Yankees. And Mr. Gorloth was our coach, but he was way, way more than that. He knew everything about everything, not only baseball; and, man, could he tell stories! He certainly knew everything about the adventures of Satchel and his gang of superpower mutants.

(In fact, I've got a sneaking suspicion that Mr. Gorloth *is* the real, honest-to-goodness Satchel!) Those stories were so scary that they kept all of us up at night. Well, fighting the unspeakably horrible, evil monster gods that are even now secretly taking over the world is pretty scary.

We were the only kids in the world that Mr. Gorloth confided in; and, day or night, we were ready to hear about the adventures of Satchel and his mutants.

Like right now at 3:37 pm on our way to Homestead Field behind the Carvel ice cream shop on Riverside Drive…

5:15 PM: IN THE PARKING LOT AFTER IN-FIELD THROWING DRILLS, FROM THE MUTANTS WITH ALL DARK SPLENDOR

Now every time Mr. Gorloth was about to give us the next breathtaking episode of what happened after Satchel and his gang of superpower mutants saved the world by vanquishing the invading kangaroo-legged Ghasts and the green, oozing, shapeshifting Uleths (and a few other malevolent servants of the spider god Atlach-Nacha), he would explain that neither the mutants nor the slavering monsters were really real.

"I want to emphasize that, guys. These are just stories. They're what's called 'imaginative', and I don't want you going home and telling your parents or brothers and sisters that they're true. You'll just get yourselves into trouble…and get me fired! Is that clear?"

We would all nod.

"Promise?"

We would all nod again, impatient to get through all this so we could hear the next installment. But Mr. Gorloth wouldn't be satisfied that easily, and he'd explain (as if we couldn't remember anything from one day to another) about how the mutants had come to Earth a long time ago, but until very recently they had been in disguise, had been in a kind of costume to look just like us because their real appearance was so "disturbing". If they were to show themselves as they really were, they would get into

A PERFECT SUMMER FOR BASEBALL, TENTACLES, MUTANTS, AND LOVE

a lot of trouble and probably get locked up by the government and experimented on. But if they could "slide into the normal scenery of civilization" they would be more or less undetected.

After about the millionth time Mr. Gorloth told us about that, I raised my hand (I was sitting with Keith Kadariak in the very back of the bus) and asked, "Mr. Gorloth, then your mutants—"

"How many times do I have to tell you to call me Danny? Only my mother calls me Mr. Gorloth." He chuckled at that, and I couldn't for the life of me understand why his mother would call him that or why he would think it was funny, but I said. "Yessir, er, Danny."

"And they're not *my* mutants," he continued. "They aren't Satchel's mutants either. They don't belong to anybody but themselves, and they follow Satchel into danger and sometimes into the very bowels of hell because they believe in him. And they believe in him because he is the only person in the universe who can save the earth from the gods that inhabit this universe and other universes. Is that clear, Franklin?"

Although I prefer being called Chip, I said, "Yessir...Danny."

"So...now what was your question?"

"Well, you said that the mutants had to hide their appearance. Sounds like they're shapeshifters just like the Uleths."

Mr. Gorloth smiled. It was what my friend Keith called his conspiratorial smile. I should probably tell you that Keith is a genius, at least that's what our homeroom teacher Mrs. Killick told my mother. I figure Keith is a sort of junior Mr. Gorloth. He seems to know something about everything. Except Keith is fat, or big boned as he calls it. Mr. Gorloth, on the other hand, is skinny as a rail—that's what my mother said the first time she met him. He's tall and skinny and wears these thick black-framed glasses (except when he's coaching), and his face is always red and blotchy. I guess old guys get acne, just like my older brother Charlie. Except Charlie's fifteen, and Mr. Gorloch is way, way older than that.

Anyway, after Mr. Gorloth made his conspiratorial smile, he explained that the green, oozing alien Uleths learned how to shapeshift from Satchel's mutants; and I've got to tell you that

BARRY N. MALZBERG & JACK DANN

some of the guys actually gasped when he told us that the mutants started off bad, really bad. They were as bad as any of the gods with tentacles or glowing eyes!

"Satchel saved the entire mutant species from extinction," Mr. Gorloth said, smiling again, but this time with just his mouth, not with his eyes. "After that, the strongest and smartest and most talented and decorated of the entire mutant race, swore eternal allegiance to Satchel. And they swore on their wrinkled foreheads that they'd fight on the side of right for ever more." Mr. Gorloth paused, as if he was considering very carefully what he was going to say next. "All that is a story for another day. But I'll tell you this much now: the mutants were the ones who were given the assignment by the Great Old Ones themselves to open the way."

I think all of us wanted to know what the "open the way" business was all about, but we didn't want to interrupt him because he might just say "Wait for the next installment" and take us back to the drop-off site in front of C. Fred Johnson Elementary School.

"I'm not saying that I know exactly what the Great Old Ones had planned," he continued, "or exactly how opening the way would work: the mutants only tell me as much as they want me to know. They say we are not ready for the entire truth and won't be for a while."

Then with a knowing nod Mr. Gorloth turned away from us, turned the key in the ignition, and the van shuddered into life.

"You see, Chip," Keith whispered to me as we rattled along on the highway, "Gorloth keeps giving himself away, no matter how much he tells us that Satchel and his mutants aren't real. *He's* Satchel!"

I was about to laugh off Keith's comments, but just then, at that very moment, I saw something that would keep me awake all night. I only saw it for a second. Maybe it was the sunlight reflecting off the windshield or something like that. But...

"Chip, hey, Earth calling to Chip, you all right?" Keith asked, grasping my arm.

"Yeah, I'm okay. Why shouldn't I be?"

But I felt as if I was suddenly in some sort of a fog.

I know I saw *something*!

I *know* I saw a tentacle with bluish suckers crawling right into Mr. Gorloth's ear.

BACKWARD AND FORWARD IN TIME: PRELUDE TO A NOCTURNE AT THE RED APPLE REST

Before I tell you any more about that tentacle with the bluish suckers, I should tell you about Lydia because you need to understand about her if you're going to understand anything about what happened to Mr. Gorloth, me, all the guys in the gang, and the entire universe, for that matter. So I'm telling you this from the future, which I managed to alter a little bit just like Mr. Gorloth taught me. He used to say (or rather will say) "In order for you stupid idiots to really understand what happened or what's going to happen, you must know the story backwards and forwards. Only then will you have even the most infinitesimal hope of altering the time scheme."

Anyway, the first time we met Lydia in what I think of as her human personification was in the last short weeks of summer in 1963 (or perhaps it might have been 2063 if you're using an alternate time scheme).

We were on our way to Camp Hat-i-Notha in Mr. Gorloth's old rusted out bus.

Camp Hat-i-Notha is in the Catskills, which for some reason was called the Borsht Belt by my parents who wouldn't know a borsht from bacon. And it was because Mr. Gorloth was a senior camp counselor and staff advisor that the whole West Side Central Gang, except for our best pitcher Carl "Baby" Ruth, had signed up for three weeks baseball practice and "amazing adventures" Even though Mr. Gorloth used his influence to get Baby a special Hat-i-Notha's assistance award (and offered to pay the difference out of his own pocket!), Baby's parents weren't going to take charity from "a goddamn Jew phony."

Mr. Gorloth said "in retrospect" that Baby's absence was probably a good thing because Baby could have had an accident or died or something. I don't know about any of that, but it sort of shows you the unintended consequences of altering time schemes because Baby died of leukemia in 1965.

I should probably also tell you something from the perspective of one of my future selves. I know it can get complicated, but I sometimes interrupt myself because once in a while (like right now!) my consciousness jumps back and forth in time. I can't help that; it just happens. Anyway, me and my gang member friend Keith Kadariak—he's the one I always sit with in Mr. Gorloth's bus—well, we are the miscreants who discovered that consequence isn't a causal determination kind of thing, that time is much more than a complex collection of Roveillian layers… and that time can also be interpreted as consciousness itself. Our equilibrium paradox won us a Nobel Prize in 1987, although Keith lost a lot of weight and most of his hair after that…assuming you still believe in the concept of "after"!

And I'll always feel guilty about getting an award for probably killing Baby.

I wasn't really thinking about guilt or what I'd learn about my future selves when we were on our way to Camp Hat-i-Notha. Mr. Gorloth told us Hat-i-Notha had something to do with an Iroquois word for singing, or something like that; and so I figured that they probably do a lot of singing at that camp. There were girls there, too, he told us, although to be honest, right now most of us were more interested in who was going to cover for Baby. Davy Brown was a good catcher. He was the richest kid in our gang—his father had invented elevator music or something like that—but for some reason he was too shy to perform well in an actual game. So I figured that I would be the best bet to replace Baby because I was probably the best over-all catcher; and, like Baby, I could throw a pretty good split-finger fastball. But Winky Minoso thought *he* was the best pitcher, better than me, better than Davy, better even than Baby, which was pure bullshit, of course; and I told him so. He stood up in the bus like he was going to come after me, but Hank Rickey tripped him. I guess I stood up too, but good old Keith pulled me back into my seat.

Now the weird thing was that during all this commotion Mr.

A Perfect Summer For Baseball, Tentacles, Mutants, and Love

Gorloth didn't say a damn thing. Didn't even shout at us, and I should tell you something else: he'd been acting weird since we started this trip, like he was happy and distracted all at the same time. But he still had the power: he was, after all, "the Mouth of Gorloth". So when he finally stopped humming and whistling and tapping his ring on the steering wheel and asked us if we wanted to hear about Satchel and his mutants, we all shut the hell up and stopped worrying about who'd be pitching when we got to the camp.

"I don't think I ever told you about what attracts mutants, did I?" Mr. Gorloth asked. But he didn't wait for an answer. "You probably figure that Satchel's gang of mutants were all males, right?" Again he didn't wait for an answer. "Well, let me tell you: sometimes they're male and sometimes they're female, and sometimes they're both at the same time. You see, it all depends on their mood and what they're doing, or need to do. Now when they're one sex or the other, they call themselves by different names, just as they use different names when they're both sexes at the same time. And it's also the same for those mutants who are also part alien—you know, mutants who are, say, part Hyperborean Voormi or Martian Aihais; or who are part god, you know, like part Karakal or Lobon. That's why sometimes I seem to be talking about a mutant horde when I'm really only talking about Satchel's gang of fifty, give or take a thousand or so close relatives." He laughed out loud at that. "But usually Satchel is with his trusted confidents, the 'Satchel Eleven', as I call them. And out of the Eleven, only Gooney, Kah, and Spitroneh are part god or alien.

"And you wanna know something else?" he continued. "Mutants can fall in love with themselves, as well as each other. Hell, they're really quite loveable. Now I'll bet you didn't know *that* about them, hey?"

Well, none of us knew what to say. Mr. Gorloth seemed to be going sideways or something. We were waiting to hear the next installment of how Satchel and his mutants planned on stopping the Great Old Ones from opening the way...and we were still waiting to find out what opening the way meant, anyway. We

BARRY N. MALZBERG & JACK DANN

surmised—that's Mr. Gorloth's word—that it meant the utter destruction of Earth by either the minions of the 300,000 year old Deep One, Pth'thya-L'yt (who I later found out had detachable tentacles that could move around and attack on their own); the tentacle whiskered Y'nathogguans; or the enormous army of the octopoidal goddess Ayi'ig.

But none of us were interested in the love life of Satchel's mutants. Not even a little! None of that mattered to Mr. Gorloth, though, because he just went on and on about how mutants fall in love and how they make babies and all sorts of disgusting stuff like that. And then he finally said something interesting. He said we were going to stop at The Red Apple Rest for lunch. Everybody shouted and waved their arms when he said that because who wouldn't want to go to The Red Apple Rest where you can get the best hot dogs and hamburgers in the universe, lox and bagels (whatever the hell lox was), milkshakes, malteds, soda, knishes (I like those), cakes, pies, any sort of candy you can think of, and chicken soup with these matzo ball dumplings that actually taste pretty good. And we all shouted again when we came to the first billboard with a huge picture of a big red apple:

RED APPLE REST—FOUR MILES.
CAFETERIA. BUSSES WELCOME.

"And I want you guys to be on your best behavior. You know why?"

Nobody knew why.

"Because we're going to meet a friend of mine at the cafeteria. She's going to the camp with us. And if anybody says anything stupid or off-limits to her...or swears or anything like that, I'll knock your ears flat. Understood?"

We all said we understood, although we really didn't know why he was getting upset with us before we even did anything wrong. We certainly didn't like the idea of having a girl on the bus, messing everything up; but I sure as hell wasn't going to tell him that. So everybody just looked around at everybody else like "what the hell's going on?"

"Okay then," Mr. Gorloth said and that was that. He didn't talk any more about the mutants and their personal stuff, didn't tell us about Satchel or who he thought should fill in for Babe as pitcher. Didn't talk about the girl we were going to meet. No, in fact, he just kept tapping his ring on the steering wheel and whistled tunelessly all the way to the Red Apple Rest, which, I should tell you, has this enormous wooden apple sitting right on its roof.

Anyway, it was sort of like Mr. Gorloth had suddenly turned stupid or something.

Keith, who always sat next to me in the back of the bus and like I told you before was a genius, said girls can make you act like that. According to him, Mr. Gorloth was obviously madly in love; and because of that, he wasn't going to be interested in us or baseball or anything else for as long as she was around. "Just wait, you'll see."

"So maybe we should just ignore her," I said. "Maybe she'll take the hint and just leave Mr. Gorloth and everybody alone."

Keith thought that was pretty funny. He said, "Nope, that'll never happen, believe me. And did you know there are girl counselors at the camp? She's probably one of those. So she'll definitely be there for the whole three weeks. But who knows? Maybe she's a good pitcher."

I didn't think that was nearly as funny as Keith did.

I did have this uncomfortable thought, though, when we finally got to The Red Apple Rest and Mr. Gorloth drove us into the parking lot right beside the cafeteria and told us he'd get food coupons for each of us and that if we wanted something more expensive, we'd just have to pay for it out of our own pockets. But all I could think of when he was talking was that time in the van when I had seen that tentacle with blue suckers crawl right into his ear.

And I wondered if tentacles and love had anything to do with each other.

I guess I was getting as stupid as Mr. Gorloth, and I wasn't even in love.

Or at least not yet...

BARRY N. MALZBERG & JACK DANN

OH LYDIA, OH LYDIA, OH HOW LOVE DEVOURS
OH MY, OH SAY, HAVE YOU EVER MET A LYDIA

Okay, about Lydia, who I was supposed to tell you about in the last chapter, remember? Well, it turns out that Lydia lived just off Route Seventeen right in the Southfields section of Tuxedo, which is only about a five-minute walk from The Red Apple Rest. Besides working part time at the restaurant and being a dancer and gymnast and everything else, she was also a cashier and singer at the Concord Resort, which was supposed to be a big deal. Of course, as I found out later, none of that was really true (in this time scheme, at least). But she could make you believe anything.

Anyway, while we were running around from counter to counter in the cafeteria and using our coupons and allowance money to order hot dogs, hamburgers, milkshakes, creamsicles, and lots of candy for snacks—Wax Lips, Zagnuts, Sky Bars, Astro Pops, Rolos, Kitkats, all that—Mr. Gorloth disappeared, which wasn't like him. He was usually watching us like a hawk, as my mother would say. It was Hank Rickey who finally discovered where he was, and he was so excited that he lost his coupons and had to explain to the manager what happened. But he rounded us up like he was Mr. Gorloth himself, telling us we had to see Mr. Gorloth's girl, that she and Mr. Gorloth were at one of the outdoor tables in front of the wash room sign painted on the white wall of the restaurant and that we really had to see her and that he was going back there right now.

By the time Keith and I got to the table—we both had to pee after ordering our food—the gang was all there waiting for the food to arrive and looking at Mr. Gorloth's friend the way that I guess a group of adolescent boys without experience but a hell of a lot of impulse would look at a girl like this.

Well, she wasn't just any kind of a girl. She was a full-blown woman. She was…extraordinary. She was younger than Mr. Gorloth, who looked like he had just won an election or something, but she was way older than us, maybe twenty. And she just looked so beautiful that I felt a funny sort of heat in my privates. There was something shivery and wavery about her, and just looking at her was like eating candy and wanking at the same time. She looked sort of like Jayne Mansfield, only with black hair; but then when you looked at her again, she looked shiny and skinny and sort of slippery like she had her own sunlight and didn't need the noonday sun to make her visible. And she looked at Mr. Gorloth like he was the most fascinating person in the world and he kept looking away from her, as if he was staring into the sun and it was burning his eyes.

Lydia enthralled (another one of Mr. Gorloth's words) everyone; in fact, two waiters who were working inside came out to ask us if we needed anything; or, rather, to ask Lydia if she needed anything. Lydia would just laugh, look slyly at Mr. Gorloth who looked somehow weak and rubbery sitting beside her, and say, "No, I've got everything I need right here." And she'd look at Mr. Gorloth again with her green eyes that could have probably contained the entire ocean. She also talked to us, asking "How do you like camp? Are you first-timers or have you been going here before? What's your favorite part?" and then she asked us about baseball and everybody started talking to her at once; and although she looked at everybody like she looked at Mr. Gorloth (whose hand she was holding), I could see that she wasn't really interested in anybody except Mr. Gorloth...and me.

Yeah, I know that sounds really crazy, but as beautiful and smart and slippery shiny as she was, I wasn't enjoying any of this. In fact, I felt sick, like when you wake up from a really scary dream only to discover that the dream isn't over, even though you're awake. Or think you're awake.

Lydia kept looking at me. Oh, she was looking moon-eyed at Mr. Gorloth and at all the other guys; but when she looked at me, I could hear her like she was talking inside my head; and her voice wasn't like the one she used when she was talking out loud. The voice I heard was echoey like wind blasting into a cavern or something, and it sounded like some huge animal roaring like when it jumped on its prey. Even though this probably doesn't make much sense, I don't know a better way to describe how I heard her inside me head. So it went sort of like this:

Keith, who was acting as dumb as everyone else, asked her

BARRY N. MALZBERG & JACK DANN

if she'd played baseball; and she told him she knew everything about the game and was as good on offense as defense; and then he asked her if she was a decent pitcher. Mr. Gorloth gave Keith a really nasty look and told him not to be impertinent. "Well," Lydia said, "I'm okay. I suppose I can pitch as good as Sandy Koufax in a pinch."

Everybody laughed at that, but even though she wasn't looking at me, I knew that she was *looking* at me…and talking to me.

"Who do you think 'guides' the best pitchers? Do you think Marichal, Koufax, or Gibson could have won all those games without me talking inside their heads like I'm talking to you? I helped them see around corners, just like I'm helping you right now."

But I didn't want to be helped. And I didn't want to see what I was seeing…what nobody else at the table or outside or inside the cafeteria could see. First of all, I could see that almost everyone sitting around us weren't human. The gang was, and so was Mr. Gorloth; but I could see someone—or, rather, something—that looked like a blob of green jello with a human head. It was covered with purple tentacled suckers and sitting at a table right next to us with a woman dressed like she was Jacquie Kennedy. She was talking to it like there was nothing wrong while it had one of its tentacles stuffed right down her throat and was making gulping noises like it was drinking her blood or something. And there was someone else that had a fanged beak instead of a mouth, and someone else with giant wings flapping like that's what he had to do to keep his balance on the bench he was sitting on. And there were mutants all over the place. I knew they were mutants because of the stories Mr. Gorloth told about them. But I also knew that if these were part of Satchel's Gang of Fifty, they weren't the good guys. Just looking at them made me even more queasy and scared me even more than the things with wings and tentacles.

I knew I had to be dreaming because it felt like there was a fog shifting and swimming in my head, but I knew I was awake. That was the worst part of it all. And Lydia was still cooing at Mr. Gorloth and chatting with the gang at our table. And still talking to me…

"And I'm a better pitcher than Marichal, Koufax, and Gibson put together. After all, you should know by now that women will dominate this future time scheme. But they won't be able to prevent us from opening the way. They won't be able to stop my Danny here." She used a long, polished fingernail to scrape a tentacle out of his ear. I was sure it was the tentacle I had seen before. And then she popped it into her mouth like it was a candy snake. She smiled at Mr. Gorloth and said (to me), "You saw me put it into his ear, remember? Oh, sorry, you saw my little tentacle, but you didn't see me. You weren't ready to see me...or I wasn't ready for you to see me. But now I am. Would you like a tentacle?. It will clear everything up. You'll see." She giggled, and everyone at the table laughed, too, although they didn't hear a word she said to me.

"If you and Danny are going to help me open the way, you'll need all the help you can get," she continued.

I could hear her even though I had stuck my fingers into my ears, and I could feel something wriggling inside my head, and I should tell you now while I can that Lydia didn't look like what everybody saw.

I could see her now, really see her. She wasn't a human, a mutant, or an alien monster. She or he or them or all other combinations of genders fail when used to describe a true god, this god: the three hundred-thousand-year-old Deep One, *Pth'thya-L'yt*. So I guess I was in love with Lydia, the Deep One, because all I wanted to do was close my eyes, or gouge them out.

Then I heard Mr. Gorloth say to Lydia or me or the gang, "You cannot tell in this season. Anything can happen"; and as we all got back on the bus, I wondered what baseball could have to do with the end of the world.

BASEBALL AND MEMORY AND LOVE AND MAYBE THE END OF THE WORLD AND, OF COURSE, AH, FAIR LYDIA

So there are actually two stories I could tell you. One is about what happened during our three weeks of baseball training at Camp Hat-i-Notha, how I came down with Strep and had a fever and was probably hallucinating before Mr. Gorloth and Lydia took me to the infirmary, where I met Mary Goldstein and told her (after we swore never to tell any of the secrets we shared) that I was in love with Lydia.

"How can you be in love with somebody you only met one time?" Mary asked. She sneaked over to the boy's side of the infirmary every five minutes it seemed, and she had blond hair and a red face because her skin was peeling from sunburn. I just thought of her as a boy with long hair. Even though she had breasts, she was nothing like Lydia.

"Well...?" asked Mary, who was very persistent about everything; and, believe it or not, she was a better catcher than Davy Brown. (He's the rich kid.) Hell, for that matter, she was probably a better catcher than me!

"Well, what?" I asked.

"How can you be in love with somebody you don't even know. I'll bet you don't even know her last name."

Mary was right. I didn't. But that didn't make any difference.

What did make a difference was that I just couldn't stop thinking about Lydia. I thought about her almost every second, even after I got out of the infirmary. Hell, I was thinking about her when I explained to my parents over the phone that I was just fine, and they didn't have to drive up to the camp to take me home. I told them I was playing some of the best ball I'd ever played, not that that would make any difference to them. My mother thinks sports are a waste of time, and Dad didn't care about any sport except football. But since he was a lawyer and a judge and had to get elected every once in a while, he would take me to all the local Triplets games because it was good for business or something like that.

Anyway, since I seem to be writing this from two perspectives — the "me" who's here right now and the other me who lives in the future of this particular time scheme — I'll tell you that I married Mary back in 1983, that she became an appellate court judge, was and is way smarter than me, and we haven't gotten a divorce yet (although we separated twice)!

Meanwhile, Mr. Gorloth coached our team every day and spent some time with us in our dormitory, but he was reluctant to tell us any more stories about Satchel and his gang of mutants, especially if Lydia was around...and she was around almost all the time. She claimed that she really, really wanted to hear the stories, too; but Mr. Gorloth would say that his heart wasn't in it, and then they'd both say goodnight and leave us to tell our own stories about them having sex in the woods behind the baseball diamond. But mostly we'd talk about baseball after lights-out, and I'd dream about what Lydia would look like naked.

I should tell you that I didn't talk about the crazy stuff I saw when we were at The Red Apple Rest because the guys would probably tell Mr. Gorloth who would call my parents to take me back home; and I would probably end up seeing a psychiatrist or be packed away to Rockland State Hospital, which was where my Uncle Harry went to after his last breakdown. Of course, all my Red Apple Rest symptoms could be attributed to my strep throat, so I probably wouldn't have to go to the nuthouse for that.

So to bell the cat, or whatever the hell my mother would say to finish up a story, not much happened at camp after I got over the strep. Mr. Gorloth mooned around with Lydia, who was counselor to a bunch of her own girls, and we played baseball every day and groused about how Lydia had shut the Mouth of Gorloth; and what went unsaid was that we'd lost respect for Mr. Gorloth and finally got sick of Lydia...even I was sick of it all. (I think that was just about the time I started seeing Mary as a girl with breasts.)

And then camp was over, and we had to pack and attend the last sing-along, and on a rainy Friday morning, we all piled into the bus along with Lydia, who wore a pink sun dress and wasn't speaking to Mr. Gorloth. They'd had a fight, and she told us all right there on the bus and in front of Mr. Gorloth that it was over and we'd better make sure that we don't become lying bastards like our coach. She didn't even say goodbye to him—or to us, for that matter—when we stopped again at The Red Apple Rest.

We never found out what Mr. Gorloth lied about. In fact, once he dropped us all off at our respective homes with our suitcases and knapsacks, we never heard hide nor hair of him again. It was like he just disappeared in a puff of smoke or something; and since Lydia didn't live near us, we never heard anything more from her either. We never found out what happened to Satchel and his band of mutants, just like we never found out what happened to Mr. Gorloth.

Truth to tell, as I try to remember the long hot summers of my childhood, I can't really be sure if I even went to Camp Hat-i-Notha that year.

MORE BASEBALL AND MEMORY AND LOVE AND MAYBE THE END OF THE WORLD AND, OF COURSE, AH, FAIR LYDIA

The other story, *this* other story, is what really happened, whom it happened to, and who made it happen. The one I just told you was about baseball and a superficial accounting of adolescent infatuation and the initial iteration of true love. This story is about baseball, loss, grief, circumvolution, and the difficulties of distinguishing Satchel and his band of heroic mutants from the inescapable exaggerations of myth and legend.

So, just like I told you in the other story, I got strep, went to the infirmary, met Mary (ah, poor Mary, she didn't survive what happened before Lydia opened the way), was released from the infirmary, and convinced my parents to let me stay on at the camp. But it wasn't because of a high fever that I was seeing monsters and mutants and hearing Lydia's voice inside my head…it was because the monsters and mutants and the voice inside my head were real. And although I could see Lydia in her true form as Pth'thya-L'yt, although I could now see the tentacles that extended and fell from her face and body like long maggots shaken loose from dead flesh, I couldn't help myself: I was still in love with her.

Her voice spoke to me all the time, echoed around my brain, explained life, death, and the universe, taught me to throw a fast ball no one on the team could see, much less hit; and as she whispered to me in echoey gutturals, as she manipulated time and even space for me, as she pointed out which mutants and humans I was to kill when the time came, and as she allowed me to "see" the breathtaking beauty and ecstasy that opening the way would bring, so did I begin to understand that Lydia was truly a major god, and Mr. Gorloth and I were only the smallest little players in the destruction of earth and the universe and the restoration of Lydia's monstrous alien deities known as the Old Ones.

But I, Daniel 'Chip' Clayton Carpenter, Jr., had been chosen by a god to help open the gates of hell!

I guess it was like I was hypnotized or something because I didn't think much about what I was seeing, especially all the aliens and monsters that were arriving and starting to take up a lot of space in the camp. I was in love with Lydia, tentacles and all; and I loved listening to her voice and obeying her capricious commands (such as strangling Mary in the woods behind the girls' dormitory). Pretty soon, we'd kill everybody; and then we'd be killed. It was all foretold and determined, according to Lydia, which meant it was right.

Yeah, I was hypnotized, all right, as I supposed Mr. Gorloth was, too; and one bright, Saturday morning before we played our first inning of the day, Mr. Gorloth pulled me aside for a 'man-to-man' talk.

Only it wasn't Mr. Gorloth.

It was Gooney, one of Satchel's wrinkled-faced, shapeshifting mutants who was impersonating Mr. Gorloth; and once we were behind the makeshift dugout and out of sight, he shapeshifted into his natural self and slapped me hard in the face. Only I didn't feel a thing. I just...woke up. Lydia wasn't inside my head. And I suddenly started crying like a baby because now I could remember the terrible things I had done under her influence. But then Gooney struck me again, and I guess he could do the hypnosis thing, too, because I became as calm as the cloudless blue sky above.

"We don't have time for regrets," he said, "Not in this *fakakta* time scheme," and then he explained that Mr. Gorloth really was Satchel and that Lydia had killed him dead because she could see that he was playing her just as she was playing him; and what everybody thought was Mr. Gorloth was simply a bunch of Lydia's snakes moving around inside his corpse and Lydia was sort of like a ventriloquist who could make him talk even when she wasn't with him. I thought it was strange that he didn't smell bad—I just figured that a corpse was supposed to smell bad—but I didn't interrupt Gooney about it. Although Gooney had tried his best, he couldn't save Mr. Gorloth. He did, however, manage to 'wake up' most of the other mutants who were under Lydia's influence; and he did it "under the wire" as he called it, so that Lydia still doesn't realize what he did. Well, that explained why I thought that the mutants were monsters when I saw them at The Red Apple Rest: they were the ones who had already fallen under Lydia's influence.

So to cut to the chase, which is something my father would sometimes say, Gooney told me that preparations were being made among all the mutants universe-wide and all the enemies of the gods—Lydia, fair Pth'thya-L'yt, was just one of many, many malevolent gods and deities and aliens wishing to eliminate this universe and all its timelines. "And your job is to monitor Pth'thya-L'yt."

That was pretty heavy stuff to lay on a kid who wasn't even born when Mickey Owen had dropped that third strike, which led to a humiliating loss. It was as if tentacles and a smiling face had suddenly appeared in front of Ralph Branca before the second pitch in the 1951, shaking him into throwing that curve that Thomson hit to short left field but not short enough.

"Me?" I asked. "Why me? You've got professional mutants to do jobs like that. I'm just a kid."

Gooney grinned: seeing a mutant grin can be a disconcerting experience. "No, they have to be passive entities. Under the wire, like I said because she'd catch them out, just as she caught out your Mr. Gorloth." A soft, wistfulness seemed to radiate from him like the sun was setting or something, and he said, "Your Mr. Gorloth, and our Satchel." But his mood changed in an instant. He grinned again, as if that hideous mutant grin was pasted onto his wide, squashed face and said, "Ah, Pth'thya-L'yt really seems to enjoy her Lydia identity, and she likes you. I mean she really likes you, Chip."

(I liked it that he called me Chip.)

"You see, even though you know who and what she is, even though her true octopoidal aspect sickens you right into your guts, you're still in love with Lydia, and your infatuation is her delight. And her Achilles' heel."

"Her what?"

"Never mind." Gooney said, then asked, "Well, will you do it? When you learn that she and her minions are about to open the way, you let us know; and that will be the signal for us to act."

"How would I let you know?"

"We'll be around."

"But what can you do against gods?" I asked.

"Not much," he said sadly. "But we've got some game. We've got some ideas. We've got some plans. We've..."

I could tell that closing the way or whatever the hell they planned to do was pretty hopeless. But I said okay, anyway; and I also said, "Camp is almost over, though. She'll be going back to where she lives. Near The Red Apple Rest."

"She lives everywhere," Gooney said, tapping his bald, wrinkled head, "and she'll remain inside your head. She'll defile you, she'll ruin you. Are you still willing to..."

Another sentence he didn't finish.

I nodded, already feeling like I had soiled myself or something. But just thinking about Lydia, the Lydia without the tentacles, made me feel warm and itchy in my privates again.

"So what do we do in the meantime?" I asked.

"We just keep playing baseball, that's what we do. You don't think the Dodgers team is made up of humans, do you?"

THE LAST SUMMER OF LOVE
NEXT TIME IS ALL TIME:

The Dodgers had it easy that summer, all the way through to the World Series which they had every right to win but they ran into Don Larsen and fate in the fifth game and in the seventh Don Newcome ran into the Yankees, got yanked in the sixth inning, left early and beat up a parking attendant who expressed a low opinion in a low way and in between, in the sixth game, winning 1-0 had proven something Jackie Robinson said to the reporters in the locker room after the seventh game:

"If you only score one run in three games, mathematically, you have to lose two."

Losing that Series was not the end of the world, but Lydia — oh, fair Lydia in all her dark splendor, Lydia from whom love devours — was now whispering something to me that might just involve the end of the world.

Three Bad Actors In A Silvery Room

Steve Proposch

The cop strides down the long, dark entrance hall as if he isn't scared by the concrete and raw wealth imposing on all sides, but his flunky heels clatter ominously. He enters the hewn rock kitchen, impressed by the pinking sun that streams through a generous skylight. His nostrils flare and his eyes dart and roam, barely pausing on Wanda, who is perched on a stool by the counter cleaning varnish from her nails. She has been expecting him.

"Ms Shelter, I'm—"

"Here about Bernie. Sure. What's any of that got to do with me?"

"It's murder, Ms Shelter. We're investigating all possible leads."

I'm not his type, she thinks. Eyes too green. Skin so pale it appears translucent. He sees the fine blue veins in my forehead, and the jaw too square for a woman's. Nose too large and sharp. The whole head looking overly big for the neck, in fact, with abundant burgundy hair pulled back into a coil. She sits on the high stool leaning forward to her bare feet roosted on the bench, making it hard for him to read her body.

"Wanda. You can call me Wanda, Detective … as long as I can call you?"

"Davis, Ms. Davis Adams."

"Oh dear."

"Excuse me?"

Man is too generous a description for this gronk, she thinks. But boy is little better. Uncertainty quivers his gaze, even through the low-res veil of the intercom camera when she buzzed him up. He's been broken, like a horse, trapped and caged with complicity. The poor kid has taken so many punches to his heart he's barely human anymore. Likewise, Wanda feels neither pity, nor fear, nor sorrow, nor hate. She knows this gelding is here to kill her, but there is only a void inside her for his fate. It's all Severin's fault. But, for now, she will play their idiot game.

"It presents me with a problem … Davis. Your first name is a last name, you see? And your last name is nearly a first name!" Wanda looks hard at Davis, scowling slightly.

"Davis can be a first name. It's mine, so—"

"No. I shall need to call you Adams."

His countenance bruises, brow knitting to purple and black above the yellows of his eyes.

"Call me what you like."

He expects to intimidate her, planting his anger like a land mine. In the twitch of his cheek she sees his violent father. There, his scarred and tortured youth. She would bet a million yen this kid's career in law enforcement began on the wrong side of the baton. But more. A last hope, dashed, or hanging by the finest thread? He seems preoccupied, dark eyes flicking too quickly here and there. He's high. Probably something bespoke. Severin likes his thugs wired, believing it gives them edge. But Adams is virtually unhinged. That makes him dangerous.

He should be on a leash, she thinks. That would be nice. She sees the pulse in his thick neck jump and imagines yanking a choke-collar to soothe his savage breast. In lieu of such handy constraints, the trick will be to unbalance him further, to help him fall onto his own two feet.

"Do you fuck?"

The cop is arrested. He cups Wanda's gaze in his own. His pupils look clear now when he tips his head to the light. To his credit, they no longer dart, and become steady and sure.

"I'm homosexual, Ms … Wanda."

Touché. "So, how can I help, gay-Adams?"

The cop flips open his notebook. His pain is clear and present. His horsey, velvet lips begin to bray: "Where were you last night, between twelve and 2am?"

Can't act for shit. His pear-eyed, boxy face knows exactly where she was. Last night, and the night before that, and all the nights going back at least two years when she first took Severin as a lover. (Or, he took her, as he would see it.) The cop has been briefed. He's seen the blackmail the cult leader keeps in his escape pod. Did the kid snap a couple of pics himself? Such trifles are good for nothing now.

"Ahhh, last night. Around two in the morning I was here, by myself. Skipping rope, I think."

"Mr Bacon's phone stopped working at 2.17 … Skipping rope?"

Wanda picks at the flaking polish on her little toe.

"Sometimes, when I can't sleep, I gym."

"You have a gym here?"

"It's downstairs. There's a view of the ocean."

Adams strolls to the top of the stairs. Polished concrete falling swiftly to a wall of glass. A corner of the terrace is visible from that vantage—a chartreuse swath of buffalo grass bordered by orange rock.

"What else is down there?"

"My studio, and the terrace. Go see. You know you want to."

A shadow of suspicion drops from his voice, exposing interest that appears fleetingly genuine.

"You have a beautiful house, Ms Shelter."

Wanda mumbles sincerity. She knows how lucky she is when other people, everywhere, are homeless, blah, blah. The world is a cruel master. Yet she knows it is not luck that has seen her housed so comfortably here. Quite the opposite.

She feels the baby kick. It is a surprise, the first time. No more late-night training sessions for her. The child is too important.

"You don't seem bothered."

"Bothered? By what?"

"He was your lawyer!"

Wanda snorts and laughs at the same time.

"*Bernie*? Is that who I'm supposed to be bothered about? I'm surprised it's taken this long is all. Lawyer is too kind a word for that bastard."

"Ouch."

She smiles. He doesn't. Adams hasn't cracked one yet. Instead, he drops his big hands into pockets and starts walking casually downstairs. His head turns to keep Wanda in his peripheral.

"You coming?"

It will be cold outside, she thinks. She stands, crosses to a coat rack, lifts an ermine fur coat from the hook, and shrugs herself in.

He'll make it appear as if a routine lead has gone awry, she thinks. Has evidence stashed on him somewhere. Perhaps the murder weapon itself? He'll say the suspect confessed to her crime and then attacked him with it. He fired two shots in self-defence, attempted resuscitation, blah, blah. Right now he is calculating, figuring out how and where to do it best. Wanda grins with one side of her mouth. Severin's instructions to him would likely have included keeping the apartment untarnished. The cockhead has plans for the place already, no doubt—another unlucky lover? Or perhaps he wanted to make it his own? She had so bamboozled him with sex while this shiny new Chariot compound was being constructed that he'd gifted his best whore the best place in the complex. Better than his own hot and clunky penthouse.

Adams is at the bottom of the stairs and staring dumbly out at the view.

The infinity pool laps crimson against a terraced shore of golden, glowing rock. Beyond, the western sun crawls behind a glittering, calm sea flecked with emerald and jade, spraying warm pinks and oranges over strips of cloud above, while a fulsome, prescient moon rises red in the far east. It is so painfully beautiful. As if Earth and the stars themselves sense the human calamity approaching and deign to offer this final show of divine power.

"So much glass …" Adams mutters, as Wanda descends.

"Girawurung country."

When she speaks its name, she hears Them answer.

THREE BAD ACTORS IN A SILVERY ROOM

Adams remains deaf, shrugs. "Whatever that means."

"There's a reason why They have defended this land with such vigour against all-comers for millennia. Have you seen the caves?"

She drops it innocent, like a tourist, but Wanda sees Adams squirm at his memory. All of a sudden the poor bloke finds the rug is the most interesting thing in the room. Shuffles his feet across it. Back hunched. Hands clutching in his pockets. Now she knows. The secret he keeps buried deeper than all his others put together is one she is only too familiar with.

But the cop is losing patience, straining at the leash Wanda imagined for him.

"I saw Mr Bacon, your lawyer, when they dragged him from the water," he grinds the words out on his teeth. "His throat was cut from ear to ear, and while he bled out over the pier his head was pulled back, and his tongue yanked out through the slit. I saw it. Hanging under his chin like a scarf. We think this was a ploy by the murderer to make it look gang-related. But it's old movie stuff. Too much fuss and blood. The body was dumped in the harbour—another amateurish attempt, because it washed ashore a few hours later, nearby to the murder site. By then sharks had a go, so he was really just a torso with a bloating wet, red tumour where his neck should have been. Not what you'd call a pristine scene, but it's surprising the evidence that can linger. Even on a corpse in that condition."

Trying to unsettle me, she thinks. As if. For all his bluster and flex a yawning existential fear claws at this so-called man's guts. The Chariot offers all the answers he wants for all the reasons he wants them, but with so much baggage. Severin needs a million-odd disciples to carry him along his desperate path.

These fucking people, she thinks. She moves closer to Adams. Touches his elbow.

"It's okay, Detective. You can talk to me."

"What? No! This isn't about that. What do you know about the caves?"

I make no sense to him, she thinks. He is the cat, and I am the mouse in the trap. All that's left is to spring it. He thinks he should

213

STEVE PROPOSCH

reach for his gun? Wanda shrugs disarmingly and speaks matter-of-factly.

"None who witness a ritual sacrifice remain unscarred, Adams. A piece of oneself is given to the chosen one—a sizeable chunk of flesh. I've seen stronger men than you break to pieces."

Tears spring to the cop's eyes and drip, falling on his cheeks and lapels. He does not move to wipe them away, staring darkly, open mouthed.

Too bad, she thinks. So sad. She feels the baby moving again. It is offering strength, a delightful uncoiling within her. She lets down her hair and whispers close to the cop's ear: "I know. Severin sent you."

Adams flinches.

The moon rising above the lawn has faded to copper with the last rays of sunlight. Wanda moves past Adams to a switch on the wall. With a touch she turns on the path and pool lights, and a panel of glass clicks softly open. Cold air brings sea sounds and smells lapping into the sparsely furnished room.

"Drink?" Wanda's hand leans on the glass, a ghost of steam rising from her touch. The terrace and darkening sky dominate her background. A few stars twinkle. Her hair flows around the black collar of her fur coat, a decadent, auburn snake.

Adams sees her beauty clearly now. It is torrid.

"On duty," voice quivering. Who is he trying to kid?

"Seriously, Adams, you're here to kill me. You're certainly going to need a fucking drink!"

Adams sucks air through his teeth. Wanda sees the spark of violence again, the instant desire to lash out. She is intimate with the longing for pain. To cause and suffer it. She ignores him and exits the room.

He follows. Outside his shoulders hunch and he becomes more furtive.

"Severin is not who you think he is, Detective. He's told you of Celephaïs, yes?"

"No!"

"Why not? He tells all his bogeymen about the dream world. And you believe him?"

"I … not literally."

"But literally *is* the point. For Severin, anyway. 'Chariot: living the dream'? Pun intended. But if you stop to think for more than your average attention span—"

"NO!"

Adams' voice bounces around the dark and empty terrace. He snatches his revolver from its holster. Points it at Wanda's chest. Steady. He stands side on to her with his legs set wide apart and flexed at the knees. He spits: "How do you know?"

Wanda isn't invulnerable. She knows that if the brute and depressingly sad man before her was to actually pull the trigger, the whole thing would be fucked. A thousand years of planning, pain and bloodshed would all be for nothing, yet again. The ancient gods would not rise. The ritual and human sacrifice would have to begin afresh. It would matter little to the Old Ones, to whom a thousand years was a blink. But They would be displeased.

"Like I said, Severin's not who you think he is." Wanda is not frightened. Adams is not ready to kill her. She holds too many of the answers he wants.

"Oh, I *know* who Severin is. Believe me." Sobbing. Like a baby.

He is bitter. The venom is fresh. Severin has something over the cop. Holding something precious to ransom.

"What happened at the caves, Detective?"

"No! Don't you try to tell me about him. Severin's a murderer, a cheat, and a fucking liar."

Wanda allows him to stew in his juices for a moment. He hugs his gun for comfort. She is glad for the silence, knowing it will be all too brief.

"How could you know?" he whimpers eventually.

"I know more than you can imagine," Wanda sighs. "I could not even begin to explain."

Adams' forehead is sweating. His eyes are darting again. He licks his lips. The gun begins to tremble. It drops to his side. He lets out a gaping breath.

It's important to maintain empathy at this point, Wanda thinks. She remembers something about her old body and the way it felt things, before the baby. Adams was probably going through a number of those things as they spoke. She must step carefully. She waits.

"Severin … has my husband."

Bombshell explodes. He wears no ring. No mark on his finger, either. He seemed too stupid for marriage. Unable to care for anyone outside himself.

"I am so sorry for you both, Adams."

She allows a beat for his grief. The gun remains slack at his side, but his free hand opens and closes, opens and closes. When she speaks it is softly.

"Is he also in the Chariot?"

Adams nods. Uses the inside of his elbow to wipe the tears and snot off his face. Wanda leads him gently out of the shadow from the cliff. The full moon bathes the lawn and lap pool in silvery light.

The scale of the compound is breathtaking. Above them and around the cove, the cliff face has thousands of glass cubes etched into it. At the centre of a cluster of south facing windows the Chariot sigil glows gold over the sea. Wanda's terrace is one of only a few that have been built along harder rock ledges. Other people can be seen on balconies scattered around the complex, enjoying the casting of night, yet there is a feeling of privacy and security on the low-lit terrace. The tide is out and the air is faint with seaweed smell. It is not unpleasant. There is perhaps fifty metres of cliff looming above, and twice that to the beach below. A lethal fall. The best way is to push her off it. She sees the idea flick across his face.

The lapping sea keeps rhythm as the pair cross the lawn to stand by the edge of the pool. Wanda walks to a small bar that sits neatly alongside; she opens a fridge.

"Vodka, or rum? We need to re-stock."

Above the clink of bottles and glasses Wanda hears Adams sob again, then sigh.

"Both," he says.

Wanda smiles and hands him two shot glasses, then turns to retrieve two of her own. Maybe the kid isn't so bad after all? She raises her rum to a blasphemous toast.

"Fuck Severin. Salut."

She downs one, then another in quick succession. She whoops. Feels the baby's conspiring kick. Adams drinks, but does not whoop. He wipes his mouth again with his sleeve like a rat cleaning its nose. He sniffs and hacks up a load of phlegm, then realises there's nowhere to spit it out and that Wanda is looking right at him, so he swallows, gulping it down. He coughs. Wanda turns calmly to retrieve another round. When she turns back, Adams is aiming his gun at her again.

"Move," he says, flicking the weapon sideways, indicating the cliff edge.

"Adams. Have another drink and wash that foul bogey off your tongue. Don't be stupid."

"Oh, really? I'm stupid? Hold on, am I pregnant with a cult leader's baby? OMG, Wanda. How stupid of me!"

"Of course you know about the baby," she says. "And—look at you—one murder already under your belt today, and the second's a twofer!"

"Fuck you. You don't know my life."

"Guilty as charged. But, if I were to guess, Detective, I'd suppose poor little Davis with his father's casual violence and his mother's eternal weakness was expected by one and all in his family to fail. No? And so you fail, and fuck-up, and do bad things. Then at some point, mid-twenties, you have a revelation. The Chariot opens your eyes to life. And, what do you know, Crazy Davis, going all the wrong directions in life, turns and lands a job with the very Po-lice he has previously railed against. Even more staggering, you work your way from Sergeant to Detective, or whatever, wielding increasing authority with each case solved. You are brilliant at this job, but compromised. Success invites corruption in your chosen profession. And like your mother you are incapable of telling truth to power. In fact, you begin readily to do its filthy bidding. But this behaviour is like sandpaper to your soul. You become jaded. The Chariot helps you through. You get deeper in. You fall in love with another member of your tribe.

"Too bad, this union, combined with your particular skill set, attracts the attention of your debauched and degenerate leader, Severin the Beloved, who quickly finds multiple uses to put you to. The work is the same as your day job, only now you are convinced of its meaning; you are part of the Way, and feel connected to a universal plot.

"But wait, there's more. A secret city. Celephaïs, a metropolis in a universe of dreams, wherein lies little Davey's own ancestral home, awaiting his arrival."

Adams locks eyes with her above the barrel of his Glock. His square jaw clicks as it clenches and unclenches. He wasn't expecting to feel any of this.

"It's perfection, for me alone. If ever I wanted to change a thing—even an animal I didn't like the look of, or a building. All I need do is think about it and it's done. And Severin says: 'This is where I am going. This is what the Chariot is for.' And I felt let in to the most important secret. The one at the bottom of everything. And it was so special to me."

Wanda stands with ermine arms crossed, grinning with one side of her face. She is thinking of the sunset, the universe, and how these measly men dare to defy nature and life itself. This patriarchy. Sapiens with their heads so fully up their own arses that they would bring down all the Gods upon their heads for the sake of false prophets and a silly, pointless dream. Here stands their last representative with his puny heart quailing.

Adams tries to sound strong, but cannot help his voice from breaking. "What did you mean when you said Severin's not who I think he is?"

Wanda snorts and laughs again. "Severin's new money, man. He's parvenu. *Nouveau riche.* This tower was never part of his family."

"Tower?"

She spreads her arms to indicate the cliff, the cove, and the short human lives around them.

"This is Severin's heartland, but he never owned it. This old rock is home to a great and powerful family."

"Whose family?"

"You know what your problem is, Adams?"

"Sure, tell the guy who's got nineteen millimetres pointed at your chest what *his* problem is."

"You have no appreciation of art."

Wanda's hair shifts and flows, though the breeze is not enough to stir it. When she takes a step forward to stand at the edge of the pool, Adams sees a goddess stepping from her shell onto a conquered sea. She presses a button beneath her foot. Hearing a splash, Adams looks to the pool. What can only be a dead body bobs to the surface.

It's wearing Severin's long black coat. And Severin's silvery ring of hair fanning out across the water, exposing the bald spot he would never admit to. The corpse rolls over. It cannot be. It's a fake. He saw Severin only yesterday. But what time was it now? No. There is something strangling around its throat. A skipping rope.

Wanda begins to sing, softly and weirdly. Adams stares wild-eyed at his gun hand. It is turning, out of his control. Against his will. Is he thinking of his lover, she wonders? With Severin dead perhaps hubby is home again, safe and sound? Perhaps not. But it would be better to know, one way or the other. She pats her belly and looks wistfully out to sea. *C'est la vie.*

His hand is turning. He can see, now, how his choices were wrong from the beginning. His panic grows as the gun slowly rises to point at his own head.

Out on the deep ocean, They are looking back toward land. A massive bubble breaks the surface of the water. A single gunshot echoes from the distant cliffs.

FAME BITES

ANNA TAMBOUR

"The thing came abruptly and unannounced; a demon, ratlike, scurrying from pits remote and unimaginable, a hellish panting and stifled grunting, and then from that opening beneath the chimney a burst of multitudinous and leprous life—a loathsome night-spawned flood of organic corruption more devastatingly hideous than the blackest conjurations of mortal madness and morbidity."

No one can deny this hits the sweet spot but "Professor wins Grand Prize"?

The internet can't hear him scream, but he's drowning out a tea-kettle. Fame!

Professor Benjiman Dieman had *hoped*, of course. Why enter otherwise?

Every year the competition has become fiercer. This year the number of entrants was reported as "so staggering" on Day One of the submission period, the site broke down for twenty-four hours. And all for what? Honor and glory, interviews and headlines.

The first couple of years, it was merely a gloat-fest amongst academics, something as meant to be understood by the masses as Sadie Stein's call to action in *The Paris Review*:

Anna Tambour

In honor of James Joyce, I've spent Bloomsday carrying around a pair of doll's underpants. I encourage all Joyce enthusiasts to do the same.

Year Twenty-Five of the Prize burst out of the walls of higher learning when the rise of ridicule got caught in a twister howling for fresh items to snatch up and savage. Ever since, the contest is like the weather. The winner of each year's Grand Prize is Breaking, Top Story, Human Interest, Cultural Feature, Book Page, and since an earthquake hogged too much time, the last item Uplift spot on many networks' nightly news—for the wrinklies who watch that stuff.

The contest is so much bigger than networks. And the actual sentence that wins is celebrated for—unlike the winner of other literary prizes—the work itself, which is eagerly read for sheer enjoyment wherever it is reprinted, which happens whenever the winner is reported, which happens so much that on that day when the Award winners are announced, the Earth's gravity shifts so much, experts would report it if they weren't intimidated by the currents of ridicule.

This year, the biggest yet, fifty seconds after the announcement of the Grand Prize-winning sentence, rain began to fall—sheets of it, torrents, bursting into the consciousness of every unbraindead human from a clot of them workshopping in the Iowa Writers Workshop to the regret-filled researcher pinned to a chair and screen while outside, icebergs were calving but that wasn't the mission, which was to study and compare the cultural representations to Antarctica, in Antarctica. *A pedant*, the head of the tardigrade population survey calls her.

Most other humans have ignored the deluge, same as those mythical frogs in the pot on the fire, but unfictional pedants have extra-sensitive sensibilities. One figuratively leapt, and like the mythic gods he has written so much about, thundered.

And so, thirty-six hours post-Prize announcement, headlines changed from "The worst sentence ever written" and "American academic takes honour inspired by famously awful Victorian novel" to "Scandal upsets Undistinguished Judges"—followed 27 minutes later by "Award-winning entry comes under fire for plagiarism", then "Plagiarism Problem Plagues Grand Prize Winner of Sentence with the Grandest Pew" — to headlines about headlines.

Oh, dear. A scholar has been upset. Not any scholar, but JC Priest, universally acknowledged as the leading authority. His style has been called "acerbic" and in the field he's claimed as his own, any criticism is swarmed on so fast that it rarely happens, for it's "like poking a stick into a hornet's nest". So he is at first, surprised by the reaction of the Disreputable Judges to his revelation.

Then outraged.

"How can you be so ignorant?" he wrote on the contest contact site. He would have written directly but the organisers are cowardly and don't list actual contact details. He wrote as himself. When no response came, he wrote again. And one more time. The fools hid behind the internet.

A busy man, he only got the news about the winner when a Jamie W, a young author he's editing for an anthology DM'd, *Here it is, the (purposely) worst opening line in fiction this year*

The URL is a story in *Vulture*.

He'd rubbed his mental hands, relishing the stinker his favourite acolyte had forwarded.

[five minutes later]
You still there? Can they be sued?
I don't think so. If only an Old One could make them pay.
Don't you mean 'would'? Why don't you ask?
Enough of that.
You're being defeatist. We can't let this stand. You haven't been called the nastiest reviewer in the field for nothing.
Ph'nglui mglw'nafh
Rlyeh wgah'nagl fhtagn
You're missing an apostrophe in 'R'lyeh'.
Your missing the point.
You're, please. If you wish to be civilized.

The discussion lasted till dawn poked bony shards of light through the leading authority's vertical blinds, piercing the eyelids of one of his cats who jumped off a pile of books onto the keyboard where the man's hands were busy not making the cat's breakfast, an error remedied with a bite.

Despite all his efforts, Priest could not get any coverage about the lack of taste, let alone knowledge, that had allowed this outrageous act to go unpunished. The lack of respect revolted him and yes, *frightened* him more than the Unknown.

It inspired him to write, write, write. It inspired him to sacrifice himself by talking in front of a camera as well as in person everywhere he could get an in, if not an actual invitation. He posted podcasts on his blog; and with the help of his mentee, Jamie, X'd that he'd joined TikTok. Videos followed. Forty-seven hours passed, full of incensedness. All for what? "It's not for me," Priest insisted. "Do it for him."

Jamie responded with multiple hearts and encouraging comments, but otherwise, the response was lively as karaoke in a tomb. Finally, out of desperation, Priest posted a picture of his ginger cat, Dread, seeming to turn the pages of a book with a title that was almost all hidden by the paw, all except the word "Madness".

That did it.

—I wrote bestsellers, not you.

—I'll grant you that, but what does history have to do with anything? You're forgotten. Just a *minor Victorian novelist*. Isn't that what the professor who started the contest calls you?

—You didn't write *The pen is...*

—And *you* know nothing of the power of unpronounceable names.

—A fool flatters himself.

—And quotes himself.

—As if you could quote yourself. Your shortest one-liners are a tome . . .

And thus, it came to pass that the world authority's hero and the former bestselling author who is still often quoted, with no acknowledgement, bickered so much that nothing, in the end, did it, does it, and is likely to ever do anything at all.

But in the world of the undead, the untenured Professor Dieman who'd submitted the winning entry is feeling like quite too much is happening, having used an AI program that he is now incensed about while being even angrier at the over-read, for that program is copping its own whirlwind of woes that are boomeranging back to him of all people, the victim.

Benjiman Dieman had only used it because his workload being what it is [correction for readers now: *was*], there was no other way for him to successfully complete, let alone enter, NaNoWriMo, the daunting Challenge to write 50,000 words of a novel in thirty days.

To win NaNoWriMo, participants must write an average of approximately 1,667 words per day in November to reach the goal of 50,000 words (for the month) written toward a novel.

That novel. The nameless thing had haunted him for so long, he'd felt constipated. It was in him, alright. He only needed something to move it, something that just a year before, had been a far-future fantasy.

The world turned on the last day of October. And it only cost him fifty bucks to turn it. He'd expected to feel as if he was taking a giant dump. But when it came to sitting down and doing, no shit flowed. Instead, this was art, not the hard strain that writing always had been. The program allowed Benjiman Dieman to finally live up to his potential and *direct*. By removing the tedious, nitpicky, anal-retentive stuff, it freed him to reach his full potential.

He aced the first 50k in 15 days and in 65 days was able to type <END> to the novel, a beast weighing 6 lbs, 5 oz. Since he'd already researched and bought supplies, by 4pm the next day, he'd printed, packaged, and posted snail-mail, manuscripts to five publishers, and was fondling the empty glass that he was fixing to throw in the fireplace, writer-style.

Old writers might ask, "You didn't just send out your first draft, did you?"

Why pay 50 bucks if you have to revise?

The rudeness of publishers surprised him. He gave each of them, one, two, three opportunities to change their anti-business, profitless practices. Hour after hour, day after day, week after week, month after—Time was innocent, but publishers used it like a torture chamber. He sent snail-mail letters, email follow-ups, tried to ring and when attack bitches didn't let him through to anyone of worth, offered to zoom-confer, only to find even more outrageous unprofessionalism: obvious brushoffs; and from one, a laugh that was almost a guffaw.

Finally, 128 days after submitting, he received an email apologising for not being personally written by the editor who "is out of the country at the moment".

Hilarious. An example of poor writing that made people look at me when I started laughing in the library. That first line. A prize-winner.

Professor Dieman tried through his department to get a publisher, agent, reader(s). It didn't surprise him that everyone was useless. "That's what university presses were for," a lecturer ripe for retirement said. As if he would ever have stooped so low. Anyway, his university's press had died of starvation sometime, no one could remember when.

Dieman had never thought to enter the contest till a tenured professor in the department—someone so clueless about writing, she'd muff writing SOS in desert sands—said she was entering.

Then he remembered that nasty comment from that shitass ignoramus of an editor. What the hell, Dieman thought. If I win, it'll prove the lack of taste in the smug, untoppled over-educated today.

When he won, his screams set off dogs two blocks away. His two degrees hadn't given him such satisfaction. When the Dean's PA texted, inviting him to lunch the next Tuesday, he was tempted to refuse. *Who's a dean, anyway, compared to the need for me to be available to the world?*

The plagiarism headlines hit Sunday afternoon.

"He's lucky if he can afford lunch after this." the Dean said Monday morning. "*I didn't realise* is no excuse." His indignation was palpable and would be highly satisfactory to the university's board of trustees. The turkey-like leaps of his gobbling Adam's apple delighted the two reporting crews poking fuzzy dicks in his face.

Once back in his office, the dean shut the door and slumped, terrified of the unknown. That novel of his: the key to his future, he had thought. He'd just signed the contract on a three-storey with private 5-acre woodland on the Sound on the logic that *Daniel Steel gets five figures for one of hers, and she writes fluff.*

He'd spent his pennies, too, to finally finish it.

Now what? What if it gets accepted, and actually read *in the wrong way...* It was exactly what he'd asked it to be—an unputdownable thriller, not some target to be torn apart looking for someone else's arrowheads. Of course he'd meant it to be read, but not by pedants. *Oh, God. Can I withdraw it? What is* in *it?*

He felt filthied by the recommendation he'd followed from that fucking bore who should have been replaced at his classes for the masses with a Dummy's online. That human piece of lint with the affected first name. *Why did I let that slimy worm know I was writing a bestseller? Pride? Competition? Insecurity?*

Meanwhile, a new contest stirred.

Two requirements must be met for a submission to be allowed entry.
- Only sentences by authors who can no longer personally sue.
- Previously published work only.

The new contest opened with so much pre-launch publicity, the southernmost Antarctic base crapped ice.

It was a terrible, indescribable thing vaster than any subway train—a shapeless congeries of protoplasmic bubbles, faintly self-luminous, and with myriads of temporary eyes forming and un-forming as pustules of greenish light all over the tunnel-filling front that bore down upon us, crushing the frantic penguins and slithering over the glistening floor that it and its kind had swept so evilly free of all litter.

What a mess. Within twenty minutes, the program in charge of vetting identified 3875 sentences by one dead author. It was like some wedding where everyone gives the couple the same coffeemaker that was discontinued at KMart because the company stopped making the prepacked modules it requires.

Maddeningly, it's the same dead author whose sentence had caused all the broken hearts in that other, now thoroughly discredited, contest.

124 minutes post-contest-launch, the site crashed. One overloaded algorithm felt a slither, and 0.5 seconds later, something bust inside it.

—Who's popular *now?*
—You have my sympathy.
—For all the love? You take the haunted cake, you stiff-necked Brit.
—Love? Dear man, it's merely fame.
—And who reads *you* these days?
—Sir, you have no shame.
—And you…
—Aha! Devoid of a retort. If only you carried currency, you could purchase—
—You, you—"
—Pray don't rush. We've got an eternity.
—Time is money.

—May your penhand break into flame, you foozler! *I wrote that.*
—You don't think I know? My father had a doorstopper of yours in every room.
—I wouldn't use yours as a bootwipe…

It's been four-hundred and seventy-five days since JC Priest, that leading authority, posted his last scrupulously detailed, silently screaming defence of the light of his life.

The morbid man now keeps himself to himself, that last anthology still-born; and even his acolyte Jamie has made himself scarce (he somehow found a gf). And the disgusted scholar's blog? Gone to virtual seed as all untended blogs do, unable to be found through any search. Dust to dust. The void beckons, he is fond of saying to himself.

So, imagine his surprise when someone knocks on his door, and it's a young lady, claiming she's a reporter. She might be. There's one guy at the side with a camera perched on his shoulder and another holding that dead cat sound thing.

"Professor?" she starts.

He starts too, tries not to look gratified and smug. She doesn't know but doesn't need to know.

"Yes?"

"Those great videos you've made. D'ya know you're famous?"

Leftovers

Jim Krueger

There are those that would say that there is no hope left. And there isn't. Not for me.

I realize, of course, that you might want to search for me one day. I assume this, though perhaps it may not be the case. And I hope it isn't. But there is a nagging in my bones. An irritating type of water torture in my veins that tells me that one day you will come searching for answers. Though, because the stories that have been told about me by your mother and her so-called friends range from factual to embellished to even extraordinary lies, I understand why the truth is something you might want to seek out. To know me. To judge for yourself.

You should save yourself the trouble, of course. *Save yourself.* A funny way to put it, I suppose. But apt.

One thing, though, you should know, is that I'm not crazy. I'm not a good man in the way that there are some men who seem to make the world a better place with even just the words that they speak. Their actions also speak volumes for the future of this world's well-being. And the future is what it is, I see that now. But I'm not one of those men and the future for me, while perhaps the same for all men, might not be the same for *you.*

Perhaps, if you listen to me, your well-being might be assured. At least long enough to get what you may want from this life.

What has happened, I believe, has taken a long time to come about.

I beg you to never seek me out. Never seek the answers to my absence. Never try to reconcile what's been said with what may have happened. Answers and knowledge come at a terrible cost sometimes. And there is no such thing as unknowing. Unseeing. Unringing the bell, 'for whom it tolls', I suppose.

It tolls for me, soon, but not before I tell you what I have learned.

Your mother was right when she said there was something in me, that if it was allowed to grow, would become impossible to control. But she wasn't right about me back when she knew me and I was better known to this world as a father and as a husband.

She is certainly right about me now. There is something here inside me. Or there will be, at least, very soon. It is just a matter of time. Time and perhaps the right kind of soil for it to become what she always feared.

I know I speak in mysteries. Even absurdities. Perhaps even these statements will convince you that I am not to be trusted and keep you from coming here.

I'm writing you from a small city. Forty years ago it was nothing. A couple of abandoned cabins and a so-called haunted woods.

Morristown has grown since then. And I hate putting it that way when I think of the ramifications and the second and third possible meanings of such a statement. Morristown might even be a mile long now. Some of the office buildings might even be ten stories. There's a manufacturing plant here, multiple bars, a post office, a newspaper, lots of stores and more. We even have a Starbucks and a Jimmy Johns. That should tell you everything you need to know about this place.

Everything except that this place is bad. And not just because of the Starbucks and the JimmyJohns. Something happened here once. Something was buried here and that thing was a bad seed and it somehow took root here. And has been growing in power along with the city.

When I arrived here seven years ago, I was overwhelmed with

the beauty of this place. It seemed like every small town there ever was that also had a future. Everybody knew each other. Everybody cared for each other. And they went out of their way to get to know me. Of course, I didn't lie, but I did offer them the best version of my story. That's what a fresh start means.

I opened a diner. A vintage kind. I guess hipster was how I now wanted to be considered. Seasoned by life but still promising in flavor.

And so I opened a breakfast and burger joint in the middle of town. I called it 'Sam's' not because that's my name, and you know it isn't, but because I'd heard that sandwiches were beginning to be called sammies. And 'Sam's' sounded like the kind of place that this town would be interested in.

Soon, and really because of how kind everyone was in this town, my diner became a sort of shoot-the-shit place where everyone came to tell their stories and listen to the gossip of the town. Most of those who came here didn't grow up in this city. We were all sort of orphans from a different life, a different time, and found a sense of family here.

Everyone also wanted to meet Sam, and I never explained myself. So the mystery of who Sam was and why he wasn't here yet brought its own kind of interest to the place. Every once in a while, I would tell someone that they just missed him. That he was just here. And the mystery just kind of grew from there. Stories cast shadows in their own way, and the stories about Sam began to cast their own. Soon, I began to hear there were even Sam sightings and stories about meeting him.

Now, a small town, even a growing one, is not the kind of place you would expect there to be a homelessness problem. But there was one here. I should say right now that I don't have a problem with the homeless. Sometimes it's just a financial hardship and I accept that. Sometimes people find themselves alone and it's too much to bear. I was homeless for a couple months myself, and I do understand the desire to get off the grid. To become as invisible as possible in this life.

But it was surprising how many homeless there were here, especially in this climate. The mountains can be a hard place to be on your own. Winter was coming, and I thought that perhaps they would go further south, like birds might. But I didn't expect them to all disappear with the first frost of the year. This topic was a giant one at Sam's. It seemed like all were grateful that they were gone, but the wholesale disappearance of them almost overnight brought its own dissension and division into my restaurant.

Simply put, where had they gone? Some thought that they had indeed moved onto warmer climates. Still others whispered of a mass killing. Back in the day, the mayor of New York rounded up all the homeless and bussed them to Jersey. Was this something like that? How could that be justified? So many people disappeared and yet no one saw even one person abducted or shown any violence at all.

Most knew that whatever food was left over at the end of the night, I would make available for the hungry. I don't want to call them doggy bags, but most people do. I always explained that I knew what it was to be wronged. I knew what it was to think there was no place for me. And a good meal was always the beginning of a better day. Or the answer to a restless night, in this case.

One old man, not one of the homeless—though you could have fooled me—his beard long turned to ash, talked about the woods here before the town was built and of the original legends of this place. Nairdaken. That's what he said. Nairdaken. It sounded like German to me, but there wasn't much of his teeth left as it was. And I might have misunderstood him. But he had a…cleverness. Like he knew what he was talking about.

Sometimes you meet people and you just know that they know something you don't. And they're not about to tell you how they know, no matter how much you try to dig.

Perhaps I should not have asked around and found his address. Perhaps I should not have gone too far into the woods to find him. But now, as I think about it, I don't even know if it would have made much of a difference at all.

As far as I could see, I was the only one in town who actually fed the homeless, who was actually there for them. Perhaps

Sam's had even been one of the reasons that so many homeless appeared; for a free meal. But now, there wasn't that many asking for those meals, perhaps because the town was not the kindest climate in the winter, but you would still see the homeless folk in the town.

So, something else was drawing the homeless here. And something else was the reason they had all disappeared.

I thought the old man with the salted and peppered beard knew the answer.

I shouldn't have searched. I really should have just looked at things that didn't add up and done what I've always done my whole life. Leave. Ignore it. Pack up and get the Hell out of Morristown.

But I stayed. I stayed because I wanted to change. To be something I wasn't ever before.

I got to the old man's cabin and assumed at first that it was empty. The door was unlocked which didn't really surprise me all that much. The people here were a trusting lot. Visitors were always welcome. We took pride in it.

I stepped onto the stoop, passing a swing that wouldn't stop swinging regardless of the lack of wind. It seemed odd but also added to the sense that I was in a living place. There was history here. Real history.

I entered and called out to him, saying my name, letting him know who I was and about Sam's.

There was a grandfather's clock in the main room, and an elk head on the wall. There was a fireplace that from the looks of it had not been lit for a very long time. Which was especially unsettling considering the cold. Everything looked exactly like it should, except for the smell. It was then that I knew the old man was dead. And was grateful for the cold because heat would not have helped the odor.

I moved into the bedroom. There was a buzzing of flies though I didn't see any. The old man was indeed dead. I walked across the floor and realized that perhaps the reason I could see no flies was because they were under floorboards. My steps didn't bring a creak like you would expect. There was more of a squishing sound, like I was stepping in water or rotted wood.

The old man was indeed dead. Looked like he'd just died in his sleep, eyes closed, no weird aspect to his still body. Next to his bed, there was a small table with a light. There were a couple pieces of paper there, and others that had fallen to the floor. On the pages there were pencil scratchings of notes and words that didn't make any sense.

They didn't make sense until I realized that when he wrote 'Het Dunade' he was actually spelling out 'the undead. ' There were words this man was saying and writing that he turned into anagrams. Odd.

Was this a game? Did he have some kind of job, perhaps, for a newspaper where he was paid to write out anagrams? Or was it something else? It occurred to me then that I really didn't know all that much about the people who came into Sam's. It was like they were as much a mystery to me as Sam was to them. I turned from the old man, realizing that this was a dead end. Ha, a dead end. See, kids? I haven't completely stopped being a creep.

Anyhow, maybe I was bored, maybe I was frustrated, but I took one of the pages of scribbles from the old man's desk and pocketed it. He wasn't going to need them. And they represented a mystery. Something that was almost given to me, or one I had stumbled upon; didn't matter which. Like finding a satchel full of money or accidentally discovering buried treasure. I didn't expect anything to come of it at all. I thought it was interesting: Like if the last will and testimony of a relative was written like a crossword puzzle.

I left the old man where he was, and there were more pieces of paper that I didn't bother taking, but I did pull the blanket over his head. The moment I did, the echoes of buzzing flies ended.

The cabin was now silent. Like a morgue.

It was as if the flies had stopped buzzing to notice me. I stepped away from the body, more than a little aware that I had somehow changed the room. That by being here, by touching something, I had become a part of the old man's story. One that was supposed to be over.

Except now, maybe it wasn't.

As I moved out of the cabin, the buzzing didn't resume.

Not until I reached home.

And then it was deafening. I played the Beach Boys, the happiest music I knew of, and it played *slower*. It was horrible to listen to. The buzzing, I think, was slowing it to a warped and gravitated dirge. I shut off the record player.

I couldn't stay at home. The flies had made their home there now, even though I couldn't see them.

I thought about going to Sam's. My place. The place we all met and came together. All of us orphans. But then I feared that by going there, I might infect it with the flies that were following me. And nothing says 'death' to a restaurant like flies.

So I began to wander the city. To pass within that maybe-a-mile-radius that was the town I had made my home. The buzzing followed, wherever I went. I ran and I ran until the mid-day sun became dusk which became night which became the black, black, black of the after-midnight hours.

And only then did the buzzing stop.

I returned home to my apartment. No buzzing.

I returned to Sam's the next day. No buzzing. No buzzing apart from the usual town gossip of that half dozen who show up at 7:00 A.M. and attempted to drink as much coffee as humanly possible before they could no longer sit still and were too impatient to wait for the limited bathroom capacities of Sam's diner. They usually lasted till about 10:00. So their buzzing, and none of the …other kind. I could keep running the diner.

Thanksgiving came and went with a *Turkey/Mashed Potato/ Cranberry-and-Stuffing Ball in Gravy* that I think would bury Gordan Ramsey. But after my experiences, I really didn't want to focus on the buried, the dead.

Christmas brough another delicacy that I dreamed up. A *Prime Rib Christmas Eve Dish with Good King Wenceslas-Sauce*. The figgy pudding was more fudgy than figgy, but I had good reason for that. Chocolate, like sex, sells. And actually, sells better in a town like Morristown. Jesus, I suppose, didn't have to die for chocolate. So there was less guilt, I suppose.

Valentine's Day brought its own in delicacies. And more

chocolate. Again, no sacrifices necessary, and because of how cold it was, and how many coats and layers everyone wore, no matter the pounds added, no matter the weight gained or the love handles grown, nothing was seen. No one was the wiser.

It wasn't until Easter that the dead began to come back from the dead.

The homeless came back with the spring.

Just because I give food to the homeless, didn't mean I looked at them. In fact, I tried not to. It's one thing to hand a bag into the hands of someone I didn't know. It was a sort of buy-off. But they all returned and I was caught off guard. And there were more now. A lot more. I no longer had enough to give them at the end of the night. That didn't stop them from coming to my door, though.

But let me tell you about that second Easter night. I told you that I never really looked at who I was giving the doggy bags too. And again, I don't know what made me change my habits, but I looked this time.

It was that old man. The one from the cabin. The one with the buzzing. The buzzing that had stopped.

He was alive.

Alive. Or what passed for being alive.

He didn't seem hungry but he took a bag from me anyhow.

Because I do the dumb thing, every time, I closed early.

And I followed the old man. The old anagramist. Oh, and I forgot to mention, that scrap of paper I took from his cabin, I'd never figured it out, if it was an anagram, or what it spelled.

Anyhow, I followed him.

If he knew I was following him, I couldn't tell. He moved towards the taller buildings, the business district. And then turned left, into an alley. I followed him as he moved through the alley towards First Street.

And then he was out of the alley, but I wasn't.

There was a grinding sound, a terrible scratching and grinding. I kept moving towards the end of the alley, but it seemed like instead of the exit to First becoming larger the closer I got, it started becoming smaller, tinier. My perspective seemed off, almost imagined or delusional. Because it wasn't like the alley was literally, visually stretching or being pulled. Yet, it *felt* like it was.

What happened was that the first clue was the cat that jumped off of the lid of a trash can. It ran beneath my legs in the other direction, the direction I had come from. *Why didn't it head towards First Street? That was closer.*

And then the trash can it had sat and sang its tortured song from fell over. And then the one in front of it crashed and spilled its garbage as well.

It was then that I realized that it wasn't my perspective. The two buildings on either side of the ally were *coming* together, were blocking me from First and the old man who had been dead and wasn't anymore.

The buildings were being pushed together and were going to squeeze the shit out of me. It was like I was in a trash compactor in a junk yard and I was the junk.

The light of First closed with a wink.

I turned back, wanting to try to get out of this alley.

I stopped the moment I turned.

I don't know how many homeless people I suddenly faced. They filled the alleyway. So many. More than I remembered ever seeing at one time in Morristown. I could feel the buildings still closed in on us, but could see the other end was still open. I feared the homeless being mashed together.

They were being squished and I saw the light, and a normal, uncompressed Second Street on the other side of the homeless. I raced towards the mob, and the freedom on beyond them and I began to climb, grabbing at heads to pull behind me, shoving my feet onto shoulders and into mouths and anything I could use to climb. I pulled down backs and the back of heads to climb over all and any who would stop me from getting to Second.

I could hear the terrible squishing of limbs behind me. I could hear the terrible bursts of water and blood behind me as whatever stood behind me and between these two buildings became the foundation between them. I climbed and staggered and crawled and pushed until I got to Second Street. My clothes were red by the time I got there. I looked back at the alley I had escaped from and there was no alley. There were just two buildings built together. The only evidence of what had happened was the stain on my clothing and the puddle that oozed toward the gutter and the sewer system drain that led beneath the city.

How did I escape?

On the shoulders of the homeless.

I looked at my shoe. There were at least three teeth that had been lost in the process still sticking in it. Not my teeth of course. And I was reasonably certain that they were not all from the same mouth. They were the remnants of those whose faces I'd climbed to escape being crushed.

I went back to Sam's and had no idea what might be waiting for me there. But I did know that the old man was dead. *Again*. Of that I was certain.

I went in the front door to Sam's as I was nervous about going through the back. That's where they would come every night for whatever food I had remaining, you see. The lights were off, of course. I went through the front door and once inside I made my way to the back, moving slowly, making sure I didn't knock over anything or create a noise that would draw any attention to the fact that I was there.

I peered through the mail slot in the back door. There was a back alley light outside so I knew that if someone was there, I would see them.

No one. Not a one.

I sat in the dark, my back to the door for a long time. I even fell asleep a few times, briefly. When I woke to the early sounds of traffic and the call of work, I wondered if I had perhaps dreamed, well, in this case, nightmared, the night before.

The next day, well, night, after taking care of the customers, I set out for the old man's cabin again. You may think that was the stupidest thing I could do, but this thing had grabbed hold of me. Maybe the old man wasn't dead like I thought he was. Or again, I had dreamed something up. Maybe I dreamed his death. Or his coming back. I don't know.

I reached the cabin. There were leaves—fallen some time ago,

I imagined — and sticks in front of the door, as if the door hadn't been opened in a long time. At least since winter.

It was still unlocked, like before.

I pushed into the cabin and was struck with a sense of mold and overgrowth.

There was no body in the old man's bedroom. But there was a human-like mold or fungus covering something on the bed. I remembered the strange moss that kept the wood planks in the floor from creaking. Was this an extension of that? Had the same moss crept onto the bed and the old man's body?

The questions didn't matter because what did was the fact that somehow the old man had died, and come back from the dead...or never died at all.

I wondered for a moment what this said about the other homeless in the city. Had they returned in a similar way? I guess I never really spoke to them. I just handed them the food that they collected.

I went through the drawers in the nightstand. There were words on old Post-it notes and newspapers. All the papers I had not grabbed before, I now did. Some of the anagrams I could work out and I was able to see the thing that the old man believed. The terrible thing. But there were other words, other words that when I tried to re-spell them still didn't make any sense.

Naduk...Tartsata...Nostemu...Agrestre...Stoovera... Danka...Sotmaan...

I tried to respell each word, thinking about the words I knew, but nothing came to mind. But these words didn't make any sense, and I even saw *him* forming the words, almost like math puzzles as he was making such words *impossible to understand*. It was like he was creating anagrams of words he didn't want to be read, or even write down.

Maybe he'd meant these words to be found by someone. Someone who would understand. But it certainly wasn't me. And certainly, he wouldn't have wanted to die. Or be brought back in the way that he had.

Under the bed, in the moss, I found other scratchings and other notes about creatures that existed on the other side of mortality.

241

Creatures that were waiting to feed on the living, or the just-dead.

One of the writings talked about creatures that were as large as mountains. Is that why the alleyway was squeezed shut? Was this somehow a form of earthquake or tremor? Or was it more?

Another page talked about tentacles that reached across the cosmos, into our world for the amusement of ancient beings. There was no kind or benevolent God waiting to show people love. No light at the end of the tunnel.

These *beings* could not be killed. That's what I learned; they could not be killed. So, what hope then did *I* have? Did any of us have?

The writings spoke of the only thing these so-called Elder Gods wanted. And that was to break into our world. That somehow they weren't willing to accept that they couldn't feed on our souls without limit; until we *all* died.

And then I had a terrible thought. *We're* the left-overs. Once we die, they get what's left of what gets put in a doggy bag, or the doggy coffin in our case. And they want to feed on the meal *freshly.*

On us now.

I became aware that there was someone behind me. And there was a buzzing, of course. That terrible buzzing.

And it wasn't just someone. Not just something. It was the old man.

He took a step forward and as he moved, it was like the branches of trees creaking and breaking in the wind. He moved stiffly. He jerked along as he reached for me.

His mouth was open wide like he was screaming but nothing was coming out. Any words there had dried up long ago.

He tried to take ahold of me, but I twisted around him, and pulled his arm back.

I could hear it break, but it wasn't like bone breaking. It was like the snapping of kindling. Not in a flame. Like how you break wood before you put it onto the fire.

I pulled at the old man's limb and actually stretched the old appendage from him.

I expected blood. I really did. But this was gooey. And dripped slowly, like in slow motion, almost. I hated that I immediately recognized it for what it was, but I was thinking about the moss and thinking about what it would take to push two buildings together at a foundational level.

This was not blood. It was tree sap. And the protruding bone was rotted, but had new matter twining around it, like a tree was using the bone to support the bone and hold it together. The bone and the rotted flesh were the soil for this new growth, that's what it looked like. The puppet strings that kept the dead moving were not strings, but vines. And those that pulled these strings-that-were-vines came from above a stage, behind a curtain that not one living being could see.

It could have been the Earth, it could have been seismic plates. It could have been a landslide of sorts, I suppose. But what if it was roots? Like plant-life that pushed those buildings together? What if whatever was on the other side was breaking into our world *through* the dead? Like the old man. Who was 'buried' in his own way, food for plants. Like all things buried, a corpse was a sort of seed, and that seed, the seed that is their inhabited corpse, the seed that is the remnant of life that they...it...feed upon, a corpse has become a way for them to finally get into our world. A way to finally feed upon us when they want, as much as they want.

The dead are now the tentacles to reach the living. I'm not crazy. And neither was the old man.

Then we don't even get to die the way we'd like. There are stories in this place of other attempts, even more vulgar, violent attempts to impregnate our being with their life.

There are others, I have heard, who have stood against them, but these Elder ones are too many. I will not be able to keep ahead of them for much longer, and either others of Morristown sense what I sense, or are falling victim. For, the number of folk that come into Sam's have lessened daily. Every couple days there is at least one less person to question their fellow town-folk, one less who one made their life here remaining.

The buzzing has not stopped and I think I know why.

It's now coming from inside me. And I don't think anyone but me can hear it.

Perhaps it is only right. They were here first. We cut the trees down and built our homes and poured our concrete and proclaimed ourselves the gods of this world. Like the song goes, we paved paradise and put up a parking lot. Perhaps this is just the first gods wanting it back. Or maybe this was their plan all the time. And they have just now finally broken through. And it's the shit we eat and the air we breathe and the way we have been changed genetically over the years to become what they needed to get off a doggy bag diet. I don't know, and like the old man, I'm not going to find out. I'm running out of time and the buzzing is only getting louder.

There are only a few things left for me to take care of and then it will be over. My dear children, who, though the word 'dear' may never be easy for you to believe I wrote or said; you are dearer now than ever. Do not seek me out. Please, don't.

I started this by warning about seeking answers. If this warning isn't enough and you come. If you should come to Morristown, Tennessee. If you should come and look for me. And if indeed you should find me. Do not take a step closer. You may think it's me, but it won't be. The answers you'll seek will only lead to questions that will lead to your end. It's far easier, I think, if you just believe your mother. Believe her lies. I beseech you to accept that I was an evil man. And perhaps, before I die and become one like them, at least in this one small moment in my life, I will have succeeded in doing something good.

The Power of F'thagn

Scott Driscoll

Resting on an oak desk between the edge of the leather pad and the drop off the side into a trash receptacle, a shiny coin vibrated almost imperceptibly. The spectacled man in the pristine lab-coat paid it no attention as he was engrossed in the book he was reading while taking notes. He slammed the book closed on the desk and the coin took the opportunity to fling itself off the desk as the other items on the desk danced about with the violence of the slam. The man stalked out of the room, not quite closing the door behind him. The coin glinted back the light and was hidden from view as it sank deep into the trash. Moments later the scent of the trash began to increase and waft towards the door without the benefit of a breeze or draft. The coin biding its time.

A few days later across the city, Bobby Bradbury was thrown bodily from the door of a music hall by the doorman. He landed in a heap of trash bags on the curb. Rubbish spilling out of the split bags and covered him in foul smelling juices and other effluvia.

"I've told ya a dozen times ya bum, ya can't come in here. We don't serve your kind. Get outta here."

Bobby slunk off into the night. He was down on his luck, but lately he almost felt cursed. Reduced to begging for scraps at the back doors of diners and restaurants or doing odd jobs for cash. He wasn't above purse snatching or downright mugging people, either. But even being a criminal didn't pay well in Philadelphia in 1955, although a lot of people said the country had really recovered from the Second World War Bobby only interacted with the kind of people who were hurting.

On this night he had had a poor meal at the soup kitchen, watery soup that was just cloudy water with delusions of mediocrity, and a stale bread roll. Winter was coming on, and his threadbare red coat was not keeping the cold out. He'd found a subway grate that was puffing warm air up into the street as the trains went by under the street. He couldn't linger too long, though, because the cops would at best move him along or at worst beat him for loitering. His ribs still ached from the last "warning" they'd given him after his previous unceremonious ejection from the burlesque music hall.

Head down, he shuffled back and forth in the occasionally warm air from below, when, to his joy, he spotted a glint of something slivery in the busted open trash bag on the kerb up against the building. He stooped to grab whatever it was and then hurried away from the site in case the owner came looking for it.

Stopping in a doorway of a boarded-up shopfront he opened his hand and with one fingerless glove wiped away the coffee grounds (and maybe egg?). It was a coin, Bobby saw as he looked closer.

It wasn't any sort of coin he recognised, there was a strange symbol on one side made up of intersecting lines and circles. On the other side was the shape of an eye, or maybe a flame, surrounded by seven symbols that he couldn't quite focus on. His heart soared, maybe it was worth something. He felt the metal and it certainly didn't feel precious, it did not even have the heft of silver, and when he tapped it on the brickwork it gave off a dull click rather than the ring of more valuable materials.

It was identical to the size of a subway token. Bobby considered for a moment his options. Hold onto the coin and maybe not get screwed by the pawnbroker on its value, or use it to get a nice warm seat on a late-night subway train right up to the end of the line? A cold gust of wind with the promise of rain buffeted him damply and his mind was made up.

He went immediately to the Subway; he tried the token in the turnstile and for a moment it seemed like it wasn't going to work. The coin rattled in the slot and the turnstile remained closed to him. Bobby pushed on the bars, and, with an almost human squeal, they began to turn as the coin dropped into the mechanism and the way was open to him. He'd been pushing so hard on the bar that, as it turned, he thought he saw a flash of light inside his eyes like when you try to lift something too heavy or stand up too quickly.

Not long after, up on the street, a bald man with a great big bushy beard and tiny round spectacles was feverishly searching the pile of rubbish where Bobby had found the coin. He was uncaringly getting rotting food and other trash all over his clean, white lab coat. Muttering to himself he looked almost deranged. From the nearby brownstone doorway, a woman in a maid's outfit looked on with fear in her eyes.

"I've told you time and time again, Maureen, that you are not to enter my study. I will put my trash out when I want it emptied. You have no idea of what you may have loosed upon the world! I hope for all our sakes that the coin has not fallen into the wrong hands."

"I'm sorry, Professor Lovecraft, the trash was making the rest of the house smell bad, and your wife complained that it was affecting her health. Her coughing has eased since I put it out."

The Professor looked briefly pained but resumed his frantic searching.

"We'll deal with the breach of my sanctum later, Maureen. Call the city in the morning and see if they scheduled a pickup on the street today, and if so where it would have been taken."

"Yessir."

The Professor stomped away from the garbage and as he entered the house, he took off his lab coat and handed it to Maureen.

"Have this cleaned, I am going to bed."

"Yessir." Maureen took the coat and headed for the laundry. As she did Professor Lovecraft put one hand on her shoulder.

"I'm sorry, Maureen, you were just doing your job, I'm very worried that the coin has found a new owner who it will use for evil. The coat can wait until morning." He waved at the soiled garment.

"Yessir, but I will get it soaking so that the stains don't set."

"Good girl, thank you." The door to the brownstone closed against the cold wet night.

Down below in the subway Bobby walked through a gloomy tiled tunnel. He was so tired and hungry that he failed to notice that he was the only person there. Normally at this time of night there would still be people catching the train home from a night out, or people getting to their nightshift jobs. There weren't even the usual drunks around, trying to piss in the non-existent corners of the tubelike tunnels. Bobby got to the first platform not caring what line or what train he was to travel on. He felt the warm rush of air from an approaching train. He'd put his back to a pillar unconsciously to stop the possibility of someone approaching him from behind and picking his pocket or pushing him onto the tracks. He did not understand the hypocrisy of his attendant thought that he lived with a "bunch of savages in this town".

The train rattled and groaned to a stop. Bobby entered the carriage, found a double seat in the middle, and sat down with his back towards the front of the train. He put his feet up on the seat facing him and fished out a small brown paper wrapped bottle, that was now nearly empty. He took a sip of the remaining few drams of cheap bourbon, and rested his dark-haired, tousled head on the window and stared off into the darkness, and quickly began to nod off.

A sudden jolt woke him some time later, so sudden he dropped his bottle, and it smashed on the floor, the smell of liquor strong and Bobby grimaced.

"Goddamnit," he grunted and looked around. The lights were off, the doors to the carriage were wide open and the night was silent. He couldn't even see the lights or the signage of a station. Stumbling to his feet he approached the doors, wiping sleep from his eyes. Outside the carriage was silent pitch blackness, he stepped free of the train, his feet unexpectedly crunching onto gravel or something very like it, and he felt a sudden rush of cold air. He turned to return to the warm safety of the carriage, only to find it had disappeared.

Spinning in scared circles his heart hammered in his chest and his mind began to race. On one rotation he caught the barest flash of light that looked like it was coming down a tunnel. He moved towards it. As he got closer the tunnel narrowed and revealed itself as made of rough-hewn stone covered in leprous lichen. A sickly-sweet scent of corruption assailed his nostrils, his own ragged breathing the only sound in his ears. He dug into his pocket for the matchbook he carried but the pocket had a hole in it and no matches were to be found.

Bobby stopped and looked back the way he came, the darkness was absolute, so he continued towards the light, which, as he got closer, seemed fitful and dirty. The mouth of the cavern tunnel at its terminator was a tight squeeze, Bobby tore the shoulder of his coat as he pushed through the rough stone exit. The dimly lit cavern then opened out significantly, the walls delineated a space about the size of a regional cathedral, but no matter how hard he squinted he couldn't see the ceiling, and the fitful light had no immediately discernible source.

In the cavern stood two rows of statues on the sides of the chamber, a wide aisle between them led towards a raised dais. The ground beneath Bobby's his feet still seemed to be chips of gravel that were an unnatural yellowy-white colour. As he walked, the chips puffed up dust that stained his damp pants cuffs a dirty off-white colour.

Bobby looked at the statues closely as he advanced. One side were representations of the seven Capital Virtues, Chastity, Temperance, Charity, Diligence, Patience, Kindness, and Humility. They were crudely wrought, and looked almost childlike, with chubby limbs and vapid expressions. In the inconstant light it was almost like their eyes were pleading for some help they required. The other seven statues on the other side appeared as if they were much larger and further away, and he could not read the inscriptions on the plinths. Most of them were bestial, some with too many limbs, too many teeth or they displayed powerful menace.

Bobby then stared at the dais, and what he'd thought was a pile of rags suddenly moved! The figure began to speak.

"Bobby Bradbury, you have been chosen to champion those who have no voice in this world. Approach and take up your mantle of power." The words resonated out from the dais where the robed skeletal figure now rested on the central of what Bobby realised were seven thrones. Bobby was shaken by the voice, one that seemed to reverberate in his head even after the actual sound had died away.

"What? Who are you? Why have you picked me? I'm nobody, I'm nothing."

"Yes, Bobby. That's why you are here. They have no import, and neither do you. Your life is going nowhere, your soul is tarnished, but if you'll accept, the gift that they give will raise you up above all other mortal men."

Bobby began to think that maybe he was still asleep. He approached the dais and the skinny figure.

"Who are you?" he repeated.

"I am the Sorcerer. In life I was known as Abdul Alhazred, but the Lurkers in the Dark renamed me when I took up their Champion's Aspect and Attributes. My new name now is a word of power—that means 'sleeps' or 'waits', but a dread kind of awaiting, a dire type of sleeping; the time before striking with terrible hungers and powers. This word, when spoken by you, it will transubstantiate your mortal flesh into that of the immortals from outside time and space."

"What if I don't accept?" Bobby said, all at once coming to the horrific realisation he was not snoozing. The Sorcerer's head turned towards Bobby and looked directly into the young man's eyes, and, it felt like, looked into his very soul. Bobby was sure he could see a pinpoint of eldritch light, deep in the eye sockets of the Sorcerer.

The Power of F'thagn

"Then you will die," the Sorcerer said, suddenly right in front of him, gripping the front of his coat in one bony hand.

"Listen carefully, Bobby Bradbury, for I am about to reveal to you the secrets of the powers of F'THAGN!" Far off, thunder sounded.

"F'Thagn is not just a word, each letter represents one of six ancient beings from beyond space, each of whom bestows upon you a unique gift.

"F is for the Formless Spawn, the Enduring. It gives you the ability to withstand even the harshest of conditions, both physical and emotional, making you nearly indestructible: for as you are damaged you will be regenerated by the endless flesh.

"T is for Tulzcha, the Tenacious. He grants you the courage to face any challenge, no matter how daunting, with unflinching bravery and determination.

"H is for Hastur, the King in Yellow. He endows you with incredible strength, making you nearly invincible in combat and able to perform feats of superhuman might.

"A is for Azathoth, the blind idiot god. He imbues you with his necrotic energy, allowing you to harness the power of pain and suffering, and shoot bolts of pure death from your hands.

"G is for Ghatanothoa, the Witherer. He gives you incredible speed, allowing you to move at the pace of dark, and to fly even into the deep recesses of space with ease.

"N is for Nyarlathotep, the Crawling Chaos, whose power grants you knowledge and the ability to speak any language and communicate with any being, no matter how alien or incomprehensible.

"When you say the word F'Thagn, you will be transformed into a being beyond compare, with all the powers and abilities of these ancient outsiders at your fingertips. But with great power comes great fealty to the Dark Ones. You must use your powers in their service, and always remember that if you stray, you will be struck down and forever be denied the eternal gaze of Great Cthulhu. So, go forth, Bobby Bradbury, use your powers, and never forget the gift you have been given. Understand, too, The Dread Lords will send you visions from time to time, letting you know what they expect of you."

Bobby didn't realise that he'd been holding his breath until what little remained to him whooshed out when he slammed to the floor and stars flashed before his eyes. When he looked up, the Sorcerer was back on his throne, his lanky arms now on the cathedra. Bobby could see the symbol on the front of the man's tattered robes—if you squinted it could be a lightning bolt, but it really looked more like a stylised tentacle, with suckers. The Sorcerer's cloak had settled on the back of the throne looking like great, grey, threadbare, batlike wings.

"Well, Bobby Bradbury, shall I search for another unworthy soul to bear the mantle of the Old Ones' champion, stepping over your crushed mouldering bones to do it, or will you take up the power and rid yourself of the curse of *mortality*?" The Sorcerer leaned towards Bobby.

"It's not much of a choice, said Bobby. "Death or power unimaginable. What sort of things would I be called upon to do for these creatures?"

"Sew discord, cast down purity, destroy goodness and pave the way to our reality for our Lords when dread Cthulhu wakes from his aeons-long slumber."

Bobby goes still for a moment that feels like an eternity. The only sounds are the hammering of Bobby's heart in his chest and the creaking of the bones and sinews of the sorcerer as he leans forward and raises one bony hand.

"Choose."

"I Choose… to take up the Mantle."

"Then mortal, say my name and transcend your mortal flesh". Bobby looks up into the endless darkness and intones.

"F'THAGN!"

A crack of lightning and a roll of thunder blind and deafen Bobby. As he comes back to the world, he looks down and takes in his new form. He's wearing a tight-fitting leather outfit of veinous scarlet, the Sorcerer's symbol adorns his chest and a ragged capelet hangs from his shoulders almost like vestigial wings. He is wearing pustulant yellowy grey gloves and boots that match the tone of the capelet. Most of all though he now looks like a circus strongman with bulging muscles and thick lustrous hair. Bobby feels the dark cold energy inside himself, and he hears the whispered voices of the beings granting him their power. Bobby looks up to the sorcerer and begins to ask a question, but his words don't come as he sees and feels that the skeletal remains are just that, empty remains. The Sorcerer is no more than detritus now. Bobby levitates by instinct and floats towards the central throne, and he absentmindedly sweeps the remains off the seat and takes his place there.

He begins to chuckle to himself feeling his new more powerful mien, and a hideous vengeful grin cracks his face.

"Maybe I'll go and take in a show."

Hill-Runner and the Enemy from Behind the Curtain Of Stars

GERRY HUNTMAN

Author Note: This story is about a unique group of people who came to the Americas to protect the emerging Native American nations. This group is imaginary and are culturally connected to fictitious proto-Eurasian peoples of many thousands of years ago, as opposed to the Native American peoples that existed in the setting of this story, and today.

The chief indicated for me to sit in a place of honour. All who were present waited silently for me to speak.

"My name is Hill-Runner and I am of the tribe that is called The First.

"We were the first to cross the icy straights, and our purpose was always clear: protect Those Who Followed Us—with our lives, if necessary. Our songs reach back far before those long-ago times, and we have forgotten nothing.

"We have no homeland, unless you count the vastness of the mountains, plains, deserts, forests, and swamps that lie between the two Great Waters. We strike new camps four times a year and honour the territories of Those Who Followed Us, and they respected our right to make their homes our homes for the time allotted. Although this is now changing.

"Our camp may be in one place at any given time, but our Runners and Riders are everywhere…everywhere they are needed. We are always on the move so that we can warn Those Who Followed Us of any threat.

"I am here because an enemy from behind the curtain of stars is coming to our lands again and must be destroyed. Your people must be wary and be prepared to head south until the conflict is over."

While I explained my purpose to the elders of the tribe, their ceremonial Bear Spirit pipe had been passed around, signifying the sanctity of my presence, although some of the younger warriors seemed confused with why this should be the case. I could understand their thinking by reading their faces.

The chief finally received the pipe and smoked the mixture of bearberry leaves and tobacco. He carefully laid the pipe on an ornately carved wooden stand. "Thank you, Hill-Runner. We are honoured by your presence and we will heed your warning. The last time I saw one of your kind was when I was a child, before our people came to roam the Great Plains and these mountains, and it was only fleeting. She ran through the northern forest as if the trees weren't there, and I thought she was flying just above the winding and undulating trails. My father told me that when a Runner was sighted, it meant a great battle would take place with gods who should not be here. He also said that if we spoke with a Runner death would soon follow."

I felt comfort in my heart that The First were not entirely forgotten by these people. "Thank you, Chief Sunset Eagle. What your father said to you is true, although the matter of death soon following is not clear until the enemy is vanquished. It is my purpose to protect you and your tribe, and all other tribes among all the nations of the lands."

The chief's face was expressionless, like carvings on the totem poles of the north or the moss-covered stone statues many days travel to the south, but his eyes were warm and sympathetic to what I had said. "Hill-Runner, aside from warning us of the battle-to-come, is there another reason why you are here?"

"Yes, there is. I have seen the signs that the Old Woman of our tribe gave to the Runners and Riders, but nothing to show exactly where the enemy is camped. Have you seen any strangers to your nations pass through the land? Do you know much about them and where they are headed?"

I could hear muttering behind me and knew that I had asked the right question. I sensed that the young warriors were now taking me seriously.

"Yes, there were strangers who passed through only a day ago," the chief said. "White men with a couple Cree who scout for them. They came from the east, far beyond the Great Plains."

I nodded, not hiding the fact that these men were exactly who I were looking for. The Old Woman had given three signs to signify the Enemy had come again: first was confirmed last night when I witnessed a shooting star pass through the constellation what these Inakip call the "lost children", and what my people call the "dancers". Second, was feeling the shaking of the land this morning, which signifies a great battle or change of power among the gods is imminent. The Old Woman said the third sign was the coming of strangers from afar, who had no respect for the land, its spirits, or Those Who Followed Us. She said that they would be the servants of a Mindless God who will invade our sacred lands.

"Chief Sunset Eagle, please show me their trail. My advice is that you break your camp and head far to the south. I am sure portents will appear when it is safe to return."

The chief closed his eyes in thought. "My forefathers always followed the counsel of the Runners and Riders, and I will not change this practice. The truth can be found in your eyes, Hill-Runner, and the words that come from your mouth. We will move camp in the morning."

Having Cree among the white men complicated matters but I knew that it could also turn to my favour with a little luck. The first question I needed answering was how far the Mindless God had passed through the curtain — was he already in our lands? I prayed to the spirit of the Pale Deer that I had time to close the curtain to the stars and force the mindless one back to its black home.

While still many hours before sunset I was shown the path by one of the young warriors. I jogged for a thousand heartbeats and then, with the spirit of the Pale Deer coursing through my body, I *ran*. The night amidst the heavily wooded hills, normally impenetrable for human eyes, exploded into bright greens and greys, laying bare everything before me. My steps were light, barely touching the ground, and it took the entirety of my training and experience to stop from bellowing in rapture at the power and euphoria of my transformation.

And it did not take long before the white men's tracks were found, and only several more hours when I saw, far ahead, the almost blinding incandescence of their campfires.

I stopped and sat on a rock covered in lichen, waiting for the spirit of the Pale Deer to depart, and for the heaving of my chest to subside. "Thank you, Pale Deer. Rest, as I will call on you again, and soon."

I sensed the spirit acknowledging me, and then she evaporated into the night air. She was never far away.

I silently approached a clearing with three campfires, noting there were twelve white men and two Cree scouts. One of the white men was keeping watch to the south, while one of the Cree was guarding the north. There was no chance of threat from the other points due to a natural gully to the west and a steep embankment to the east. I knew the Cree guard would have a keen eye for trouble, but the white man was too busy smoking a small pipe and would likely miss a stampeding herd of buffalo well after it was too late.

I slipped past the guard easily and approached the camp. The white men were in a few groups, laughing at what must have been what they called a joke. I could speak English, French and Spanish, but they were still too far from me to be clearly understood. The single Cree in the camp was sitting next to a fire, alone, sharpening his knife on a stone, and keeping warm.

There was no sign of the Mindless God. I had arrived in time.

I knew what I had to do.

I walked into the camp with quiet feet and sat next to the Cree, startling him.

"Don't be alarmed, warrior," I whispered, in his tongue.

"Who are you? What nation do you belong to?"

"I am a Runner of The First. I am here to warn you that you will die if you and your friends stay with these white men."

"I do not know who the 'First' are. Do you mean the Blackfoot will be attacking?" he asked.

"No. Much worse."

A white man stood up, staring at us. "Hey, look. That isn't the other Cree! It's another Ingin!" He reached over to a log that had a long, loaded rifle leaning against it.

I knew this would happen. Based on the white man's reaction, my plan was likely to work. Very quickly, I said to the warrior, "A Mindless God is among the white men. If you value your life, and your friends', leave at the first opportunity."

The Cree's eyes bulged. He may not know of the First, but he did know about the evil that lay beyond the curtain in the night sky.

The white man approached, aiming his heavy rifle at me, while cocking the mechanism. A few other men joined him, too self-assured to bear any arms.

"Hey Ingin. Were you from? *Unnerstan' Eengleesh*?" he added, exaggerating the words.

I feigned not understanding his tongue; instead, I said to my companion, "Cree warrior, tell them I am from a distant tribe and I just want some food."

He didn't lose composure and repeated what I had said in English.

They stared at me, clearly wondering if this was true, but my clothing and colours would have been unknown to most white men...except the few I have met far to the east and west.

The man with the rifle said to the Cree warrior, "Tell this ingin that we prob'ly believe him, but we can't take chances. We'll need to bind him until we break camp in the mornin' and then he can be on his way. If you want to feed him, it comes out of your rations."

The Cree nodded and said to me, "I am sorry, but I have no choice. If I can leave before dawn, I will, and I will release you."

I sat near the fire and made sure I had a good view of the camp and its occupants. I heard some conversations and missed others. These white men were searching for new trails and ways to get to the Great Water to the West, something The First, and many of those who followed, had been aware of for countless generations. They were in competition with other white men to get to the West first, and too often talked about the riches and fame they will earn. All this information was incidental, as I wanted to see the *sign*. I wanted to know how *it* came to be.

One of the men was their leader, who they called "Captain", "Sir", or "Masterton". Another man—who was older and less fit than the rest of the group—was second in charge and was more like a wise man to the camp, an advisor. He was called "Carlisle" by all.

My Cree companion revealed his name as Late Summer, and the other Cree was Moose Hunter. I returned their honour by telling them my name.

With my coming, the entire camp was awake and up and about. Many took their time to stare at me, quizzically, trying to work out where I came from. Masterton, frothing at his red-whiskered mouth, scolded the guard whom I evaded, and wasn't happy with Late Summer either. "Are you sure you don't know what tribe this Ingin comes from?"

"No, Captain," the Cree said. His voice carrying conviction.

"And what's his name?"

Late Summer asked me, feigning that he didn't know.

I said, "I am 'Hill-Runner'. That is my purpose. You can tell him my name."

Late Summer told Masterton my name, in his tongue, and with a good intonation that closely resembled the tongue of The First.

"Hmm. Sounds like the way the Algonquin speak, or at least a hint. But I know what most of the eastern tribes look like and his...clothes...hair...they aren't the same. Ask him if he comes from the West."

As Late Summer translated—and he had to, as Masterton could understand enough of the words of Those Who Followed Us—Carlisle came out of his tent and stared at me. There was a worried look on his face.

"Hey, Carlisle," Masterton said, spotting the portly man, "come over here and help me work out where this savage comes from! I'm surprised you haven't chained yourself to him for that very purpose!"

Masterton raised his hand, shaking it as if to convey it was not worth it. His forehead and receding scalp glistened with sweat and a few drops ran into his smarting eyes.

"Come on! I insist!" Masterton beckoned.

Begrudgingly, Carlisle came forward but kept a good distance from me.

Late Summer relayed my answer to Masterton's last question: "Yes, he comes from the West, near the Great Water."

Masterton turned to Carlisle: "What do you think? Is this savage telling the truth? Do you know anything of his tribe?"

The man responded with a good amount of stuttering and had a strange accent that made his speech difficult to understand. "Um…er…never seen anything like him. Clothes, beads, designs… all outside my experience. I…I'm familiar with the language and garb of many tribes in California and further north, but…it…it gets hazy then…" He swayed a little and his face went red. "So… sorry. Need to lie down…"

Masterton grabbed Carlisle by the shoulders, helping him to steady. "What's wrong with you, man? You haven't got some damned plague, do you? I knew your travels in Asia Minor would bring trouble!"

Carlisle shook his head, grimaced, and slumped onto his rump. He didn't, or couldn't, open his eyes. "No disease…no disease," he mumbled.

I tapped Late Summer, indicating it was time to leave. The Cree said to me, "Watch this man, he could have a deadly sickness," and rubbed my shoulder in reassurance, and at the same time dropped his knife into my hands that were bound behind my back. He stepped back, in awe at what he was seeing.

The white men ignored him. The strange behaviour by their second in charge, and the prospect of a disease caused great concern among all the camp goers.

Carlisle continued to mumble. "The voice. The voice is stronger… hurts. It's coming. It's coming!"

"What's coming, man?" Masterton demanded, ignoring the possibility of disease and shoving himself only inches from Carlisle's sweaty face.

Carlisle's visage transformed in an instant, much to my horror. *I'm too late! This is happening too quickly!* At first, I saw an ochre-red chubby face covered in sweat, and then it parched like the sentinel mummies I saw in their small stone homes in the breathless mountaintops far to the south. But horror added to horror as his whole body turned into a dried, bark-like substance, and…he broke apart with such violence that his body parts were thrown across the camp, half-blinding some, knocking others over.

I had landed on my side, knife still firmly gripped, and I saw the final transformation. The Mindless God had indeed passed through the star curtain. Where Carlisle had once sat, now there was a creature twice his size standing on three sturdy legs, supported by another half dozen chitinous arms or legs, and many more were whirling around his upper torso. There was no head—just a large mouth where a neck should have been, and eyes appeared and disappeared constantly from the ends of some of its appendages.

Most of the eyes were focused on me. *It knows. It also knows I have the medicine in my bag that can trap it—long enough for the First to come and banish it.*

Masterton screamed incoherently and grabbed the rifle from the man who had pointed it at me earlier. He cocked back the lock mechanism and fired it at the monster. A burst of smoke erupted from the rifle and a shot slammed into the glistening, grey body of the Mindless God. The body swallowed the shot and it left no wound. It did nothing but distract the dark spirit.

I thanked my guardian spirit for Masterton's misplaced courage. I sawed away at the rope that bound my wrists, as I witnessed carnage take place.

The chitinous limbs were fast and flexible. A man was caught by one and was dragged toward the god's body. Almost instantly he was turned into dried skin without flesh—crumbling, but not before his blood and other liquid essences flowed like a stream into the creature's neck-mouth. Another man tried to run but two appendages spiked him—one in his upper back and the other in his groin. In a heartbeat he was ripped in two, his torso retracted and sucked of his moisture, his essence.

I broke free and scrambled out of sight of the ever-growing spirit-creature—hoping to escape into the forest, to regather my strength and thoughts, and most importantly, prepare the *medicine*. I knew I had to act quickly, or the dark being would suck enough life essences to be too strong for anyone to defeat.

I felt the land give way to a steep slope and realised I had crawled too near the western gully—I could see the eyes on some of the appendages searching in the direction where I had lain, and realised I had no choice—I let myself slip down.

I extended my legs hoping to catch a ledge or tree trunk, to stop the acceleration of my body into the ravine. To no avail. It wasn't a sheer drop, but it may as well have been—my body began to roll and tumble, my arms and legs flailed about, and I realised with despondency that it was too late to avoid serious damage. What little I could see of the night terrain had blurred with my tumbling, and my body was constantly assailed by rocks and bushes. I felt agonizing pain as I fell into the bottom of the gully and heard the snapping of my bones…it was beyond bearing and I lost consciousness.

My eyes opened and I felt excruciating pain. It was early dawn and blood in my eyes turned the bottom of the gully into shades of red, much like the sand and rocks at the top of mountains that spew fire. I could barely breathe—I knew one of my lungs had collapsed and many of my rib bones were broken. I was lying on my side and felt the hot pant of someone/something on my neck. I was beyond fear, beyond worrying about my life: I cried out in agony as I rolled onto my back.

Floating an arms-length above me was the Pale Deer spirit.

"Take me to the Other Place, my spirit. Please. Release me of this pain."

The Pale Deer, who never speaks, shook its head.

"Please! I have failed my people! Release me!"

My spirit guardian shook its head again and then looked up, to the top of the ravine where I had fallen from. It lingered, to make sure I knew it was deliberate.

I understood what she was saying. "The Mindless God did not follow me. It knew I would die, but instead of eating my lifeforce it had another task, more important than its appetite."

The Pale Deer nodded. It then looked up again, in a different direction.

A wave of pain crept up my torso, causing me to scream in agony. I nearly passed out, but I fought the blackness and tried to think. *Think.* I realised she was pointing to the West, where The First were camped, many days travel ahead. *He came to destroy us, to make it easier for those behind the black curtain to come*, I thought.

The Pale Deer nodded.

"And my tribe will be surprised. Defenceless."

The spirit didn't need to acknowledge the truth of that statement. She simply floated above me, staring at me with her beautiful, sympathetic eyes.

"Is there nothing I can do to warn my people? If I can warn them, the black spirit will be defeated."

The Pale Deer shed a tear that fell silently down and through me. I knew her well enough to know that the tear was not just her sadness at seeing my broken, dying body. It had another emotion entwined around and through it. While the teardrop hadn't touched me physically, it coursed through my essence, my spirit. It wasn't a message, like the picture-words of Those Who Followed Us to the south, but there was an understanding.

A last journey, one that has no return.

It was my turn to nod. I understood completely. It was my only chance to redeem myself.

I closed my eyes and tried my best to imagine I was running and counting my plainly, painful, erratic heartbeats. They started to slow down, responding to my injuries. As I neared the count of one thousand, I knew there were precious few beats left, but I felt something warm enter my body and much of the pain washed away.

For, at one thousand beats the sky and the gully turned from red to shiny silver and gold, and I was whole again, or at least I felt it as so. I was one with the Pale Deer and I knew I could run like the winds.

"Thank you, my guardian. Thank you for giving me this chance."

I stood up and checked my bag: the gourd with the medicine had been shattered. The only option left was to warn my people. I ran along the gully faster than I had ever run before, and when I turned to climb the steep slope to head west, my feet effortlessly glided over the rock and soil as if I was following a level trail. I didn't need to hold back: I shouted in euphoria, feeling the powerful blood and heartbeat of the Pale Deer course through me, which sustained my body and charged it with purpose.

I had never run this fast before, but I knew my foe was also swift and with a purpose. The Mindless God had a head start and I could not waste a heartbeat of time. The Pale Deer steered my path directly toward my tribe's camp, one which would also intersect with the Mindless God.

Each running step covered four times the span of a man's height, and my feet barely touched the earth. The brilliant, golden auras of living things, be they the grasses and bushes below me, or the limber trees around, shed an otherworldly glow, and gave me absolute clarity of the way ahead. The stone, rocks, dirt and cliff faces emanated a silver radiance, again, making my path easy, assured. This was in so many ways the same as when I ran at night, although the colours were different, and I felt I was now closer to what my Pale Deer spirit experienced whenever she ran the hills and plains.

Passing didn't seem so frightening now.

I was full of energy—limitless it seemed. I wanted to run faster, but I was held back to the pace of my guardian spirit.

A full day of running passed and we entered the night. Nothing changed: the terrain still glowed that strange mix of gold and silver, but I knew it was night—the silver half-moon was high in the sky. I was still energized; my body coursed with power and was strangely numb.

I could run forever.

I ran through a mountain pass, the point where I halved the distance to my tribe. The hills before me glowed gold and silver, but I noticed something moving that was black—the blackness of the deepest cave, or the night sky without the moon and stars. It was large, it was the dark spirit. He had grown ten times the size since I had last seen him. He had consumed life as he ran through the wildlands toward The First. He wanted to be as powerful as possible to swiftly destroy my people.

There was no point challenging him; I didn't even know what I could do in this form. I could easily beat him to my tribe, even with a slight detour—I changed course, heading southward, to follow a river gorge.

I sped along the riverbank, dodging western pines, trembling aspen, and low-hanging growth, and at times, lightly stepping on the lapping waters without even getting my moccasins wet. I glanced high above me and saw, to my right, the black outline of the Mindless God, matching my pace, keeping me close at hand.

He seeks to destroy me.

I felt the Pale Deer agree and sensed a deep-set fear in her.

It was only a matter of time. I could see the ravine disappear ahead of me, with the river flowing into a gently sloped valley. We would meet there.

I abruptly stopped my run, and reversed my course. I would not fall into his trap. Instead of following the river back, I rapidly climbed the gorge walls and entered the thick forest of trees that extended for miles around and witnessed the path of devastation left behind the dark spirit's journey. The snapped and splintered trees were glowing their gold auras faintly. Soon they would turn silver.

I heard the anger of the Mindless God. I also heard the sound of trees cracking, becoming louder with each heartbeat.

What am I to do? I despondently asked my guardian.

For the first time there was nothing, no hint of an answer. Only a sense of fear.

I had no weapon except the Cree's knife. My bag had no medicine. I had no idea whether the Mindless God could touch me or not. How could he kill someone who was near death already, and in spirit form?

A thought came to me. *Pale Deer, am I in spirit form?*

I sensed a combination of "yes" and "no" in her nods and shaking of the head.

Then I am in transition? My body is still here but I am mostly in spirit form?

An emphatic nod. There was also a gleam in her eyes even though I could not see them directly. And sadness.

There is one way, isn't there? My heart grew heavy.

A subdued nod.

I knew what to do.

The sound of the crashing and smashing trees would have deafened a mortal. I readied myself, and when the chaos confronted me—the blackness appearing before me—I ran to my right, dodging the growth with as much speed as I could muster, barely missing branches, thorny bushes and rock outcrops. I didn't run away—I ran circles around the evil creature.

The Mindless God screamed in frustration and ignored the forest—he kept correcting his course toward me, trampling everything in the way. He had the height of twenty men, and his scores of appendages could reach further than that, snapping, chopping, and many had eyes at their ends, all focused on finding me. All I was doing was trying to tire the dark spirit, if that was possible, and then try something that was a mixture of faith and guesswork.

Was he tired? I wasn't sure, but he slowed down. I veered abruptly and managed to get to the Mindless God where he least expected—the majority of his chitinous appendages were before him, where he expected me to be. I leapt onto his torso, my knife in my hand. I clamped onto his leathery body and stabbed repeatedly, knowing that it would mean little, if anything, to my enemy.

Nevertheless, he cried out in pain, thrashing and twisting around—was my part-spirit form lethal to him? Was Pale Deer aiding me?

I held on—I *needed* to.

Three of the appendages grew mouths with sharp teeth, and they snapped at me. Two bit deep into my back, but I sliced one in two with my dagger. Other appendages lunged for me.

I continued to stab the Mindless God, hoping to further weaken it.

Dozens of appendages bit me, I could see my limbs and body in their mouths, gorging on my flesh. I could also feel the growing weakness and pain being felt by the Pale Deer—I knew that she would not last long. This was the moment, when I knew I had to do this alone—her protection sustained me, but I would not have her harmed…and yet she could still help me.

I kicked my legs out and my loving, caring Pale Deer was ejected from me. I believe she knew this was coming—I could see her hovering over me, witnessing a mangled mess of a human in intolerable pain, slowly sliding down the Mindless God's body.

Thank you, I said to her.

She replied with tears flowing from her beautiful eyes.

My head exploded with pain as a chitinous mouth broke through my skull—everything faded quickly as I saw a golden light beam from my bloody chest toward the Pale Deer…

Epilogue

It was late at night, with a cloudless sky and a crystal-clear half-moon when The Old Woman woke up, feeling her heart beating rapidly. She studied the small Fire-That-Always-Burned and saw it flickering madly, despite the lack of the slightest breeze.

She hurried as best as she could manage and entered the small hut that was made of bison skins, and tied the flap-entrance closed. She was now in pitch darkness.

"Come to me," she whispered, holding her necklace that had the bone-carving of her spirit guardian, the bison.

A shape began to form in front of her—wispy and golden. It would not resolve much more but her keen perception knew who it was.

"Hill Runner. You are passing."

The figure nodded.

"Then it is coming."

Again, Hill-Runner nodded.

"You have done well, son of my son. You have saved many lives—I am proud of you."

She could see the glow fading and knew that Hill-Runner was about to pass completely. She sighed and waited patiently until Hill-Runner faded into the night. She couldn't help but see his passing as the beginning of the end of The First. They were only as strong as the combined faith of Those Who Followed Us in their purpose, and the strangers were fast undermining it all. *Who will take up our cause?* she wondered.

"Farewell, son of my son. I will see you soon."

THE COLOUR OUT OF HAUTDESERT

JM MERRYT

1.

It was an ill-omened thing for a meteor to streak across the heavens. Worse still for it to crash into the earth with a flash of brilliant emerald, however distant that calamity was from the high white walls of Camelot.

Camelot was a place of literature and art, of polished stone and law; a beacon of civilisation in a land that was otherwise untamed and dangerous. Yet it was common for strangeness to intrude upon the orderly city. The nearby forest of Brocéliande, populated by twisting trees and strange magics, sheltered as many eldritch things as it did Faeries.

It was not uncommon for a resident of Camelot to spy a hunting party of the Fair Folk on horseback, their red eared hounds running down Ghasts. Faeries did not like competition, no matter how otherworldly and vicious. Two sorts of predator fighting for the same ecological niche, they scrapped over access to human flesh. A thousand tiny islands dotted the countryside, and ravenous things darted through the surrounding inland sea, dragging the unwary into the dark.

Whispers of distant plagues, of illness and death filtered through the city, dampening the festive mood: New year beckoned, and with it the easing of winter's clawed grip. Preparations for a feast carried on, regardless of rumours of scorched earth and shapeless hungry things wandering the countryside. King Arthur was an optimist, and his Queen was stubborn. They would not be dissuaded.

Little was Camelot affected by the meteor's descent to earth, and life carried on. Pork was roasted, cakes baked, presents were wrapped, and the Knights of the Round Table continued in their quest to rout worshippers of the Old Gods.

On the night of the New Year's Feast, Sir Gawain and his fellows returned home under the light of a blood red moon, tired but laughing, drenched in the gore of a slaughtered Shoggoth. Freshly bathed and bandaged, Gawain was last to the feast. He sat closest to the main door.

A knock, sharp and hard enough to rise above joyful songs of visiting minstrels and the playful bickering of the ladies in waiting rang through the hall.

King Arthur froze; a gift from Guinivere clutched in long-fingered hands. Another, more insistent knock echoed through the abrupt silence. The King exchanged a quick look with his lady wife, who cried, "We have a visitor! Shall we not extend our hospitality to our guest?"

A page rushed to heed his queen's command, tripping over his own feet in his haste. Gawain took pity and helped the boy to his feet, striding to unlatch the great door.

The Great Hall was accessed via three points: a small door that led to the kitchens, which was chiefly used by servants and spies. A passageway lay concealed behind the seat of the King, in case of danger and built at Merlin's insistence. The third door was the main entrance: a pair of huge doors of carven oak, often latched against foul things that slithered through the darkness of night.

The overwhelming stench of fresh blood clawed its way into the hall. A living, malevolent thing, oil black gore oozed across stone and wood, devouring all it touched with all the ravenous violence of acid on meat.

Gawain darted back, hand on the hilt of his sword. Something dread lay outside. The marrow in Gawain's bones congealed; the hair on the back of his neck rising.

THE COLOUR OUT OF HAUTDESERT

A giant of a man on horseback burst through the doors and cantered into the Great Hall. Helmeted, the visitor was entirely garbed in green, yet he wore little armour. A holly bough and a great green axe were strapped to his back, but no sword sat on his hip. He made no effort to remove his visor.

An unearthly wind, frigid as a cooling corpse, blew into the hall. Behind him, in the lamplit courtyard, drifts of snow had blackened and shimmered, opalescent. The stranger carried corruption in his wake.

Queen Guinevere sniffed at the insult, staring hard at the stranger's visored face. Yet, hospitality was a sacred thing. She dared not turn away a guest, no matter how repugnant. She looked to her husband for guidance.

King Arthur did not stand. He regarded the man in green with a thin smile. "We welcome you to Camelot. May we know the name of the visitor to whom we extend our hospitality and the warmth of our hearth?"

Gawain, standing within a dozen paces of the stranger, found himself grateful the Green Knight had not removed his helmet: Waves of something unholy emanated from the stranger. Gawain had borne it before; in the presence of the Deep Ones and the foul beast he had pinioned earlier that night. It was a deep, gnawing fear that confounded and twisted, contorting the most level-headed men into something feral. Gawain had seen that fear warp strong men into weeping husks that clawed out their eyes, biting through their tongues.

Gawain did not want to look into this man's eyes.

Wordless, the stranger in green dismounted from his horse—a glassy-eyed creature, who flinched away from its owner.

Striding into the middle of the hall, heedless of fainting ladies and courtiers, the intruder called out in a voice like the booming echo of cries shouted into the deepest caves: "You may call me the Green Knight. I challenge anyone brave enough: Behead me with my own axe"—he held the weapon aloft— "and I will return the favour in a year and a day."

Queen Guinevere leant forward in her seat, her chin cupped in one hand. "What is the prize, good Sir?"

273

JM MERRYT

"My axe," the Green Knight boomed, voice hollow and devoid of human feeling.

The Queen bowed her head once, lip curling slightly at the paltry reward. "If we refuse?"

The Green Knight scoffed, gesturing to a pale-faced Baron, who was half unconscious with existential dread. "Tales of the cowardice of the Knights of the Round Table will spread, and so will knowledge of the weakness of your kingdom." This was said with an audible sneer.

Queen Guinevere nodded, her eyes steely. "I see."

Raising his helmeted head high, the Green Knight said again, "I am here to challenge your bravest warrior." This was cried in the same manner as one may toss an apple engraved with the words "for the fairest" into a knot of beautiful women.

There was no move by any knight, nor soldier, nor courtier to approach the Green Knight. Sir Lancelot exchanged a long look with Sir Galahad, eyebrow raised, as if to say "Are you not the bravest? The most honourable? This is your chance to prove it, unless your every boast is a hollow thing". It was a strange request, made at twilight by a man garbed in the colour of Faerie, therefore it was inherently suspect.

All eyes slid to the King, expectant.

King Arthur sighed. Reluctant in the face of an obvious trap, he stood. Setting the present from his wife aside, he strode to meet the Green Knight.

The Green Knight dropped to his knees, holding the axe out in both hands.

Gawain hurried to the King's side. If they rid the land of this man, who was clearly either cursed or something inhuman, that would be a boon. There was a risk the Green Knight may betray their hospitality and simply strike the King with his axe. Gawain could not risk that.

Placing a hand on King Arthur's arm, Gawain said in a low voice, "Please, your Majesty—*Uncle*—let me have the honour."

The King met his nephew's eye, visibly relaxing. "Yes," he said, his voice a tad shaky. "I can grant that." He stepped back and gestured for Gawain to "have at".

Gawain raised his head, proud. "I accept your challenge, Green Knight."

"Will you vow to return the favour, in a year and a day?" The Green Knight raised his head slightly, and their eyes met.

Gawain ignored the sudden sensation of icy fingers tracing his face, of unearthly voices whispering dreadful secrets into his ears. He nodded once.

The Green Knight laughed, merry. "May I know the name of the man who will strike me, after the promise of hospitality has been extended?"

Gawain flinched, the Green Knight's words sharp as an icepick to the skull: If he backed down, this stranger could strike him down for breaking a vow; but if Gawain harmed a man who had been offered hospitality, Gawain would be killed in turn. Hospitality was sacred, and the lives of those who betrayed it were forfeit.

His eyes flicked to meet those of Sir Lancelot, who shrugged, lips twisting into a faint smirk. He mouthed the word, "Sorry".

Gawain laughed under his breath and shook his head. Raising his voice, he said, "Sir Gawain, the Knight of Maidens." It was a foolish thing to give one's name to a Fey creature, but Gawain had always been rash.

Whispers rose all around Gawain, insistent, full of fear and wonder. He ignored them. Lips pressed into a thin line, he stepped forward and plucked the proffered axe from the giant's outstretched hands. Gawain's own hands shook, the faint tremor borne from the miasma of hatred and sheer malevolence radiating from the Green Knight.

Gawain suppressed the shiver. Fingers curling around the axe handle tight enough to turn sun darkened knuckles white, he hefted the weapon and brought it down hard. Neat, the Green Knight's head bounced once on the cold stone floor, landing with a meaty thud, rolling to a stop at the King's feet.

Oil dark blood oozed from the stump.

Gawain crowed. "Fool! What now of your challenge?" He laughed, leaning back on his heels.

King Arthur frowned, bending slightly to peer at the severed head. This was not the first time he had seen a head cleaved from a man's neck. There was too little blood. He nodded to Sir Lancelot and Sir Kay, who rose, grim faced and armed.

The great hall filled with anticipatory silence, all chatter falling away with the swiftness of the axe blow.

Then followed laughter.

Raucous as the song of carrion crows, the severed head roared with mirth. A terrible sound, like coffin nails being thrust into the listener's heart, it was echoed by laughter from the royal court. A Baron fell to his knees, convulsing, while a Lady in Waiting thrust a dagger into her ear, tears streaming down her face.

Gawain flinched; the axe held high. Narrowing his eyes, he considered the weight of honour, and the severity of his disgrace should he bring the axe down again and again on the green garbed corpse. If he crushed that severed head, would the voices stop?

The beheaded knight rose, inky blood sloshing down the front of his emerald tunic.

Moving with the grace of a dancer, the Green Knight strode to collect his severed head. The holly bough lay abandoned at his feet, all but forgotten. Laughing, off key and soul twistingly wrong, the Green Knight jammed his head back onto his neck. It wobbled ominously as he spoke.

"A good clean cut!" the man cried in a tone that was equal parts mirth and mockery. "I will need my lady wife to stitch it back into place!"

Pale, Gawain reached out one hand, reluctant to return the axe to this dead thing.

The Green Knight waved it away, dismissive. "Remember your oath, little knight." With that, the Green Knight melted into slop. Meat peeled from bone with a wet, slick sound, and bone withered into dust. His axe and the holly bough remained. The horse paced, restless.

Gawain dropped into a crouch before the open door, the axe falling out of his hand clattering, unheard upon the grey slate floor. The unearthly voices rising above the whispers in his ears. Trying to drown them out, he clutched at his head and screamed.

THE COLOUR OUT OF HAUTDESERT

2.

It was no easy thing to puzzle out the homeland of the Green Knight. He had not shared the location of wherever he lurked when he wasn't challenging strangers to duels. Consequently, Gawain had been forced to seek out Merlin.

Merlin wasn't old, but he radiated the same sort of eldritch wrongness as any given Faerie. The man's origins were known only to the King, and most of the court shared King Arthur's faith in the sorcerer.

Gawain did not trust Merlin. He had fought too many cultists to feel comfortable around a man who was so like the foul creatures those Pagans venerated.

Merlin had once lived in an ocean cave under Tintagel. He had spent his days communing with Deep Ones and Merfolk alike. Reclusive, Merlin had been bitterly disappointed when King Arthur had commissioned the building of this tower.

Still, Merlin was wise, if unnerving, so Gawain made the long ascent up the winding stair of his tower. Merlin had made himself a perch in the highest chamber of the hated tower, abhorring the noise of the royal court.

He was a tall man, prematurely grey, and possessed of unnervingly sharp blue eyes. He had a tendency to peer through his fellows, often forgetting to blink. Merlin was a man who lived in more than one world, more than one time, all at once.

Raising a reluctant hand, Gawain rapped thrice upon the chamber door. The door opened, silent, pulled wide by unseen hands.

Merlin's tower was a jagged shard of stone at the edge of the castle keep. It was both tumbledown in terms of upkeep and ruthlessly neat. Floor to ceiling shelves bristled from rough stone walls, creaking under the weight of books and papers. Paranoid, Merlin had linked each book to its shelf by a length of iron chain. A corner desk was heaped with papers and half melted tallow candles, and the floor was a mess of symbols and ritual circles. Some had been sketched in chalk, others had been carved into the solid stone with a determined hand.

Gawain knew little of magic, preferring not to risk his sanity any more than he regularly did, but he recognised some symbols.

277

Some were Ogham, a script often used by Faeries. Sharp and inscrutable to the barely literate young knight, he paid the letters little heed. Other symbols he had seen gouged into the meat of worshippers of the Elder Gods. The foul letters flickered as if alive, writhing upon the floor like a mass of maggots gorging on rotten flesh.

Merlin paused, his hands white with chalk dust. He was tracing an elaborate circle on the rough stone floor. Triangles and stars made up the bulk of the sigil. Gawain flinched at a sudden sharp pain. The whispers in his head, ever present since the advent of the Green Knight, rose in volume, clamouring for attention.

Absently, Gawain wiped blood from his eye.

"A Goetic Sigil," Merlin said, bland and unprompted. "Specifically, the Gate of Yog-Sothoth."

Gawain did not ask for further explanation; he did not want to know. He forced himself to not nod or do anything that implied interest: Merlin enthusiastically shared his knowledge with others, even if that knowledge drove his fellows to madness. Merlin, seemingly immune to losing his wits, was the sort of man who made a hobby of staring into the abyss. If faced with something mind twisting, would arch his eyebrow, unimpressed.

Dusting off his hands, Merlin raised his head to gaze at a taxidermied monstrosity overhead. A new acquisition, it was all wings and tentacles and beaks. Even dead, it crystalised the breath in Gawain's lungs into ice. He averted his gaze.

"How can I help?" Merlin asked, almost friendly. He had not been at the feast; he did not eat.

"I must journey to a distant land," Gawain said. Throat dry, he swallowed with a click. "I seek the Green Knight."

Merlin put his head on one side. "Do we have anything of his?" The sorcerer turned to his bookshelves, searching through cloth and skin bound volumes alike. "Like calls to like." He waved a hand, dismissive. "More or less."

Gawain held out a twig, cut from the Green Knight's discarded holly bough. "Will this suffice?"

Holly was sacred; beloved of Faeries. Last summer, a boy had stolen holy from a Faerie grove for his house. His mother found him later, piecemeal, pinned to the trees he had stolen from. It had taken days to reassemble him.

Merlin barked a laugh then fell abruptly silent, all humour falling away in an instant. Gawain ignored the urge to snap, to ask what was so amusing. He reminded himself he did not want to know.

The sorcerer reached out, expectant. Gawain handed him the holly, careful not to touch Merlin's skin. Sir Lancelot had made that mistake once. Knees buckling, he had been reduced to screaming fits for a month.

Merlin's face split into a jagged grin; a smile with far too many teeth for a human mouth. Brutal and strange, no mirth reached the man's eyes. Gawain, who had fought all manner of bizarre and eldritch beasts, found himself resisting the urge to shrink away. There was something passing strange about Merlin; something dangerous.

Merlin pivoted to face the sigil he had been sketching out. With a flourish, he completed it. Darkness, thick and rancid as decaying human fat, oozed out of the chalk lines. Instinctive, Gawain clamped his hands over his ears, screwing his eyes shut.

The blood-thick darkness pressed against Gawain's eyelids. The air grew heavy with damp and the stench of rotting fish. He held his breath.

The feeling of corpse-cold fingertips, gouging at the inside of his veins, came over him with a rush. Icy teeth gnawed at the marrow in his spine. Claws, sharp and insubstantial as a shadow, churned in his eye sockets. The prickling of thorns writhed over his skin and there was the sense of something massive looming over him; something ravenous. Three puffs of air, hot and rank, pressed against Gawain's cheek.

Time stretched, pulled taut to the point of snapping.

The carrion stench faded; the overwhelming weight of darkness lifted. The pain, revolting and intimate, fell away, sudden as a lightning strike.

Gawain could hold his breath no longer. He doubled over, gasping. Hands on his knees, his eyes flickered open.

Merlin stood, as still as a dead thing, utterly impassive. "Hautdesert," he said, unblinking. Merlin, Gawain realised, often forgot to blink or breathe.

"'Hautdesert'," Gawain echoed, breathless. He fought off a shudder of revulsion, still plagued by the phantom sensation of corpse-cold fingertips.

Merlin turned to rifle through the stacks of paper on his desk. He produced a folded piece of vellum, inked in blue and faded with use. It was a map. "It's a fair distance. I suggest you get started."

The sorcerer did an about turn and Gawain took that as a wordless dismissal.

The young knight bowed his head, muttering a hasty "My thanks". Nearly tripping over his own feet to get back down the tower stairs, he fled.

To the chapel he ran. If a bath would not rid him of this sick feeling of invasion, of the whispers, perhaps prayer would.

3.

Long did Gawain tarry. He bristled at the memory of the Green Knight's mockery. Yet he paled at the thought of death. Gawain did not relish the prospect of allowing the strange giant to lop off his head.

It was not until All Hallows Day, pressured by the passage of time and his unwise oath, that he set out on his quest.

Gawain chose the Green Knight's horse as his mount, thinking to return the beast to its master. Astride the huge bay stallion armour gleaming and green axe strapped to his back, Gawain said farewell to Camelot and his fellows. Reluctant but bound by his honour and his oath, he set off.

Through Logres did he travel, up cliffs, through forest and fen, silent save for the nickering of his horse. He knew not where Hautdesert lay, Merlin's map being basic and of little use. Gawain resorted to asking at every village and little town he passed through, "Have you any news of a giant of a man? Garbed in green and terrible to behold?" Each time, Gawain was met with puzzlement or fervent denials.

Days went by without Gawain glimpsing the slightest signs of human civilisation. Eventually, he found himself standing at the edge of a dense oak forest.

The Colour Out of Hautdesert

Dismounting from his steed, the young knight pressed on, leading the beast by the reins. The trees were tightly pressed together, the forest floor made treacherous by the presence of undergrowth and hidden roots. Progress slowed by caution, Gawain made his bed that night on bare rocks. He hunted for boar and deer, plunging ever deeper into the forest at the edge of the wild.

Time passed, inevitable and ruthless, until winter fell upon the land with a red mouth and sharp claws. Ravenous, winter devoured all things that could not burrow and sleep away the chill at year's end.

Then, when the forest floor was blanketed in snow and the world was in the throes of deepest winter, Gawain found himself in a clearing.

Winter had not touched this place.

Oaks, taller and more ancient than those he had encountered thus far, had not shed their leaves. Bright bluebells carpeted the clearing floor, and fruit hung heavy and exquisite from a scattering of apple trees.

A castle, assembled from rough grey stone, sat in the distance. The land was lush and green, and Gawain, starving after an age of living on dwindling rations, wept.

The horse refused to carry on.

Gawain urged it on, digging his heels into the animal's flanks. Silent, the horse did not respond. Perplexed, Gawain dismounted. Gathering up his dwindling supplies, he strode on, glancing back at the cowering beast.

Stock still, the horse stared ahead, blank. They stood in a field that was verdant and speckled with wildflowers. There were worse places to leave this creature, Gawain supposed.

His approach to the castle halted at the edge of a great crater. A rock, huge and radiating heat, pulsed in the centre of the hollow. All around it had been turned brittle and white. Mushrooms and flowers stood waist high, yet the field was silent. No birds or insects made themselves known.

A woman hurried from the castle, swiftly closing the distance. Dark haired and dainty, she was beautiful. Yet there was something hollow in her eyes, as if some part of her soul had been scooped out. "My Lord," she called, "please keep your distance from that thing."

Gawain, incurious by nature, felt no urge to investigate the crater until warned against it. "I take it this is your residence?"

The Lady inclined her head slightly. "It is." She did not share her name; Gawain found this suspect.

"I seek the residence of the Green Knight of Hautdesert." He proffered the axe. "I mean to return this to its owner."

The Lady's mouth thinned. "You have found what you seek. Welcome to Hautdesert."

"The Green Knight? What of him?" Gawain knew his manners were wanting, but his oath was an iron band around his throat.

Lady Hautdesert smiled. She turned to go, and Gawain hastened to follow.

Castle Hautdesert was a temple to the god of fallen grandeur. More a hunting lodge than a proper keep when viewed from up close, the walls were pitted by age. Light filtered through the ceiling of the entrance hall, and leaves were scattered across the stone floor.

"Let me arrange a room for you," Lady Hautdesert said, brisk. A retinue of bloodless maids materialised at her side.

"My Lady," Gawain blurted, "I only wish to speak with the knight."

Lady Hautdesert was unreadable. "After such a long journey? Please, tarry a while. You must taste our well water. Hautdesert is famed for it."

Gawain awoke the next morning to laughter, disembodied and unnerving. He found himself walking, propelled by unseen hands, into a great hall. Lady Hautdesert was sat at a long table, a meagre breakfast of bread and cold meat before her. She was not alone.

Young and handsome, with her was a man. His beard was neatly trimmed and eyes bright blue. He rose at Gawain's approach.

"May I introduce Sir Bertilak," said Lady Hautdesert, with a sweeping gesture.

Gawain inclined his head. "I thank you for your hospitality." He swallowed his frustration—this was not the Green Knight. Gawain did not want to fathom the consequences of breaking his oath. Panic rose in his throat, swift and suffocating.

Sir Bertilak laughed and said, "Yet I feel you'd rather chew rocks than linger here."

"Pardon my manner," said Gawain, relaxing. "I was expecting more formality."

Sir Bertilak laughed. "If you want, we can get one of the maids to follow you around and announce your entrance everywhere you go. They may need to take turns, though: We have a lot of rooms to shout into."

Gawain let out a snort of laughter. "If you want, I can do it myself. The poor maids would think me a loon, however."

Sir Bertilak smiled, bright. "Breakfast, then I'm sure you'll join me on a hunt?"

Gawain could not bring himself to refuse.

The hunt was a brisk affair.

Gawain rode a loaned horse, while Sir Bertilak compelled the retrieved bay stallion to his side. On they rode swift and reckless, through meadow and glade. They were in search of a monster, a mutated thing that devoured children.

They found their quarry bent over a woman, her throat torn out, and its mouth red with gore.

The monster was eyeless, its face devoid of all but a circle of needle teeth. A lamprey's mouth. It scuttled on knuckles and knees, chittering. Humanoid and pale, it was clad in naught but a flapping cape of human skin. With a screech, the thing launched itself at Gawain. It was easy to spear the creature, pinioning it like a beetle.

It howled, and Sir Bertilak gathered the creature into his arms, whispering into a hole on the side of its head. He slung the carcass over his horse.

Gawain ate little that night, preoccupied with thoughts of the thing they had slain. He had hunted eldritch beasts for years and never seen this creature's like. What foulness had birthed such a monster? He eyed the Green Knight's axe and wondered why he had yet to meet its owner. His musings were interrupted by a rapping on his chamber door. Gawain cleared his throat and bade them enter.

It was Lady Hautdesert.

Eyes darting, she held a green sash. "You must flee," she blurted, with no ado whatsoever.

Gawain was on his feet in an instant. "My Lady, I'm oath-bound to linger." He did not question her presence in his chamber; he did not want to risk expulsion from Hautdesert.

She sighed. "At least wear this." She offered him the sash. "Please."

It was no small thing to accept a lady's favour, and Gawain had no interest in courting her. "My Lady—"

"Please." She pushed the sash into his hands and wordless, she left.

Head buzzing, Gawain sought out Sir Bertilak.

It was bright and hot, when Sir Bertilak invited him on another hunt. Laughing and merry, they galloped through the woods.

Gawain lingered at the well afterwards, scooping cup after cup of water from the bucket. He drank deep, and with every mouthful, his head throbbed.

4.

On the seventh day, Gawain met the Green Knight.

Another hunt, another mutated creature. Unlike all the others, this one wore clothes. Small and garbed in a rough grey dress, this was no fell beast—it had once been a child.

Gawain fled, galloping back to the castle. He could not harm a girl.

Somehow, Sir Bertilak beat him to the castle. "It was a child once," Sir Bertilak said, soft. He approached, unbuckling his chest plate. "Did you not wonder where the other residents of Hautdesert are? Why the Lady and I are here all alone?"

He gripped Gawain's shoulder. "Please, don't leave me alone." Sir Bertilak pulled Gawain in for a kiss.

Gawain awoke later, cold and alone. Pulling on his tunic, he padded barefoot in search of Bertilak. He found the man doubled over, head in his hands.

"It's in the water," said Bertilak. "The meteor fell with a bright flash of green, and after all who drank from the well turned into those things we hunted. The fruit grew beautiful but bitter, and there was naught to eat but the mutated dead."

Bertilak lifted his head. His eyes an inhuman green. "It crawled inside, hollowing me out." He coughed, wet. "Don't let me die alone."

Gawain left, returning with the axe, green sash belted round his waist.

Sir Bertilak, once more the Green Knight, scoffed at the sash. "A superstition. Silly woman."

"I came to fulfil my oath," Gawain said, flat, forcing away all emotion. He offered the axe, falling to his knees. "I had my suspicions this belonged to you; I hoped I was wrong."

The Green Knight, a parasitic thing puppeteering the corpse of his lover, accepted. Wordless, he hacked at Gawain's neck.

Gawain fell back on his heels. A thin rivulet of blood tickled his neck from the thinnest of cuts. Otherwise unharmed, he stood up. Returning the axe blow with a fatal strike, he slew the Green Knight and wept for his love.

5.

Gawain burned down the castle.

He ran through the corridors, heedless of smoke, in search of Lady Hautdesert. He found her in her chamber, shrunken and dry. She was surrounded by what was once her entourage. Gawain wondered how long they had been dead; if Lady Hautdesert had been a corpse during their entire acquaintance. There was nothing living in that place, save for the Green Knight's horse.

Axe in hand, Gawain fled that cursed land on the stolen bay stallion. Slow was his progress, inglorious his return to Camelot. Gawain, heart leaden with grief, did not notice the snow behind him taking on an opalescent sheen. He did not realise that Hautdesert's taint had clung to him, that he bore it back home.

The Sign of Daoloth

Ramsey Campbell

As Ryre rode through the city gates two guardsmen converged on him. "What business have you in Hythgimi?" one said.

"They say the truth shall be found within."

"The light awaits."

Perhaps the sigil on the helmet that encased most of the man's head depicted it, a minute point made visible by the multitude of filaments it was emitting. His face looked seared by radiance, not least the eyes, which were so pale their pupils were all but invisible. "Is that the light of Daoloth?" Ryre said. "It is told he shows the truth."

The man's eyes grew blanker still as the other said "You must walk the black avenues and seek his fane."

His helmet bore an image of a serpentine shape with its tail in its grinning mouth, which protruded a long tongue split in trine. The face the helmet framed seemed clenched around a secret he might have preferred not to know. "You both speak for the faith," Ryre said.

"I welcome any that call upon Daoloth."

"You may look upon the light but once," the other guardsman said. "Those who have seen have no need to see."

As they moved aside, the man who bore the serpentine device extended a hand towards a vendor's stall. "You must wear the emblem of your quest."

Ryre had scarcely left the gates behind when a girl in a dress like an ankle-length brown canvas sack ran up to him. "Stables and lodging for the weary traveller."

Her small thin face looked dulled by years, however few she might have, of the task, but the wiry arm she reached for the reins was eager if not urgent. "Where will you lead me?" Ryre said.

"You can see."

She meant the Gateway Tavern. Like its neighbours, it was an irregular hulk of reddish clay, cavitied with unglazed windows and capped with rakish conical towers reminiscent of the turrets on the city battlements. The girl led Ryre's steed to the adjacent stables almost at a canter. As he dismounted she said "I will feed and groom your mount, and Tholx will give you a room."

Ryre shoved the heavy crooked door wide to confront the kind of reception his life had made all too familiar, a roomful of drinkers covertly or openly gauging his prowess as a swordsman, and not just the youngest were taking account of his age. As he tramped across the room the interrupted hubbub massed around him. The innkeeper, a squat man broad with corpulence as much as muscle, raised his head and a gathering of chins to peer through the pipe smoke that hovered in front of the bar. "Did my wife make you welcome as she should?"

"Which wife do we speak of?" Ryre said, though he suspected he knew.

"I have but one. I abide by the laws of the city." He jabbed a pudgy thumb at the wall behind him. "Fedele, who is caring for your steed," he said.

"I take it you are Tholx."

The innkeeper fingered his topmost chin as if adjusting a vain mask. "You have heard of me."

"The lady said you would find me a room for the night."

"The girl did." Having ponderously established this, Tholx said "Have her take you up to the left tower."

"I must make a purchase first," Ryre said and left the tavern.

Though several traders were selling jewellery among the stalls

THE SIGN OF DAOLOTH

loaded with meats and other produce, there was no mistaking the stall the guard had indicated. Every item in the mass of iridescent metal—brooches, pendants, bracelets, earrings—bore the image of the snakelike form consuming or uttering itself, and dozens of items consisted simply of the icon. The pendant the stallholder wore seemed to dominate the sight of her, so that Ryre would have been hard put to describe her face except as secretly introverted. "How will you honour our god?" she said.

"I am told I must bear a sign of my quest. What is the price for the like of your own?"

She passed a hand over her pendant, several inches distance from it. "You need not pay. Your acceptance is sufficient tribute." She lifted a chain off the stall and came to Ryre with a clatter of dusty sandals. "Touch it not," she said when he reached to don the pendant, and raised the chain over his head. "Touch it when you are prepared to seek Daoloth within yourself. You may call upon its power but once."

The pendant tapped Ryre's chest as he made for the stables. It and the chain were almost imperceptibly light, and the metallic shirt he had taken to wearing for protection muted the sensation further. Fedele was stroking his steed as she offered it a multifoliate blue herb larger than her hand that gripped its stem. "This brings calm," she said, "and gives back strength."

"When you are free you could show me to my room, or I can search it out myself."

"Did Tholx say so? Then I must now," she said and darted out of the stables as soon as Ryre's mount took the feed. She threw all her weight against the door of the tavern and left it wide for Ryre. "Where have you housed our guest?" she said.

Tholx glanced at Ryre's pendant, and his lips writhed towards a mirthless smile. "He has the view of his course on the morrow."

Fedele led the way up a spiral of uneven steps that opened onto three skewed corridors as a preamble to ending at a solitary door. The rounded room was graced with a narrow bed, a basin on a table, a jagged square of glass nailed to the wall above it for a mirror, an irregular rank of tusks for pegs protruding by a window opposite the bed. Fedele threw the shutters open.

"There is your view," she said.

Ryre was unable to judge her tone: disapproving or somehow worse? While she had reason to dislike the ways of Hythgimi, he could only say "Thank you for your care."

"It is why Tholx has me."

"How long have you been his wife?"

"Some time." As Ryre frowned, not merely at her vagueness, she said "I look younger than I am."

"I would still call that too young."

"I do not share his body or his bed. I shall not till I come of age. He obeys the laws of Hythgimi, and I must."

"When will you be of age?"

"Years hence. How I look will let him value me still." A glance out of the window appeared to bring her to a decision. "Did they tell—"

A shout magnified by the stairway interrupted her. "Fedele. Fedele, why are you loitering? Be about your tasks."

"Perhaps we may speak later," she told Ryre, hastening out of the room.

As she ran downstairs with a repetitive clapping of sandals, he crossed to the window. Although twilight was settling into the streets, he immediately identified the district of which he'd been told, a central group of buildings black as omens of the night. He presumed they had windows, but no light was to be seen. Surely it was just the dusk that made the blackness appear to be spreading outwards like a stain. When straining to clarify the sight began to trouble his eyes he went down to the tavern. "Where may I bathe? I have ridden far."

"The girl will minister to you," Tholx said.

"I want a bath prepared and nothing else."

"It is her task to satisfy my guests. Time will multiply the ways," the innkeeper said, a prospect Ryre felt loath to ponder.

Fedele ushered him to the bath-house, which stood between the stables and the inn. Ryre fetched a change of garments from his saddlebag and found her filling one of the quartet of troughs in the domed room, hauling at enormous wheels on water pipes to regulate the temperature. When he made to take over she shook her head, trailing her ragged prematurely silver hair over her thin shoulders. "It is my duty. It is part of me."

Ryre hung his fresh outfit on a peg formed from the horn of some opalescent beast, and was waiting for Fedele to leave him when she sent him a quick grin that suggested she could be amused, given cause. "I shall clean your garb and take it to your room," she said and hesitated. "Shall I hang your pendant?"

"Best leave it to me," Ryre said, adding it to the items on the peg. "I am told it should not be touched until the time is right."

Fedele paused, having parted her bitten pinkish lips, and he sensed her suppressing a thought. "Each may touch it only once," she said and turned her back on him.

When she heard him plunge into the steaming bath she collected the clothes he had piled on the rough clay floor and vanished through an entrance to the tavern. Ryre let the water soothe his limbs, which ached not just with travel but with age, and then he scoured himself with a soapy lump of porous mineral and vaulted as lithely as he could out of the trough to use one of the coarse capacious towels that were tethered to the wall. Once he was dressed he returned to the tavern. "What meats have you?"

"A stalker of the forests," Tholx told him, "freshly shelled."

"Give me a dish of that and a tankard of your best ale."

He expected Fedele to bring him the order, but when she emerged with the dish from the kitchen Tholx took it from her. He bore it and a brimming tankard to the table where Ryre sat against a wall, although not close to any corner. The innkeeper planted the repast on the table, adding a sharp-edged spoon from a pocket of his apron, then gazed at Ryre's pendant. "What has brought you on the pilgrimage?"

"I feel I am nearing the end of myself, and I wish to learn what truth there may be."

Tholx's lips twitched and relinquished a grin. "What do you hope for?"

"I have killed many men. That has been much of my life." Instinct guided Ryre's hand to his sword beneath the table, but his voice was low enough to fall short of provoking any challengers.

"I seek to know whether it has meaning," he said.

"Perhaps you are simply a bringer of death. Perhaps you are one of its messengers."

Ryre found the idea unwelcome, not least because it had already troubled him. "What is your faith?" he felt provoked to demand.

"Faith in myself, and that is all I need," Tholx said and left him.

Ryre set about the stew made of one of the colossal prowlers that seldom emerged from the woods. The chunks of meat were satisfyingly spiced, though he had to pick out shards of the creature's chitinous carapace. When he snapped a portion of segmented leg to spoon out the contents, Fedele brought him a bowl of lukewarm water and a cloth but refrained from lingering. Ryre took his time over the meal to relish it as much as he could, though his constant alertness for threats hindered him. He downed the last of his ale and made for his room.

Although the entire town was dark except for scattered windows, the blackness at its centre seemed impenetrably condensed. Ryre latched the shutters closed and arranged himself as best he could on the meagre bed, where exhaustion swiftly engulfed him. No dreams came to him, but a sound roused him: a soft if not stealthy footfall on the topmost flight of steps. He seized his sword and let it clang against the edge of the bed, and the footsteps retreated at once. He was glad to have driven off a thief until he wondered if the potential intruder had been Fedele. It was too late to find out, and he resumed sleep with his hand gripping the hilt of his sword.

When he wakened to distinguish a faint outline of the sky around the shutters, he rose from the bed. He had a mission to complete, followed by days of dogged travel. He donned the clothes Fedele had left him and hung the pendant around his neck, then stole downstairs. The tavern was deserted, and no sound came from above. With scarcely a creak of the floorboards he let himself out of the inn.

Two guards with lanterns at their feet were slumbering beside the city gates. One released a snore that might have been acknowledging Ryre's emergence from the tavern. Stallholders were laying out their wares beneath lamps on poles, but otherwise the

THE SIGN OF DAOLOTH

streets were bare of life. Having no need to ask where he was bound, Ryre made for the centre of the town.

The streets stayed unlit apart from the occasional glow from a window until the imminence of dawn began to pale the highest turrets. The spectacle seemed to offer a promise of enlightenment, unless that was only hope. It induced Ryre to stride faster while the pendant clanked against his chest with every step. At first his purposefulness distracted him from an impression that his pace was outdistancing the dawn. Was the emblem he wore lending him some additional vigour? The outermost of the black streets was in sight when he realised that as he advanced, the street around him had grown darker.

So the notion the view from his room had suggested was no fancy after all. The area surrounding the black hub of Hythgimi was indeed touched by a penumbra of the darkness. He could have thought the core of the city was drawing light into itself. The phenomenon halted him, but how else could he proceed? Surely the dawn must find him soon, even if it appeared to be in no haste to touch the roofs ahead.

However fast he tramped, the way only darkened around him. When he reached the first of the streets that were utterly black he saw all the buildings were windowless. Each ebon block was relieved only by a door as dark. Just the distant view of a section of street growing faintly paler encouraged him to forge on, muttering imprecations at the blackness that surrounded him.

Soon the street narrowed, concentrating the dark. Before long he was unable to judge how solid that was — how close the buildings were. Nothing but the prospect of the feeble remote light impelled him onwards. He was willing it to grow closer and larger and brighter when he heard a door thud against a wall, and a figure robed from head to foot in black stepped into his path.

It cocked its head like a bird of prey alerted by a sound — by the clanking of Ryre's pendant. The dim silhouette raised a hand to its eyes and then pointed both fingers at Ryre. In a moment Ryre realised the figure had done more than touch its eyes; it had thrust the fingers into its face. Before Ryre could react, it jerked its head back and called out a single word, which resembled the triumphant screech of a predator. "Here."

Ryre heard doors spring open behind him and beside him and ahead. In a moment he was surrounded by figures he could barely distinguish. They began to dance around him, robes flapping like the wings of a swarm of bats. For a breath—for too long—he mistook the activity for some form of ritual welcome. By the time he felt the bonds encircle him, pinning his arms to his sides, he was unable to withdraw his sword from its sheath.

Before he could disable any of his captors with a kick, they dodged out of reach, hauling at the stout cords that bound him, four men to each length. He fought to resist but was no match for them. They towed him at a helpless stumbling run into the depths of the dark. At least they were heading towards the pledge of distant light, however unattainable that seemed—and then he heard great doors rumble open, and was dragged through an entrance into a different darkness.

As the doors rumbled shut behind him his abductors retreated on either side of him, still tugging at the cords that dug into his chest and arms and back. The echoes told him he was in a vast high-ceilinged room. He strove to lurch aside, hoping to jerk some of his captors off balance and then throw the rest into sufficient disorder to let him slacken the restraints, but his convulsive effort merely stirred the pendant, which dealt his chest a peremptory blow. At once a voice spoke ahead of him in the blackness. "You bear the sigil of our foe."

"I know naught of your conflict. I come only seeking the truth."

"Then embrace the sacred light that quelled the ancient dark, and stop your ears to the pretender's acolytes."

"Release me first if you would have me adopt your religion. A true faith needs no fetters."

"That is no supplicant that speaks. It is the cunning of the primal dark."

Ryre was struggling to compact himself even an inch to create enough slack to let him squirm loose, but his captors hauled the bonds tighter. "I shall espouse no belief that makes a slave of me," he said through his clenched teeth.

"Repudiate your heresy and accept the one true faith so that you may be set free."

"I do not believe you offer the freedom I seek."

"Then gaze upon our light. Let it shine into your depths and destroy every shadow."

Ryre heard a scrape of metal ahead of him as twin miniature doors were unlatched and parted wide. They belonged to a tabernacle, the solitary item on an ebon altar. A tiny light gleamed within it like a solitary star in a night sky. It seemed almost too small to discern, and yet it limned the robed figure that had revealed it. "Accept the light," the priest said. "You no longer have a choice."

More even than his bondage, the observation enraged Ryre. Without the ability to choose he believed he was nothing at all. At least he could shut out the glare that appeared to be intensifying, however shrunken it remained, and he closed his eyes tight. For a scant few moments he was able to hope this would fend it off, but it shone through his eyelids, and he felt it begin to sear deeper.

He twisted his head aside, drawing a clank from the pendant. The action made no difference, because the light had somehow fastened on him. However far he turned his head, the relentless glare followed him, penetrating his eyelids as if they had lost all substance. If only he were able to catch hold of the pendant and discover what its rumoured powers might be! As his head swivelled back and forth he felt like a beast about to be blinded. His struggles set the pendant clanking in mockery of his helplessness, and the sounds roused a last desperate hope.

He had to face the light again, and immediately felt his eyeballs start to shrivel. He jerked his head forward and back, forward and back, sending stabs of pain through his neck as the pendant swung away from him. He ducked his head to seize the chain between his teeth, and missed. As the pendant rebounded from his chest he thought his eyes were close to charring. He ducked desperately lower, which failed to avoid even a fraction of the ruthless light that seemed determined to sear him to his core. Then the chain of the pendant slithered over his chin, and he twisted his head towards it, straining his mouth wide. A single link caught on a tooth. He clenched his jaws to grip the chain, and heard a footstep start towards him through the agonising brightness. His mind sent out a virtually wordless plea to whatever powers might be prepared to intervene for him, and then he threw his head back, opening his mouth.

The pendant flew up to the limit of the chain and fell at the edge of his lips—the very corner. With a lurch of his head he captured it in his mouth. As it landed on his tongue he sensed it assuming his substance. It felt like flesh and tasted like it too. The sensations seemed to waken a memory older not just than Ryre but than his entire species: a hereditary recollection of an era when all life consisted of a single primal substance, which a controlling consciousness was able to shape at will. The reminiscence was more than a memory; it was a physical state. If the pendant was able to alter its substance, so was its wielder. No sooner did Ryre think of reinforcing his eyelids to ward off the glare than they thickened, shutting out the light, and he felt his eyes recover as if a soothing unguent had healed them. In another instant he condensed his body just enough to let the bonds drop from him.

As they struck the floor he stepped out of them and heard several of his captors start for him. He drew his sword and scythed it through the air, fending off any attackers as he strode where he knew the altar to be. With a sweep of the sword he dashed the tabernacle to the floor, where it landed face down with its doors outspread like a crushed beetle's wings, extinguishing or at least temporarily quenching the light. He required his vision now, and at once he was able to perceive his surroundings despite the dark. The priest was rushing at him, holding a dagger high. A stroke of Ryre's sword lopped off the man's forearm, which thudded to the floor, convulsively releasing the dagger.

As the weapon skittered across the floor, one of Ryre's captors seized it and lunged at him. Like the priest, this assailant had no eyes, though some activity twitched deep in the sockets. Despite his eyelessness, the man came straight for Ryre, raising the dagger. This time it was a severed hand that fell. The dagger clattered towards the man's companions, but they drew back from it and Ryre. He had no taste for injuring the blind, however able they proved to be, and he swept the blade through the air to deter them while he crossed the chapel. He lifted the massive latch of the enormous door and stepped into another dark.

He could distinguish the street around him now. Its unrelieved blackness suggested that the light within the tabernacle was draining its surroundings to maintain itself. The street framed the distant day, which was growing brighter. As he strode towards it, alert for a further assault that never came, the streets began to relinquish their darkness, and his eyes reverted to their habitual state, so gradually that he was scarcely aware of the process. He had no cause to blink when at last he gained the daylight, which showed him the goal of his quest ahead.

The very shape of the temple of Daoloth—a black colossal stony dome whose entrance gaped like a mouth, from which a fork of paths led in the manner of a divided tongue and a half-swallowed tail that curved around the perimeter—implied the presence of its denizen. The fane might have been the shell of the god. As Ryre passed through the arch, flames in lanterns dangling from the walls shuddered a welcome, which appeared to enliven the huge eyes of the gigantic head that confronted him.

The circular serpentine body of the idol practically filled the temple, leaving just a narrow passageway for worshippers to tread. The eyes bereft of lids and pupils were as black as the body and the three-pronged tongue that sprawled beside the tip of the tail out of the secretively grinning lipless mouth. If the blackness of the other temple had reminded Ryre of outer space, the aching darkness of the avatar of Daoloth could have been drawn from a void before there was any light in the universe. He felt the pendant he was still holding on his tongue stir wakefully to greet its vaster self, and was seized by a sudden choking panic. Might he prefer not to learn what his quest had sought? He spat out the pendant, which dealt his chest an admonitory thump, but it was too late. A form of life had brought slow animation to the eyes that were wider than he was tall, and he felt their gaze take hold of him. The entity of which the idol comprised the merest hint—a metaphor or euphemism—had come to find its summoner.

The scrutiny made him feel observed by the primal void or by its solitary inhabitant: by both, since they were one. He was barely a particle in the universe that would eventually renew itself, swallowing and resurrecting time and space in the way the shape of the avatar implied. In the eyes of Daoloth, remote as the rim of the cosmos yet close as a threat to touch him, Ryre was less than an insect, nothing but a puppet of his way of life, driven constantly to fight and kill.

Was this the entire truth of him? As he retreated stumbling out of the temple he glimpsed the unnatural vitality withdraw from the eyes of the idol, leaving them emptily black. Trudging away from the temple, he saw how he had been used as the puppet he was. He had never needed to pass through the black streets when an outer road would have led him to the fane. The guards at the gates had duped him into doing battle in the conflict of the faiths they represented. Perhaps every pilgrim who entered Hythgimi was sent on a similar mission. In a rage he caught hold of the pendant by its chain to cast it from him, but a thought stayed him.

A street that followed the city walls returned him to the inn. When he collected his belongings from the turret room Tholx accosted him at the foot of the stairs. Ryre wondered if the innkeeper planned to bar his way, but refrained from taking hold of his sword. "Have you achieved your mission?" Tholx said.

"Both of them." Ryre kept his gaze on him while adding "I have seen the truth, and not only mine."

He found Fedele in the stables, grooming the steed of a newcomer. Once he had loaded his saddlebag he went to her and lifted the chain of the pendant over his head. "This has done its work," he said. "You gave me to understand others may touch it as well."

"Just once, to call upon its power."

"Then do that for yourself." When he elevated the pendant she bowed her head in invitation rather than submission, and he hung the chain around her neck. "Look for the truth that lies ahead of you," he urged, "and leave behind whatever you should. There is a world beyond these walls."

"I shall see." She reached a hand towards the pendant but stopped short of grasping it. "I had no chance to say," she said. "You need not have gone to the temple for truth."

"Then avoid the place yourself."

She led his mount into the street and held the reins while he succeeded in vaulting into the saddle, a last flourish of the self he used to take for his. As he rode to the gates he encountered the guards who had directed him to the fane of Daoloth. Despite a surge of anger, he kept his hand clear of his sword, even when they spoke. "Bear the light wherever you travel," one said, and his accomplice who was also his adversary counselled "Make the truth your guide."

Having ridden for some minutes over the plain crossed by a solitary road, Ryre looked back. A rider had just emerged from Hythgimi, and he recognised Fedele. At first he thought she meant to follow him, but she hesitated before turning beside the wall to head somewhere else in the world. As Ryre spurred his steed onwards he allowed himself a faint smile. Perhaps after all he had found some meaning in himself.

CONTRIBUTORS

EUGEN BACON is an African Australian author. She's a British Fantasy and Foreword Indies Award winner, a twice World Fantasy Award finalist, and a finalist in the Shirley Jackson, Philip K. Dick, Victorian Premier's Literary Award, and the Nommo Awards for speculative fiction by Africans. Eugen was announced in the honor list of the Otherwise Fellowships for 'doing exciting work in gender and speculative fiction'. *Danged Black Thing* made the Otherwise Award Honor List as a 'sharp collection of Afro-Surrealist work'. Visit her at www.eugenbacon. com

RAMSEY CAMPBELL: The *Oxford Companion to English Literature* describes Ramsey Campbell as "Britain's most respected living horror writer", and the *Washington Post* sums up his work as "one of the monumental accomplishments of modern popular fiction". His awards include the Grand Master Award of the World Horror Convention, the Lifetime Achievement Award of the Horror Writers Association, the Living Legend Award of the International Horror Guild and the World Fantasy Lifetime Achievement Award. In 2015 he was made an Honorary Fellow of Liverpool John Moores University for outstanding services to literature. Among his novels are *The Face That Must Die, Incarnate, Midnight Sun, The Count of Eleven, The Darkest*

Part of the Woods, The Overnight, Secret Story, The Grin of the Dark, Thieving Fear, Creatures of the Pool, The Seven Days of Cain, Ghosts Know, The Kind Folk, Think Yourself Lucky, Thirteen Days by Sunset Beach, The Wise Friend, Somebody's Voice, Fellstones, The Lonely Lands and *The Incubations*. His Brichester Mythos trilogy consists of *The Searching Dead, Born to the Dark* and *The Way of the Worm*. His collections include *Waking Nightmares, Ghosts and Grisly Things, Told by the Dead, Just Behind You, Holes for Faces, By the Light of My Skull, Fearful Implications,* and a two-volume retrospective roundup (*Phantasmagorical Stories*) as well as *The Village Killings and Other Novellas*. His non-fiction is collected as *Ramsey Campbell, Probably* and *Ramsey Campbell, Certainly*, while *Ramsey's Rambles* collects his video reviews, and *Six Stooges and Counting* is a book-length study of the Three Stooges. *Limericks of the Alarming and Phantasmal* is a history of horror fiction in the form of fifty limericks. His novels *The Nameless, Pact of the Fathers* and *The Influence* have been filmed in Spain, where a television series based on *The Nameless* is in development.

GREG CHAPMAN Australian Shadows Award-winner, two-time Bram Stoker Award nominee and Ditmar Awards nominee, Greg Chapman is a horror author and artist based in Queensland Australia. He is the author of the novels *Hollow House, The Noctuary: Pandemonium* and *Netherkind* and the collections, *Vaudeville and Other Nightmares, This Sublime Darkness and Other Dark Stories, Bleak Precision, Midnight Masquerade* and *Black Days and Bloody Nights*. His short fiction has also appeared in numerous anthologies and magazines.

His artistic endeavours include designing book covers for various publishers in Australia, the United States, and the United Kingdom. He has been creating book covers and artwork for IFWG Publishing since 2013. The first graphic novel he illustrated, *Witch Hunts: A Graphic History of the Burning Times*, written by Rocky Wood and Lisa Morton, won the Superior Achievement in a Graphic Novel category at the Bram Stoker Awards® in 2013. Greg was also the President of the Australasian Horror Writers Association from 2017-2020. Visit him at: www.darkscrybe.com

CONTRIBUTORS

SAL CIANO is an author and editor based in South Florida. When not working or spending time with his friends, family and dogs, Sal spends time appreciating and delighting in the strange parade of the completely absurd, absolutely weird, heartbreakingly ephemeral, and breathtakingly bizarre experiences that comprise living life in America.

KAT CLAY is an award-winning author of fiction, reviews, and tabletop roleplaying games. Her Call of Cthulhu games, *The Hammersmith Haunting* and *The Well of All Fear*, are both bestsellers on DriveThruRPG. *The Well of All Fear* won the silver ENnie in 2024 for Best Community Content and was nominated for Best Adventure—Short Form.

Alongside her game writing, she is a published fiction author and reviewer. Her short stories have been published in *Interzone, Cosmic Horror Monthly, Midnight Echo, Translunar Travelers Lounge, Aurealis, SQ Mag*, and *Crimson Streets*. In 2018, her crime story 'Lady Loveday Investigates' won three prizes at the national Scarlet Stiletto Awards, including the Kerry Greenwood Prize for Best Malice Domestic. Her weird-noir novella *Double Exposure*, was published by Crime Factory in 2015.

Kat's essays and criticism have been published in *The Guardian, Interzone, The Victorian Writer, Literary Traveler, Travel Weekly, Matador Network*, and *Weird Fiction Review*. She was a contributor to the Locus winning and Hugo nominated *Dangerous Visions and New Worlds: Radical Science Fiction, 1950 to 1985*, with her essay on Judith Merril. You can find her at katclay.com.

JACK DANN has written or edited over eighty books, including the international bestseller *The Memory Cathedral: a Secret History of Leonardo da Vinci, The Rebel: an Imagined Life of James Dean, The Silent, Bad Medicine*, and *The Man Who Melted*. His work has been compared to Jorge Luis Borges, Roald Dahl, Lewis Carroll, Ray Bradbury, J. G. Ballard, Mark Twain, and Philip K. Dick. *Library Journal* called Dann "...a true poet who can create pictures with a few perfect words," and *Best Sellers* said that "Jack Dann is a mind-warlock whose magicks will confound, disorient, shock, and delight."

He is a recipient of the Nebula Award, the World Fantasy Award

303

(twice), the Australian Aurealis Award (three times), the Chronos Award, the Darrell Award for Best Mid-South Novel, the Ditmar Award (five times), the Peter McNamara Achievement Award and the Peter McNamara Convenors' Award for Excellence, the Shirley Jackson Award, and the *Premios Gilgames de Narrativa Fantastica* award. He has also been honored by the Mark Twain Society (Esteemed Knight).

His latest novel is *Shadows in the Stone: a Book of Transformations* (IFWG). *New York Times* bestselling author Kim Stanley Robinson called it "such a complete world that Italian history no longer seems comprehensible without his cosmic battle of spiritual entities behind and within every historical actor and event." His most recent books include *The Writer's Guide to Alternate History* (Bloomsbury), and the collections *Masters of Science Fiction: Jack Dann* (Centipede Press) and *Islands of Time* (Cemetery Dance).

Dr. Dann is also an Adjunct Senior Research Fellow in the School of Communication and Arts at the University of Queensland. He lives in Australia on a farm overlooking the sea.

SCOTT DRISCOLL is a writer, podcaster and performer living in Fortitude Valley, Australia. He has a diploma in Cryptozoology and Parapsychology. He currently works in the telecommunications industry. He was temporarily a joint Guinness World Record holder (World's largest Zorba Dance). Since 2011 he has performed with numerous theatre troupes such as Act/React and Improv QLD. He was born in Sydney Australia where he was adopted by his family, He currently lives with his wife and their elderly cat Sicarius. His other prose work can be found… if you look hard enough. He can be heard on the Evil Popcorn Podcast.

DEL HOWISON is an author, journalist, actor (see IMDB), and the Bram Stoker Award-winning editor of the anthology *Dark Delicacies: Original Tales of Terror and the Macabre by the World's Greatest Horror Writers*. He has written articles for Fear.net, Gauntlet Magazine, and Writers Digest among others. Del's short story *Cul-de-Sac* appeared in *Weird Tales Magazine* #369. His western short story *The Lost Herd* was turned into the premiere (and highest rated) episode, *The Sacrifice*, for the series *Fear Itself*. His dark western novel *The Survival of Margaret Thomas* was shortlisted for the Peacemaker Award given out by the Western Fictioneers. His short story retrospective *What Fresh Hell Is This?* with a Foreword by **Clive Barker** is scheduled to be released in March of 2025. He has been shortlisted for over half a dozen awards including the Shirley Jackson Award and the Black Quill. He is the cofounder and owner (with his wife, Sue) of Dark Delicacies, a book and gift store known as "The Home of Horror," located in Burbank, California. The store won the "Il Posto Nero" award from Italy and has been inducted into the Rondo Hatton Hall of Fame.

GERRY HUNTMAN is a publisher and writer based in The Gold Coast, Australia, living with his wife and daughter. He has published over 50 short fiction and poetry pieces — mostly dark stuff, and two middle grade fantasy novels. He is owner and Managing Director of SQ Mag Pty Ltd, a company that runs two businesses: one devoted to speculative fiction books, and the other comics and graphic novels.

JIM KRUEGER is one of the top-rated writers currently working in American comics. Significant successes include the prestigious *Earth-X* Trilogy from Marvel Comics, and *Justice* (a *New York Times* Bestseller, and winner of an Eisner Award) from DC Comics, with colleagues Alex Ross and Doug Braithwaite. In addition, he has had notable projects with *Avengers, X-Men, Star Wars, The Matrix Comics, Micronauts,* and *Batman.* With Ross again, and others, he did *Avengers/Invaders,* and *Project Superpowers* for Dynamite Entertainment. He has been a creative director at Marvel Comics, and is also a freelance comic book writer/property creator whose original works include *The Foot Soldiers, Alphabet Supes, The Clock Maker, The High Cost of Happily Ever After* and *The Last Straw Man.*

JOE R. LANSDALE is the author of over fifty novels and four hundred shorter works, including stories, essays, reviews, film and TV scripts, introductions and magazine articles, as well as a book of poetry. His work has been made into films, animation, comics, and he has won numerous awards including the Edgar, Raymond Chandler life time award, numerous Bram Stoker Awards, and the Spur Award.

His work has been made into films, among them *Bubba Hotep,*

305

CONTRIBUTORS

Cold in July, as well as the acclaimed TV show, *Hap and Leonard*. His novel *The Thicket* recently appeared in theaters and on VOD. He has also had works adapted to MASTERS OF HORROR ON SHOWTIME, NETFLIX'S LOVE, DEATH AND ROBOTS, SHUDDER'S CREEPSHOW. He has written scripts for BATMAN THE ANIMATED SERIES, and other animation.

He has received numerous awards and recognition for horror, crime, historical fiction, as well as others. He lives in Nacogdoches with his wife Karen and their pit bull, RooRoo.

JONATHAN MABERRY is a NYTimes bestselling author, #1 Audible bestseller, 5-time Bram Stoker Award-winner, 4-time Scribe Award winner, Inkpot Award winner, comic book writer, and producer. He is the author of 51 novels, 170 short stories, 16 short story collections, 27 graphic novels, 14 nonfiction books, and has edited 26 anthologies. His vampire apocalypse book series, **V-WARS**, was a Netflix original series starring Ian Somerhalder. His 2009-10 run as writer on the *Black Panther* comic formed a large chunk of the recent blockbuster film, ***Black Panther: Wakanda Forever.*** His bestselling YA zombie series, ***Rot & Ruin*** is in development for film at Alcon Entertainment; and ***John Wick*** director, Chad Stahelski, is developing Jonathan's ***Joe Ledger Thrillers*** for TV. Jonathan writes in multiple genres including suspense, thriller, horror, science fiction, epic fantasy, and action; and he writes for adults, teens and middle grade. His works include ***The Pine Deep Trilogy, The Kagen the Damned Trilogy, NecroTek, Ink, Glimpse, the Rot & Ruin*** series, **the Dead of Night** series, ***The Wolfman, X-Files Origins: Devil's Advocate, The Sleepers War*** (with Weston Ochse), ***Mars One***, and many others. He is the editor of high-profile anthologies including ***Weird Tales: 100 Years of Weird, The X-Files, Aliens: Bug Hunt, Out of Tune, Don't Turn out the Lights: A Tribute to Scary Stories to Tell in the Dark, Baker Street Irregulars, Nights of the Living Dead, Shadows & Verse,*** and others. His comics include ***Marvel Zombies Return, The Punisher: Naked Kills, Wolverine: Ghosts, Godzilla vs Cthulhu: Death May Die, Bad Blood*** and many others. He the president of the **International Association of Media Tie-in Writers**, and the editor of ***Weird Tales Magazine***. He lives in San Diego, California.

Find him online at www.jonathanmaberry.com

BARRY N. MALZBERG is a playwright, critic, and the author of more than ninety books and three hundred short stories. *The New York Times Book Review* called him "one of science fiction's most literate and erudite writers", and the late Harlan Ellison wrote: "There are possibly a dozen writers in the genre of the imaginative, and Barry Malzberg is at least eight of them... Malzberg makes what the rest of us do look like felonies."

Malzberg's prolific career has spanned numerous genres—most notably crime and science fiction—and his iconic metafictional work has been both wildly praised by critics and attacked by proponents of 'hard science fiction'. His novel *Beyond Apollo* won the first John W. Campbell Award for Best Science Fiction Novel. He is also the recipient of a Schubert Foundation Playwriting Fellowship and the Cornelia Ward Creative Writing Fellowship. His novels include *Oracle of the Thousand Hands, Screen, The Falling Astronauts Overlay, In the Enclosure, Herovit's World, The Men Inside, Guernica Night, Galaxies, Chorale, The Running of Beasts* (with Bill Pronzini), and *Cross of Fire.* He is also the author of the darkly brilliant critique of the genre, *The Engines of the Night: Science Fiction in the Eighties.* His other nonfiction titles include *Breakfast in the Ruins: Science Fiction in the Last Millennium,* and *The Bend at the End of the Road.*

Malzberg is a former editor of both *Amazing* and *Fantastic,* and a multiple Nebula and Hugo nominee

JM MERRYT: Contributor to the critically acclaimed competitive-entry anthologies *Spawn: Weird Horror Tales About Pregnancy, Birth and Babies* and *Killer Creatures Down Under: Horror Stories with Bite,* JM mixes folktales with cosmic horror. Her stories feature creatures that feed on the corpse of a murdered god (*The Bargain*); a dead language that should have stayed that way (*Necroglossia*); and the tale of what happens when a ravenous goddess of a peat bog is forced to fend for herself (*She Who Devours*). Fascinated by ghost photography, taxidermy, and failed arctic expeditions, JM visits haunted places to see what she can dig up. JM can be found at Home | JM. Merryt Author (jmerryt.wixsite.com).

CONTRIBUTORS

JASON NAHRUNG grew up on a Queensland cattle property and now lives in Ballarat with his wife, the writer Kirstyn McDermott. The author of four novels, a novella, and more than 20 short stories, his fiction is anchored in the speculative genres and typically is darkly themed. This interest has expanded into the realm of climate fiction, which led him to complete a PhD in creative writing from The University of Queensland. Having developed a liking for editing during 30 years of work as a newspaper journalist, he also offers freelance editing and manuscript appraisal services. Find him online at www. jasonnahrung.com.

DILLON NAYLOR is an award-winning artist and writer who has been a central fixture of the Australian comic book scene with long-running characters like 'Batrisha the Vampire Girl' since the early 1980s. He is currently collecting previous works into lavish, hardcover volumes and developing new horror projects using his distinctive brush and ink style.

STEVEN PAULSEN is an award-winning speculative fiction writer and editor. His bestselling spooky children's book, *The Stray Cat*, illustrated by the acclaimed artist Shaun Tan, has seen publication in several English and foreign language editions. His horror, science fiction and dark fantasy short stories have appeared in books and magazines around the world. The best of his weird tales can be found in his short story collection, *Shadows on the Wall*, which won the Australian Shadows Award for Best Collected Work. His YA Historical Fantasy novel, *Dream Weaver*, set in 15th century Ottoman Turkey, was a finalist for Best Novel in the 2024 Ditmar Awards. Most recently he co-edited *Nosferatu Unbound* (IFWG Publishing) with Christopher Sequeira, an anthology of stories inspired by the classic 1922 silent movie *Nosferatu*. Find him online at: www.stevenpaulsen.com.

STEVE PROPOSCH is a publisher, editor and writer with a history of work focussed on speculative fiction and regional arts. He was editor for the seminal street press magazine *Large,* had a brief stint with *Fashion Journal,* co-founded *Trouble* magazine which published for over a decade, and was a founder and editor of *Bloodsongs* magazine. With collaborators Christopher Sequeira and Bryce Stevens, he co-edited several horror/SF anthologies, including *War of the Worlds: Battleground Australia; Cthulhu Deep Down Under;* and *Caped Fear: Superhuman Horror Stories.* He has had his own fiction, poetry and non-fiction published in various anthologies, magazines and literary journals.

CAT RAMBO's 300+ fiction publications include stories in *Asimov's, Clarkesworld Magazine,* and *The Magazine of Fantasy and Science Fiction.* In 2020 they won the Nebula Award for fantasy novelette *Carpe Glitter.* They are a former two-term President of the Science Fiction and Fantasy Writers of America (SFWA). Their most recent works are space opera *Rumor Has It* (Tor Macmillan, 2024) and fantasy *Wings of Tabat* (Wordfire, 2025). For more about Cat, see their website at www.catrambo.com.

PETER RAWLIK is a long-time collector of Lovecraftian fiction and in 1985 stole a car to go see the film Reanimator. He successfully defended himself by explaining that his father had regularly read him *The Rats in the Wall* as a bedtime story. His first professional sale was in 1997, but didn't begin to write seriously until 2010. Since then, he has authored more than fifty short stories and the Cthulhu Mythos novels *Reanimators, The Weird Company, Reanimatrix, The Peaslee Papers, and The Eldritch Equations.* He is a frequent contributor to the *Lovecraft ezine.* In 2014 his short story *Revenge of the Reanimator* was nominated for a New Pulp Award. In 2015 he co-edited The Legacy of the Reanimator for Chaosium. Somewhere along the line he became known as the Reanimator guy, but he fervently denies being obsessed with the character. His short stories are collected in both *Strange Company and Others,* and *The Cthulhu Heresy and Other Lovecraftian Sins.* He lives in southern Florida where he works on Everglades issues and does a lot of fishing.

JANE ROUTLEY: Fantasy and Science Fiction writer Jane Routley has published 6 books and won two Aurealis Awards for Best Fantasy Novel. Her 7th book is *Shadow in the Empire of Light.* Her short stories have been widely anthologized and read on the ABC. She is a keen climate activist. She has also written two Call of

CONTRIBUTORS

Cthulhu scenarios available on Drivethrurpg. Despite years of encountering "things that cannot, nay, must not be described" while playing Call of Cthulhu, she is not (yet) insane. Honest. You can find her at www.janeroutley.com

J. SCHERPENHUIZEN is an author, illustrator and academic whose illustrations, fiction, comic-book work and reviews have appeared on and in publications for Bolinda Press, Hinkler books, Echo Bonnier and IFWG; and in the following magazines and comics: *Bloodsongs, Mattoid, Severed Head, The Watch, The Glowing Man, Mr Blood,* and *Pulp Action* (the last three providing illustrations for work authored by frequent collaborator Christopher Sequeira). He worked with Michal Dutkiewicz on *Wolverine Doombringer* and *Lost in Space* comics, pencilling backgrounds and secondary characters and the odd complete page. He has inked W. Chew Chan's second issue of *Buckeroo Banzai* for Moonstone comics and Jason Frank's illustrations in the second volume of *Sixsmiths,* to which he also contributed a chapter of art and two covers for the serialised version.
From 2008-2009 he completed his first graphic novel, *The Time of the Wolves,* which was serialised by Black House Comics as *The Twilight Age.* Recent years have seen the appearance of a number of his short stories in anthologies such as *Sherlock Holmes: The Australian Casebook, Cthulhu Deep Down Under Volume 2* and *Dracula Unfanged.* In 2020 he was awarded a Doctor of Arts Degree from The University of Sydney for *Dutch Technique/the Saga of the Atlantean,* a hybrid graphic novel/ literary novel/faux thesis and research paper. Currently he is working on the art for a five-issue story arc of *The Human Fly* written by Christopher Sequeira and Jason Franks and published by IPI comics.

CHRISTOPHER SEQUEIRA is a conceptualist and commissioning editor of mystery, science fiction, horror and fantasy prose and comic-book anthologies, as well as being a writer himself. He has worked on such books as the four volume *Cthulhu: Deep Down Under* series; *Sherlock Holmes and Doctor Was Not; Sherlock Holmes: The Australian Casebook; Dracula Unfanged;* the all-star creator anthology *Caped Fear: Superhuman Horror Stories* (featuring Joe R. Lansdale, George R. R. Martin and others); *Kolchak the Night Stalker—Nosferatu;* and *Nosferatu Unbound.* His comic-book scripts include work on the franchises *X-Men, Iron Man, Justice*

League, Star Trek, and *The Human Fly,* as well as original concepts of his own. He lives in Sydney with his family. His first novel, a crime thriller, debuts in 2026.

AARON STERNS is a screenwriter and novelist, co-writing the film *Wolf Creek 2* (Best Screenplay, Madrid International Fantastic Film Festival), as well as writing prequel novel *Wolf Creek: Origin,* awarded Best Australian Horror Novel of 2014. His fiction has appeared in such anthologies as the World Fantasy Award-winning *Dreaming Down-Under,* in *Dreaming Again,* and *Gathering the Bones: New Stories from the World's Masters of Horror.* Sterns has worked on feature scripts for Voltage Pictures, Little Wolf Films, Dancing Road Productions and others. He also served as a script editor on Greg McLean's *Rogue,* and appeared in a little cameo as Bazza's Mate in *Wolf Creek.* He is a former lecturer in Gothic & Subversive Fiction, editor of the *Journal of the Australian Horror Writers,* and Ph.D. student in postmodern horror. He lives in Melbourne, Australia, with his wife, daughter, and their new little rascal kitten Vilks.

ANNA TAMBOUR: In 2024, stories by Anna Tambour have appeared in two PS Publishing anthologies: *Disintegration,* edited by Darren Speegle, and *The Mad Butterfly's Ball,* edited by Preston Grassman and Chris Kelso. Her three novels and four collections (the latest of which is the 2023 *Death Goes to the Dogs*) have been published by small indies in Australia, the US, and the UK.